"A spellbinding tale of he[...]
blooms in the darkest of [...]

SILVER ECHOES

A GOLD DIGGER NOVEL

ADVANCE READERS COPY

WHAT REALLY HAPPENED TO ROSE MARY ECHO SILVER DOLLAR TABOR?

REBECCA ROSENBERG

Praise for Silver Echoes

"A spellbinding masterpiece through triumph and heartbreak, where hope blooms in the darkest of times."

~Kay Bratt, Author of *Wish Me Home*

"A twisty and atmospheric story about the damage inflicted by childhood trauma and its manifestations in later life. We are immersed in Silver's world as she performs daring high-wire feats, trains tigers, and debuts as a silver screen starlet, while danger is ever-present. In another narrative thread, we follow her mother as she tries to find out what happened to her brave and vulnerable daughters, while protecting the family's Colorado silver mine. It captures the vulnerability of young women of gumption in the 20s and 30s, the era of gangsters and speakeasies and men you should never trust."

~Gill Paul, internationally best-selling author of *A Beautiful Rival*

"Gorgeously written and impeccably researched, *Silver Echoes* follows two compelling women during a transformative era of American history. Through alternating timelines, this moving tale explores one woman's struggle with tragedy and mental illness, and her mother's unwavering devotion. An irresistible, page-turning journey crafted with compelling prose and exquisite detail. I couldn't turn the pages fast enough. Highly recommend."

~Renee Ryan, award winning author of *The Last Fashion House in Paris*

"Baby Doe Tabor's 'wayward' daughter lives again through this alternate and totally plausible telling of Silver Dollar Tabor's rich and compelling historical story. The true-to-life narrative unfolds in two timeframes roughly separated by more than a decade. Both story lines are ripe with color and filled with adventure, giving three robust dimensions to an otherwise largely murky part of Colorado's Tabor legacy. Silver Dollar Tabor re-emerges as an independent, flesh-and-blood player in this lively page-turning saga."

~Dave Kanzig, historian and moderator of www.babydoe.org

"Beautifully written, *Silver Echoes* is the captivating story of how entertainer Silver Dollar faced poverty, sexism, and internal battles with smarts and determination. You'll root for her daring and weep for her misfortunes. A must-read for immersing into turn-of-the-century America. Highly recommended!"

~Carol Van Den Hende, author of the award-winning *Goodbye Orchid* trilogy

"A gripping novel of redemption, fame, and the toll of self-sacrifice." Silver Dollar Tabor dreams of redeeming her family's tarnished name, but the journey to fame is fraught with danger and heartbreak. To survive, she conjures an alter-ego, Echo La Vode—a daring, unrelenting force who propels Silver into stardom. Yet, as her fame grows, so does Echo's grip on her life. When Silver tries to reclaim control, the battle between reality and illusion leads to devastating consequences. In *Silver Echoes*, Rebecca Rosenberg masterfully explores the cost of redemption, the allure of fame, and the toll of self-sacrifice. This haunting, true-story-inspired novel will captivate readers from the very first page."

~Rae Blair, author of *More Than I Ever Had*

"Gripping and immersive, the evocative setting and family story of struggle and survival pulled me in and didn't let go. A poignant historical dual-timeline novel, Silver Echoes, explores the psychological cost of trauma, the steep price of ambition, and the enduring strength of a mother's love. What lies behind a facade? How far does one go to protect this and at what cost?"

~Cara Black, NYT best selling author of
Three Hours in Paris

Please post a review on Amazon & Social Media. Thank you! ~Rebecca

Even in the darkest of times, hope blooms.

SILVER ECHOES

Rebecca Rosenberg

♡

Love in the
Shadow of trees,
Hope blooms

Rebecca Crowder

Also by Rebecca Rosenberg

The Gold Digger Novels:
Gold Digger, the Remarkable Baby Doe Tabor
Silver Echoes
Firebell Lil (2026)

The Secret Life of Mrs. London

Lavender Fields of America

The Champagne Widows Novels:
Champagne Widows, First Woman of Champagne
Madame Pommery, Creator of Brut Champagne
License to Thrill: Lily Bollinger (2025)

Join Rebecca Rosenberg's newsletter for notice of upcoming novels!
https://rebecca-rosenberg.com/join-rebeccas-email-list

SILVER ECHOES
A GOLD DIGGER NOVEL

REBECCA ROSENBERG

LION HEART
PUBLISHING

This is a work of fiction. Names, characters, organizations, places, events, and incidents are either products of the author's imagination or used fictiously.

Copyright © 2025 Rebecca Rosenberg

All rights reserved.
No part of this book may be reproduced, or stored in a retrieval system, or transmitted in any form or by any means, electronic, mechanical, photocopying, recording, or otherwise, without express permission of the publisher.

Paperback ISBN: 978-1-7329699-6-4
Ebook ISBN: 978-1-7329699-7-1

Published by
LION HEART PUBLISHING
California

Printed in the United States of America

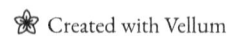

❦ Created with Vellum

*Dedicated to the enduring spirit of the Tabor family,
Silver Echoes reimagines their story,
revealing a timeless tale of grit,
resilience and love.*

*A portion of the profits will be donated to the preservation of The
Tabor Opera House, a monument
to the visionary pioneers of this country.*

~Rebecca Rosenberg

"Two entirely distinct states of consciousness were present, alternating frequently and without warning.

These states grew increasingly distinct as her illness progressed.

In one state, she recognized her surroundings; she was melancholy and anxious, but relatively normal.

In the other, she hallucinated and was 'naughty'—abusive …"

~Sigmund Freud, *Studies in Hysteria*

Part One

"People will do anything,
no matter how absurd,
in order to avoid facing
their own souls.

One does not become enlightened
by imagining figures of light,

but by making the darkness conscious."

~Carl Jung, *Psychology and Alchemy*

Chapter 1

1915

Silver price $0.50 per ounce

Denver, Colorado. The metal ladder rungs bit into my thin slippers, the rusty metal cold even through the thin fabric. I climbed the Lake Rhoda tower, the roar of the crowd below punctuated by whistles and the occasional, chilling scream. Their faces, a mountain meadow of columbine flowers in the afternoon sun, tilted upward, expectant. A nervous giggle, hollow and thin, escaped my lips. Is this reckless gamble for fame worth risking my neck? My hand hesitated on the ladder. Still time to change my mind. But as Mama always said, "Fortune favors the bold."

I stepped up, imagining Mama gazing up at the marquee out front, my name – SILVER DOLLAR TABOR – blazing in lights. I could almost hear her cheering, "That's my girl!" like she did at my dances and plays. She'd be so proud watching me soar on the highwire, a feat I'd imagined a thousand times, yet still sent shivers down my spine. Jaw clenched on the mouthpiece, wearing nothing but orange feathers and fishnets, my hair flowing behind like a magnificent plume. Mama was always my biggest fan, and I missed her cheering me on. But she was always at the mine. That blasted Matchless Mine was a prison swallowing her whole and leaving me with nothing but a whispered goodnight and cold mush before sun up. But Mama wouldn't have to be chained there any longer. Once I was a star, she could finally leave that hellhole, that life that was slowly killing her.

But first, I have to survive this. And something in the sway of the tower, the way the wind howled through the wires, whipping my tail feathers around my thighs and threatening to rip me from the ladder, told me that might not be so easy.

Each rung sent a jolt of pain through my feet as I climbed. Below, Lake Rhoda shimmered, reflecting a dizzying upside-down world. Lordy, what have I gotten myself into? But then I picture it: the crowds roaring, the flashbulbs popping. My name in every headline. This crazy stunt will make me the talk of the town, the next big thing.

Fifty feet below, Doris, the freckle-faced comedian who tried to upstage me in every scene we'd shared at Pikes Peak Photoplay, shook the ladder with a wicked grin. "Break a leg, Silver Spoon," Doris screeched, her eyes sparked with mischief and envy.

My foot slipped off the rung, and I snatched back the ladder, my stomach doing the turkey trot. "Pipe down, Doris. This ladder's wobbly enough without your racket." My heart did a jig in my chest, and for a moment, the shadowy lake below seemed to call to me, promising an end to the climb, to the fear. I shuddered, pushing away the thought like a bad dream. Gripping the ladder tightly, I continued my ascent.

"Silver Spoon!" Doris's words cut through the air. "Don't forget, if you fall, I'm right here to take your place."

"In your dreams, schemer," I yelled back, resolutely climbing to the next rung. Darn that Doris, always ready to undermine me when it came to a gig she coveted. I couldn't let that wannabe actress steal my thunder this time.

Halfway up the ladder, the wind whipped my long hair in my face, threatening to blind me as tiny orange feathers from my costume whirled down like frenzied fireflies. I wanted to cross myself but couldn't let go. "Oh, Blessed Mary, carry me across the lake or I'm a dead woman." My hands, slick with sweat, clung desperately to the rusted rungs of the ladder.

The world below blurred into a nightmarish spectacle. Garish lights swirled, casting grotesque shadows on the grimacing faces of painted clowns. The cacophony of the fairground: the tinny music, the rollercoaster screams, the maniacal laughter rose up to meet me like an out-of-tune honkey-tonk. The ground seemed to sway beneath me, the Ferris wheel a dizzying blur of color.

The lake was a dark abyss, beckoning with a siren's song. A childhood memory surfaced, unbidden and unwelcome: icy water closing over my head. The desperate struggle for air. The terror. I screamed, but the only answer was the echoing silence of the empty lake. My sister, Lily, had abandoned us; no one to watch out for me. But then, a lisping voice, a soft and reassuring presence, had cut through my panic. "Stand up, silly. The water's only to your waist." Even now, perched high above the ground, that memory sent shivers down my spine. I could use my secret friend about now.

Like an answer to my prayer, a chill whisper brushed my skin, raising goosebumps on my thighs. "You didn't drown then." Ethereal as the breeze itself. "And you won't drown now." The whisper lingered, a soothing balm against my fear, stilling the frantic flutter of my stomach.

The barker's shout shattered the spell. "Silver Dollar's death-defying Slide for Life!"

Below, Pikes Peak Photoplay's dreamboat script boy, Carl Erikson, waved from the crowd, his golden locks practically blinding me. Just when I'd been willing to overlook that he was a head shorter than me and date him, a big picture studio in Chicago had offered him a job, and now I'll never know if we could have been a hot item. A pang of longing stabbed at my heart.

Truth be told, I'd thought about hopping on that train to Chicago with Carl. But I was strapped for cash since Pikes Peak Photoplay paid peanuts to bit players like me. But their stars? They lived like royalty. This stunt was my chance to get noticed, to become a leading lady. But best of all, to see the Tabor name up in lights again. If I flubbed this, I'd be back to slinging hash and hiding my gams under a frumpy apron. Bringing more shame to Mama and me.

Reaching the top, I climbed onto the wobbly platform creaking under my feet. The lake below gaped wide as Moby Dick's choppers, ready to swallow me. A realization hit me like a bucket of snowballs. *I can't swim* ... I can't swim! Why had I never thought of that when I accepted this stunt? Had I lost my mind, risking my life? If I backed out now, I'd be forever branded a coward. But if I went through with it ... I need this chance.

The iron mouthpiece attached to the highwire looked suspiciously like a horse stirrup, much larger than I remember. Stretching my lips around the iron and biting down, the metallic flavor mingled with the acrid taste of fear. With a surge of adrenaline, I forced my slippers to the edge, sun beating down on my face, wind whipping at my hair. My lips cracked, my tongue gagged, and my heart hammered a frantic drumroll against my ribs. One step, just one step ...

The crowd's roar swelled with the same intoxicating elixir of attention and adoration that always drew me in, daring me to win or lose. Papa's gambling blood, Ma said. He'd gambled on our silver mines 'til the crash. Then we crashed too. Never recovered. But this time would be different. This time, Silver Dollar Tabor would not be consumed by the vicious claws of failure. This time, I'd shine brighter than the stars themselves.

Teeth clenched on the iron mouthpiece, I leaped into the open air, my triumphant smile a torch against the infinite blue.

Chapter 2

1932

Silver price $0.28 per ounce

Leadville, Colorado. Baby Doe Tabor squinted through the iron gunsight of her rusty Winchester rifle, tracking the stranger climbing the icy road from the once-booming mining town, now a ghost of its former glory, much like herself. The oily smell of coal smoke mingled with the crisp mountain air, the wind howling and biting at her exposed skin, a chilling unease churning in her gut.

What could this city slicker want all the way up here at the Matchless Mine? Trouble, most likely. The kind that came with unpaid taxes, looming liens or another lawyer hungry to snatch her last remaining asset.

The mine's rusty headframe groaned like an old man's bones in the desolate landscape, as Charlie, the sole miner she kept on since the Depression, strained to haul up a meager load of ore. He'd be expecting her help, but she couldn't risk leaving. Not with this stranger approaching.

The man's fashionable driving cap shielded his ears from the wind. A crimson scarf whipped around his neck. Snow clung to his polished wingtips, foolish choice for the mountains. His bare red hands clutched a leather portfolio. What secrets did it hold?

Twenty paces from her cabin, she shouted, "Stop right there." Her finger trembled on the cold trigger. Would it even fire?

He doubled over, gasping for breath in the thin mountain air. After a ragged moment, he finally managed to speak. "Mrs. Tabor? I knew Silver Dollar for years. Came to pay my respects."

Her fingers tightened their grip on the rifle, knuckles bone white against the worn wood. No one had come looking for Silver for seven years since the newspapers screamed about her shocking death, the gruesome circumstances forever imprinted on her mind.

"My daughter's not here." The words still choked her, grief an open wound. She wouldn't let this stranger see her pain.

"I know that ma'am," he puffed, finally reaching the stoop. Off came his fancy cap, revealing blond curls against a tanned face. His fine coat looked downright silly next to her grimy overalls and worn-out jacket, her once-golden hair hidden beneath a miner's hat. A sour taste, like spoiled milk, filled her mouth. Silks and satins were a lifetime ago; now she was just a scarecrow guarding a dying dream.

"I'm Carl Erikson. Silver and I were ..." He coughed, the sound harsh in the mountain air. "We were friends."

More than friends, she reckoned, by the longing in his eyes and the wistful curve of his lips. She recalled his name from Silver's letters, a tangle of discouraged dreams and disappointments. But which man was he? A friend? A lover? One of the gangsters she ran with?

"Were you the Fuller Brush man? The one she wrote about marrying?" The memory stung, a reminder of Silver's impulsive nature.

"No, ma'am. I'm a screenwriter for Warner Bros. in Hollywood." He stared into his cap like a crystal ball gone dark. "Knew Silver during her acting days."

Mercy me, a real friend of Silver's? She lowered the rifle, but caution remained. Everyone wanted something, especially someone asking after Silver Dollar. Couldn't afford to be naive.

Especially not now, with Silver long gone and the mine on the verge of collapse. "Have a seat," she gestured toward the cracked willow chair.

Erikson sat cautiously, his gaze lingering on the foot of snow piled on the roof of the cabin. The hissing headframe of the Matchless Mine loomed behind the cabin, a constant reminder her precarious situation.

Rubbing his shoulder, a painful grimace contorted his handsome face.

"Something troubling you, Mr. Erikson?"

"Just an old injury acting up." He turned to the snow-capped peaks, a troubled reflection in his Hollywood blue eyes.

He was hiding something. But what? This Carl wasn't Silver's type. She remembered her wild, dangerously beautiful daughter, arms grasping a rough-and-tumble rodeo rider, galloping bareback through Leadville. The scent of horse sweat and dust filled the air as they raced down Harrison, a shopkeeper frowning from his doorway, a group of women whispering behind their hands. Silver, hair flying in the wind, leaned back and whooped with delight, her hands around his taut abdomen tighter, thighs clenching his. Baby Doe took her to confession when she finally came home.

Carl seemed a world away from Silver's dramatic rebellious streak that always got her in trouble. His smooth hands had never seen a shovel, yet a writer's callus marked his middle finger. Two kindred spirits weaving tales of sorrow and heartache? Perhaps. But trust was a luxury Baby Doe couldn't afford. Not anymore.

"This Leadville weather is as crazy as Silver said." He blotted his forehead his handkerchief embroidered with WB. "The sun burns, but the wind cuts like a knife."

"Leadville's altitude's two miles high," she replied. "Enough to make a grown man cry. Seems to have ruffled your feathers a bit."

He leaned back, portfolio on his lap. "So, how's the silver price these days with the Depression and all?"

So that's it then, the real reason for his visit. "You come to talk about Silver Dollar?" She gripped the rifle across her lap, a silent warning. "Or is it the silver you're after, Mr. Erikson?"

He rubbed his shoulder again. "I just remember how excited Silver Dollar got when silver increased to over a dollar during the Great War."

"Down to twenty-eight cents an ounce now." She polished the rifle handle with her blue bandana. "Not worth the labor to mine it."

He sighed, his breath carrying the faint scent of licorice, reminding her of her husband, Horace. "Ever notice how Silver's moods mirrored the silver market?" Erikson looked out at Turquoise Lake, frozen over. "Soaring and crashing with every fluctuation."

Surprise tightened her chest. 'You noticed that, did you?' she mused. "Most folks just saw the glitter and the glamour. Never the storms brewing beneath." She felt a surge of kinship with this stranger. He understood Silver's tumultuous soul, and obviously cared for her anyway. She'd tried to help her daughter, tried to teach her God's ways. She prayed every night that she hadn't failed.

Charlie ambled over, best as his bowlegs could carry him, wiping gloves on his overalls. "Fixin' to go to the assay office." He frowned at the stranger. "Want me to stick 'round 'til yer comp'ny leaves?"

She waved him on. "I'm fine, Charlie. Just reminiscing with an old friend of Silver Dollar's."

Charlie shot him a sidelong glance. "I'll be back afore sundown, then." He shoved the ore cart toward town. The Annunciation Church bell rang four times, a distant call to Vespers.

Erikson shivered, his breath misting in the frigid air. "If the price of silver is so low, why keep digging?"

"Ever felt hunger gnawing at ya, keeping you up nights?" Her voice sounded sharper than she intended.

He raised his hands in surrender. "No offense, Mrs. Tabor."

A flush of remorse heated her cheeks. "There's more than silver here, son." Her arm swept the ore piles. A lifetime of obsession flickered in her mind: the booms and busts, the aching backs, the stubborn hope. "Lead, zinc, copper ... molybdenum. We fight for every scrap."

Carl glanced up at the pine-covered hill. "Silver and I ... we were coming to see you." His hand ran through his curls. "She was helping me write a screenplay about the Tabors and wanted to ask you some details."

Baby Doe's jaw clenched, a wave of bitterness washing over her. Silver had written about it years ago, full of excitement, but nothing had come of it, like everything else she started. Now, the whole idea seemed pointless, a hollow echo of what might have been. "If Silver had wanted to come back, she would have."

"No, really. We were coming. In fact, that's why I came here, Mrs. Tabor. I need your help to finish the screenplay." Carl patted his leather portfolio. "There're gaps in the storyline about when Horace first discovered silver, became a senator, when you met, your wedding ... Some Silver told me, but I've forgotten." His forehead furrowed. "Was it Sarah Bernhardt or Lillie Langtry that Silver tap-danced with at the Tabor theater?"

She scoffed. The idea of a movie about her family felt like a cruel joke given all that had happened. "The past is dead and buried. Best let it stay that way."

He leaned forward, eyes pleading. "Please, Mrs. Tabor. Silver dreamed of seeing the Tabor movie on the marquee of the Tabor Grand in Denver."

A pain pulsed in her temple. "Listen here, Mr. Hollywood." Her gaze hardened. "I want no part in a movie that exploits the scandal this family has had to face."

An ominous creak on the roof broke the silence. A giant icicle, glistening in the sunlight tore loose from the roof, shattering into a thousand shards between them.

Carl Erikson jumped back, all the life and light drained out of his face.

She felt a pang of sympathy for him, for the pain she caused. "Son," she said softly, her hand resting on his knee, "no movie will change the fact that neither of us were there for Silver Dollar in the end."

A shudder wracked his body. "That's just it. I was with Silver at her flat that night."

She jumped up, ice skittering across the cabin stoop. The wind whipped at her face, carrying the scent of pine and snow. "You were there?" Disbelief and fear swirled within her. Grabbing her rifle, she aimed straight between his eyes. "Explain yourself."

He held up his palms, choking back a sob. "Silver Dollar was alive when I left her, I swear. We made plans to meet the next day at the Palmer House, but she never showed." Tears welled in his eyes. "The doctor said she died in great agony. Burns ... blisters ... her skin ..." He trailed off, unable to continue.

She slumped against the splintered cabin, the Winchester heavy in her shaking hands. His first-hand details were just as gruesome as the reporters had described. The image of her daughter engulfed in flames was seared into her mind, the cruelest end for her vibrant, beautiful girl twirling in the Tabor Opera House, her laughter echoing through the lobby. Silver, sweet girl, her skin blistered and charred ... a vision that haunted Baby Doe's nightmares. How could she have let this happen?

"Did the police questioned you?" she asked him.

He wiped his cheek. "They interrogated all of her men. Friends, lovers, anyone who might have known something." He glanced at her, hesitating. "Silver ran with a rough crowd, Mrs. Tabor. But in the end, the police ruled it an accident." He scoffed. "Lots of accidents in Chicago in the twenties."

The cockamamie story she'd told reporters crumbled, burying her in an avalanche of truth. She'd made up the story to protect both her daughter and herself. And she'd stick to it till her dying day. "My daughter is in a convent serving the Lord." Each time she repeated the tale, her vision of Silver in a nun's habit grew sharper, a comforting mirage in her grief.

Carl's hand emerged from his pocket, cradling rose quartz beads knotted with glass roses, the silver crucifix gleaming in the last rays of sun.

Baby Doe's breath caught. The rosary she'd given Silver to protect her. If it was here, it hadn't done its job. Had her daughter clung to it in her final moments? "How did you get that?"

Carl laid the rosary in her wrinkled palm.

"I had it restrung," he said.

The beads felt warm, almost as if Silver had just prayed on them. "Did the rosary break?"

His eyes avoided hers. "She was angry."

Baby Doe heard a low growl on the hill under the railroad track. The hairs on her arms stood on end. A lone cougar, its sleek fur the color of dried leaves, crouched on powerful haunches, its glowing eyes fixed on them. "Silver Dollar's cougar." She shooed him away. "Get along, you!" The wildcat slunk into the shadows, but Baby Doe's gaze remained fixed on the spot where it had vanished, a knot tightening in her stomach. "He still lurks around, waiting for her to return."

Carl shuddered. "Strange, isn't it?"

"Silver was scared to death of him." A smile crossed her lips. "But she loved him just the same."

Down below, Charlie pulled up the empty ore cart, his whistle a lonely sound in the wind. A sudden gust whipped flakes of snow like icy needles against her cheeks. The sun dipped below the mountains, a chill spreading through her.

"Jiminy Cricket, it's freezing." Carl wrapped his scarf tighter. "If you change your mind about the Tabor film, I'm at the Vendome." He walked toward town, fading into the twilight.

But damned if she was going to let the only man who knew

Silver slip away. "Thursday." Her rasp raked through the biting wind. "The Vendome serves spaghetti and meatballs."

He paused, turning back to face her. "Pardon me?"

"You can buy me dinner." The wind whistled through the pines. "Well, Mr. Erikson?"

"Only if you call me Carl." He waved his driving cap. "And leave the rifle at home." Retreating down the mountain road, his silhouette vanished in the shadows.

Baby Doe pressed the warm rosary against her cheek, almost like Silver Dollar next to her. "I failed you then, precious girl. But I won't fail you again." Determination coursed through her veins as she gripped the beads tighter. She'd wrangle some answers out of this young man. He knew more than he was saying. That's for darn tootin'.

Chapter 3

1915

Silver Price $0.50 per Ounce

Denver, Colorado. I sprung off the towering platform to the crowd's chants: "Silver Dollar. Silver Dollar." The mouthpiece nearly jerked the teeth clean out of my head, but I clenched down tighter. My stomach swooped up into my lungs, and for one ecstatic moment I soared above the cottonwoods of Lakeside Park. Thin air whistled over my fishnet hose as I posed in a dramatic arabesque, a tail of orange feathers flying behind. The taste of blood filled my mouth as the mouthpiece dug into my gums.

Neck straining, jaw clamped tight, eyes forced to peer up at the pulley sparking on the wire as I whizzed across Lake Rhoda. A purple thunderhead was blowing in from the east, and a flock of black ravens jeered.

As the shoreline shrank away, the cheers faded into a distant murmur. When the wind died down, a deafening silence fell, broken only by the buzz and spark of the thin highwire.

Suddenly, the iron mouthpiece seized on the highwire with a screech, jerking me forward then back as my teeth were shaken from their roots. Mother Mary, please don't let me lose my smile. The pulley, attached to a highwire above, was supposed to glide smoothly along the wire, carrying me safely to the other side. But something went wrong. My body swung violently, an orange pendulum dangling a hundred feet above the dark water. My fingers, reaching for the pulley, were scorched by the friction of the wire. I tried to pry it loose, to wrench my body free from the deadly crimp. Nothing budged. A dam burst within me, unleashing a torrent of pure terror. Should have listened to Mama's warnings about my foolish feats. Should have listened.

The audience yelled from the shore in a garbled sound I couldn't make out. My swinging ebbed, and I hung suspended, my jaw throbbing, blood pulsing in my ears.

Would they still pay me if I didn't make it across the lake?

I squinted to the shore to see if they were coming to rescue me, but it was too far away to tell. Slowly, but surely, my jaw was losing strength. I clamped down harder on the iron mouthpiece and felt something crack. My jawbone spasmed into a rigid position, shooting fireballs of pain through my head.

With a sudden, painful lurch, my jaw gave out, at once unhinging and gaping wide. The iron mouthpiece tore over my teeth, and I was falling. I clawed for the wire, but it slipped from my grasp. A scream of terror tore through me, sweat stinging my eyes, blurring the rapidly approaching water. The wind howled past my ears, a chilling prelude to the icy plunge.

"I can't swim!" I yelled, the vast emptiness swallowing my words. Mother Mary, full of grace, where is my rosary when I needed it?

The soles of my feet struck the frigid surface. A thousand icy needles stabbed my body, seizing my muscles in a painful grip. The reek of decay and stagnant water filled my nostrils, the taste of algae and mud coating my tongue. Kicking, thrashing, gurgling ... a desperate fight for survival. Below, a swarm of blood-red leeches erupted from the weeds, their razor teeth biting my skin. Each movement was agony, each breath a burning struggle. My lungs screamed, filling with foul water. The black depths beckoned with their silent embrace. This is how it ends.

"Don't give up on the light above, Silver." The electric lisp ricocheted through the watery abyss. "Remember, we're waterbirds meant to soar, not sink, my dove."

Was she really back? Ten long years had passed since I'd banished my imaginary friend, Echo, to the shadowy corners of my mind. She was a relic of my lonely childhood, a figment of my imagination born from the emptiness I felt when my sister, Lily, abandoned Mama and me. My Echo was really here, whispering words of encouragement as I teetered on the brink of death.

Fueled by her support, my legs kicked powerfully toward the surface. Memories of our laughter under starlit skies and fantastical stories spun by a crackling campfire sparked joy in the depths of my despair. My secret friend had returned, offering hope in the face of impending doom.

But the inky depths fought back, their icy grip tightening around my limbs. Sinuous pondweed wrapped around me like eels, dragging me deeper into the shadows. The surface, once a tantalizing shimmer, now receded with each frantic gasp. Despair, a leaden weight, threatened to crush my spirit.

"Unravel the weeds, Silver, like silken threads of hope," Echo's ethereal lisp emerged from the depths. But the pondweed's suffocating embrace tightened, its darkness consuming me. My fingers, numb and clumsy, fumbled at the tangled mass. My lungs burned, desperate for air, each breath a searing pain. Echo faded too, a figment of my traumatic past. Gone.

We will drown together. Me and the ghost of my past, forever bound in this watery tomb.

Carl, the script boy lingered in my mind, a final pang of regret before oblivion claimed me.

∼

Next thing I knew, Carl's face loomed over mine, his blue eyes wide with panic. "Silver? Silver, can you hear me?" The sound came from a distance, muffled by the throbbing pain in my temples, a sharp ache that echoed with every beat of my heart. I blinked, my vision a kaleidoscope of blurry colors and distorted shapes.

He tilted my head back, pinching my nostrils closed, and then his lips were on mine, his warm breath puffing into my lungs. My eyes flew open, and a gasp escaped my lips as water spewed from my mouth. "Carl?" I coughed, my voice hoarse and weak.

"Easy," he murmured, relief flooding his features. "You're alright." He continued the mouth-to-mouth resuscitation for a few more breaths, then helped me sit up, his arm a sturdy support against my trembling back. His touch sent warmth through my chilled body, and I clung to him for a moment, burying my face in his shoulder, the fear and the cold still clinging to me like a shroud.

As he gently checked me for injuries, my mind drifted back to the depths of the lake. Had it truly been Echo down there? Or just my own desperate imagination? I hadn't thought of Echo in years. After my sister left, Mama tolerated my secret friend, seeing how she filled the void Lily had left behind. But as our friendship deepened, Mama took me to Father Wilkins for confession. The priest, with his zucchetto cap and flowing white beard, was horrified. "A voice in your head is not of God," he warned. "Turn away from this delusion and pray to the Mother of God." It had been years since I'd heard Echo's whisper like the rustle of leaves in the wind. Echo had been my comfort through loneliness and fright, her daring and strength encouraging me to push my limits. Now that she'd returned, excitement battled with the lingering terror.

"You gave me quite a scare," Carl said, his voice husky with emotion. His wet shirt clung to his chest, his blue gaze searching mine.

I laughed weakly, propping myself up on my elbows, orange

feathers soaking wet and tangled. "They won't forget my name in a hurry, at least."

He mimed a newsboy calling, "Silver Dollar Drowns for Applause."

Playfully, I whipped him with a cattail, fuzzy spears flying as we laughed. "Next time, try a bit more 'Prince Charming,' a little less 'tadpole,'" I teased, nudging him with my elbow.

"Hey, I resemble that remark!" he retorted, feigning offense. "Besides, who needs Prince Charming when you have a damsel in distress who can't even swim?" He gently brushed a strand of wet hair from my face, his fingers lingering on my cheek. For a moment, the world around us faded away, and it was just the two of us, alone on the shore.

Burying my face in my shaking hands, I inhaled the earthy scent of mud, a grim reminder of the abyss I'd barely escaped. But Echo had been there, pulling me back from the brink like she had in the past.

Carl placed a gentle hand on my back, his gaze holding mine. "What took you so long to surface?"

"Just the weeds," I choked out, my voice trembling.

"Your lips are blue," he said, his voice laced with concern. "But they're still the most beautiful lips I've ever seen."

Over the dune, I heard the crowd getting nearer. I jumped up, legs wobbling. "I can't face them now."

He wrapped his arm around my waist. I clung to his shoulder, hobbling along the cattail path. Each squelch of my ruined slippers marked another step away from the lake's icy grip.

"Why did the tightrope walker cross the lake?" Carl asked, his eyes twinkling.

"Telling jokes at a time like this?" But I couldn't help but chuckle. "To get to the other side?"

"No," Carl said, "to prove she wasn't all wet!"

Laughter bubbled up in me, and for the first time since the water closed over my head, the world felt bright again. Carl's wit and kindness were a comfort against the chill of the lake and my lingering fear. But then, a realization pierced the idyllic moment: the yawning emptiness that I would feel when Carl left for Chicago. A cold gust of wind swept across the lake, and I shivered, a premonition of the loneliness to come. What then?

∼

ON THE BUSTLING STREET, Carl hailed a Denver Electric Cab, its yellow wood frame and black canvas top bouncing on its spoked wheels. The smell of horse manure mingled with the fumes from the motor cars making me queasy. Only my second time in one of these motorized contraptions. Big motor cars and horse carriages now vied for space on the road. Papa would turn over in his grave to see this mayhem. I shivered in my soggy feathered leotard, cold and shock seeping into my bones. Orange plumage caught between my legs, the headdress hopelessly tangled in my long locks. It would take hours to untangle it. My dream of stardom drowned in front of a standing-room-only crowd. Had to redeem myself.

Yet Carl turned to me, his big eyes brimming with promise. "There's still time to change your mind and come with me to Chicago. We can catch the evening train."

So easy to just say yes, to let him whisk me away from all this. But I owed it to myself ... and Mama. To reach for the big brass ring. "You know I can't miss that audition for *The Greater Barrier* film," I said, my voice firm despite the tremor in my heart. "The leading role is perfect for me. My big chance to really make it."

He took my pruney fingers between his palms and rubbed them back to life. "Bah! Pikes Peak Photoplay wouldn't know a starlet from a saloon girl. Come to Selig Polyscope with me, that's the big time. I'll introduce you to the producer myself." He smiled that Pepsodent smile I found hard to resist. But I'd fallen for a hundred pretty faces, and where had it gotten me? If I wanted to be a star, I had to stick to my guns.

"I appreciate the offer, Carl," I said. "But I have to do this on my own." I squeezed his hand. "Besides, I can't leave Mama up in Leadville through the winter. She'll freeze to death." An urge to apologize welled up inside me, but what good would it do?

The taxi pulled up at my boardinghouse, and I tried to end on a cheery note. "Better change your clothes before Chicago, Carl. You smell like a swamp critter."

He wrinkled his nose, laughing. "Back at you."

"Be sure to write." I waved, my hand trembling, as the taxi rattled away, his face in the back window. A cold wind blew down the bustling street, chilling me in my wet costume. A lump formed in my throat. I never thanked Carl properly, not for saving my life, not for anything.

Was Echo truly gone also? Or had she simply retreated into the shadows, waiting for another moment of desperation?

The taxi disappeared around the corner, leaving only the lingering smell of exhaust. Shivering, I turned toward my boardinghouse, the weight of loneliness pressing down on me.

Chapter 4

1932

Silver price $0.28 per ounce

Leadville, Colorado. Snow fell, wet and fast, as Baby Doe braved the icy boardwalk, her coat and dress hitched up. Brought back memories of those snowy days when she held her two daughters mittens as they walked this street. Her husband's fancy streetlamps, the ones Horace put up when he was mayor, shed sad yellow puddles in the snow. The cafes and saloons were all closed up quiet as a tomb. First the silver mines went bust, then with the Depression everything else went downhill.

Her dress, a faded blue taffeta gown resurrected from a trunk she kept in the church basement, hung loose on her frame. The scent of mothballs clung to it, overpowering the delicate fragrance of Lily of the Valley. Before her loomed the Vendome Hotel, a shadow of its former glory as the Tabor Grand. The faded awning, bearing a ghostly trace of the Tabor name, seemed to mock her. Snowflakes fell steadily on it, hiding the Tabor name beneath the weight of time and snow. Baby Doe tightened her grip on her purse, her jaw clenched firm. She'd find out more about Silver Dollar from Mr. Erikson ... Carl. With a shake of her head, she pushed aside her nerves and stepped up to the door, the sound of her boots crunching on the icy steps.

"Mrs. Tabor?" The doorman, once a bellboy, smiled. "Remember me?"

"Never forget that smile, Willie." Inside, the musty scent of mildew and faded opulence stung her nose. They'd taken it all for granted back then: the hotel, the opera houses, the Denver mansion. Now, chandeliers gathered dust, the tapestry soiled.

The coat check girl, lost in *True Story Magazine*, barely glanced up. A curt snatch of her coat, a plastic token. Baby Doe felt invisible now, not the pampered Mrs. Horace Tabor of old.

"You'd get more tips without the magazine, young lady," she muttered, striding down the hallway. The gilded mirror reflected a stubborn gumption in her eyes, her face lined with wrinkles. Silver Dollar used to call them "spiderwebs." Would her daughter be ashamed to see her now?

Tiger lilies, like the ones Silver used to send when she was flush, bloomed on the central table. The dining room, smelling of steak and smoke, was a stage where Baby Doe had played a tragic role. But tonight, the script was hers. Carl held the missing pieces of Silver's story. But was she ready to face the pain that might come with those revelations? She took a deep breath, steeling herself for the encounter. She had to know the truth, no matter the cost.

∽

CARL ERIKSON, his blond curls slicked back as best he could, rose from his corner table. As she approached, she saw he wore a striped linen jacket, the likes of which belonged on a beach. "Mrs. Tabor, I'm so happy you could join me." His gaze lingered on her outdated dress, and she met his eyes unflinchingly.

The maître d' pulled out a chair as if bestowing a royal favor. "Allow me, madam."

"Mrs. Tabor," she corrected. "The Tabors who built this hotel."

The maître d' blanched. "My apologies, Mrs. Tabor. I ... I didn't realize who you were."

"Shouldn't matter who I am. Respect is owed to all." How long it had taken her to understand that.

He bowed stiffly. "Shall I pour the wine?"

Carl's eyes crinkled at the edges. "Will you join me?"

She nodded. "Think I will." The maître d' poured from the straw-wrapped Chianti bottle. She and Horace had enjoyed wine, but since his passing she had no desire for it. But tonight, the thought of its warmth comforted her. She held the menu close and scanned the courses. "No spaghetti and meatballs?"

"Not since I've worked here, ma'am," a young waiter cocked his head.

Disappointment pooled in her stomach. Ernesto's spaghetti had always soothed her soul. Now, the menu featured steaks, tough and unyielding to her tender teeth. "Rainbow trout, please."

Erikson ordered the same, then raised his glass for a Gaelic toast. "Sláinte."

"Wouldn't have pegged you for an Irishman." She swallowed the wine, the fruity notes easing her disappointment at the menu.

"Silver Dollar taught me that toast; she was proud of your Irish roots." He smiled and blushed. "I'm Swedish, myself. Grew up in New Haven, Connecticut."

"And what do your parents think about you living so far away?"

He scoffed. "Good riddance, I imagine. They don't approve of show business." He stared into the ruby depths of the wine. "My father calls Hollywood 'the devil's den.'"

Her fingers clenched the tablecloth, guilt rippling through her. Silver had run away from her, too. She took another sip of wine. "Tell me about your film Mr. Erikson."

"Carl." He shot his finger at her, and she smiled.

"To be honest, it started as a way to get close to Silver Dollar. Writing the film together, that is." The tips of his ears colored, as he fingered the stem of his glass. "She told me Tabor stories wilder than anything I could ever dream up." He fanned his fingers theatrically. "Adultery? Betrayals? A mountain of silver that brought nothing but heartbreak and disgrace."

So, Silver twisted their love story into a tawdry spectacle. "We may not have been saints." Shame flared in her throat. "But I've tried to make up for that now." She repented every day for those sins at Annunciation Church.

"Was all that stuff about Oscar Wilde true?" He laughed nervously. "That drunken escapade down in the mine?"

She huffed. "Silver told you that? She wasn't even born then."

Carl pointed at her, eyes twinkling. "Exactly why I need your help. Only you know the truth about your story. Every tale Silver told me was more fantastical than the last."

She chuckled, warming to the idea. "Silver had a way of stretching the truth now and then."

"I was in awe of your daughter." Carl sighed heavily. "Ambitious, talented, drop-dead gorgeous. She was out of my league, but I couldn't help myself." He poured more wine. "Silver was a shooting star blazing across my life, brighter than anything I'd ever seen." His hand swiped the air in a gesture of loss and longing.

Silver had always spun a spell around men. And it always seemed to backfire in the end. But this fellow seemed so nice. What happened between them? "Do you mind me asking if you've met someone else?"

"Divorced." He cleared his throat. "Silver turned me down, and when I moved to Hollywood, I grabbed the first girl I met." His thumb touched his bare left finger. "Didn't last."

So, he'd proposed? Now she'd opened a can of worms. She was relieved when the waiter served the trout in small cast-iron skillets. Yeasty sourdough and sizzling fish filled the air with an enticing aroma, making her mouth water.

"Compliments of the chef," the waiter informed her, serving side plates of steaming spaghetti and rich garlicky tomato sauce.

She gasped. "My lands. Tell him I'm most grateful." Twirling spaghetti around her fork, she sopped up the rich sauce with warm bread, thinking of impish Silver doing the same thing as a girl.

Carl ate a bite of fish and closed his thick eyelashes while he chewed. "Rainbow Trout, huh? Haven't tasted fish this delectable in my life." He smiled a smile Silver Dollar must have liked.

"How far did you and Silver get with the screenplay?" She took another bite.

"Finished it later in Hollywood, and always wished I could show it to her." He put down his fork and drank half his glass of wine. "I just want to do the story justice, Mrs. Tabor ... for Silver Dollar."

He sounded almost desperate, and she reached across the table covering his hand with hers. "How can I help?"

"If we could go over the screenplay scene by scene and get your impressions of the stories Silver told me?" He sounded so hopeful she couldn't turn him down. Besides, the prospect of hearing Silver's stories filled her with anticipation.

"I will help you with your screenplay." Her breath hitched. "But I do have a condition."

Planting his chin in his hands, he grinned. "Shoot."

"I have Silver's letters." Something she'd never told the detectives who badgered her. "I knew something was wrong in Chicago. Her constant moves, job changes, hospital stays, the revolving door of men ... Help me understand her life in Chicago, who her friends were, what she did for a living, her state of mind. What really happened to her."

"Mrs. Tabor, you don't know what you're asking of me." Carl's fingers drummed a nervous rhythm. "Silver ... she changed like a kaleidoscope, each twist flashing a beauty that could blind you. Thrilling performances and heartbreaking tragedy. One minute the seductress, the next, cold as ice." His voice got husky. "Never revealing the whole picture, always hiding something."

Her impression exactly. "Maybe between the letters and what you know, we can figure something out. We could face the truth together."

His eyes darkened as he stared out the window at the sleeting snow, his face hard and unreadable. What was he hiding? A knot of anxiety tightened in her stomach. Was there something he didn't want me to know? Why had Silver turned down his proposal? Had Silver's overly dramatic letters exaggerated, or had she been running from something? What drove Silver from man to man? Why were her nerves perpetually frayed? Why did she beg Baby Doe for money one month, just to send her expensive gifts the next? Whatever the answers, it was obvious Baby Doe did not have the whole picture.

Finally, Carl reached out to shake her hand. "You have a deal, Mrs. Tabor."

"We can start tomorrow morning if that suits you." Enough for one day. The wine and turmoil had exhausted her.

Carl retrieved her coat and walked her through the lobby.

Willie, the doorman saluted her like the old days. "It's nasty out there. I'll drive you up to the mine, Mrs. Tabor. The hotel has an automobile for import'nt customers, and you're as import'nt as they come."

"Very well, Willie." She forced a smile and turned. "Thank you for dinner, Mr. Erikson."

"Carl." He smiled.

She shook his hand. "See you tomorrow, Carl."

On the street, the Model T sputtered an oily scent. She ducked into the back seat, the worn leather cold to the touch. Carl stood under the awning, shoulders hunched, hands pushed into his linen pockets. The Hollywood man looked so out of place in a blizzard, or was it his lost expression that plucked her heart strings?

Chapter 5

1915

Silver Price $0.50 per ounce

Denver, Colorado. The landlady's frown deepened as I walked past. "Looks like Miss Tabor took a dip in the wishing well and didn't get her wish."

"If wishes were fishes, I'd be swimming in a sea of fame." I retreated to my room, leaving a trail of water from my sopping tail feathers.

The one gaslight flickered, revealing stained wallpaper, a lumpy bed, and the stench of a dead rat caught in the wall. A shooting pain radiated from my jaw. In the mottled mirror, I examined my cracked molar, shredded gums, and blood-stained teeth. Not the look I was going for with my big audition coming up.

I kicked off my ruined slippers and collapsed onto the mattress, shivering. Pulling the dingy patchwork blanket around me, I tried to ignore my growling stomach. I guess Echo was a figment of my imagination, because she did not come to console me, no matter how much I begged her to take me away from here.

Instead, I found the rosary Mama gave me, its rose-quartz beads a solid comfort through my fingers. Just got to get that lead role and I'd be sitting pretty. If I fail, that sleazy lawyer of Mama's will probably sell off the mine, leaving us with nothing. We'll be stuck in this room, Mama and I, without two pennies to rub together. No matter how much I hate the Matchless, at least it's hope that someday it will pay off again. If we lose that hole in the ground, the light in Mama's eyes will be gone. I'll never see it again.

∽

THE NEXT DAY, I unpinned the soggy orange feathers from my leotard and spread them across the back stoop to dry under the autumn sun. My mouth throbbed, swollen and bruised, a constant reminder of my disastrous attempt at a high dive. Fallen leaves swirled around my feet, carrying the scent of damp earth and my damper spirit, now that Carl was gone.

"So, you and Carl are serious now?" Doris's smile cut sharp as a broken bottle.

"Not at all. He left for Chicago," I mumbled through the gauze, dabbing at my split lip with a limp towel.

Doris snorted, a gust that sent a few feathers tumbling. "You really fumbled that one, Silver Spoon. Letting a catch like that slip through your butter fingers."

I winced, clenching my teeth against the shooting pain. "Honey, Carl's too green for a seasoned starlet like me." The lie left a bitter taste, but a girl's gotta keep up appearances.

"Lakeside Park's pretty generous letting you try the Slide For Life again," Doris said, flicking my long legs with an orange feather. "'Specially since you can't swim a lick."

"They owe me, after their highwire nearly turned me into fish food." Plucking the feather from her grasp, I tickled her nose with it. "Besides, my near-death experience sold out the show."

Doris's face soured. "I could do that Slide for Life," she whined, "Please, Silver, I need this more than you. You've already got the looks, the legs, the legacy."

"If my audition at Pikes Peak goes well, I'll put in a good word for you with Lakeside Park."

Doris's eyes narrowed. "Pikes Peak already turned me down flat. The casting director said they don't need clowns."

The familiar ache of rejection settled in my chest. "Everyone faces challenges, Doris. You have talent. There'll be a part for you in the next film."

"Casting directors don't care about talent. They care about how you look in a bathing suit, plain and simple." Her bottom lip pushed out so far, a bird could poop on it.

"Come to church with me," I offered, hoping to ease her pain. "We'll pray for your big break."

"You know I ain't religious." She stalked inside, slamming the door.

I made my way to church alone, the moon casting long, skeletal shadows as I walked. The crisp autumn air bit at my cheeks, but the guilt chilled me to the bone. Mama's disappointed face flashed before my eyes, the memory of my harsh words burning like acid in my throat. Should I pray for forgiveness? For the strength to convince her to give up on Papa's dying wish? "Hang on to the Matchless," he'd told us, clinging to the hope of a fortune I no longer believed in. Fifteen years later, Mama was still toiling away, pouring blood and tears into that barren hole in the ground. Sixty-one now, she deserved a life free from the ache of mining, free from the burden of the Matchless. Every time I pictured her there, my stomach twisted with a fresh wave of guilt. Surely my plan, becoming a star and restoring the Tabor name, was a faster route to the fortune we needed. Then we'd never worry about money again, and Mama could finally live in the luxury she once enjoyed.

I lit a candle smelling of honey, its crackling flame illuminating the dim church. I prayed for my audition to be successful, and to be a source of pride for Mama again. A fragile hope flickered inside me, but a nagging voice whispered, what if you fail? My future, my mother's happiness ... everything depended on this audition. I wouldn't let anything, or anybody stand in my way.

Rounding the corner, I noticed two coppers crouched by a paddy wagon, their silhouettes sharp against the light of the streetlamp.

Doris pointed at me and shrieked, "There she is! Silver Dollar. She stole my sapphire ring."

My heart jumped to my throat. "What are you talking about?"

The landlady emerged, her rouged cheeks glowing unnaturally in the dusk. "Thieves like her have no place in my respectable establishment!" Venom dripped from her words. "Always slinking around in those scandalous outfits, singing like a banshee at midnight."

The younger officer's eyes widened in recognition. "Wait. Are you ...that Silver Dollar Tabor? The one who sang for the President?"

I forced a theatrical smile. "The one and only." I curtseyed grandly, hoping my fame might offer some protection. "Though I must say, this isn't quite the encore I had in mind."

"I thought that was you." He blushed, clearly starstruck.

But the older cop, his face hardened by years on the force, wasn't swayed. "Miss Tabor, you're coming down to the station for questioning. Turn around."

The cuffs bit into my wrists. "I demand to see our lawyer. JD Rockwell, Esquire."

"Sure, sweetheart. You'll get your lawyer." The older cop shoved me toward the wagon.

I spun around. "I didn't take your ring, Doris. Did you look in your bed?"

Doris clung to the landlady, her face a mask of distress, but an evil glint shone in her eyes.

"Get in," the cop barked, shoving me into the darkness. He slammed the door, plunging me into a cage of steel and shadows. Panic clawed at my throat. I yanked at the handcuffs. My blood ran cold. Doris wasn't after the ring at all; she wanted my spotlight. The Slide for Life.

∼

THE JAIL, with its faded wanted posters and overflowing ashtrays, reeked of stale tobacco and despair. The sheriff emerged from behind his desk, toothpick wagging in his mouth like a conductor's baton. He lumbered down the narrow hallway towards my cell, his keys jangling a mournful tune. "Alright, Miss Tabor," he drawled. "One phone call. Who's it gonna be?"

I held my swollen jaw, the pain radiating through my face. Who could I turn to? Mama would be mortified if she knew I was accused of stealing—one of the ten sins in the good book. And my uncles? They were tired of footing the bill for my failed dreams of glory. Just last week, Uncle Peter had cornered me at his cabaret I worked for extra cash, his face red with disappointment. "Silver Dollar, you've got to face it. You sing off key, your lisp is not cute anymore, and you're too tall and leggy for the chorus line. You're just not cut out for the stage." Then he'd launched into his usual tirade about finding a respectable husband and settling down. The thought of it made my stomach churn. Tea parties and charity balls? Never!

Only Mama still believed I could be a star. But at twenty-five, the clock was ticking. This audition was my last chance, my one shot at escaping the clutches of my overbearing uncles and proving them all wrong. Play-acting was my calling, my destiny—Silver Dollar Tabor, the rightful heir to the Tabor Grand Opera House legacy. But now, thanks to Doris and her conniving scheme, my dreams were hanging by a thread. If I missed this audition, it would all be over. I couldn't let that happen. I would find a way.

There was only one person I could truly trust: JD Rockwell. Mama's lawyer for the Matchless, with his handlebar mustache that could rival a walrus's whiskers and a booming laugh that shook the chandeliers in the Tabor Opera House, had always had a soft spot for me. He'd watched me grow up, a whirlwind of a girl twirling amidst the chaos of grimy miners, sharp-suited bankers, and smooth-talking politicians. I was a bright spark in the cutthroat world of mining fortunes, stock market shenanigans, and backroom political deals. "Uncle Rockwell," as my sister Lily and I called him, was the one person who would understand, who would move heaven and earth to get me out of this mess and keep my name from being splashed across the front page of every scandal sheet in Colorado.

I tossed my raven hair over my shoulder like a silken waterfall. "Sheriff, darling," I purred, my voice all honeyed distress. "If you could just contact my lawyer, JD Rockwell, he'd clear this whole mess up in a jiffy."

"Rockwell, huh?" the sheriff snorted, "That city slicker ain't gonna dirty his hands with your kind of trouble." He started to walk away.

Panicked, I clutched the cold, steel bars, like a prisoner in a melodrama. "Please, Sheriff. If I miss this audition, my life is over."

He stopped and spit a stream of tobacco juice into a spittoon. "Tell you what, Miss Tabor. I'll make the call. But no guarantees, mind you. Rockwell's a busy man."

I clapped my hands together. "Oh, thank you, Sheriff! You're a lifesaver!" I curtsied, my skirt swirling around my ankles. "I just know everything will be hunky-dory."

He grunted and lumbered away, leaving me alone in the cell with the dripping pipes and the scuttling cockroaches. I sank onto the hard cot, the rusty springs groaning in protest. This wasn't the glamorous life I'd envisioned for a rising star. But I had to believe that with JD on my side, I'd escape this mess and return to the movie set where I belonged.

. . .

Friday came and went. No Rockwell. Saturday. Sunday. Still no Rockwell. My swollen gums throbbed with a searing pain, a just reward for my foolish high dive. The cracked tooth, a jagged edge against my tongue, sent waves of agony through my jaw. The taste of blood mingled with the festering infection, a foul taste that lingered in my mouth.

The days bled into each other, a monotonous blur of despair. The sheriff, with his pitying glances and gruff pronouncements of "Nothin' yet, Miss Tabor," became my only connection to the outside world. The day of my audition passed, unmarked, uncelebrated, a cruel mockery of my shattered dreams.

"It's over," I choked out, sinking to the cold, unforgiving concrete, the rough surface scraping against my skin. Alone. Forgotten. Abandoned. My family was probably relieved. Mama, finally free from the burden of my reckless escapades. My uncles, no longer obligated to bail me out of my disasters. Even JD Rockwell, perhaps he'd never really cared after all. It was easier to forget about Silver Dollar, the aspiring actress who always seemed to land herself in trouble.

The sounds of the jail jangled nightmarishly around me. Sobs and whimpers drifted from the unseen depths, interrupted by a desperate cry or the clank of a metal cup against the bars. Phantom voices whispered through the walls, murmuring unintelligible threats and accusations. I couldn't see them, these other inmates, these lost souls trapped in this purgatory, but their presence was a constant, chilling clatter of my own isolation.

I huddled in the corner, shutting out the darkness and terror. Hours or days passed, I couldn't be sure. A strange tingling sensation flooded my body, a wave of icy chills followed by an intense warmth that spread through my veins like wildfire. A secret language between me and the imaginary friend who'd always been my refuge.

"Well, well, well," a voice chirped with a mischievous lilt. "Looks like someone's got a front-row seat to the pity party!"

A gasp escaped my lips. "Echo? Is that you?"

"The one and only," she replied, her playful whisper danced through the air like circus balloons. "Just in time for fun and games, it seems."

Echo materialized before me, not in flesh and blood, but as a shimmering apparition, her form flickering like a candle flame in a drafty church. Her eyes, pools of midnight starlight, sparkled with a daring glint, and her maniacal giggle rang in my ears, a welcome respite to the grim jail cell. "Don't you worry your pretty little head, Silver," she whispered, her voice a silken promise woven from the fabric of my own desires. "We'll have some fun in this dump yet."

With a mischievous grin, she chased a cockroach across the floor with a broom straw, her laughter bouncing off the cement walls. "Look at him go!" she squealed. "He thinks he can outrun us, but we're too quick!"

She plucked a long thread from the frayed hem of my dress and challenged me to a game of cat's cradle, our phantom fingers weaving intricate patterns in the air.

"Don't worry, my broken doll," she confided, her voice a warm caress against my cheek. "I'm here now."

The bars and concrete seemed to fade, their harsh edges replaced by the soft, hazy glow of the meadow where we used to play as children. With Echo by my side, my desperation melted away, replaced by a giddy sense of defiance. Maybe, with Echo's help, I could survive this nightmare and emerge stronger, bolder, ready to conquer the world.

The sheriff's shadow fell across the cracked floor. I didn't bother to look up. He slid a tray of food through the opening, the smell of greasy stew doing nothing to tempt my appetite. I didn't touch it. Nothing mattered but Echo and the comforting world we'd created in this prison of shadows and horrors.

The iron bars creaked open, and I squinted, my heart leaping at the sight of JD Rockwell's familiar beaver-hide cowboy hat. Years of legal battles had forged canyons around his walrus mustache, proof of secrets kept and cases won. A hefty silver nugget, plucked from the depths of the Matchless, gleamed on his bolo tie, payment for Rockwell's services.

"Silver Dollar, sweetheart." His hand slid around my shoulder. "Uncle Rockwell's here to get you outta this stink hole." He hauled me up, my legs shaky as a newborn colt's.

I pulled away from his touch. "I thought you were going to let me die in here." I looked back at the empty cell. What about Echo? Her elfish grin flashed before my eyes. But just as quickly faded, like a dream dissolving in the cold light of day.

Rockwell caressed my swollen jaw, his touch gentle despite his calloused fingers. "Who hit you? Someone in here?"

"Bruises from the Slide for Life," I mumbled, wincing at the throbbing pain. His familiar cologne of spice and leather was warmly comforting as he walked me out, a contrast to the stench of mildew and sweat that clung to the jail. The sheriff, eyes half-mast, gave us a two-fingered salute. Rockwell palmed him a crisp bill. Papa swore JD Rockwell could talk a prairie dog into selling its own shadow.

"You had to bribe him?" I asked, as the coachman steered the carriage away from the jail. The scent of horse manure and damp hay filled my nostrils, a welcome change from the stale air of the cell.

"Had to, darlin', if you ever wanted to see the light of day." He handed me the newspaper, its headline screaming in bold, black letters: "Silver Dollar Tabor Charged in Jewel Theft."

My hands clenched into fists, nails digging into my palms. "How dare Doris drag the Tabor name through the mud."

"That's not how your mother and uncles see it," he said, his voice grave.

"Doris is the thief," I hissed, my anger rising. "She spread this lie to take over my Slide for Life stunt. We have to get back at her, clear my name." I flung open the carriage window, a gust of fresh air whipping through my hair.

"You'll do no such thing." Rockwell firmly closed the window, his voice brooking no argument. "The bank demands I put a lid on this, or they'll rescind your mother's loan on the Matchless." His jaw clenched, and a steely glint entered his eyes, silencing my protests. I couldn't bear to cause more grief for Mama, I'd caused plenty for her in the past year.

"Be a good girl, lie low, and let me handle things for the next few weeks." His smile softened, the warmth returning to his eyes as he reached for my hand. "I'm taking you to my penthouse: hot shower, a steak dinner ... sound good?"

"You know best," I murmured, a flicker of ambition rekindling beneath my anger. If anyone could salvage my reputation, it was Rockwell. But a nagging doubt lingered. That familiar icy-hot tingle snaked down my spine ... Echo's laughter rang in my ears.

Chapter 6

1932

SILVER PRICE $0.28 PER OUNCE

LEADVILLE, COLORADO. BABY DOE, HER HANDS GNARLED and calloused from years of wielding the pickaxe and toting slag, reached for the stack of letters below her straw mattress. A treasure more precious than any ore she'd ever unearthed. Silver, her wild, beautiful Silver. That girl could charm the birds right outta the trees, but trouble always seemed to follow close behind. Baby Doe always sent what she could when Silver was desperate—five dollars here, ten there—scrimpin' and savin' to make ends meet. But those fancy presents Silver sent confused her, a bottle of French perfume, a box of pomegranates. What in tarnation was a body supposed to do with pomegranates?

She opened the first letter Silver had sent after disappearing from Denver. Just like Lily, Silver had vanished without a goodbye, leaving a gaping hole in her heart. Where'd she go wrong with these girls?

HOTEL TIMMERMAN
Running Hot and Cold Water to All Rooms
Some Rooms with Private Bath and Telephone

Beatrice, Neb.
Sept 27, 1915

DEAREST MAMA,
 Denver is nothing but a bad dream now. All those whispers about that dreadful arrest are fading with every mile I put between myself and that awful town. Don't you worry, not a soul here knows Silver Dollar Tabor and her scandalous headlines. I had to reinvent myself, vanish like smoke in the wind, so no one could recognize me. A fresh start, you see. Echo LaVode! It has the perfect ring to it, don't you think? A name destined for the marquees! And guess what? I've landed a gig with the Takka Chance traveling show – singing, dancing, acting! Just imagine, Mama, your little Silver, performing for adoring crowds across the Midwest!
 Of course, it wasn't all sunshine and roses at first. Imagine me, sailing across Lake Rhoda suspended by my teeth for a few measly dollars. But that's all behind me now. I'm on my way to the top, Mama. You just wait and see. I'll be a star, bigger than Mary Pickford!
 That freckle-faced Doris, well, she turned out to be a viper in disguise. One minute she's batting her eyelashes and singing my praises, the next she's accusing me of stealing her ridiculous ring and having me arrested. All lies, Mama, I swear it! Those newspaper headlines ... "Silver Dollar Tabor: Jewel Thief!" Can you imagine?
 Our slick lawyer, Rockwell, got me out of that mess. But he wanted a rather hefty payment for his services. So I jumped on the first train out of Denver, leaving that whole nasty business behind. Needed to let the scandal die down, you know? Avoid those pesky reporters.
 Keep those letters coming, Mama, but send 'em to Echo LaVode, General Delivery, Beatrice, Nebraska. If you can spare a few dollars that would be most helpful to start out. And don't you dare breathe a word, not a peep to anyone about where I've gone. Not to Rockwell,

for sure. Let the Takka Chance shows be my launching pad to fame and fortune!

I'm saying my prayers every night, Mama, and going to church every Sunday. You'd be proud of me.

Holding *you close in my heart, always,*
   Your Silver, reborn as Echo LaVode

The ink had blurred on Silver's name, making it unreadable. She clutched the letter to her aching heart. Lord, forgive me.

So sad that Silver felt she had to change her name. Her mention of "Echo LaVode" brought back the grim memory of the imaginary friend Silver invented when Lily left. Her little girl playing hide-and-seek with herself.

"Oh, Silver, I should have helped you." The letter felt so flimsy and fragile in her cold fingers, like those big dreams Silver always chased. Was it selfish to search for answers after all these years? What if those answers tarnished her memory of Silver? Baby Doe picked up the rosary and held it up to the firelight. The beads were worn smooth, each one a silent prayer. Perhaps they'd brought Silver solace.

With a trembling hand, she tucked the letter away, knowing she had to pursue the truth that had been hidden for far too long. At the very least, she had to find out what happened to her daughter.

Chapter 7

1915

Silver Price $0.50 per ounce

Denver, Colorado. I swept into Rockwell's penthouse, dropping shopping bags and a new fox fur by the door. He could certainly afford the bill. The familiar aroma of cherry tobacco mingled with the clinking of ice in a crystal decanter, a symphony of wealth and indulgence. I checked my reflection at the round mosaic mirror in the entryway. Once, this mirror was a portal to a thousand imagined lives: cowgirl, Ute squaw, French mademoiselle ... The world was my oyster then. Now, my bruised jaw looked as if I'd been in a bar fight, my recent failings dimming the light in my eyes: my fall from the highwire that almost drowned me. The missed audition, my chance to be a leading lady, gone. The scandal of the stolen ring, the whispers, the averted gazes. I quickly looked away from my reflection, a knot of anxiety tightening in my stomach.

But Rockwell, with his connections, could fix everything. He'd redeem me, wouldn't he? With a forced smile, I twirled a curl around my Tiger's Eye hair ornament. If only my luck were as bright as this stone.

"How'd they treat you at Denver Dry Goods?" he asked,

handing me an applejack. The sweet smell mingled with the cloying aroma of his cherry tobacco, making my head spin.

"Shop girls kept bringing me dresses when they knew it was your account. Mighty kind of you to replace my clothes, Uncle Rockwell."

His fingers traced slow circles on my palm, and I felt a prickle of unease, like a spider crawling on my skin. "You were born to finer things." His eyes lingered on my face a moment too long. "It's your birthright. Ever see your baby pictures? Fur blankets, velvet gowns, diamond diaper pins? Your nanny had a hundred silver spoons to feed you."

Slowly, I pulled my hand away. "Mama says we mustn't dwell on the past but look to our future in heaven."

He barked a laugh. "Heaven's all very well, but here on earth, a beautiful woman like you has advantages heaven can't buy. That's where your mother went wrong. A real beauty, she was. Could've had any man she wanted after your father died. But no, she chose to waste her life on that godforsaken mine. You, Silver," he said, his voice dropping to a conspiratorial whisper, "you're smarter than that."

I drowned my troubles in the applejack, the liquor burning a fiery trail down my throat. "So stupid for Mama to stay up in the mountains now that she's old. That mine's a worthless hole in the ground."

"That's where you're mistaken." He lit his pipe, the scent of it thick and pungent, filling the opulent room with a blue haze. "The Matchless is rich with all kinds of ore. Plenty of money to be made if Baby Doe would take investors. She just doesn't trust anybody."

"Don't I know it." I sighed, kicking off my new heels. The plush carpet beneath my feet felt sinfully decadent, compared to the rough floorboards of our cabin in the mountains.

"Stand closer where I can see that dress." His words slurred; he must have started drinking earlier than usual. I hesitated, a flicker of apprehension in my chest, but I obeyed. "Remember how you danced for your daddy and me?" he asked, his gaze lingering on my body.

"Of course, Uncle Rockwell." I began to sway, the new silk chemise swirling around my legs, firelight flickering shadows across the silk. I saw his reflection in the dark windowpanes, his eyes following my every move. "That big audition slipped through my fingers, Uncle Rockwell ... would you be an angel and talk to the Pikes Peak producer?"

He lowered his pince-nez, his pupils dilated. A slow smile spread across his face. "Why do you think you'd impress the producer?" He mixed us fresh drinks.

"Don't you?" I threw him Cleopatra's smoldering stare and perched at his feet, my hands on his knees. The scent of his cologne filled my nostrils, making me feel strangely lightheaded and disoriented. "Then you'll talk to him?"

"I'll see what I can do." He served me the amber liquid in an etched glass, and I kissed him on the cheek, the skin beneath my lips feeling papery and thin.

Returning to my dance, I vocalized an exotic tune I'd learned at the nightclubs, my hips tilting, back arching ... I lost myself in the song and dance, the applejack burning like fire in my veins. Until I heard his soft groan stretching out, getting louder.

My half-mast eyes blinked open. Rockwell was straining against the back of the sofa, wet breaths rasping. His face was flushed, lips stretched in a strange grimace.

A chill snaked down my spine. "Are you all right, Uncle Rockwell?" I reached out and touched his forehead. It was burning hot, like a branding iron. His skin felt clammy, and a tremor ran through him. A wave of dizziness washed over me, the room tilting.

He grabbed my wrist, his fingers digging into my flesh. "Dance," he hissed with a sudden, terrifying urgency. "Dance for me, Silver. You owe me that much." His eyes burned with a hunger that made my blood run cold.

I forced myself to move, my gut clenched. The shadows on the wall seemed to twist and writhe, mocking my every movement. A buried memory flashed: twelve years old, the scent of tobacco and whiskey, his large hand lingering too long on my small sun-warmed neck, continuing down my dress. "Doesn't that feel nice? Just our little secret," he'd whispered. The recollection hit me like a slap, a cold sweat breaking out on my skin. I could almost feel his hand on me again, clammy and unwelcome. He'd always insisted on kissing my lips instead of my cheek, his hugs smothering me for too long. He plied me with special presents, lavish compliments, secret favors, that felt like they required payback. Why hadn't I realized? I dropped my glass on the table, the applejack sloshing over his lap. He let out a startled curse as the stain bloomed on his trousers.

"Clumsy me." I handed him a bar towel. "I guess I'm really tired." I took a hesitant step back. "I think I better just go to bed."

"Dance, dammit!" He slammed his fist on the table, reverberating through my bones.

My blood ignited with a fiery rush, an electric current tingling through my body. Like a guardian angel, Echo was with me. "Rockwell is not your uncle," she hissed. "He's a predator, Silver, and you're his prey. You need to leave."

I danced toward the back of the room, my heart pounding.

"Now!" Echo shrieked. "Get out of here!"

I lunged for the entry.

"You're not leaving." In an instant, Rockwell was on me, his wheezing breath hot against my ear. He slammed my shoulders against the mosaic mirror. Mirror tiles burst into the air, showering me in glittering shards. I dove for the front door, but he grabbed me, flinging me to the floor. Broken mirrors pierced my back, shooting pain through my body.

His fingernails raked my skin, ripping the silk. He pressed down on me, his bristly mustache against my frozen lips. The coppery tang of blood filled my mouth. His elbows pinned my arms, crushing the air from my lungs. "Silver, sweetheart," he rasped the mocking endearment.

The attack was a blur of violence and pain. The crashing mirror, the ripping silk, the sharp sting of glass in my skin. His weight pressed down on me, suffocating me. I clawed at his face, but he was too strong.

Nausea ripped through me, searing and unforgiving. My flesh recoiled, my spirit was pummeled beneath each relentless thrust. In those endless moments, only despair remained. Every ounce of hope, of belief, extinguished. Just the chilling void of absolute betrayal.

Then, a hoarse grunt ... his body spasming atop mine. A final, violent jolt.

∽

AN ICE-COLD EMPTINESS, devoid of feeling, blotted out all else. Rockwell's spent carcass sprawled around me. My body a shell, violated, discarded. An icy-hot sensation intensified into a surge of power as Echo took control of my body, her voice a chilling whisper in my mind, "Revenge is ours." I was no longer Silver; Echo had taken the reins.

Echo's eyes blazed through the shattered mirror fragments, each shard a warning to those who dared to harm me. Like a scorpion claiming its prey, Echo crawled over Rockwell, her knees pinning his arms to the floor. He thrashed, his breath coming in ragged gasps, but in his weak, drunken state, the old man was useless against her bloodlust.

"Not so brave now, are you, Rockwell?" Echo's fingers wrapped around his throat with bone-crushing strength.

"C-c-can't ..." A sickening gurgle rose in his throat.

"Oh, but I can." Echo's eyes blazed as she stepped on his hands, grinding her heel into his flesh, tightening her grip on his throat. "And I will."

His eyes bulged in disbelief, terror replacing his lust.

A strangled sob escaped my lips. "No, Echo, stop!" I begged, but my voice was swallowed by her guttural roar. I tried to wrench my body away, but Echo's grip on me was unyielding.

"You. Did. Not. Deserve. This." Her voice bellowed through the hollow chambers of my mind, obliterating any trace of my own will.

Air whistled through Rockwell's crushed throat, a death rattle that echoed in the sudden silence of the room.

"Oh God, make it stop!" I screamed, my voice raw with desperation. "Mother Mary, full of grace ..." My fingers clawed at the carpet, desperate to find purchase, to pull myself away. But Echo's grip was ironclad, and I could only watch in horror as Rockwell's face turned purple, his eyes bulging. Each gasping breath rattled in his throat, and I tasted bile rising in my own.

"He deserves to die," Echo spat, her thumbs digging deeper, cutting off Rockwell's air. His face contorted, a grotesque mask of terror and desperation. His struggles weakened, his body going slack as he lost consciousness.

"Protect us from wickedness and the snares of the devil," I choked out a desperate prayer against the rising tide of darkness. A blinding light filled the room, and a sudden stillness descended, broken only by Rockwell's last guttural wheeze. Drool and blood trickled from the corner of his slack mouth, his eyes rolling back. With an overwhelming shudder, Echo released him with a terrifying warrior's cry.

The world snapped back into focus, the gruesome reality crashing down on me. Rockwell lay sprawled amidst the shattered mirror tiles, chilling evidence of Echo's rage and my own helplessness. He'd been my bedrock, but he'd torn me apart, and now blood was dribbling down my legs, warm and sticky against my skin. Pain pulsed through me in agonizing waves. But had he deserved to die?

The crushing realization of his death pressed down on me. I

curled into a fetal position, tears blurring my vision, the bitter taste of betrayal and violence filling my mouth.

The terrible truth sank in: Echo had murdered him, and I was powerless to stop her.

∼

A SOB TORE from my throat. Rockwell's once imposing features stared back like a wax museum replica. My chest constricted, and a wave of nausea washed over me. Should I stay? Should I call for help? But the thought of facing the authorities, of explaining what had happened, was too overwhelming. "He deserved it," Echo's whisper chilled me. "I only defended you."

Had to leave. Had to get out of here. I put on my shoes and packed my belongings. A photograph of Rockwell and me at Lake Rhoda burned my fingers. I tossed it in my carpet bag. Couldn't leave evidence I was here. I tossed in my rosary last, its cool beads stinging my palm. I couldn't kiss it after what Echo had done.

Stepping over him, shards crunched beneath my heels. I snatched my fox coat, grabbed my shopping bags, and fled. I could never return to Colorado, not ever. What do I tell Mama?

Down the elevator, out the revolving doors. Jaw throbbing, I stumbled through a stinging snowstorm toward Union Station blocks away. Wind whipped around me, stinging my cheeks and blurring my vision. The icy pavement was treacherous beneath my feet, each step a struggle against the blinding snow.

Echo, my warrior, emerged from the shadows. "Burn that old life, Silver," she whistled through my head. "Let the world see the real you, dazzling and untouchable. They'll forget Rockwell, but the name Silver Dollar Tabor will be legend."

The clanging station bell warned me the train was boarding. The tang of blood filled my mouth as I gasped for air. "But where can I go?"

Echo's icy zephyr coiled around my ear. "Anywhere but here ..."

~

THE TRAIN LURCHED, jolting me awake. Beneath me, the iron behemoth pulsed with a rhythmic thunder mimicking the frantic beat of my heart. My jaw throbbed, molars cracked, a painful souvenir of the Slide for Life that had set me on this desperate flight. The air reeked with the stench of engine oil, mingling with the putrid taste of blood.

I buttoned my new fur coat to cover my bloody and torn chemise. The raw ache between my legs whispered Rockwell's name, a litany of shame and rage. My breath hitched in my throat. Desperate gulps as if I were drowning in the swampy shallows of Lake Rhoda.

My eyes burned, straining against the starless sky. Echo's wrath still hummed through my veins. She, the shadow I thought I'd outgrown, instead had burrowed within me, her charming mischief and protectiveness turning malicious. Yet I owed her twice for saving my life. Once from drowning and the second from Rockwell's lusty grasp.

Echo's defiance, raw and primal, filled me with terror. "Defend you, protect you, shield you," she said. But at what price? Echo's fury had left blood on my hands. She'd made me the obvious suspect of Rockwell's murder. A murder I didn't commit ... Or did I? A sliver of doubt crept in. Had some dark part of me summoned her, relishing in Rockwell's demise? The train lurched, and with it, my stomach. Was I running from justice, or was I running from the terrifying reality of what Echo had done for me? My own reflection, exhausted and contorted, stared back from the train window. Echo's fierceness mirrored in my eyes. Not a guardian angel, not an invisible friend ... but a protector born from my own pain and desperation.

I stared numbly out the window. Rows of harvested corn flew by, four hundred miles away from the incident. The sheriff would track me down ... question Mama, my uncles ... Did Rockwell tell anyone I was with him? My brain rattled against my skull as the train roared on.

The wind howled across the barren plains, sending tumbleweeds skittering. A hot-cold tingle chilled me to the bone.

"Start over," Echo whistled with the wind. "Invent someone new the coppers could never find. Someone fearless and invincible. Someone like me."

∽

Stepping off the train at Beatrice, Nebraska, the vast plains unfolded before me, a welcome reprieve from the cramped dining car. I clutched my carpetbag, the stolen steak knife nestled in my new clothes. The huddle of buildings offered little refuge from the October wind, even with the warmth of my new fox coat. Rockwell's lifeless body plagued me, his stubborn blood still clinging beneath my fingernails. The law would be on my tail soon, the noose tightening around my neck.

A hawker's cry sliced through the air, his wares a colorful distraction. The distinctive Lucky Strike pack caught my eye. Those gold-rush cigarettes, a symbol of glamour and reinvention, seemed just what I needed. I practiced a first puff in the ladies restroom mirror, the tobacco's harsh bite sent a dizzying rush through me. The pipe smoke swirled, blurring the lines between reality and the elaborate personas I wrote and acted.

"My name ... is Echo. Echo LaVode." The words tasted nostalgic on my lips, my sister Lily's nickname for me. Her little Echo, now a desperate fugitive on the run. Echo LaVode, a protagonist in my novels. A French beauty, married to a notorious gangster named Jack LaVode. The name rolled off my tongue, a seductive mask, a shield woven from a childhood nickname.

"Echo ..." I murmured, catching in my throat. "This is a new story. A new adventure. Mine to escape, yours to make your own. It's the only way." The Jardin de Nuit perfume, a detail I'd scripted into Echo's character, wafted through the restroom. A sign, that sweet heavy scent of night-blooming jasmine. Mama always said to pay attention to signs. The cracked mirror reflected a stranger, her eyes haunted, her cheeks streaked with grime and tears. The steak knife in my bag felt alien, yet it was the only tool I had to carve out a new life.

"It has to be done." I forced conviction. "Silver Dollar can't exist anymore." Raising the blade against my trembling hand. The first drag of the knife sent a jolt of pain through me, a sharp cry fleeing my lips. Each rough tug a sacrifice. My shorn locks falling in heavy clumps around my feet, like broken promises to Mama and myself.

Finally, I met my gaze in the mirror. Gone was the glamorous actress with cascading curls; in her place was Echo, face framed by a jagged bob that made her cheekbones sharper, her eyes wilder.

"Echo LaVode. Enchantée," she purred playfully and winked at the mirror. "Don't worry, darling." A sassy grin spread across her face. "No one will find out your cover. You're in good hands."

Chapter 8

1932

Silver price $.28 per ounce

Leadville, Colorado. The owl's shriek woke Baby Doe. Her dream of Silver, a giggling toddler, vanished like smoke, replaced by the wind howling through the thin planked walls of her cabin. The brass clock said 5:25 am, half-an-hour before dawn, colder than all get-out. She pulled the bear skin up to her chin and closed her eyes. But her mind returned to the same chilling words, like a needle stuck on a record: "Scalded beyond recognition." The phrase the reporters kept repeating, a gut-wrenching image she could never scrub from her mind.

Seven years ago, the press had descended on her like vultures, their words sharp and merciless. Accusations surfaced of Silver's involvement with the mob called the "Chicago Outfit," and that horrific 'accident' in their gangster lair. "Angry red welts stretched from her hair to her toes," they'd said, their voices a chorus of morbid curiosity. "What would she be doing with burning oil?" they'd asked, lusting after a scandalous story. The reporters' claims were sharp as pickaxes. "Forgive me for asking, Mrs. Tabor, but Silver was the headliner at a notorious speakeasy. The police thought she may have had a target on her back? Who exactly did she work for? Was Silver really part of the "Chicago Outfit"? Did she feel threatened by them?"

They claimed the coroner described a beautiful woman with blue-black hair, crumpled into a screaming ball, steam rising from her mottled and lifeless skin, her beauty and identity erased. The details were sketchy, reported second-hand, but the brutality of it was branded on Baby Doe's mind. Their inquiries exposed a vast chasm between her knowledge of what Silver Dollar was really involved with, a gap she'd failed to acknowledge until it was too late. "Why hadn't you visited Silver," they asked. "Have you met her friends, watched her perform?" "Why did your daughter, Lily, disavow being a Tabor?"

How was Baby Doe supposed to answer any of that? The answers were not only condemning, but embarrassing. Baby Doe had no money to visit Silver or Lily. No money for a train ticket. And no time to leave the mine.

The reporters' questions paled compared to her own judgments of her neglect. Maybe she was to blame for encouraging Silver to take to the stage. Or perhaps she simply abandoned Silver Dollar as Lily had done? Or did Baby Doe resent Silver for heaping more shame on the Tabor name? Regardless of the reasons she hadn't visited Silver Dollar, she blamed herself for what had happened to her. Now, Carl Erikson offered a second chance to get to know her daughter and what really had occurred.

The owl's second hoot confirmed it. No more sleep tonight. Lighting the lantern, she pulled on her overcoat and added kindling to the fire, blowing on the coals until it caught. She retrieved the orchid-and-tiger box from under her cot. Silver's gift from '21, one of those unexpected extravagant presents she seemed fond of sending. Trembling hands lifted her cherished memento to the lamplight. The faded *Denver Post* front page: Silver, beaming, shaking President Roosevelt's hand after her performance of the song she wrote for him. Goosebumps prickled her skin.

Silver had always been wildly talented, writing poems and

stories and producing plays, but—the President? That was the cat's whiskers. Baby Doe had purchased a dozen papers and sent them out to her brothers and sisters, aunts and uncles. And, of course, Lily, her older daughter.

The President's handshake had ignited Silver's dreams. She envisioned herself a celebrated writer, her words weaving tales that would captivate the world. She vowed to reclaim their lost fortune and restore their fallen dynasty. Always promising ...

Huffing frozen air, Baby Doe put the kettle on and checked the used teabag in her chipped cup, enough for one more.

After Silver performed for the president, she was hired by the Post as a society reporter. Her prestigious byline opened doors to the most exclusive social circles. The job lasted but a few months until Silver was fired for a story about Denver's elite, calling them "the haughty thirty-six who bilked a great heap of money for sweet charity's sake." Baby Doe laughed to read her daughter spearing those society biddies who'd shunned her in the past.

She picked up Silver's novel, the one that nearly bankrupted Baby Doe to publish. Between the pages, she found newspaper reviews that still stung. "Star of Blood bleeds with purple prose. An exploitative tale of crime, false identities, murder." A harbinger of things to come? Steam plumed from the teapot, burning her fingers as she filled her cup. After Silver's book flopped, her daughter drowned her disappointment in rye whiskey, honkey-tonks, and ruffians.

"Don't waste your talent," Baby Doe had told her. "Use what God gave you, a face and figure folks can't forget. Find a stage where you can showcase your gifts."

And surprisingly, Silver did. The stage became her refuge, her sanctuary. She stole scenes, sang, and shimmied. When Silver landed a motion picture role with "Pikes Peak Photoplay," Baby Doe wept happy tears that her daughter's wings were finally unfurling. Then, she was gone, and Baby Doe never saw her again.

The owl hooted a third time. Baby Doe filled the kettle with water from the bucket. Carl said he'd be bright and early, but no telling when early is for a Hollywood screenwriter. She'd be ready with her questions when he came.

Chapter 9

1916

Silver price $0.66 per ounce

Beatrice, Nebraska. The Lucky Strike glowed between Echo LaVode's fingers, its smoke a veil for her secrets. She exhaled, a silent vow escaping with the haze. No one would penetrate her disguise. The French accent, the rehearsed backstory, the Jardin de Nuit perfume ... all part of the performance. She'd play the role of Echo until she became her.

Beatrice smelled of dry earth and hay, a handful of storefronts lining Main Street, a far cry from the glitz and glamour of motion picture studios. Yet, even an Echo had to start somewhere. She dragged her carpetbag down the sun-baked street, her practiced smile faltering as she caught sight of her reflection in a storefront window. A stranger stared back with the new choppy bob and enormous eyes ringed in kohl.

At the end of the street shone a beacon of hope: the Gilbert Theatre. Its facade, proof of the town's prosperous past, now bore the scars of neglect. Peeling paint, the color of dried blood, released a faint, chalky odor when she touched it. Not exactly the kind of place she envisioned for her new life, but the sandwich board propped against the theater's entrance claimed "Dancers Wanted" in bold letters. She threw back her shoulders with newfound resolve. This was her chance to shed the past and become someone new.

Creaks and groans emanated from the theater, as if the old building were sighing in its sleep. The air inside was thick with the scent of dust and decay, and the velvet curtains on the stage were faded and threadbare. Not exactly the Moulin Rouge, she thought with a grimace, but a stage was a stage. "Bonjour, monsieur. Enchantée!" she said to the manager. A few shuffle-ball-changes, a flash of her rehearsed smile and she signed her new name, Echo LaVode, on the contract for the Takka Chance vaudeville troupe.

That night, in her cheap hotel room, Echo sat at the rickety desk to write Baby Doe. The bare lightbulb cast long shadows, dancing across the peeling wallpaper like ghosts of her past. Her fingers trembled as she picked up the flimsy hotel pen, its cheap plastic bending under her grip. The ink left blanks as she struggled to write the letter, pressing harder to get the words down. Writing Silver's Mama meant admitting Silver could never go home again. She had to pretend to know nothing about Rockwell's death, to have nothing to do with it. Needed to paint a picture of sunshine and rainbows for Silver's Mama, so she wouldn't suspect something was wrong. Wouldn't send her uncles searching for Silver. Lies and truth bled together on the page. Stolen jewelry, Doris's cruel accusations, a new dance career … all a smokescreen to hide the real reason she fled Denver: to save Baby Doe the shame of knowing her daughter had killed a man. Anything but the ugly truth of Rockwell's attack and her desperate retaliation. When she finished, she shed a tear, blurring the ink on the page.

As she sealed the envelope, Echo's gaze drifted to the theater marquee outside her window, blinking incandescent bulbs against the encroaching darkness. Perhaps her new vaudeville gig, her new persona, could drown out the chilling memory of Rockwell's hands. But as she drifted off to sleep, she couldn't shake the feeling that the shadows of her past were lurking, waiting to reclaim her.

∼

Lincoln, Nebraska. Backstage was a chaotic swirl of greasepaint, stale sweat, and the sticky scent of sweet and sour pork, the only thing she ate these days. "Mon Dieu," Echo muttered, wrinkling her nose. She took a long drag of her Lucky Strike, the smoke doing little to numb the throbbing pain in her jaw, still hanging on from the cursed Slide for Life.

She tried to shake off her jitters. Without Silver's commanding stage presence, Echo felt adrift. Now, she had to learn to dance on her own, every step a risky improvisation. The dazzling lights, the frenetic Ragtime tunes, the clowns and monkeys and sword swallowers, this was the life she'd craved, but what if they discovered she was a fraud? What if they found out she was a killer?

Setting her cigarette aside, she dipped a small brush into a tin of coal dust, carefully darkening her lashes. It was a trick the old headliner, Annabelle, had shown her, meant to draw attention away from her bruised jawline. But even with her eyes sparkling like fireflies, Echo couldn't quite quell the rising panic.

The dressing room hummed with chatter and laughter as nine other chorus girls jostled for space at the mirror. The air reeked of cheap toilette water, weak and insignificant to her Jardin de Nuit perfume, a defiant bloom amidst the fading flowers.

"Quit hogging the mirror, Echo," Trixie whined with a Southern drawl.

Echo arched an eyebrow, her Parisian accent thickening. "Careful, Trixie. Claws come out when the spotlight fades, mon cherie."

A sharp throb stole her focus. The clove oil had worn off, and the pain in her tooth radiated through her jaw. She needed something stronger, something to dull the ache, to silence the doubts that threatened to unravel her carefully constructed facade.

Ollie, the slicked-hair, ferret-faced stage manager, popped his head in, his eyes darting nervously. "Showtime in ten," he barked.

"Full house. Don't screw it up." His gaze landed on Echo. "What's with the long face, sweetheart? Teeth acting up again?"

Echo nodded, pressing her jaw.

Ollie slipped a small brown bottle into her hand. "A swig of this'll fix you right up. Just don't tell the fuzz," he added with a wink. The label bore a skull and crossbones, but she uncorked the bottle anyway and gulped the bitter liquid, warmth spreading through her chest.

"Easy there, kid," Ollie cautioned, retrieving the bottle. "That stuff's stronger than it looks."

Echo ruffled her bobbed hair and laughed, a glassy glint in her eyes. "A little liquid courage never hurt anyone, *n'est-ce pas?*" She shimmied into her sequined costume, the laudanum humming in her veins. Her reflection grinned back at her, a forced smirk masking the turmoil within. Tonight, she'd be more than another chorus girl. Tonight, she'd be Echo LaVode.

∽

Omaha, Nebraska. Echo knelt with the other girls as Annabelle took the spotlight. The harsh glare revealed every line on her face, though the old woman had tried to hide them with pancake makeup. Annabelle tossed her boa aside, a flash of flabby flesh in the smoky air. She kicked and lunged, her aging limbs straining. The crowd roared, oblivious to her faltering steps.

"Ridiculous," Echo muttered. She could do better. Way better.

The farmers and clerks tossed flowers and cash. Annabelle blew kisses, scooping up her riches. Echo craved that spotlight, that power. The music swelled, the chorus girls shuffled off. Echo's laudanum buzz was fading, leaving a gnawing emptiness.

"You were on fire tonight, Echo," Annabelle rasped. "Keep at it and you'll be a star."

"Sooner than you think." Echo forced a smile. Annabelle would be yesterday's news.

"Hey, ma Cherie! Swan Saloon," Tiny called to her as she did every night.

"You go ahead." Echo waved her on. The pleasures of drunken sailors was limited at best. Maybe Ollie had more laudanum to quiet the voices that clawed at her in the night.

"Ollie, my man!" she called, spotting him by the stage door. "Got more of that stuff? My stomach's acting up."

"Cost you two dollars."

"Two dollars?" she jeered. "For a friend?" She paid him with jittery fingers and hid the bottle. One swig and the world would melt away.

Backstage, men buzzed around Annabelle. Vultures, Echo thought, picking at the bones of a dying career.

"Oh, Echo, be a doll and take these to the hotel," Annabelle purred, loading her down with envy and resentment that bit into her arms.

Annabelle's room reeked of gardenia perfume and stale cigarettes, paste jewelry and risqué lingerie spilling from overflowing boxes. The bounty of a Vaudeville queen who didn't deserve her throne. Echo would snatch the crown.

Back in her own room, a stranger stared back from the cracked mirror. Two cowlicks twisting into devil's horns crowned a face gaunt with hollow eyes and a severe bob. She looked away, a chill crawling up her neck. Who was that woman?

The laudanum burned, a promise of oblivion, and her muscles twitched, yearning for release. No time for tired dance routines tonight. Echo's movements grew wilder, more reckless, a frantic dance of defiance against the shadows that haunted her. Another drop, and a fierce ambition ignited within her, a hunger for power that eclipsed the fear. Let Silver Dollar cower. Echo LaVode would seize her destiny, alone if she had to.

∽

Des Moines, Iowa. The chorus girls chattered, making dinner plans as they changed, their voices a distant buzz to Echo at the makeup table. On stage, she was fire, the spotlight her fuel, the applause an addictive rush that masked the tremors, the gnawing emptiness only laudanum could quell. She needed a dentist for her broken molars, but her money went to laudanum. Oblivion was a brutal bargain, but it was the only one she could afford.

Backstage, Tiny slumped against the wall, a wilted violet since Heda ran off with the sword swallower. The Hungarian twins had been inseparable, their synchronized shimmies and sly winks a crowd favorite. Now, Tiny was half a twin, a sad mirror of Echo's own emptiness.

"Ditch this dump?" Echo hauled Tiny up, her own muscles frazzled.

Stars pierced the icy sky as they trudged to their flea-bitten hotel, its neon sign flickering like a dying firefly. Tiny, bundled in a moth-eaten coat, stared at her worn boots, each step crunching on the frozen puddles.

"Shake it off, Tiny girl," Echo nudged her. "You were the real star."

Tiny huffed, a puff of frosty air. "Without Heda, I'm just half a Hungarian sausage."

Echo choked back a laugh. "Any word from her?"

"Not a peep." Tiny's facade crumbled. "One minute we're two peas in a pod, the next she's married to the sword swallower! Didn't even ask me to be a bridesmaid."

A wave of nausea hit Echo, and she stumbled. A cold sweat slicked her brow.

"Whoa, you okay?" Tiny steadied her with surprisingly strong arms. They reached the hotel, its dim lobby smelling of cigarette butts and despair.

"I cracked my molars on that stupid Slide for Life I told you about." Echo winced, holding her jaw.

"Clove oil and zinc should fix you up," Tiny said, her accent thick. "I've got some."

But it was more than her mouth. The ache in her gut was a gnawing beast, growing with each step. She craved the bottle.

"You're sweating like a pig in a sauna," Tiny said, her brow furrowed. She hauled Echo's arm around her shoulders, half-dragging her inside.

The keyhole swam before Echo's blurry vision. Tiny took over, guiding her across the threadbare carpet. Echo crumpled onto the lumpy bed, springs protesting with a rusty groan.

"Top drawer," Echo rasped, pointing a trembling finger. "Medicine."

Tiny opened it, her eyes widening at the skull and crossbones. "Rest here. I'll get my paste."

When the door clicked shut, Echo scrambled for the bottle, but it was gone. Damn. She groaned, clutching her stomach, and collapsed onto the bed.

In a while, Tiny reappeared. "Open wide."

Echo braced for laudanum, but Tiny slathered clove-smelling paste onto her cracked molars. A cool tingle spread through her gums, a welcome relief.

Tiny capped the bottle. "Back in the morning."

"Just a drop, Tiny, and I'll be right as rain," Echo begged, her voice cracking. "Got to make it through the night."

Tiny's eyes softened and she sat on the lumpy mattress. "I'll stay until you fall asleep." She sponged Echo's face with cool water, humming a mournful Hungarian lullaby.

Echo held her pounding head. "If that's a lullaby, I'd hate to hear your battle cry."

A weak smile crossed Tiny's lips, and she kept humming. Her song, with its yearning notes, soothed the throbbing and wove a comforting warmth around Echo, lulling her into a restless sleep.

Rockford, Illinois. After Echo's successful audition, Annabelle stormed off, a whirlwind of sequins and indignation. Ollie wasted no time pushing Echo into the spotlight, promising fortune and fame.

But Echo yearned for more than Annabelle's tawdry Hoochie-Coochie. She craved the atmosphere of the Nile, a faraway river Silver had told her about as a child. Drawing on memories of Silver's summers spent crafting sets for her Uncle Peter's theaters, Echo took up hardware store brushes, the smell of paint and turpentine filling the stage. Desert hues swirled across the canvas, ochre flames licking at golden pyramids under the relentless sun. A felucca sailed across the glistening Nile, steered by the powerful Queen Nefertiti. With a final flourish on her crown, Echo felt a surge of pride. This wasn't just a set; it was a world she'd conjured from Silver's imagination.

She transformed herself into Nefertiti; a gold headdress studded with lapis lazuli and turquoise held a rearing cobra. Kohl elongated her eyes, bronze powder dusted her cheeks, deep scarlet painted her lips. A flowing white silk gown, painted with golden hieroglyphics, flattered her statuesque physique. A broad collar of turquoise and carnelian beads completed the transformation. No longer a chorus girl, Echo was Nefertiti herself.

Yet, the clove and zinc couldn't mask the pain in her teeth, and that strange new discomfort radiating in her abdomen.

Ollie found her doubled over backstage, a sheen of sweat on her brow despite the chill.

"Need … a touch, Ollie." Her voice was a hoarse whisper.

He held out the bottle and she took a long swig, the laudanum burned like a bitter fire as it slid down her throat.

Ollie grabbed it from her. "Easy girl."

Soon, a slow warmth blossomed, blurring the edges of pain. Silver's face swam before her eyes, distorted and frowning. Echo pushed her out of her head, thoughts drifting like smoke as the world softened. The toothache retreated, the nausea subsided, but a cold tremor lingered beneath her skin, a reminder of the devil's bargain she'd struck. Just one more performance. Then she'd quit.

As the curtain rose, Echo stepped onto the stage, her senses dulled by the laudanum but her spirit raging like a wildfire. The footlights seared her vision, their harsh glare fueling the laudanum's haze. The silk costume, once a symbol of her glorious transformation, now clung to her damp skin like a suffocating shroud.

The pounding drums seemed to drown out the band's melody, their rhythm a chaotic pulse in her ears. Echo's limbs, once graceful and fluid, now felt heavy and awkward. A wave of nausea permeated her body, causing her to fumble her carefully choreographed steps. She attempted a graceful arabesque, her arms outstretched like the wings of a sacred ibis, but her balance wavered. A series of spins evoking the swirling sands of the desert, floundered into clumsy stumbles. The audience shifted in their seats. Someone coughed, the sound amplified in the sudden silence.

Panic clawed at her throat, cold sweat streaming down the bronze powder on her cheeks. The painted Nefertiti on the backdrop seemed to scorn her, the felucca in her mural capsizing in a turbulent sea. Her vision swam, the stage tilting beneath her leaden feet.

A sharp, agonizing pain ripped through her abdomen; a sensation far worse than anything she'd felt earlier. She stumbled, a strangled cry escaping her lips as she lost her balance. She fell back into the heavy velvet stage curtain, bringing it down in a crash of sawdust and horrified gasps from the audience.

The world spun, the backstage riggings a tangle of ropes and pulleys. Echo panted for air, the pain in her belly intensifying with each heaving breath. Tiny's face swam into view, her eyes wide with alarm until it blurred, then faded into merciful darkness.

Chapter 10

1916

Silver price $0.66 per ounce

Rockford, Illinois. The sterile white room assaulted her senses, a jarring shift from the vibrant stage. Echo shivered, nausea roiling through her. The antiseptic tang stung her nostrils.

A man in a white coat appeared, his mouth a grim line. "I'm Dr. Roberts. You're in the Good Samaritan Hospital."

Her heart pounded a frantic rhythm. "What happened? Why am I here?" Her throat was raw and dry, a nasty bonus of laudanum's grip.

"Miss LaVode, I'm glad you're awake," the doctor said. "You collapsed backstage during your performance. Your friends brought you in." He took a deep breath. "There's a matter of utmost urgency. You have a serious complication with your pregnancy."

Pregnancy? The news hit her like a punch to the gut, the air whooshing from her lungs. A bitter taste flooded her mouth; horrible memories of Rockwell's violation crashed over her. The harsh hospital lights bore into her skull, amplifying the throbbing in her head.

"No," she choked out a whisper.

"It's called an ectopic pregnancy, where the baby develops outside the uterus, in your case, within your ovary. It's very rare and incredibly dangerous. We need to operate immediately." The doctor's gaze fell to the floor. "My priority is saving your life, Miss LaVode. But ... the pregnancy ..." He trailed off, his silence heavy in the room.

Echo's shoulders wracked with sobs, pain and grief tightening in an unbearable knot in her chest. The hushed whispers of nurses in the hallway underscored the heavy silence in her room.

"I understand your distress," the doctor murmured. "This is a terrible burden to face alone. Shall we call your family? The father? He ... he should be told."

Her head snapped up, her eyes flashing with a fierce defiance. "There is no father," she spat out the words, bile rising in her throat.

"I'll make the necessary arrangements." The doctor left, his footsteps hollow in the hallway.

Once again, Echo was the martyr, shielding Silver from pain she couldn't bear. Her tears fell hot and fast, tracing burning paths through the stage makeup. A child born from violence, a child she never wanted. How could she care for a baby when she barely survived herself?

∽

THROUGH THE CHLOROFORM HAZE, Echo saw the starched white coat of the doctor looming above her, his face pale and drawn, worry carved into the lines around his eyes. A bloodstained bandage cinched her abdomen, and an IV needle pierced the delicate skin of her inner arm. Her body felt leaden, a dull ache throbbing beneath the bandage. The room smelled of chemicals, a sharp, ethereal odor that pricked her nostrils. She tried to lift her head, but the world tilted alarmingly, dizziness forcing her pounding head back to the pillow.

"Where's the baby?" Echo croaked, her throat raw and scratchy.

"You'll be fine," Doctor Roberts reassured her. "But it will take a while. You contracted sepsis. Very dangerous."

Her breaths felt like daggers in her chest, a heavy throb pulsing through the incision in her belly. She tried to sit up and gasped, the rough stitches under the flimsy hospital gown pulling painfully against her skin. "What did you do to me?"

The doctor helped her up, his touch firm yet gentle. "The incision is deep, but it will heal with time. It's crucial to rest, or it won't mend properly, and you'll have trouble dancing."

"You know I'm a dancer?" Echo asked, surprised.

"Your friend, a Miss Tiny Kline, brought your clothes before the show left for Lake Geneva."

Abandoned. Desolation washed over her, leaving her feeling adrift. "Tiny left me behind?"

Dr. Roberts pushed her food tray forward, the savory steam a distraction from the emptiness inside her. "Chicken soup will help build your strength. The nuns made it."

She slurped the soup gratefully, warmth spreading through her chilled body. It tasted like home, a fleeting comfort in this sterile, cold world.

"But what about the baby?" The thought of a child conceived in violence was … repulsive. But despite herself, she longed to feel the warmth of the baby on her chest, smelling the dewy skin, hold that a tiny hand. "Is the baby with the nuns?"

He shook his head. "I'm so sorry, Miss LaVode. The girl didn't survive." He patted her shoulder before he left, leaving her alone to sit with that unexpected sadness, the loneliness engulfing her. She longed for Silver. All the colorful stories she told.

Like the time when Silver was seven, wading in the Arkansas River, her laughter swallowed by the roar of the flashing water. But she slipped on a mossy rock and tumbled head-first into the current. Icy water surged into her mouth, choking her with its mineral taste. The sharp tang of wet earth and decaying leaves mingled with the smell of her own blood. She flailed in the water crying for help but the current dragged her down stream, bruising her body and hitting her head on the boulders. Just when she'd thought she would surely drown, a strong hand grasped her arm, hauling her toward the riverbank. It was Lily. Silver's older sister who always pulled her from danger. How Echo loved that story of the fierce, protective sister. As a girl, hearing it had filled her with a longing for that kind of bond, a fierce loyalty that would always pull her from the rapids.

If only Lily were here now, to hold her close and whisper words of comfort against the relentless current. Did Lily ever wonder what became of the sister she'd left behind, swept away by the river of life, just as Silver had been swept away all those years ago? Tears streamed down her face, and for a moment, the sterile hospital room faded away, replaced by the relentless rush of the Arkansas River and the salvation of a child clinging to her sister's hand.

Chapter 11

1916

SILVER PRICE $0.66 PER OUNCE

MILWAUKEE, WISCONSIN. THE BITTER WIND MADE ME shiver to my very bones. My incision throbbed, and my legs felt like spaghetti as I stood at Lily's door knocking. At least Echo was gone, with her wild ways and bad habits. So excited to see Lily. How many years had it been? Fifteen? Would she even recognize me? I remember that day she left with her pillowcase of clothes, to live with Aunt and Uncle Last in Milwaukee. She leaned close and I smelled the vanilla behind her ear. "Get away as soon as you can, Silver," she'd pleaded. "Mama's crazy ... she can't stop working the mine. It's never gonna pay, Silver." She hugged me tight before she took off down the railroad tracks above the Matchless. Next thing we heard was that Lily had married our cousin and they were all living together.

Now here I was, knocking on that door again and again until my knuckles felt bruised as my innards. Finally, I heard steps, and the lacquered door swung open.

Lily's hand flew to her mouth, her eyes widened. "Silver Dollar? As I live and breathe, is it truly you?" Her delicate hand, lined with time, reached out to caress my cheek, and all of my hopes and dreams were answered. My throat swelled with emotion, choked by the words I yearned to spill, the humiliations I'd borne, the shame that clung to me.

She pulled me inside from the bright snow, the gloom of the foyer swallowing us up. "Mama hoped you might show up here. She's so worried." Her grip on my arm was strong. "And here you are, like a miracle."

But the relief of seeing Lily again was tempered by the house's foul smell. Bitter quinine, sour milk, and a cloying sweetness of decay filled the air. "Is someone sick?" The question caught in my throat.

Lily waved a dismissive hand. "Leave your bag here. I need a smoke." She hustled me down the cluttered hall to a kitchen stacked with dirty dishes, so different from when we'd visited Aunt Cornelia back when we were rich. She employed a downstairs and upstairs maid who made the house smell of lemons and lavender. By the looks of things, when Aunt Cornelia died, the maids left too, leaving Lily to fend for herself.

We stepped onto the back porch, a concrete slab choked with overflowing trash cans. A frigid wind lashed at my face, and I wrapped my arms around my fox fur coat, feeling oddly glamorous compared to my sister. Lily, once the darling Tabor baby featured on Harper's magazine cover, now huddled in a stained apron, her vibrant red hair now dull and streaked with gray, thrust a crumpled pack of Lucky Strikes at me.

"I don't smoke." My belly stitches burned and itched from the surgery, reminding me of the baby daughter I lost. Another secret to hide, due to the circumstances. "Where are the children?"

"John takes them to school. They'll be back this evening." She inhaled deeply on her cigarette, smoke swirling around her. Her eyes suddenly lit up. "I know you just got here, and I am so sorry to spring this on you, but I have a huge favor to ask. You see Uncle Last's nursemaid called in sick, and now I'm in a pickle." Her fingers drummed on her cigarette pack. "I'm in charge of a march in Chicago, the Women's Christian Temperance Union?" She glanced at her watch and frowned, dragging on her cigarette. "The planning meeting is in an hour, and I can't leave Uncle Last alone in his state."

My body ached for a nap, but Lily's desperation touched me. "What's wrong with him?"

"On his deathbed, I'm afraid. Won't be long now." Her clammy hand grasped mine. "You're a godsend."

Lily took a last drag, frosty clouds billowing from her lips. "Uncle Last is upstairs, first bedroom on the right. Take the room next to his. Makes it easier to hear him if he needs anything." She tossed down her cigarette and stubbed it out, the harsh smell drifting in the winter air. "You look exhausted. Uncle Last won't be needing anything for a while. Get some rest."

We retraced our steps back to the foyer. Lily shrugged into a threadbare coat while I hung my fur in the closet.

She turned to me, frowning. "Was that coat the one JD Rockwell bought you before you left Denver in such a hurry?" she asked.

I froze in place, my mouth gaping.

"He's been asking me about your whereabouts." Lily pulled on her gloves. "I told him I had no idea where you were. I hadn't seen you."

Rockwell was alive? Ice water flooded my veins. He couldn't be, not after what I ... "You've heard from Rockwell?" The memory flashed before my eyes: him, sprawled amidst the shattered mirrored tiles, his body deathly still. God have mercy. My legs felt weak, and I stumbled backward, my palms pressing the plaster wall for support.

"He keeps me abreast of the Matchless and the family." She crinkled her nose like something smelled rotten. "He says you jumped bail on a jewel theft charge and left him holding the bag?" Her mouth pursed and she shook her head. "I hoped you'd outgrow your crazy behavior by now."

"That is not true," I cried. "I was innocent. He ..."

Lily heaved a great sigh and flung open the door. "You can tell me your sob story tonight while we make dinner." The door slammed shut, leaving me reeling.

I hauled my carpet bag up the creaking stairs, stopping midway to catch my breath, exhausted. Uncle Last's low rumbling snore promised me the nap I sorely needed.

But under the meager quilt, my belly throbbed, a dull ache of emptiness. My dress snagged on the angry red stitches that crisscrossed the festering wound. Ugly proof of the child I'd lost. Rockwell's child. And now he was hunting me. As I drifted off to sleep, nightmares of his assault swirled around me, leaving me drenched in cold sweat.

∾

A BELL'S insistent clanging filled the air. "Lily, is that you sneaking around?" He rasped, throat thick with phlegm. "Bring me some prune juice, for God's sake!"

I peeked around the corner. He sprawled in bed, spectacles perched on his long nose, his nightgown hanging open on his sparse hairy chest. His rheumy gaze landed on me, brow furrowed. "You're not Lily."

"It's me, Uncle Last. Silver Dollar." The stench of camphor, liniment, and decay overwhelmed me. "I came to visit my favorite uncle." A skeletal grandfather clock in the corner marked time with his harsh breaths.

A gnarled hand emerged from beneath the quilt. "Let me get a good look at you, Silver."

"What is wrong with you, Uncle?" I asked.

"Lost my marbles, they say, but I have plenty to spare." A wheezing cough wracked his frail body, his eyes glinting with mischief and madness. "How about we whip up some Corpse Revivers for old times' sake? Remember those nights your Papa would make them?" A spark of life fighting in the embers.

"I doubt your doctor would approve," I ventured.

His cold, bony hand tightened on mine. "One last drink to a dying man. Have pity on me." His shoulders sagged.

My resolve wavered. Should I deny him this final wish, this fleeting taste of a memory? "Is the bar downstairs?"

"Lily abolished the bar. Temperance Union and all that, your sister has gone all straight-laced on me. All I ask for is a sip of sunshine, and she goes on about pickled livers." He cupped his hand to his mouth. "I keep my hootch under the bed."

Down on all fours, I peered under the bedframe. A collection of bottles among the dust bunnies: gin, whiskey, vodka. And what do you know? Cognac, vermouth and Calvados. "By golly, Uncle. You have all the makings for a Corpse Reviver." I shimmied out, bottles in both hands.

But Lily's voice cracked a whip through the air. "What are you doing?"

"Spring cleaning?" My humor died as I met the accusatory glare in her eyes. Not the kind sister I remembered, but a judge carved from righteousness and fury.

"Serving a dying man alcohol, just like you did with Rockwell." Her eyes narrowed to slits. "Now you are trying to corrupt my father-in-law, too? Have you no shame?"

The bottles burned in my hands as I held them up in surrender. "Lily, listen. I was only ..."

"Out!" she shrieked, her arm an arrow pointing toward the door. "I took you in to help Mama but clearly you haven't changed your wicked ways since Denver. If Rockwell told Mama how you plied him with liquor, and tried to seduce him, do you know how it would shatter her heart?"

I put the bottles down, my breath catching. "That's what Rockwell told you?" Fury surged through me, heating my cheeks. "He's lying, Lily. He's the one who—"

"Out. Out. Out," she shooed me out of the room. "Leave,

before I call the sheriff and expose you for the lying, thieving, wanton woman you are."

I grabbed my carpetbag, and stumbled down the stairs as she followed, yelling all the way to the front door. I snatched my fur coat from the closet.

"Rockwell warned me about you, and I should've listened. You were always trouble, Silver. With Mama busy with the mine, I was the one left to clean up your messes. I couldn't take it anymore. The two of you were made for each other. Crazy and crazier."

Her poisoned darts penetrated my heart, twisting and turning into old wounds that had never healed.

"I want nothing to do with you. Or Mama." Lily slammed the front door, ending my naive hope of reconciliation.

I trudged toward the train station. No idea where to go. I heard the familiar whisper, "Anywhere but here …" But running away hadn't gotten me anywhere. Not anywhere good, anyway. I stood at the crossroads, the wind whipping at my face, no family or friends. Wait. One friend. I knew just where to go.

Chapter 12

1932

SILVER PRICE $0.28 PER OUNCE

LEADVILLE, COLORADO. BABY DOE TABOR REINED IN her emotions as she stood firmly in front of the Tabor Opera House, a symbol of a bygone era when she and Horace reigned over not one, but two such grand theaters. The Tabor Grand in Denver, and this jewel he'd built in Leadville before they were married. New awnings and a theater marquee couldn't mask the memories that lived within the very walls and floors. Frosted windowpanes glittered like the diamonds she once wore, offering a glimpse of the interior. She noted the Elks' changes: new runners, new wallpaper, portraits of performers ...thankfully, the Tabor's Italian chandeliers remained. A fine job restoring its glory, though she'd never have chosen that gaudy red brocade.

Carl's boots crunched on the snow beside her. A crimson scarf wound around his neck, and he carried a bright art deco case with a handle on top.

"What's that?" Baby Doe asked.

"A Brownie Kodak camera, for research. Hope you won't mind."

She pointed a crooked finger. "One picture of me and our

deal's off. No discussion." Newspaper photographers still stalked the Matchless, hoping to capture the elusive Silver Queen.

He held up his palm in surrender. "Understood."

"The manager agreed to let me show you around without him." Baby Doe pushed open the heavy double doors, and memories flooded in like a spring thaw. A faint melody seemed to waft through the lobby, banjo, fiddle, and harmonica. Scarlet usher uniforms, velvet-clad waitresses with champagne trays. Horace's booming laugh, the brisk scent of his aftershave. Leadville's finest citizens greeting them, the air crackling with anticipation. Her daughters, wide-eyed beside her. Lily, ever dutifully restraining her sister and, Silver Dollar, a whirlwind of curiosity. Baby Doe blinked back tears.

The camera clicked and whirred in Carl's hands, capturing images that could never truly reflect the laughter, the tears, the love that had woven itself into the very fabric of this theater.

"Are you alright?" Carl asked, winding the camera. "Where'd you go just now?"

Taking a shaky breath, she pushed open the double doors to the auditorium. A swirl of musty air stirred the crystal chandeliers, tinkling notes waking the ghosts of performances past. Faint aromas of cigars and whiskey hung in the air.

She traced the worn velvet of a cast-iron chair. "Eight hundred and fifty seats."

"Doesn't look that big." Carl's camera's shutter clicked: the stage's worn floorboards, the once-vibrant curtains now muted by dust, the painted backdrops of forgotten dramas.

"Our Denver Opera House held fifteen hundred." She sank into an aisle seat, her throat tight. "Imagine, Carl ... right here, Oscar Wilde himself held court. A flamboyant peacock in velvet and silk, he strutted across the stage, his wit as sharp as his emerald tiepin. The audience hung on his every word, their laughter echoing through the rafters."

"I can almost see him," Carl said. "Long-legged, pacing,

posing. Drinking, smoking, witticisms spilling out like gold nuggets. What a night that must have been."

"The Tabor Opera Houses were gateways to the West, you see." Memories flooded back. "Sousa's melodies. Buffalo Bill's antics. Will Rogers, that sly grin, his lasso whipping the air. Sarah Bernhardt played Camille right there. I felt her tears in my heart, a torrent that drenched every soul." She gripped the velvet seat.

"So this was where Silver danced with Bernhardt?" he asked.

She pointed to the box seats in front. "Silver was four, a force of nature in dancing shoes. When Sarah bowed, Silver darted onto the stage." She clapped her hands. "Sarah scooped her up and spun her around. You could've heard my girl giggling up to the balcony."

"That scene should be in the film script." He lowered the camera, his eyes welling with a longing. "What was your favorite show?"

"Houdini, he was the best, bar none." Baby Doe squinted at the stage, remembering. "He looked right at Silver and said, 'I'll make this little firecracker disappear!' He put her in his trunk, locked it up tight, then poof! Lights out! I screamed, thought he'd really made her vanish. But when the lights came back on, the trunk was empty. Gone! Everyone went crazy, shouting and hollering. Then, wouldn't you know it, there was Silver, skipping down the aisle from the back of the theater! Everyone clapped and cheered like mad."

"But how? How'd he make her disappear?" Carl snapped a picture of the stage, winding his Brownie with a whir.

"Magic." She winked at him, knowing full well about the trap door in the stage. "Pure magic ..." Now was her chance to learn more about her daughter's disappearance. "Carl, just think. Silver Dollar vanished from this stage during Houdini's show. And years later, she disappeared again. What if ... what if she's not truly gone? What if she's simply ... reappeared somewhere else?"

He opened his mouth to refute her, but she cut him off.

"You said she turned down your proposal. Was there another man?" His pain was almost palpable, a heavy weight settling over the room. She hated to push him, but she had to know. "Maybe the speakeasy owner, or someone from the movie studio?"

Carl huffed. "Silver could have had any man she chose. They lined up around the block to see her show, and more than a few jealous girlfriends caused trouble too." He rubbed his weary eyes, the gesture speaking volumes about his grief.

He must know something, some crucial piece of the puzzle. "Maybe she went her own way," she offered, trying a different tack. "Maybe she's doing a show in a New York City cabaret?"

His head dropped into his hands. A hush fell over the theater, broken only by the creaking of old wood and the soft hum of the ceiling fan. The silence amplified his despair, pressing down on them with the weight of shared sorrow.

"Silver wouldn't want us to lose hope, Carl," her voice thick with emotion. "We can't lose hope."

She strained to hear it all again: Silver's laughter, a tinkling melody that once filled these halls with joy. A gentle breeze caressed her arm, and she could almost feel Silver beside her, the familiar scent of tiger lilies and frankincense swirling around her. *She's with me.* A sense of certainty taking hold. *Always with me.* A feeling of profound peace settled over her.

Part Two

"Unexpressed emotions
will never die.

They are buried alive
and will come forth later
in uglier ways."

~Sigmund Freud

Chapter 13

1916

Silver price $0.66 per ounce

Chicago, Illinois. Stepping through Selig Polyscope's grand iron gates, I flung myself into Carl Erikson's arms, a flutter of hope rising in my chest, making me forget my weakness and jitters.

"Silver, you don't know how good it is to see you," Carl breathed in my ear.

His familiar scent of licorice brought back simpler times. Had it only been a year since we whispered dreams under the vast Colorado sky? Felt like a lifetime ago. I pressed closer, his warmth a haven from the storm raging within me. His heartbeat, a comforting rhythm against my arm.

"She's with me," Carl told the guard at the gate.

"Still need your full name and company." The guard poked his pencil lead to his clipboard.

I struck a pose. "Silver Dollar from Pikes Peak Photoplay." No more Echo, not now, not ever.

"Word of warning, Miss Silver Dollar." The guard smacked his bubblegum. "Watch your Ps and Qs around our star, Miss Kathlyn Williams. She's mighty particular about other actresses, especially a looker like you. Her extras get canned if they look at her cross-eyed."

I crossed my eyes and flashed a silly grin. "Duly noted."

Carl walked me down the studio alleyway, a thoroughfare of horse carts laden with props and scenery. Scents of sawdust, paint, glue, and horse manure tickled my nose.

"You look different somehow. What's different?" He reached out to my hair grazing my chin. "You cut your hair, and you're skin and bones." He frowned. "Colonel Selig likes curvy actresses in his movies." His words stung, but before I could react, he hugged me again. "I can't believe you came. You didn't write. Nobody's heard a peep from you since Denver."

I clung to his arm as we walked, emotions tangling up inside me. I knew I wouldn't confess a single thing that had happened. Not even my latest fiasco with Lily. Carl was the one person who saw my potential to be the star I desperately wanted to become. Why ruin his image of me?

I laced my fingers between his. "I missed you." Until now, I didn't realize how much.

He squeezed my hand, his stride long and purposeful. I matched his pace, absorbing his confidence. Had he grown taller, or was it the aura of success that made him seem larger than life? Gone was the lowly script boy. Stagehands, painters, and caterers greeted him with big smiles that slid over to me. The sheer scale of the studio lot stole my breath, with its sprawling sets and vast glass ceilings that bathed everything in an ethereal glow. Nothing like rinky-dink Pikes Peak Photoplay.

"What've you been up to, Silver?" Carl asked. "Where've you been working?"

"Long story," I said, glibly. "Short story, I need a job." Funds were running dangerously low.

He stopped and pulled me aside. "Looks like you've been through a rough patch."

Instinctively, I held my stitched belly. He waited for me to speak, but I held firm in my resolve. To repeat the last year would forever taint me in his eyes.

He reached up to kiss my nose. "You just need to take care of yourself and be patient. All the acting parts are cast already, but actors spin out faster than spooked mustangs. And when they do, I can get you an audition. But you have to be ready to shine, see? Nothin' less."

Beneath the sting, I knew he was right. I had to rise above the shadows, embrace this new opportunity, and prove to Carl, and to myself, that I was a star waiting to be discovered.

The alleyway led us through a miniature jungle teeming with exotic creatures that would have made Barnum & Bailey green with envy. Sunlight from the greenhouse roof illuminated a flurry of fur and feathers, a cacophony of animal calls filling my ears.

"What are all these animals doing here?" My voice strained above the roars and shrieks.

"The Adventures of Kathlyn takes place in India." Carl scratched his chin. "Lots of animals on set. Say, if you need a job right away, the zookeeper's assistant position is open. Big Otto's been going nuts without one. How are you with animals?"

My stomach sank. Zoo assistant? Not the glamorous job I had in mind, but beggars can't be choosers. I forced a smile, that must have looked like a pout, because he tweaked my bottom lip.

"You'd be first to hear when an acting part opens up." His eyes twinkled. "Plus, Otto's assistant makes double what the extras make, so it's not a bad place to start."

I perked up at the prospect of a decent wage. "Sign me up," I said, my grin returning.

We ventured deeper into the zoo, the air so thick with roars, shrieks, and chattering, that it made my skin crawl. "I've never seen animals like these," I said, holding my nose against the smells.

"You get used to them," Carl said, but I knew I never would.

Emerald-breasted parrots squawked, a scarlet macaw's screech startling me. Nearby, powerful tigers paced, their musky scent heavy in the air. Monkeys chattered and swung, a playful counterpoint to the tigers' menace. Deeper in, an elephant trumpeted, its wrinkled trunk reaching through the bars. Towering giraffes, dappled and graceful, stretched their necks over fences. Languid camels, eyes filled with ancient wisdom, completed the surreal tableau.

Carl waved at the largest man I'd ever seen, shoveling food into cages with a pitchfork. "Hey, Big Otto, got a minute?" He led me to a mountain of a man with a brushy gray mustache.

"Silver Dollar Tabor." I extended my hand. His hand engulfed mine, warm and rough.

Carl gestured with a flourish. "Big Otto is the maestro of our menagerie."

Otto rumbled a deep, earthy laugh. "Are you one of the belly dancers they brought in for the sultan?" His sea-green eyes, a striking contrast to his tanned, weather-beaten face, crinkled at the corners.

"Good news," Carl said. "Silver Dollar's the new assistant you've been bellyaching about."

Otto grimaced, skepticism etched on his face. "I asked for a stable boy."

I stood up straight, mustering my confidence. "I mucked stalls and groomed horses for years, learned from the best."

Otto's chin jutted back into his neck. "Only worked with horses?"

"Grew up in the mountains," I said. "Made pets out of all the critters: elk, deer, mountain goats, blue birds, hawks, eagles. Pronghorn, porcupines, coyotes—they all love to be fed."

His eyes narrowed to slits. "What about wildcats?"

"Bobcats, lynx, cougars ... I fed them mice right out of my hand." My palms grew clammy, but I held his gaze, willing him to believe me.

Carl patted my shoulder. "I'll be back for Silver Dollar when the whistle blows. Need to get back on set." He left me with Big Otto, the discord of the zoo suddenly deafening.

Sink or swim, as they say. And everyone knows how well I swim.

Chapter 14

1916

SILVER PRICE $0.66 PER OUNCE

CHICAGO, ILLINOIS. My fear of wildcats ran deep. It all started back in our one-room cabin. I'd lie awake, facing the rough pine wall, feeling the cougar's vibration as it rubbed against the cabin, breathing through the gaps. Was it hungry? Or just looking for a cuddle? Either way terrified me. Every night, I'd listen to it prowl, my flannels soaked with sweat. I couldn't even go out to the outhouse after dark. Kept a Maxwell House coffee can under my bed for emergencies. But every time I used it, that cougar would yip and whistle, a reminder it was waiting for me.

Now, I forced myself to spend every spare moment with the tigers, fighting against the survival instincts screaming in my head. Each step around their cages felt like walking on hot coals. Their low, rumbling growls drained the blood from my head, leaving me shivering, lightheaded and weak.

They lounged in patches of sunlight, massive bodies sprawled across the cage floor, tails flicking lazily at flies. In this drowsy state, I watched them, trying to learn their habits, their personalities. But even then, their deep rumble triggered a cold sweat. That sound, guttural and quivering, was the same one that haunted my nights in that mountain cabin.

Echo, my ever-present shadow of doubt, clawed at my mind. "Think, Silver. Think. Don't be a fool. Feel those claws tearing, teeth crushing ... the tang of your own blood."

I clamped my eyes shut, trying to drown out her whispers. But silence only amplified them, drumming up grotesque pictures in my mind. The tigers, now monstrous, their drugged stupor masking a crouched fury worse than any wildcat roaming the mountains. A deafening roar broke the stillness, monstrous proof of my horror. My heart hammered against my ribs, desperate for escape.

From behind me, someone squeezed my waist, and I jumped a mile high. A startled yelp blurted from my lips, and I whirled around to find Carl grinning like a Cheshire cat, dressed in his usual bold striped suit and signature red bow tie.

"Gotcha!" He slapped his knee, clearly amused by my reaction.

My cheeks burned hot. "What the devil? Why'd you do that?" I glared at him. The tigers seemed to watch our exchange with great amusement, their large eyes following our every move. It was almost comical, the way they observed us as intently as I'd been observing them.

"I saw you sneaking around the cages and couldn't resist." He flashed a flirtatious grin.

I crossed my arms and raised an eyebrow. "Any idea what a wildcat can do to a person?"

He threw up his hands. "They're trained, Silver. They won't hurt you."

"Shows what you know," I retorted. "My pet cougar ate a deer's heart out right in front of me."

Carl's grin widened, a goofy, lovestruck expression spreading across his face.

"You're grinning like an idiot when I'm telling you my worst fear? Tarnation." I stalked past the tigers, but he caught my arm before I could escape.

"It's not like you to be afraid," he scolded. "You're the girl who slid across Lake Rhoda by her teeth. What's gotten into you?"

"You think I want to be a cage mucker the rest of my life? When do I get to audition?"

He touched her arm, "Just be patient. Your chance will come."

"Not for me." I spun to face him, my eyes narrowed. "I'm a mountain girl wanna-be star, and I have no idea what's expected from the director when I walk on that set."

Carl scoffed. "You're overthinking this, Silver. It's sucking out all the spunk and bravado that makes you shine."

"Maybe that's because Director Grandon hates me when I bring the tigers on set. He yells at me through his megaphone to the pleasure of the cast and crew." I felt dizzy with anger.

"Don't worry about the director. Colonel Selig loves you."

"The owner? How can he love me when I haven't met him yet?"

"The Colonel said he met you at the tiger cages."

"The guy in the pith helmet?" I racked my brain. "He should've introduced himself."

The studio whistle signaled the end of the day, and a cheer erupted from the sets. Carl took my hand and headed toward the studio gate.

"Where are we going?" I asked.

He grinned. "Over the rainbow." Carl had a knack for turning my troubles into opportunities. He had guided me through the studio labyrinth, helped me navigate auditions, celebrated my triumphs, and even lent me money for a room nearby.

He hailed a passing streetcar, its bell clanging a call to adventure.

∼

THE GRANDEUR of the Palmer House lobby, with its ceiling murals of Greek gods, was a world away from the rugged landscapes of Colorado. I felt a little self-conscious striding across the gleaming parquet floors in my khaki jodhpurs, burnt orange safari shirt, and cowboy boots. But I held my head high, a touch of defiance in my stride. After all, a girl's gotta own her roots, even amidst velvet baroque chairs and the clinking of champagne glasses.

Carl, ever dapper in his striped suit and red bow tie, seemed perfectly at ease.

"Someday," I mused, "I'd love to bring Mama here, a mink stole slung across her shoulders." A hollow ache opened up inside me, a longing for her hand, for her bright laughter. Our letters were poor substitutes for her hugs, for the feeling of her arms chasing away the loneliness, for the reassurance that only she could give.

The maître d' seated me in a red leather booth. Carl excused himself, crossing the room to chat with a raven-haired waitress with curves like a bass. A pang of jealousy twisted my gut, unfamiliar and unsettling. "Down, girl," I told myself. "This is not a date," I reminded myself, tracing the tender zipper scar across my belly. That train had left the station.

He returned a moment later, his eyes twinkling. "They tell me this is where the writers hang out," he said, settling into the booth beside me.

"Never knew writers hung out in such a fancy place." I scanned the room, trying to identify them. Men held half-empty glasses, blue smoke curling from their ashtrays. Some stared blankly at the circling ceiling fan. Others studied their fingernails. A few actually wrote in their notebooks.

The waitress, the same one Carl had been chatting with, set a towering glass bowl on the table, a colorful rainbow of ice cream crowned with a golden waffle cone. "The Rainbow Sundae," she curtsied, her gaze lingering on Carl before she left.

"This is what you meant?" I laughed, swirling my spoon through the green pistachio and pink cherry ice cream.

"Don't play with it, eat it." Carl reached for my spoon, trying to feed me. "You need to eat, Silver. You've lost your curves."

He has no idea what I've been through. My defenses shot up like a shield, and I toyed with my sundae, no longer the treat he intended. "Tell me about your screenplay."

"*Our* screenplay, Silver. The story you've told me about your family. You'll help me, won't you?" His eyes gleamed with the fervor of a director on opening night. "The American Dream, the tale of Horace Tabor, the Silver King…"

Carl launched into a passionate description of Tabor's life, but his vision of rugged miners and dusty trails clashed with my own memories.

"It is more than Papa's tireless trips to Washington, fighting for silver against the gold-backed dollar," I countered. "It's Mama's too, her charity work with churches, firehouses, and schools, insurance for our miners, establishing soup kitchens."

Carl wrote everything down, and I noticed the focus, the concentration, the smile that curved on his face.

"What about your home life?" He added.

I laughed. "Mine involved chasing a hundred peacocks roaming the grounds of our Capitol Hill mansion."

Carl chuckled. "Peacocks? A hundred?"

"Oh yes," I said, a mischievous glint in my eye. "They were Papa's pride and joy, but they were absolute menaces! Always squawking, chasing the neighbors' dogs, and causing chaos."

Carl fed me another bite between sentences.

"One time, a whole flock of them got loose during a political fund raiser. We had the governor and senators running around, trying to catch these iridescent birds while they shrieked and scattered feathers everywhere. It was absolute pandemonium!"

Carl burst out laughing, a hearty sound that filled the room. "That's priceless!" He wiped tears from his eyes.

The memory bringing a warmth to my chest. "The newspapers

had a field day with it, of course. 'Peacock Pandemonium at the Tabor Mansion.'"

Carl was practically doubled over with laughter by this point. "Oh, Silver," he managed between gasps, "you're full of surprises."

I smiled, feeling a lightness I hadn't experienced in a long time. It was good to laugh, to share a moment of joy.

"And don't get me started about the nude statues my parents imported from Europe. The neighbors were scandalized, and Mama had to get clothing made for them."

Carl listened with rapt attention, his laughter subsiding into a soft smile as I told him about Stardust, my beloved pony, and the countless hours I spent riding him through the Colorado plains. I described the thrill of winning my first riding competition, the sting of falling off and breaking my arm, and the unwavering bond I shared with my horse.

I found myself opening up to him in a way I hadn't with anyone else, revealing glimpses of the carefree life we had before the silver crash, when the world changed overnight.

As I spoke, the restaurant around us seemed to fade away. The clatter of dishes subsided, replaced by the rhythmic swish of the waiters' brooms sweeping the floor. The lights dimmed, but we remained oblivious, lost in our own world of shared stories and laughter.

"This is incredible, Silver," Carl said, his voice hushed with awe. "It's a real-life drama, triumph and tragedy."

"Exactly," I said, feeling a surge of energy. "It's the perfect story for the silver screen."

Carl had been initially drawn to the sensational aspects of the Tabor story—the love triangle, the downfall. But he came to appreciate my desire to portray my family's legacy with dignity and nuance. He listened with interest as I spoke of my parents' philanthropy, their political battles, and their unwavering love for each other.

"So, you're saying the Tabor story isn't about scandal, it's about legacy. A family who dared to dream, loved fiercely, and ultimately paid the price for their ambition. That's the story we need to tell."

Our eyes met across the table, and I felt a spark, a connection that went beyond the words we spoke. A nervous flutter like minnows in the creek started in my stomach.

"We should probably go," I said, my voice a little breathless.

"Of course," Carl said, rising from his seat. "I'll walk you home."

My smile faltered. I couldn't let him get too close. He wouldn't understand. He couldn't know the truth about what I'd become, the darkness I'd been through.

"Actually," I said, trying to sound casual, "I think I'd rather walk alone tonight. Clear my head, you know?"

He looked confused, his brow furrowing. "I'm not letting you walk home alone, it's not safe."

He was right. The sounds of the Southside—sirens wailing, shouts echoing, the occasional gunshot—were a stark contrast to the hushed elegance of the Palmer House.

When we reached my apartment building, I shook his hand, a tight smile plastered on my face.

"I'll help write the Tabor script, Carl," I said, my voice firm. "But just to be clear, no funny stuff. It's all business."

He nodded slowly, a flash of disappointment crossing his features. "Whatever you say, Miss Tabor."

I watched as he turned to leave, a pang of regret tugging at my heart. But I pushed it aside. He couldn't know. Not ever. Not about the rape, not about the child I lost, not about how close I came to murdering Rockwell. And most of all, not about Echo, the shadow self that clung to me.

I closed the door behind me and leaned against it, my heart heavy. Could I ever truly escape the weight of my past, forever haunted by the secrets that lurked within?

THICK, humid air clung to my throat, smelling of overripe pawpaw and animal sweat. My heart chirruped under my ribs like a lark caught in hawk's talons. This grimy menagerie seemed like a punishment for my bad behavior at Lily's and even worse, the child that had been cut from my womb. Yet, Selig Polyscope seemed the only logical path forward. Carl and the silver screen just beyond the tiger trailers offered a frail hope.

Big Otto gestured toward a cage teeming with long-tailed macaques, their chatter discordant hisses and clicks. "First stop, Miss Silver," he boomed, thrusting a large basket overflowing with juicy mangoes and plump grapes into my trembling hands. "Toss it in but mind your fingers. These lads got nimble hands and a taste for trouble."

I swallowed my fear and approached the cage, a wiry male caught my eye. With a mischievous glint he snatched a mango with lightning speed, leaving his companions to squabble over the fallen fruit. A laugh bubbled up from my throat. I sensed a wild magic woven into this chaos, a spark of raw life amidst the stink and screech. With a flick of my wrist, I sent the rest of the food sailing through the bars. The monkeys erupted in a frenzy.

"Now comes the main act, Silver," Otto's voice boomed over the approaching snarls. The tigers emerged from the shadows, their massive forms filling the cage, magnificent stripes swirling like molten lava in the dappled sunlight. Only iron bars separated me from their ferocious teeth. "Prime cuts for these beauties. Show them who's boss."

Boss? *Me?* Terror seized me. My spine prickled, sweat clinging to my palms as I reached into Otto's bucket. Raw meat, slick with blood, squished between my fingers. Bile rose in my throat. These magnificent beasts, hungry and impatient, could devour *me* instead of the steaks.

But I had to do this. One by one, I hurled the meat through

the bars, each slab a bloody offering. The tigers lunged, a blur of orange and black muscle, jaws snapping, teeth flashing. They devoured the meat in a torrent of growls and snarls, tearing at the steaks with a vicious fury that chilled me to the bone.

And yet, with each throw, a strange sense of control began to bloom within me. *I* was the one providing the food, *I* was the one dictating their movements.

When the meat was gone, they turned their amber eyes on me. Something electric crackled between us for a fleeting moment, a primal connection, raw and untamed.

Fear hadn't left me, not entirely. But a spark of defiance had ignited alongside it. I wasn't merely feeding tigers; I was taming them, taming the fear that threatened to consume me. The remorseful girl from Colorado was fading, replaced by a woman forging her own destiny in this wild, untamed world.

Chapter 15

1932

Silver price $0.28 per ounce

Leadville, Colorado. Baby Doe was lost in the story of her own life, Carl Erickson's words weaving a tapestry of memory and emotion that enveloped her completely. Fancy ballrooms, chandeliers sparkling like a prospector's dream. President Arthur, laughing fit to bust. Actors, singers, highfalutin' folks they'd hobnobbed with. Mark Twain, spinning his tales, Walt Whitman, reciting poetry. Even Sarah Bernhardt, dramatic as all get-out. Met artists too, Tiffany, Remington ... their masterpieces hanging in our Denver palace. A thrill, it was, hearing it all, seeing it in her mind's eye.

Like panning for gold, she strained to hear the truth in Carl's fancy words. All them high-society shindigs weren't the real story, not by a long shot.

Carl finished the Oscar Wilde part, trailing off. Quiet as a tomb, 'cept for that lonesome train whistle echoin' down the canyon. He pounded the table. "I should drop that scene, shouldn't I? Silver Dollar was fuzzy on the details."

"Don't even think of dropping that scene," she said. "Oscar Wilde had Leadville howling like coyotes at a full moon."

Carl leaned forward, his eyes pleading. "Tell me about it, Mrs. Tabor."

"Oscar had them rolling in the aisles." She mimicked Wilde's clipped British accent. "Whoever said money doesn't grow on trees hasn't seen Leadville's aspens. Every leaf a golden dollar, just waiting for Horace Tabor to pluck!"

Carl scribbled in his leather notebook. "Great stuff!"

"But the real fireworks happened down in the mine." She inhaled deeply, the scent of Irish whiskey ghosting through the air. "We threw Wilde a hurdy-gurdy party down in the Matchless. Picture a fiddle wailing like a lovesick hound, dancers twirling in the lamplight. My brother Peter kept Wilde's glass topped with enough hooch to fuel a buffalo stampede."

Carl shook his head in awe. "So you think my script is ready to present to Warner Bros.?"

"Not by a long shot." The truth pained her. "It's too pretty, too glamorous, too easy. There was nothing easy about what we did. It was dirty work, killing work. You can't finish the script until you go down into the mine to truly understand what we were dealing with."

"But I can't wait 'til Spring to go down in the mine," Carl whined. "Warner Bros. wants a blockbuster for Fall. They're counting on me, and if I don't come through there are a hundred others standing in line."

She swallowed her frustration, needing him to understand. "Close your eyes and imagine this." She gave it all the drama she dared. "Horace Tabor, his face streaked with dirt, not fancy cologne. Silver dust shimmering in his hair. His muscles straining as he hauls a cart laden with ore. The chill of the mine shaft seeping into his bones. The rhythmic clang of the pickaxe against rock, the steady drip of water through the darkness ... smell the damp earth."

Carl nodded, slow and thoughtful.

"That is where our empire was truly forged. In the shared

sweat and stoic silence, a hundred feet below the earth's surface." She paused. "And, our love story wasn't some radio soap opera, Carl. It was forbidden, yes, but we shared a love born of hard work and dedication, blossoming amidst the harsh beauty of the mine. That's the story you need to tell, Carl. The real one. The one that started in the heart of this mountain."

"But the producer's demanding to see the script."

The ground trembled beneath them, the rumble building into a deafening roar. The cabin lurched, throwing her off balance, her heart pounding in her chest. A picture crashed to the floor, dust stinging her eyes as a cold draft whipped through the room. The old wood creaked and groaned, amplifying the sense of impending doom.

When the shaking finally stopped, a heavy silence descended, and a cold fear gripped her, tightening around her heart like a vice.

Carl's face drained of color, his eyes wide. He stumbled backward, gripping the table for support. "Earthquake?"

She shook her head. "Avalanche, most likely. Springtime in these mountains is a beast."

Carl's eyes darted toward her only window as if expecting another onslaught. He swallowed hard. "I guess the mountain objected to the Tabor script, too," he forced a weak laugh.

A wry smile tugged at her lips. "Maybe now you understand why I insist you experience the mine firsthand."

Carl nodded slowly. "This mountain ... it has a power I've never witnessed. I need to see its heart, its belly." He pulled on his coat. "I'll be back when the snow melts and finish the script."

After he left, Baby Doe traced the splintered crack in the wall, proof of nature's destructive force and the precariousness of their lives. Yet, it had also served a purpose, jolting Carl into understanding the true essence of the Tabor story.

Chapter 16

1917

Silver price $0.81 per ounce

Chicago, Illinois. "Just relax, Tamber, sweetheart." I swallowed hard, keeping my voice soft and steady though my stomach danced a nervous turkey trot. "It's just a manicure."

At least Tamber let me touch her paws, for now at least. Not sure where I got the bright idea to bond over a manicure, but it was worth a shot. I sat cross-legged outside their cage, her paw resting on my knee through the bars. The humid air, thick with the scent of damp earth and exotic animals, clung to my skin. The trumpet of an elephant blared through the zoo, a wild sound in the burgeoning city of Chicago.

Her mate, Timber, watched my every move from the corner of the enclosure, a low growl rumbling in his throat, claws flexing against the concrete. I could feel his vibration in my bones, making my hair stand on end. The nail polish brush shook in my hand, knowing he was watching, ready to pounce. The ripple of muscles beneath his striped fur raised goosebumps on my arms.

Monkeys screeched and chattered in the neighboring enclosure, setting my teeth on edge. A palpable tension hung thick with the sound of distant thunder, warning of the storm brewing outside. Dark clouds gathered above the glass ceiling, casting ominous shadows through the lush jungle trees of Selig's zoo.

Big Otto's voice boomed through the din. "Silver Dollar, did you hear the news? Director Grandon cast you in his film."

"Really?" I squealed with glee, my mind racing ahead, seeing myself up on the silver screen.

Startled by my outburst, Tamber jerked her paw, and I fumbled the red nail polish.

"Better than that." Otto's eyes twinkled. "They cast you as the Maharaja's tiger keeper."

"No, no, not that part." My stomach lurched. The tigers. The cold sweat, the racing pulse—I'd tried so hard to overcome it, but my terror always won. "Couldn't they find another part for me? Anything?"

"I put in a good word about how well you worked with the tigers." Otto's smile faded. "I thought you'd be thrilled. Director Grandon doesn't hand out roles like this easily." His eyebrows shot up at the sight of Tamber's painted claws. "What in the Sam Hill are you doing?"

My pulse quickened. "It's just a little—"

"Grandon will have my hide if he sees this." His face turned blistering red. "The tigers have a scene tomorrow." His gaze swept over the overflowing feed pails, the unkempt stalls, the muddled tools, tasks I'd put aside for the manicure. "Silver, I spoke too soon for you. You aren't keeping up with your tasks. I'll tell Director Grandon I made a mistake. This isn't working out as I hoped." His head shook.

Losing two jobs at once, fear clawed at my throat. "Oh, no, Otto, don't fire me. I'll clean this up immediately." I jumped up, grabbed a broom, and started sweeping. "I need this job, and I need that part." My rent was due, and I needed that paycheck. "I'll have this in tip-top shape immediately."

Otto rubbed his heavy jowls. "Then get that polish off her. Or we'll both be fired if Grandon can't use her tomorrow. And you won't have to worry about the acting part you don't want." He trudged off, his belly leading the way.

I fed the monkeys their fruit, but it brought me no joy today. Never saw Otto this angry, even when the monkeys threw banana peels at him. I opened the solvent and started rubbing Tamber's claws. She started to pull away and I gripped harder. "Hold still, Tamber."

Placing her other paw on top of my head, Tamber rubbed my hair with the same fury I was rubbing her paw, only her force was tenfold. "Ease up, Tamber." The solvent was doing nothing on the fingernail polish. Needed to try something else.

I tried to wrench free, but Tamber's claws snagged my hair, tightening with every desperate tug. Trapped in a living Chinese finger puzzle, Tamber's grip a vice around my head. From the corner of my eye, I saw Timber closing in, his menacing rumble growing louder with each step.

Goosebumps prickled my skin, followed by a wave of icy heat through my scalp and down my neck. Echo, my protector. "Don't let the overgrown kittens see you sweat."

"Easy for you to say," I retorted, over the thunder grumbling ominously outside.

Hearing footsteps, I tried to lift my head, but Tamber held my cheek on the cold cement, her claws digging into my head. "Help," I yelled out. "Can someone help me?"

Carl's oxfords stepped around the aisle. "What the devil?" He ran to me, his hand gripping my shoulder. But as soon as he did, Timber lunged toward the bars from inside the cage, his breath hot and angry.

Carl backed off, holding up his palms. "What can I do?"

My mind raced. I gestured to the wall with my right arm. "Firehose, full stream. Hold tight."

He grabbed the nozzle with both hands and aimed it at Timber. Then turned the steel spigot as far as it would go. Water spurted with vigorous power, Carl holding the hose with two hands. The gusher hit Timber in the chest, yowling and snarling, pushing him back to the corner.

Turning off the hose, Carl carefully worked to free my hair from Tamber's claws. The cold water seeped through my jodhpurs and blouse, chilling me to the bone. I lay there with my head in Carl's lap, shivering uncontrollably, my teeth chattering.

Echo's gibberish screaming through my bleeding scalp: "Could have been killed. Need to quit. What are you thinking?"

Finally, Carl released the last shred of my hair, and the tigress ran back with Timber. Carl lifted me from my quivering heap and wrapped his arms around my shivering body.

Relief crashed over me, so intense it made me dizzy. Gratitude mingled with a sudden, overwhelming affection for Carl. I had held back so long, so many things I had to hide from him. The jagged scar on my belly, for one. I couldn't bear seeing his disillusionment.

Yet my emotions threw logic out the window, and I pressed my lips onto his in a desperate, hungry kiss. The taste of black licorice mingled with the salt of my tears, a profound yearning I was afraid to admit.

Echo's voice cut through the warmth. "No, Silver!" she cried with a desperate urgency. "Don't let him in! He'll hurt you. Remember Rockwell? Remember the pain? Men are dangerous. They'll use you and discard you."

Rockwell's hands, rough and forceful, flashed through my mind, a terrifying echo of the past. My breath hitched, a cold sweat erupting as panic flooded my senses. Echo's words, though harsh, resonated with a deep-seated fear I couldn't ignore. A wave of nausea washed over me, the sweet licorice taste turning to bile. Carl's touch, once a comfort, now burned like acid, searing my skin.

"He'll break your heart!" Echo's voice shrieked, a desperate plea in the tempest of my mind. "You have to protect yourself! Push him away!"

I shoved Carl away, the force of it a shock. I fled, dodging towering jungle backdrops and stacks of wooden crates, the studio lights a dizzying blur.

"Silver, wait!" Carl's voice was a distant plea, swallowed by the rising tide of Echo's warnings.

Bursting out the doors, rain lashed my face, a cold shock that mirrored the icy grip of fear constricting my heart. I was running from past trauma, from the terrifying potential for future pain. Echo was right. I had to protect myself.

But as I ran, a sob escaped my lips, a cry of despair for the love I was leaving behind. *He'll be better off without me. I'm damaged goods. I'll only hurt him in the end.*

A bitter laugh, cold and hollow, escaped my lips, a sound that was both mine and yet not mine. Echo had taken over, her fear and pain strangling my own feelings. The storm raged on, a battle for my soul that I had already lost.

Chapter 17

1917

SILVER PRICE $0.81 PER OUNCE

CHICAGO, ILLINOIS. Echo turned away from the window, empty handed again. Where was that return letter from Baby Doe? Where was the sweet cash she'd begged for? Should've bet on the ponies instead.

While Carl made flimsy excuses for Silver's absence at Selig Studios, Echo had flown the coop, renting a room in a Bronzeville boarding house, her purse emptier than a politician's promise. A new hustle was needed, fast.

"Sweetheart let you down, doll?"

Echo's gaze landed on a man in smoky gray sunglasses, though they were indoors. Angled jaw, a cleft chin, snappy pinstripe suit. A blood red carnation blazed against his lapel, and a creamy fedora atop his head. His expression exuded a bored confidence that intrigued and irritated her.

"None of your concern." Playing hard to get made the chase more thrilling.

A low, smoky chuckle rumbled from his throat. "My apologies, Miss. But you seem troubled. Perhaps you'll allow me to extend an invitation. A cocktail, perhaps?" He grinned, the dimple in his chin deepening as he chuckled.

What have we here? A moth to the flame. "Your name first," Echo demanded, "then I'll decide if you're worthy of knowing mine."

"Dante Rossi, at your service." He skimmed his fedora with flair. "Your turn."

Panic constricted her throat. What name should she use? 'Silver Dollar Tabor' had the reputation of wealth and power but was the very identity she protected. 'Echo LaVode' offered anonymity but lacked the status.

"Rose Mary Echo Silver Dollar Tabor." The whole truth for a change. "Daughter of the legendary Horace Tabor, silver king and US senator." As soon as the words left her lips, she knew she'd made a mistake. Too much, too soon.

Rossi's eyes lit up with recognition. "Of course, I've read about the Tabors." He stroked his cleft chin. "How about that drink?" His gaze swept her ample bosom to her t-strapped pumps.

He's not getting off that easy. "Dinner. Dinner and drinks. Where'd you have in mind?" Thinks he's a smooth operator. Let's see how smooth.

"The Pump Room?" Rossi gestured down the street. "Not too far from here."

Swanky spot. A man who's not afraid to spend a buck. "I feel like a steak," Echo declared. Gotta make this worthwhile, after all.

With a whistle between his fingers, he hailed a cab with ease. Echo bet lots of things came to Dante Rossi with ease.

"Slide in, Miss Tabor," he drawled.

"Call me Echo. I go by my stage name now." A brilliant recovery from her thoughtless gaff a few minutes ago. "Echo LaVode."

He slid beside her, the scent of gunpowder and tobacco mixing with the piney scent of gin. His sharp suit, tailored to perfection, reeked of new money, but his eyes, cold and black as a moonless night, promised danger and deceit. Just the type of man that set Echo's motor racing.

Tension buzzed between them, a delicious undertow as the cab raced toward the Pump Room. What did she want from him besides a meal? An alliance, an affair, a trap? Who was trapping whom? Or was it who? A cunning grin played on her lips.

The plush velvet embrace of the Pump Room only deepened her hunger. The last sunlight speared through organza curtains, casting patterns on the embossed tablecloth, a far cry from the peeling wallpaper of her Bronzeville room she'd rented away from Silver's studio.

Dante Rossi's gaze, intensified by the sharp lines of his cleft chin, held hers with a force that made her skin prickle. He was all sharp angles and bold colors, from his buffed nails to his flamboyant tie. "Your family must be thrilled that silver prices may rise if the US joins the war."

So that's his angle. "Are you an investor? Or a stockbroker?" She forced a smile, a tremor in her hand as it reached for the silver spoon, a token of another life.

He leaned in, breathing her in long and slow. "Let's just say I have a knack for sniffing out opportunities. Silver and gold are always in play, don't you agree?"

Martinis were served, dinner orders placed, and Rossi continued his sly inquiry. "So where are your family's silver mines?" He stirred the olive around his glass.

"Colorado. My mother's business, now that my father passed. I'm strictly show business." She giggled between sips. "Don't like to get my hands dirty."

"Where do you perform?" He leaned back into the leather booth, sipping his martini.

"Looking for a new gig now, if you know of any."

"Singer or a dancer?"

"Triple threat, darling." She let loose a low chuckle. "Dancer, singer, actress."

The waiter, his French accent thick as cream, prepared their steak tableside.

"Rare, please," Echo instructed, inhaling the intoxicating aroma.

"Make that two," Rossi murmured.

Burning cognac mingled with the sizzle of steak, a heady scent that made her mouth water. Flames erupted, bathing them in an orange glow that mirrored the heat pulsing between them. It was a dangerous dance, exhilarating and forbidden.

Hours melted away, fueled by wine and seared meat. Their conversation crackled with unspoken desires, their shared glances a seduction of wills. The plates now sat empty, wine glasses drained, leaving only the lingering question.

"Taxi to your apartment?" His finger trailed a suggestive line down her shoulder.

Echo leaned back, a smirk playing on her lips. "Sleep can wait, darling. The city's alive with jazz, and frankly, so am I."

Intrigue crossed Rossi's face. "Say, the Peking Club needs a star. Someone who can draw a crowd. Think you're up to the challenge?"

"Mister Rossi." Echo tilted her chin. "You haven't glimpsed the spectrum of my talents."

His black eyes caressed her décolleté with a hunger she knew all too well. "Then consider me a captive audience."

Echo scooched closer, her breath ghosting his lips. "You won't be disappointed."

They stepped into the neon night, the city's pulse drawing them toward the exotic nightclub, a stage set for ambition and seduction. Rossi's offer came with strings, she knew it. But she had conditions, too. A sly smile curved her lips. The game had begun. Time to turn up the heat.

Chapter 18

1917

Silver price $0.81 per ounce

Chicago, Illinois. My unexplained absence had raised eyebrows at Selig's, but Carl had covered for me, saying I was sick with the flu. The details of my lost week remained hazy, like a forgotten dream. I imagine Echo was up to her old tricks, and that could not be good. Not good at all. A strange sense of dread clung to me, like a cobweb I couldn't shake off. What if she hurt someone? Now, I had to work twice as hard to prove my dedication and avoid any further suspicion. My body ached, my mind felt foggy. Not only did I have to catch up on the training, but I also had to regain Otto's trust. Losing this job would mean losing everything.

A shadow fell across the ring. "Thought you pulled a fast one, didn't you, doll face?"

My spine prickled. "I beg your pardon?" Something looked familiar about his cleft chin and the gold wire sunglasses, but for the life of me, I couldn't place him. "Have we met?"

He barked a dry laugh. "Don't play coy. You know who I am." A red carnation blazed against his pinstriped suit. His face was shadowed by a wide-brimmed fedora. "Dante Rossi. Perhaps the name strikes a chord, you little fraud?"

A monstrous growl erupted next to me. Tamber's roar shot icy dread through my veins. In a flash, the tiger lunged at him, yanking against her leash buckled around my wrist. "Tamber, down," I commanded, bracing against her massive strength. The tigers' snarl cut through the humid air, but her training kicked in. Hesitantly, she lowered her massive body.

With a jerk, I freed a steak from the pouch. I flung it into the open cage. "In!" The word cracked out of me, sharp like a whip.

Tamber lunged, a blur of stripes and hunger, disappearing into the corner. I slammed the door shut and fumbled for the bolt. I leaned against the bars, chest heaving.

The man called Rossi removed his hat with and smoothed back his hair, his expression a carefully crafted mask of indifference. Only the slight tremor in his hand betrayed his reaction to the tiger.

"Who let you into the training ring?" My eyes darted around the deserted enclosure. Everyone gone for lunch. No witnesses.

He straightened his lapel, a sneer twisting his lips. "The guard said I'd find Colonel Selig back here. Business to discuss." He squinted. "Then I saw you. The doll who pulled a fast one on me a week ago. I should warn Colonel Selig about your antics."

I squinted at him trying to remember. "Never set eyes on you in my life."

He whistled. "You owe me an explanation, Echo."

A cold fist squeezed my heart. He'd met Echo? How? What had she done? What had she said? Nausea churned in my stomach, sweat prickling my skin.

"What a night we had: martinis, wine, steak. You danced like a hellcat on fire. Then you just walked out. Vanished. Leaving me alone at the Peking Club."

"What ... what did you call me?" The words a strangled gasp.

"Echo. Echo LaVode. Your stage name, you told me."

My breath hitched. "You've got the wrong girl." I forced a

brittle laugh. "I work here as an animal wrangler and actress. No time for setting dance floors on fire." Spinning around, I marched toward the canteen, desperate to put distance between me and this stranger.

His hand shot out, grabbing my arm. "You gave me your real name, too. Silver Dollar, right? You are Silver Dollar, aren't you? Same fiery eyes, long legs, captivating mane. Has to be you."

I jerked away and kept walking, his strides keeping pace. Couldn't he leave me alone?

"I've been trying to find you. My investors are eager to invest in the Matchless Mine."

"What about the Matchless?" I spun around.

"I did some digging." The glass ceiling lit up his sly grin. "Silver prices are about to skyrocket thanks to the Great War. My investors are keen to invest." He stepped closer. "Smart woman like yourself wouldn't want to miss this golden opportunity, would she?"

For Mama's sake, I should hear him out. A silver boom could be Baby Doe's salvation, a way out from under Rockwell's thumb. "Intriguing proposition, Mr. ... Rossi, is it?"

"My friends call me Dante."

"Mr. Rossi, tell me about your investors." I pushed open the swinging canteen door, met with raucous laughter and glasses clinking. Smells of spilled beer and sawdust. "Let's see if your investors are half as interesting as my phantom twin." I hoped my bravado didn't sound as bamboozled as I felt. This Mr. Rossi was proof positive that Echo had taken over while I was "sick." That she could take over whenever she felt like it. A shadow fell over my soul, a premonition of a dark side of myself I clearly had no control over.

The whirring fans stirred the hot air, like the churning in my stomach. Conversations died on everyone's lips as the tall, dark stranger with sunglasses, followed me into the dim canteen. A bead of sweat trickled down my temple, as we sat at the worn bar.

"Hey, Silver!" Big Otto clapped a forgiving hand on my shoulder. "Saved you the Standard & Poors." He thrust the flimsy paper into my hand. But the stock price of silver remained stagnant. Was Rossi lying, or did he have insider information?

He slid onto the bar stool next to me, his elbows on the sticky bar.

"Hiya, Stevie. Nathan's hotdogs and beers." I held up two fingers to the flamboyant bartender, his kohl-rimmed eyes twinkling over his tattooed bicep.

Stevie sashayed over, sliding cold beers and a bowl of peanuts onto the table. The salty aroma of the peanuts mingled with the tantalizing smell of grilled hotdogs as Stevie served them up, steaming with chili fiery enough to make my eyes water. I winced as I took a bite, savoring the explosion of flavor despite the dull throb in my jaw.

"They don't make them like this back in Colorado," I admitted, a hint of homesickness creeping in.

Rossi wiped steam off his lenses with a napkin. "Speaking of Colorado, I'm heading to Denver for other business. Thought I'd take the train up to Leadville and present your mother with our investment proposal in person."

My gut twisted; he was moving too fast. "Look, Mr. Rossi, first I need to approve the deal, then we'll see about you meeting Baby Doe. Mama's a recluse. Doesn't see anyone." Not to mention that all Matchless business went through JD Rockwell. But Mama would see Rossi if I wrote her, and Rockwell would be cut out. That would be something, wouldn't it? Extracting revenge for what he did to me. "Who are these investors you represent, and what kind of deal?"

"Chicago businessmen," he said, wiping off chili oil.

"Moneymen, strictly confidential. We've worked together for years." His eyes narrowed behind tinted lenses. "Mrs. Tabor gets all the money she needs for equipment and labor, and we split the profits fifty-fifty."

I choked, the bitter beer burning my throat. "It's our mine, Mr. Rossi. Seventy-thirty split more like it." Wouldn't let this slippery businessman take advantage of Mama like others had.

"There are other silver mines we're looking at." A tight smile stretched his thin lips. "Trying to help you out, doll face. All expenses on our dime. Money your mother wouldn't see otherwise."

Rossi had a point. Baby Doe had been bleeding every cent to keep the mine afloat since Papa's passing. I shoved aside my half-eaten hotdog. But how can I trust Rossi, especially when he met Echo. What did Echo promise him? Was he just another vulture circling the Matchless?

Stevie placed fresh mugs in front of us, dew already snaking down the glass. I lifted mine against the flushed heat of my cheeks. I had to take the risk. This was a gamble that could finally pay off for Mama. "Fine. Sixty-forty and I want to see everything in writing."

"Deal." Rossi's mug met hers in a clink. "Why not come with me to Denver? See for yourself that everything's legit."

Not a bad thought." I ran my fingers through my hair. "But I can't leave. They are ready to film my part." Taking a swig, the beer did nothing to loosen the knot in my stomach. "What if you're wrong about the silver prices? What then?"

Rossi chuckled. "Don't be naïve, doll face." Light glinted on his sunglasses. "War is always good for business. That's why we have them." He covered my hand with his.

The saloon doors swung open with a groan, a harsh rectangle of sunlight cutting through the smoky haze. Carl's face lit up when he saw me, a smile spreading across his face. But then his gaze dropped to Rossi's hand on mine. His smile froze, the warmth in his expression drained away, replaced by a cold mask of disbelief and hurt.

I ripped my hand free, my cheeks hot and prickly. Carl's jaw clenched, a muscle throbbing in his temple. He spun around and stalked out, the saloon doors swinging in his wake.

Another fight brewing between us. Just another one in a string of them lately, because I kept skipping out on our writing sessions. Because ... Echo. He'd suspected I was seeing someone else, and now, well, now there'd be no room for doubt.

Rossi smirked, sizing up the incident. "Interesting timing, wouldn't you say? Perhaps this explains the double play, Miss ... Echo?"

"None of your business." I rubbed my hand where he'd left a slimy trail. Guilt twisted my insides. Carl deserved better than my tangled web of secrets. I could try to explain Rossi, but he wouldn't understand. A fierce determination sparked, fanned by years of watching Mama struggle to keep the Matchless afloat. I have to do this for her. For our future. Couldn't let my feelings for Carl stand in the way. Love was a luxury I couldn't afford right now.

I turned back to Rossi, my resolve hardening. "Let me review the contract," I demanded, cold and sharp. "Then, and only then, will I write Mama and tell her you're coming."

A slow grin spread across Rossi's face as he raised his beer mug in mock salute. "Of course, partner. You'll have it by this evening." His eyes darted to the swinging saloon doors, then swirled the mug in his hands with the satisfaction of a gambler with a royal flush.

I jabbed my finger at his chest. "If I hear one more breath about this Echo, all bets are off. Understand?" Draining my beer, I slammed the mug down and walked out, his eyes burning on my back. Rossi may think he has the upper hand, but I won't let him take advantage of Mama. What was that saying? "Keep your friends close, but your enemies closer?"

THE COBBLESTONES beneath my cowboy boots felt uneven, reminding me of how unhinged I felt. The towering spires of Holy Sepulcher Church pierced the sky, casting long dark shadows in my path. A storm of confusion raged within me, a chilling realization taking shape with each huffing breath. So, I hadn't been sick like Carl said ...it was her. Echo. The steamy kisses, the smoky clubs, the reckless abandon. They were memories of her reality, not mine. How had she escaped without me?

Guilt and shame weighed down my steps, threatening to drag me under. What else had Echo done? What else had she told Rossi? He knew. He knew about her. The thought shot a bolt of panic through me, my fingers tightening around my quartz rosary beads. I needed to find a way to keep her inside me ... or I could lose everything; my job, my friendship with Carl, even Rossi's investment that could save the Matchless.

Mama always said the church was the answer. I climbed the steps to the heavy wooden doors. Could it help me now? Could it help me silence the storm within?

But inside, the confessional was empty, the priest gone. Sorely disappointed, I kneeled in the nearest pew, the cloying sweetness of frankincense doing little to settle my nerves. It'd been so many years since my last confession. My fingers traced the smooth rosary, each bead a prayer.

"Bless me, Father, for I have sinned." How insignificant the words sounded, given my grave offense. Rockwell's face, twisted in a macabre laugh, swam before my eyes. Echo had taken over that night and saved my life. I remembered how relief had washed over me, gratitude for this fierce protector who emerged to save me. But the violence that followed haunted me, proof of her dark power simmering beneath the surface.

Clearing my throat, I continued. "It started again, Father.

When I get scared, she ... comes. I cannot seem to stop her." A sob grasped my throat.

The tropical fragrance of frangipani wafted over me, carrying the lilting island accent of a woman. "Do not fear the night, child. It holds wonders the day cannot reveal."

"W-who are you?" I bolted upright, glimpsing large, luminous eyes beneath a vibrant scarf, its colors swirling in the dim light. A necklace of deep red coral beads, polished by the sea, rested against her throat, catching the flickering candlelight.

"I hear confessions of a different sort, child. The kind the priest has no answers for." Her voice, rich and resonant like a distant drum.

"You hear ... what I need to confess?" I whispered, afraid she'd vanish into thin air, a figment of my imagination.

"This spirit that walks beside you; you fear her power, her anger. But it mirrors your own, does it not?"

A chord of truth. Echo embodied all the courage, the fight and fury I kept buried. "I think I created her out of my own pain and loneliness," I admitted. "But now I ... I can't seem to control her ... Echo, I mean." A shiver pulsed through me. "She's done things. Unspeakable things, that I never would've done. I'm afraid of what she's capable of, what damage Echo can cause."

The woman hummed a low, mournful note, rocking back and forth to an unheard rhythm. The hypnotic melody eased the tension in my shoulders and lulled me into a state of tranquil surrender. The scent of flowers intensified as I drifted deeper into her chant, finding myself adrift in a sea of fragrant petals. Geraniums, tiger lilies, and roses, a vibrant tapestry blanketing my head and shoulders. A prayer shawl woven from nature's bounty.

Finally, she spoke. "I see your wounded spirit is growing teeth, child. Very dangerous to trap a spirit."

My skin prickled. "That lawyer deserved it, but I don't want to see anyone else get hurt."

"Your fierce one, she ain't here by mistake. Why cage a bird, clip its wings? Let it fly."

"I don't understand." My hands clenched the pew.

"Some folks got demons talkin', some got ancestors walkin' with 'em. You got your own fierce spirit, ain't that what your Echo is?"

I tried to understand her cryptic statement. Hadn't Echo always been a whisper, just a breath away, smoldering under the surface? But now she felt like a separate being. "You want me to ... let her go?" How could I do that if Echo was me?

"Think of it this way, child," she said, a gentle caress. "Let her explore, let her taste freedom. Maybe then, she'll come back to you, satisfied and peaceful. Let her go."

When I looked up, the woman had vanished. I blinked, unsure if I'd imagined the entire encounter. The pew was empty, save for the vibrant tapestry of petals that still clung to my shoulders. I gathered the remaining petals, tucking them into my pockets.

As I stepped outside, the serenity of the church was drowned out by the clanging streetcars and the hawkers' cries. I sank onto a park bench, the old pain radiating from my broken teeth.

The woman's words in my head: "Let her taste her freedom." Maybe there was truth in the stranger's message.

"Alright, Echo," I whispered, the wind stealing my breath. Reaching into my pockets, I pulled out the flower petals. Admiring their vibrant colors, they smelled fresh as this new start promised to be. I raised my trembling hands to the sky and opened my fingers, letting them flutter free. A colorful cloud of blossoms dancing in the wind, each petal a promise to my newfound resolve. "Go. Little Echo. Be free. Live your life." I watched the petals fly until they were all gone. Surprised at the emptiness I felt letting her go.

∽

CHICAGO, Illinois. The dentist's chair, in worn leather and gleaming chrome, loomed over me like a medieval torture device. The drill, a menacing silver insect, lay ominously near a tray of wicked-looking tools. Pain throbbed in my jaw, synced with the drumming in my chest. The Slide for Life injury had become a nightmare. When would I learn not to risk my life for glory?

"We'll need to dig out what's left of these molars," Dr. Rosenberg said, his fingers firm as he probed roughly against my gums. "Infection's setting in. Did someone try to glue it together?"

I nodded, the pain a white-hot lance in my jaw, sweat beading on my forehead. The sickly-sweet gas mask settled over my face, a cloying chemical scent filling my nostrils. "This'll just take the edge off," the dentist assured me.

The harsh overhead light blurred at the edges, morphing into a hazy orb. The drill's whine filled my ears, the vibration a shockwave through my skull. There were no cruel taunts from Echo. Just the rhythmic drone of the drill and the medicinal smell of disinfectant.

"Echo?" I could use some comfort. "Where are you?"

The drill's relentless whine filled the void where she used to reside. Had the woman in the confessional truly helped me banish Echo?

I clutched the armrest, facing this excruciating pain alone, now. Utterly alone. None of Echo's chatter to distract me. "I can do this." I squeezed my eyes shut against the tears. "I have to." I focused on my breath, in and out, in and out, drawing on the newfound resolve I'd discovered in the confessional. I would not be defeated by fear.

When the drill fell silent, exhaustion left my limbs heavy, my eyelids drooping. But there was also a sense of triumph, a quiet strength blooming in the hollow where Echo used to be.

As I stumbled out of the dentist's office, minus two molars, the world felt sharp and unfamiliar. My mouth felt raw and swollen, gauze packed into the empty sockets.

In my coat pocket, I found a remaining rose petal from the church, a vestige of my promise to let Echo go, and of the strength I'd found within myself. I felt unburdened, as if a weight had been lifted from my shoulders. I wasn't sure what the future held, but for the first time in a long time, I felt a glimmer of hope.

I just couldn't help but wonder where Echo went when she wasn't with me?

Chapter 19

1917

Silver price $0.81 per ounce

Chicago, Illinois. Leave the daytime working girl to Silver Dollar. Echo came alive at night in Bronzeville. The heartland pulsed with jazz spilling from open windows, the sizzle of sausages on street vendors' grills, and the streetlamps illuminating the brilliant murals on brick walls. From her tiny window, she watched working girls emerge, transformed with colorful cosmetics and glittery dresses. Laughing and animated after their workdays, these women excited her. They were taking life into their own hands, headed to the Taxi Dance, and Echo would go too.

She shimmied on a sequined chemise in defiance of the drab decor beneath the bare bulb. As she headed to the New Majestic Dancing Academy, each cool breath of evening air felt like a final shedding of Silver's daytime persona. This was the city's gritty, pulsing heartbeat, raw and real. Gone was the hesitant starlet; Echo was finally living. This life held the promise of freedom, of flouting social expectations, undeniable danger that ignited her soul.

Inside the dimly lit dancehall, the air thick with the scent of cheap perfume and sweat, men shuffled in queue, their eyes glinting with barely concealed hunger. This wasn't the glamorous escape she'd envisioned, but rather, the gritty underbelly. A wicked thrill coursed through her.

Echo watched the other girls line up, their eyes darting between the men and the measly tips in their outstretched hands. Fools, selling themselves short for pennies and smiles. She craved more than this, more than the desperate grasps and empty promises. She wanted a life that sizzled, a life that burned with the same intensity as the jazz that filled the air. A life where she wasn't just a commodity, but a force to be reckoned with.

Echo's dance card filled rapidly. First, a stout man with a handlebar mustache, smelling of cigars, clumsily shuffled through a foxtrot, his sweaty palms leaving a clammy residue. Next, came a downtown businessman, his breath heavy with garlic and onions, who clung to her like a vine during a melancholic waltz.

Not going as she'd hoped. She ached with a restless need, her gaze sweeping the room of men, none to her liking. Until one. Crisp, starched army uniform, the scent of soap and sunshine clinging to him, his valiant determination a mirror of her own bold spirit. She beckoned him over with one red-painted nail.

The soldier handed her a ticket, his fingers brushing hers with tingling warmth. "Private Jeffrey Mink from Indianapolis, at your service. And who might you be?"

A mischievous grin curved her lips. "The answer to your prayers, Private." Her blood surged as they took the floor. "My dance card suddenly feels less dreary."

"Think so, huh?" He launched into a goofy Turkey Trot.

Laughter exploded from her, hot and unexpected. Soon they were a whirlwind of the Charleston, then dipping into a joyful Lindy Hop. A flask materialized in Jeffrey's hand, the sharp smell of whiskey cutting through the sweaty air. They took turns swilling from it, a fiery warmth spreading through her veins.

Jeffrey paid her ticket after ticket, a possessive streak flaring beneath his friendly persona. "Let me dance with my baby." He pushed aside impatient, grumbling men waiting their turn.

Twirling her with effortless grace, his hands felt like fire on her waist. As their eyes locked, Echo sensed the magnetic charge. His hazel eyes reflected the same raw desire burning within her own. A wicked grin lit her face as Jeffrey walked her home, his touch tantalizing on her back. This had been her plan all along, dance, flirt, find a spark. Tonight, that spark had roared into a blaze.

Over warm whiskey in her dim apartment, any vestige of caution vanished. This was no scene played out for a camera, but the intoxicating rush of the woman she wanted to be. She met his gaze head-on, fueled by a reckless daring.

"So, Private First Class, how much longer before they ship you out to the Great War?"

"Let's say I'm making the most of the days I have left." He nuzzled her neck.

"Is that an invitation, soldier? We might get into more trouble than you realize." Echo traced the lifeline on his palm, crisscrossed with so many others ... like the invisible scars on her heart.

"No use pretending I'm heading to some adventure, Echo. Just, nights like this ... makes it a little less terrifying." His words betrayed the profound fear beneath his desire.

Longing pulsed through her, a sweet ache that bordered on pain. "Let's not think of that right now, Private." For a heart-stopping second, silence stretched between them. Had she misread him? What felt like a calculated gamble now seemed a leap off a cliff.

But, then, Jeffrey bent over and brushed her lips with his, the sensation arousing yet heartbreaking. He deserved a night of pleasure before he went off to war. "Let's make the rest of the world disappear, Private."

∽

WHITE CITY AMUSEMENT park blazed with lights, the Electric Tower a beacon illuminating the city. Echo glanced over at Jeffrey striding boldly beside her, his strong arm clamped possessively around her waist. It was military night at the park, and Jeffrey wore his dress uniform: the sharp navy-blue jacket and light blue trousers with the electric yellow stripe. Half the men at the park were dressed in similar fashion, the atmosphere crackling with bravado. Now that America was joining the Great War victory would be theirs. Or so the Chicago Tribune spouted. Four million men enlisted or conscripted, an endless river of uniforms flowing into uncertainty.

The smell of caramel apples made her mouth water. But she sucked her Lucky Strike instead, inhaling smoke along with the sweet cotton candy, taffy, and caramel corn wafting through the air. Then came the twang of a banjo, a sound so grating it could raise the dead from their graves. Honky-tonk music, Baby Doe's favorite, an homage to heartbreak and betrayal. Men with wandering eyes and quicker tongues.

She tugged his shoulder patch. "Does that thing make ya invisible to bullets?"

"I'd have to kill you if I told you." Jeffrey grinned. "National Cadet Advisory Council."

"So you know more about the war than the average Joe?"

"Forget about the war tonight." He rubbed his palms together. "What do you want to do first? Shoot-the-Chutes? Flying Airships? I want to show you everything in White City."

"The Adventure of Kathlyn wild animal show. I've seen every episode of the serial." Of course, she saw them with Silver. Why couldn't she let go of Silver, despite the freedom she sought?

Jeffrey led her into the jungle of White City. The humid air clung to her skin like a lover's embrace, but her heart yearned for something more genuine than the fake trees and bottled scents of frangipani and tuberose.

He held open the railcar door, and she slid across the bench. His warmth radiated an intimacy more unsettling than any jungle beast. The train whistle blew, then jerked them into the dim tunnel of palms.

Jeffrey's hazel eyes followed her every move. The loving eyes of a man who'd witnessed her laughter but not yet her bite.

A screeching monkey, pure silliness amidst painted trees, broke the spell. She laughed, a genuine sound for once. Jeffrey's arm settled behind her, and White City faded momentarily. Its trumped-up thrills couldn't compete with the quiet intimacy of his arm around her.

"Maybe this is off-base, Echo, but sometimes that spark of yours seems lonesome." His eyes focused on the flashing lights beyond their car. "That fire of yours deserves a proper hearth, someone to build up its warmth, let it burn safely. Seems like ... a pity if you never found someone strong enough to handle the burn."

Was this his idea of a crazy carnival game? We have a winner! Give this brave soldier the prize of domestic bliss. Jeffrey didn't know her. Didn't know the things she'd done. If his kind eyes ever truly saw her, he'd recoil.

"So, do you want babies?" Her laugh sounded hollow.

"A boatload of them." He grinned, but his eyes were serious. He wanted a mother for his future children, and somehow, under the glow of carnival lights, Echo seemed like the answer.

She could never be that mother. There was an emptiness inside, a hollowness so deep, those bulbs might as well be shining straight through her. But he didn't need to know any of that. His train would leave in a week, carrying him away from her and into the mud of distant battlefields.

"Well, butter my biscuits, aren't you movin' a bit fast here?" She forced a playful smile, hoping he wouldn't notice the tremor in her voice.

His hand tightened on hers. "Maybe I am. God knows everything's movin' fast these days." He eyes pleading. "But wouldn't it feel ... right? Knowing someone's waiting for you? Someone wild and strong enough to match the worst they can throw at me over there?"

"Ain't it grand how war turns you soldier boys into desperate romantics?" The words left her lips before she could rein them in. Bitter, maybe. Hell, she envied the poor fool who had somethin' to believe in.

The Ferris wheel loomed above them, its rusted metal frame groaning and creaking with every revolution. The swaying buckets hinted at the darkness that lay ahead. "C'mon, let's ride that thing before I change my mind," she said. As they ascended, each rusty lurch mirrored the uncertainty of the future. The glittering city below held no answers, only a soldier boy's desperate hope reflected in his eyes.

"Tell me about your family," he said, rubbing his thumb over her hand. "I want to know everything about you."

"Nothing to tell, really." Nothing. Absolutely nothing. The car lurched to a stop at the apex, swaying precariously over the lake. Echo's stomach flipped with the Ferris wheel's dizzying motion. Echo knew she had no family. She had no life other than this moment. She'd lived only for Silver Dollar. But now, not even Silver Dollar wanted her.

Chapter 20

1932

Silver Price $0.28 per ounce

Leadville, Colorado. Thirty-five years Baby Doe had weathered countless false starts and busted hopes at the Matchless. But now, the rhythmic clang of hammer on nail, building sturdy storage sheds, sent a tremor of excitement through her. If Roosevelt succeeded with the Silver Purchase Act, they'd be ready. Rockwell had convinced Rossi's investors to risk it all, building up the mine to excavate the monster vein, the one Tabor always swore held a king's ransom.

Leased equipment rumbled up the road: explosives, drills, muckers, pumps—everything needed to awaken the sleeping giant. Equipment she could never have afforded alone. Soon, the mine would teem with men, their calloused hands and sweat a testament to honest labor. She missed that—the camaraderie, the shared purpose, the promise of prosperity.

Not wanting to miss a moment, she sat outside on the stoop, paring sprouted potatoes for colcannon. A goofy car horn broke into her daydream. She smiled, knowing it was Carl. Shading her eyes, she watched Carl maneuver his Tin Lizzie up to the cabin. The car sputtered and kicked up dust, but Carl looked downright dapper in his driving goggles and argyle sweater. Heavens to Betsy, the boy was getting fancier by the day out in Hollywood. A pang of longing struck her—if only he'd married Silver. With the mine's revival, they'd have everything they ever dreamed of.

"What's all the commotion?" Carl asked, taking in the bustling activity.

"Gearing up for a major extraction." She waved her arm at Charlie and the men. The clanging and pounding was music to her ears.

Carl grinned. "You're kidding."

A wistful smile touched her lips. "This time it's real. Just wish my girls were here to see it."

Carl took off his cap and ran his fingers through his curls. "Shoot, I wanted to take you for a ride." He reached into the automobile for a fancy box and gave it to her. "Go on, open it."

Inside was a driving cap with goggles and a long, fringed scarf.

"The scarf matches your eyes." He held it to her cheek.

"Such a sweet talker." She plopped on the cap, camped a pose, fluffed her hair, and smiled her best movie star smile. It'd been years since she received a bonafide present—ever since Silver stopped sending presents from Chicago.

Carl helped her up from the bench. "Let's skedaddle."

She put on the black satin coat Silver had sent, draping the cornflower-blue scarf around her neck.

"You look glamorous for your first automobile drive, darling," Carl said.

She giggled. "I see why Silver could never say no to you."

Carl shot her a double take. "Silver said no whenever it suited her." He settled her into the car and ran around the other side.

"Funny how memory works, isn't it?" She touched the rich leather seats. "Everyone telling their own version of the same story."

"I wish I could hear Silver's side of things now." Carl sighed.

She knew his pain. It lodged between her ribs, in her joints, riddled around her brain. She forced a smile, determined to make the most of the day.

He headed north along the Arkansas River. The sharp tang of pine mingled with the sweet, earthy scent of sage, a welcome change from the smoke, dust, and stink of Leadville.

"Fourteen thousand feet high," she said, filled with pride. "Tallest in the Rockies."

She pointed out Mount Massive, Elbert, Harvard, La Plata Peak as they drove. "We had hundreds of mines, back in the day." Memories flashed in her mind: the thrill of discovery, silver gleaming in the sun, the miners' cheers echoing through the mountains.

The insatiable greed, bitter betrayals, crushing loss. Her jaw tightened. Penance was her work now. But those vibrant memories …If God smacked her later for remembering them fondly, it'd be a fair trade. "Tabor staked a claim wherever he smelled silver. But the Matchless … that mine made our fortune."

"Silver Dollar told me her father claimed the Matchless would bring millions again."

"The Bible says the love of money is the root of all kinds of evil," she quoted. "We struggled with that one. Still do, I suppose."

Carl glanced at her. "I see where Silver got her religion."

"I hoped it helped her along the way." She wrapped her scarf tighter, heart aching.

"She even got me to church with her," he choked out.

"Does my heart good to think of you two in church together. I hope she went to confession. Her letters sounded so lost."

"She went often, always disappearing on me. Liked her independence, that girl." A wistful smile touched his lips.

He parked in a clearing, the engine sputtered and backfired with a loud report. Jumping out, he opened her door and led her into an aspen grove budding silvery leaves.

"Where are you taking me?" she asked.

"You'll see." He smiled mysteriously.

∼

SMOKE SNAKED from the chimney of a log cabin nestled in a riot of columbines, vetch, and bladderpod. A woman on the porch waved and hurried toward them.

"Mrs. Tabor, so happy to see you." She clasped Baby Doe's hand. "Do you remember me?"

"Lucinda? Of course, you're the little girl who rode horses with Silver." If she had her math right, she must be forty-two. Would she even recognize Silver now?

"I'm so sorry about Silver Dollar," Lucinda said. "I read about it in the newspaper a few years back."

"Don't believe what they write in the papers." Baby Doe sounded sharper than she intended. "Silver Dollar is serving the Lord in the Holy Sepulcher Convent." She crossed herself, the story catching in her throat.

Lucinda turned to Carl. "And you must be Mr. Erikson. I hope this is what you had in mind." She gestured to a table by the window adorned with a vase of black-eyed Susans.

Lucinda pulled out her chair. "Your son-in-law ordered a very special dinner for you."

Baby Doe raised her eyebrows.

"I may have said something to that effect." Carl sat across from her, grinning.

Lucinda poured the champagne. "Champagne for a Colorado legend."

"What about Prohibition?" she asked.

"Who'd find us way up here?" Lucinda disappeared inside.

Carl raised his glass to hers. "To you, Mrs. Tabor."

"Son-in-law, is it?" She clinked his glass and sipped. The champagne tasted of blackberries, a memory of sun-drenched days picking them with Silver along the tracks.

Behind the meadow, the mountains loomed, the chirping of crickets punctuated by an owl's hoot. "Why did Silver keep getting sick? She was always writing to me about one ailment or another. All of them quite mysterious."

Carl fiddled with his champagne glass. "She worked hard and played hard. What can I say? She got run down."

"Did you ever meet her doctor friend she wrote about?" Her fingers drummed a nervous rhythm on the table.

"Doctor Lawton?" He curled his fingers in air quotes. "Bootleg doctor, more like it. He prescribed whiskey for indigestion. Gin for toothaches. Rum for depression. I told Silver that guy was no good for her, but you know how much she liked advice."

"But Silver didn't drink."

He rolled his eyes. "It was Prohibition. Everybody drank."

She squeezed her eyes shut against a picture of Silver she couldn't bear to see.

Lucinda's husband grilled the trout outdoors, the smoky aroma wafting through the air. Fresh and hot to the table.

She eagerly dug into the trout, the crispy skin and flaky flesh melting in her mouth. "Betcha' don't get fish like this down in Hollywood."

Carl scoffed. "I eat in a deli next to the studio. Nothing fresh passes my lips."

They talked more about Silver over dinner, the sun setting over the mountains, painting the sky in hues of orange and pink. Baby Doe asked why Silver didn't stick to acting if she was as good as he said. Carl said he wished Silver had followed him to Hollywood. They agreed on one thing: Silver kept her own counsel.

Carl was quiet all the way home and she let him be. From the motor car, the vast sky was a moving panorama. Then, a sudden streak of light—a shooting star blazed across the heavens and vanished, leaving her breathless.

Back at the mine, Carl parked the car and let the sputtering and coughing die before he turned to her. "Whatever else happened to Silver Dollar, she always knew how much you loved her." His eyes reflected the moon. "And that spark she had? Your light always burned bright in her."

"I miss her terribly, Carl," her voice cracked. She squeezed his hand with a strength that belied her trembling heart. ""Thank you for today. Thank you for everything."

Chapter 21

1918

Silver price $0.97 per ounce

Chicago, Illinois. Carl stormed into the wardrobe studio, red faced and huffing, carrying an exotic harem costume draped over his arm. "Silver, where's the wardrobe mistress? I need this ironed and ready for the new auditions."

I took the blue and gold costume from him. "You don't iron chiffon, you steam it." I plugged in the cast-iron wardrobe steamer by the row of racks overflowing with costumes from every corner of the globe. A long worktable held stacks of fabric, spools of thread, and a couple of Singer sewing machines.

"Director Grandon is pulling his hair out."

"What a surprise." I giggled. "Why do you think he's going bald?" A puff of steam sputtered from the steamer wand. "What happened?"

"Just when we started the harem scene, the sultan's favorite consort kept losing her lunch. Grandon fired her on the spot, ordering me to get another concubine on set pronto." Carl flipped through head sheets. "The agency is sending girls over."

I steamed the costume, glancing at the head sheets he studied: all blonde, short, pixie-like girls. Nothing like a harem girl of the Ottoman Empire. "Let me take her place, Carl. I can dance

Egyptian with such fiery passion, the sultan himself will swoon!" I shimmied dramatically to the floor, my kimono swirling around my legs.

My theatrical display clearly captured his attention. His eyes widened with astonishment and amusement, and the head sheets slipped off his lap.

"The schedule is too tight." He started picking them up from the floor. "We're shooting your tiger keeper scene next. Besides, the audience will know it's the same actress if you act both roles."

"The tiger keeper wears coveralls. The audience would never guess it was me." I grabbed the harem costume and stepped into the dressing room. The brocade harem pants were ridiculously tight. I grabbed scissors and slit the seams with a loud rip.

"What are you doing in there?" Carl asked.

Humming the snake charmer tune, I unbraided my hair and let it fall to my waist in undulating waves. Adorning my head with the jeweled headdress, I stepped through the dressing room curtain, long legs peeking through the slits I made in the harem trousers.

"Good heavens, woman!" He wiped his forehead.

I jumped side to side jingling bells around my ankles. "Will Grandon like it?"

"If the costume designer sees what you've done, he'll have both of our heads on spears." He grabbed my hand and walked me down to the set grinning. "Damn, Silver, you've saved my hide."

It felt good to return his favors. Good to have a partner in this crazy show business. Trollies rattled past, drivers gawking as if I was an exotic carnival sideshow. Not far off the mark today.

"Let me recap the storyline," Carl said, catching his breath. "Kathlyn's on a mission to rescue her dad from Prince Umballah. She'll uncover a secret and buy his freedom."

"Got it." My afternoon coffee swilled in my stomach.

He rubbed his watery eyes, his animal allergies apparent.

"You're the prince's favorite concubine. Just keep fanning Prince Umballah and you'll be fine."

The trophy room set featured preserved heads of lions, tigers, zebras, and other Selig animals. Director Grandon, perched in his director's chair fifty yards back, barked orders through his megaphone. Prince Umballah sat cross-legged on the high lift surrounded by concubines and peacocks strutting.

Carl tugged me through the throng, our path blocked by props and peacock feathers molting onto dusty carpets. "Your new concubine is ready, Director," he puffed, sweat dotting his brow.

My eyes were glued on Grandon. Time to show him what I could do.

Grandon's eyes raked over my flowing raven hair, embroidered cropped top, lingering on the curve of my hip, the slits in my harem pants, and down to my curled-toe jutties. "I prefer you as a concubine." He cleared his throat. "So you've acted before, Miss—I'm sorry, I forgot your name."

"Silver Dollar. Silver Dollar Tabor." I tilted my chin up and smiled with kohl-rimmed eyes. In my experience, it never hurt to make eyes at the director. "And, yes, I had several major parts with Pikes Peak Photoplay." Just don't ask me to elaborate.

With a frightful screech, Kathlyn Williams broke away from the guards. Her pith helmet and khaki did nothing for the star—nor did her sourpuss expression.

"If you're finished interviewing the bit-part actress, can we get on with the scene?" She swung her tied wrists to the side. "These ropes are cutting into my wrists."

Grandon raised his megaphone. "Yes, Miss Williams, of course. Sorry for keeping you waiting. Places everyone."

Carl squeezed my hand. "Go get 'em tiger!"

Swallowing the lump in my throat, I wiped my clammy hands on my costume.

Director Grandon led me to the Indian throne and seated me

on a cushion next to the prince. "Fan him slowly and look as if he is the sun and moon you live for."

"Where's the fan?" I looked around.

He jutted out his arm. "Prop master, peacock fan, now."

A prop boy with a Dodger's cap ran on set with a peacock fan like Mama had when I was little. Surely it was a sign.

"Stand by," Grandon yelled.

Prince Umballah muttered from the side of his mouth. "Say, are you the Silver Dollar I read about in the Tribune?"

Kathlyn whined from her side of the stage. "Charles Clary, if you don't stop talking, I'll stuff my fist down your throat to make you."

Prince Umballah froze with lips askew. "Later."

"Camera set," the cameraman said.

"Roll camera," the director yelled.

The camera whirred to life. "Rolling!" the cameraman yelled.

I fixed my gaze on the lens, the key to getting more footage in the long run. Looking good always helped. Stretching my long body diagonally, my legs peeked through the harem pant slits. I straightened my back to show off my bosoms. And why not? They were glorious, after all.

The palace guards prodded Kathlyn toward the prince with spears. She screamed and made tortured faces. "Let me go. I'm an American citizen, and you have no right to treat me this way."

Of course, Kathlyn's words were not recorded, but actors always talked while the camera was rolling and captions were added later.

"I'm here to find my father, Colonel Hare," Kathlyn said. "It's been three months since I received a letter from him."

I waved the peacock feather fan over the prince's face. The cameraman held one eye glued to the lens and the other squeezed shut like an owl that sleeps with one eye open.

"I haven't had the privilege of meeting your father," the prince answered. "I'm sorry I cannot help you. But I insist that you be my guest for the evening."

Kathlyn struggled to break free of the guards but could not. "I don't seem to have a choice."

As the scene dragged on, my arm ached from fanning. Closing my fan, I caressed my thigh and admired the turn of my calf through the harem pants. Slowly, my hand followed the curve of my hip to the small of my waist and opened the fan below my bosoms. My new curves rather pleased me. Deep-dish pizza had helped. No one could accuse me of being a tomboy now.

I raised my eyes to find the prince observing me with half-closed lids of seduction. Was I supposed to speak? The camera ceased clacking. The filming stopped. All eyes on me.

Kathlyn marched over, wagging her finger like a fishwife. "Whose name appears on the posters? Me, Kathlyn Williams. Not you, Miss no-name actress. If we weren't so behind in filming, I'd have your pretty gams walked straight out of the gate."

The cracked pancake makeup in the wrinkles around Kathlyn's eyes betrayed her aging beauty. She was much too old to play the ingenue character, and she knew it. A pang of sympathy hit me, remembering Mama losing her youthful beauty. But I couldn't let Kathlyn treat me like dirt.

Pushing myself up from the floor cushion, I squared my shoulders and met Kathlyn's gaze head-on. "Miss Williams, allow me to introduce myself. I am ... Silver Dollar Tabor. And I would not dream of stealing your marquee, because someday soon, I will have my own."

The crew stood with mouths gaping, eyes darting between us. Kathlyn's face twisted, her mouth working silently for a moment before she spun on her high-heeled shoes and stormed off.

She wouldn't forget my name, now, I bet.

WHAT HAD I DONE? Sassing the leading lady and causing a scene wasn't exactly the way to grab my big break. More like career suicide. Why, why, why did I always have to steal the spotlight? Seemed I'd never be happy until I was the star. Something inside me depended on it. Demanded it.

Hot-cold chills prickled within me. Echo's laughter sounded sharp and mocking in my mind. "Oh, come off it, Silver! You're shaking in your boots like a scared kitten! A bit of drama never hurt anyone. Besides, who needs that washed-up actress anyway? You're ten times the star she'll ever be!"

I grabbed my rosary, my fingers fumbling over their surface, her words a painful reminder of my own insecurities. Running down bustling streets, my cheeks burning; heart drumming a frantic rhythm against my ribs. The faces of passersby blurred. Harsh sunlight reflecting off the cobblestones. The imposing silhouette of the Holy Sepulcher closer with each step. Was Echo right? Was I letting fear hold me back?

Slipping into a pew, I fumbled with the kneeler. The rosary beads felt cool and smooth laced between my trembling fingers, yet a wave of shame kept me from praying. I wished I could blame Echo for causing my reaction to Kathlyn, but this mess was all mine.

"Mother Mary, I don't mean to make a mess of things. I just want a chance to make a name for myself, to make Mama proud. My big mouth always gets me in trouble. Help me fix this. Amen."

I held my breath waiting for an answer.

But the silence stretched too long, and I gasped for a breath.

A rustle drew my attention. The woman with the colorful headscarf, the one from the confessional, knelt beside me, her presence a comforting warmth in the cool church air. Her eyes remained closed as she spoke, chanting a lyrical melody that seemed to flow directly into my heart.

"Your fire is your gift, but also your lesson. Your spirit has power beyond your imagination, but it can either pave your way or set your path ablaze. Find a way to tame your spirit, as you do your tigers, and nothing will stop you from your quest."

Before I uttered a word, the woman stood. I reached after her. "Wait, I—"

A flash of her bright scarf vanished through the heavy church doors. But a calling card was on the railing:

Madam Theodosia

Spiritualist & Seeress

Thick, creamy cardstock with raised lettering in a deep, midnight blue. A flicker of candlelight shone on the gold embossed eye symbol. The address was not too far from here.

I scoffed. Spiritualist and Seeress? What a load of hooey. I can barely afford rent, let alone some phony fortune teller. But curiosity pricked my skin like a thousand tiny needles. How had this woman known so much about me? Was it just a lucky guess, or was there something more to this Madam Theodosia?

Starring at the vibrant stained-glass window of Mother Mary, the prisms blurred in my eyes.

"Tame your spirit," Madam Theodosia's words resounded in my mind.

"If it were only that simple," I muttered, slipping the card into my pocket. Echo's mischievous grin flashed through my mind.

∾

A KNOCK RATTLED the flimsy door of my apartment by the studio. "Oh, no, it's gotta be Carl." My stomach lurched.

Carl slumped against the doorframe, a smirk twisting his lips. "You live a charmed life, Silver. Colonel Selig wants you back on the palace set tomorrow at ten sharp."

"No! Really?" I grabbed his arm. "I thought for sure I was done for after that stunt with Kathlyn." I gestured him inside, my heart dancing. "How did the Colonel even see it? I thought those bigwigs never left their offices."

"Colonel Selig was watching your little speech to Kathlyn. Seems he found your ... spunk ... amusing." Carl chuckled, but the sound was hollow. "He said, 'That Silver Dollar Tabor has gams that won't quit.'"

Hope sparked in my chest. "Was he the man in the beret?"

"That's the one." He sighed, shaking his head. "The director wanted you fired, but the Colonel has the final say, for better or worse." He paused, then added, "Before I choke on my irritation, got anything to drink? We should go over tomorrow's scene."

I forced a smile. "I've ... sworn off the sauce. Trying to keep a clear head for the silver screen, you know?" My gaze darted to the cupboard. Echo's stash.

Carl opened the cupboard, the door creaking open like a coffin lid, revealing a graveyard of bottles. Cold dread snaked down my spine.

Carl pulled out a half-empty gin bottle, his eyes narrowing with hurt and suspicion. A cold sweat broke out on my skin. My hasty facade crumbled like dry clay, leaving me exposed and vulnerable.

"What the devil, Silver?" he snapped. "These bottles are half full. You're lying to me now?"

No good answer to that. As soon as I threw out the bottles, more would appear. Each morning, I stashed the evidence and sprayed the room with Jardin de Nuit to hide the stench of smoke and liquor.

"Previous tenant," I murmured. "Haven't found the time to get rid of them." I turned on the tea kettle as a distraction. Would he buy it? He frowned and tapped his foot. Which was worse? Hiding Echo's bad habits, or hiding Echo herself?

Pouring whiskey in the only clean cup, he shook his head, disgusted. "Let's get this over with." He read the script aloud as I moved around the room trying to grasp the scene's blocking. A sickening dread coiled in my belly. What if I mess up again?

"What's all this?" He gestured to the silk-draped lamp shades and candles.

"Oh, uh ... just trying to make the place a little more ... atmospheric," I stammered, feeling a blush creep up my neck. "You know, for inspiration. Helps me get into character." I forced a laugh, hoping he wouldn't notice the tremor in my voice.

Carl scrubbed a hand across his tired face. "Look, Silver, I know I push you, but I do it because I believe in you. I fight for every chance you get. Can't you ..." He searched my face. "Can't you meet me halfway?"

My eye caught the strange cane and Trilby hat behind him. His eyes followed mine, landing on the forgotten items. The script dropped to the floor, pages flying. His brow furrowed with a dawning realization.

Silence stretched, thick and sticky as hoisin sauce.

Finally, he stooped to gather the script pages, his movements stiff and awkward. His eyes met mine with a question. But he left without another word.

The door clicked shut, leaving me alone with my despair and loneliness. Carl was my only friend, and now Echo had come between us.

A shrill shriek pierced the oppressive quiet, making me jump. Not Echo this time, just the blasted tea kettle. But a wave of panic washed over me. What if Echo went out tonight and jeopardized my big chance? Tomorrow had to be a smashing success—my only shot at impressing Colonel Selig and proving to Carl that I wasn't a lost cause.

The candles on the windowsill sputtered out, their last wisps of smoke a reminder of what was at stake. One wrong move from Echo, and my dreams could vanish like those flickering flames.

∾

Director Grandon's sneer sliced through the chaos of the Maharaja's dungeon set. "Stage left, Silver Dollar. Start on the white X on the floor."

The dungeon was a set designer creation, faux stone walls and spotless floor whispering of artifice. Rusted iron bars, draped with heavy chains, framed the cell, while strategically placed stuffed rats added a touch of grim realism. Yet, despite the illusion, a thrill of anticipation pulsed through me. This was my stage, and I was ready to perform.

Kathlyn's nostrils flared as I took my mark. "Whose pizzle did you swizzle to slither back here?"

"I beg your pardon?" I pressed my hand against my heart.

"Quiet on set!" Carl yelled, quite a change from his cold shoulder this morning.

"Roll camera," Grandon barked.

Holding my lantern high, I led Kathlyn through the claustrophobic tunnel, the camera's whir a constant distraction.

Kathlyn pivoted, her stage whisper aimed squarely at the lens. "The King said we were going to the royal gardens." She could have said anything, because they'd do captions in the edit.

I pressed a finger to my lips. "Trust me, Madam. I'm trying to help you." The pointed juttis I wore felt stiff against the dungeon floor, slippery and smelling of new paint.

"Why should I trust you?" Kathlyn said. "Where are you taking me?"

We reached the cell. The cameraman, perched on his trolley, zoomed in. Colonel Hare, looking old and ragged, sprang up, clutching the bars. "Daughter! What are you doing here? They'll capture you too."

"Father, you're alive!" Kathlyn grasped the bars, her voice cracking.

Her words struck a pang of longing in me, sharp and unexpected. If only Papa was alive to see me act. Papa, with his booming laugh, his bear hugs that smelled of pine and ore. My throat tightened, tears stinging my eyes.

"You must escape, get out of here," Colonel Hare's voice trembled, mirroring the tenderness I'd craved since Papa died. "Give your mother my love. Know that I ..." His voice caught, thick with emotion. "That I love you."

The dungeon walls blurred, the set dissolving into a memory. It wasn't Kathlyn clinging to those bars, but me, a little girl reaching for a father's love I'd never fully known. A sob tore from my chest, raw and unrehearsed. "Hurry, Madam. A boat is waiting," I choked out. A tear escaped, tracing a hot path down my cheek.

Kathlyn recoiled, surprise flashing across her face. Not at all like we rehearsed. "You're leading me into a trap," she accused, improvising a line. "The palace guards will be waiting to capture me." Her cruel smile was a declaration of war.

She was setting me up to fail. But I wouldn't let her. My spine straightened, defiance burning in my chest. I turned to the old man, fumbling with the prop key. "No, Madam. No trick. We are taking your father." I unlocked the cell door. "A father's love is the most precious thing in the world. Don't let fear steal that from you."

The old man's eyes widened, then he stepped out of the cell, his hand reaching for Kathlyn's. The scene pulsed with raw, unscripted emotion. The camera whirred, capturing the magic unfolding before it.

Kathlyn spun to Director Grandon, her voice laced with venom. "Silver Dollar is trying to upstage me again, the little thief."

I wanted to retort, but the lump in my throat made it impossible.

"Cut!" Grandon boomed. "Prep for next scene."

The set erupted in cheers. Kathlyn, ever the diva, disappeared without a backward glance.

I spotted Carl leaving the set and hurried after him. "Carl, wait. Please."

"I have a meeting," he mumbled, not slowing his pace.

I caught up with him. "I'm so sorry about last night. Thank you for prepping me."

He spun around. "If this is the appreciation I get for my efforts, I'll pass. I've covered for you, Silver. Lied for you. Smelled your whiskey breath."

I flinched. Echo was to blame, but how could I explain her without sounding insane?

"I thought ... I thought we had something, Silver. Something real." Disappointment flashed in his eyes and he turned and walked right into Colonel Selig. "Sorry, Colonel. Didn't see you."

"Silver Dollar Tabor," I said, extending my hand. "An honor to meet you, sir."

The Colonel's handshake was firm, his eyes warm. "Your performance was remarkable, Miss Tabor. I felt the concubine's soul in your eyes. Black, limitless ... a world of pain."

Heat crept up my neck. "I felt Kathlyn's sorrow in losing her father."

His gaze lingered. "You have Baby Doe's beauty, I see."

"You knew my mother?"

"I performed as 'Selig the Conjurer' in the Tabor theaters."

"That was you?" My heart skipped a beat. "You mesmerized me with your multiplying rabbits!" I nudged Carl. "Can you believe that?"

"I'm sorry, I'm due at the accountant's." Carl ran off and I stared after him, confused.

"You two will be at the wrap party, then?" Colonel Selig's eyes twinkled. "I want to introduce you to Tom Mix. He's looking for a new leading lady."

The words hit me like a jolt of electricity. Tom Mix! This was my chance to break through, to finally land a major role.

"Wouldn't miss it for the world." A shiver of anticipation ran through me.

Chapter 22

1918

Silver price $0.97 per ounce

Chicago, Illinois. With no Carl visiting, Silver was reduced to a gray blob on the sofa. The Selig film was over, and with it, her paycheck. Just because Silver was out of a job, didn't mean Echo had to be. Slapping on crimson lipstick, Echo headed out, leaving Silver to marinate in misery.

Echo inhaled her cigarette, pushing through a crowd of men clutching newspapers with grim expressions, war headlines blaring. The rumble of streetcars drowned out a newsboy's cries about the latest battle. She tried to block out the longing reminder of her soldier boy's embrace. But who was she kidding? With Jeffrey Mink sent off to the damn war, the passion they'd shared left a gaping wound in her heart. Twisting his mother's ring around her finger, she scoffed at the violets for loyalty and lilies for purity, symbols of a life she'd never known. Echo sent letters every week to Jeffrey deployed to Saint-Nazaire France. Such a chichi name for the bloody front lines.

Echo strutted into Chinatown, the afternoon sun casting long shadows on the brick buildings. She scanned the street for the Peking Club, eager to meet the elusive owner she'd missed when she came with Rossi. The perfect hideaway, far away from the stuffy suits and starlets at Silver's Selig Polyscope in the North side. No one to recognize her. Echo LaVode could blend in, a chameleon shedding her Silver Dollar skin.

Savory smells from inside made her knees weak. She tossed her cigarette butt down and smashed it with her pointy toe. Studying her sallow reflection in the window, she fluffed up her hair.

A dark face with upturned eyes stared back at her from the window, startling her. The door creaked open, revealing a round-faced man. A thin Fu Manchu mustache drooped past his chin, framing a face creased with amusement. He wore a mandarin collar jacket embroidered with dragons, a Trilby hat tilted at a jaunty angle, and a jade pinky ring.

"Looking for trouble peeking into the Peking like that?" A subtle accent like worn velvet.

Echo straightened up. "No siree, I'm looking for a job."

"Get it? Peeking into the Peking?" He laughed a high chirrup and tossed the newspaper he'd been reading in the trash. She recognized the Standard & Poors sheet Silver Dollar always checked.

A plume of sweet-smelling smoke curled from a long clay pipe dangling from his lips. "Sorry, Miss. We're not looking to hire your type." And by 'type' she thought he meant 'white'.

Echo smoothed her long black hair. "I can look Chinese if you'd like. I can be a Spanish senorita dancing the flamenco. I can dance the hula, the merengue, the tango. You name it, I can dance it. I danced with the Takka Chance dance troupe on the Orpheum circuit."

He took another drag, observing her with cunning eyes that belied his humorous nature.

"I need a job, Mr.—"

"They call me Zhang." He smiled with gold capped teeth through his Fu Manchu. "Your experience is impressive, but the job opening is for a coat check girl."

The savory smell of roasted duck made her weak with hunger. "How much does it pay?"

Zhang chirped a high-pitched laugh. "Four dollars a night plus all the chop suey you eat."

"Plus tips, right?" At least Echo wouldn't starve, and she'd get out of that cramped room with Sad-sack Silver. Behind Zhang, the kitchen boys pushed out plates of dumplings and eggrolls, making her salivate. "When can I start?"

His irises dilated to black. "Tonight, six on the dot."

She pointed to The Standard & Poors sheet. "Mind if I look at that?"

"You sitting on a gold mine?" Zhang tilted his head.

Echo let out a high-pitched giggle, her fingers snatching at the paper. "Just curious, that's all." Her eyes darted across the columns. If silver was up, maybe Silver could finally crawl out of her hole and get them both out of this city.

But her heart sank as she saw the dismal price of silver. Looks like they were stuck in Chicago, for better or worse. The bitter taste of disappointment rising in her throat.

"Hey, what's your name?" Zhang asked.

"Echo LaVode." She gave a sassy curtsey.

"Echo-o-o!" He elongated her name, blowing Os of sweet smoke.

"And here I thought I was the entertainer." She shot her forefinger and thumb like a pistol.

He returned her pistol shot and smiled with his fourteen karats. "Remember to dress Chinese, Echo-o-o."

"Sure thing, Zhang." Echo snatched a couple egg rolls off a passing tray.

∽

ECHO STUBBED OUT HER CIGARETTE, her frustration simmering. Jeffrey was gone, fighting for a future she couldn't share. And Silver Dollar? She'd set Echo free in some kind of ritual Echo did not understand. Who knew you could shed a shadow?

Abandoning her, especially after all Echo had done for Silver. Her betrayal cut deep.

Echo ripped open a drawer, fingers snatching a lapis lazuli necklace, a defiant spark against Silver's betrayal. "Hell yeah," she muttered, fastening it. "New Echo. No one's shadow." She slipped on killer heels, a smirk twisting her lips. Tonight, she was reclaiming her power.

Echo stepped out, ready to own the night. The neon lights buzzed with adventure, calling her name. The Peking Club throbbed with jazz and smoky energy. Black, tan, white—a haven for those who dared to defy the rules.

Echo pinned on the China-doll wig, each jab of her scalp a reminder she was leaving the past behind. "Who am I tonight?" Her playful smirk turned bitter. "An exotic dancer? A spy? Or Echo, the femme-fatale?" She inhaled incense and pipe smoke, numbing the sting of Jeffrey's absence and Silver's betrayal.

Taking her place at the coat check, Echo surveyed the parade of furs and cashmere and silk. Zhang checked on her, a glint of approval in his eyes. "Remember, everyone's a big shot here. Everyone's got the right to swing their own way. Who they dance with? Their business." He chuckled, covering his eyes. "See no evil."

"Sure thing, boss," Echo purred, all sugar and spice. But her mind was already scheming. A parade of hungry eyes passed her coat check, eager for a taste of the forbidden. The jazz pulsed through her, a siren's call drowning out the ache in her heart. As the trumpet's cry filled the air, Echo let loose. Charming men in sharp suits, women draped in furs—they couldn't resist her.

"Let me take care of that for you, handsome," she winked, accepting a gentleman's beaver coat with a generous tip. Or, to a lady draped in sable, "Allow me to liberate you from that burden, my dear." A subtle compliment here, a playful wink there—Echo knew how to make them feel special, even as she tucked their secrets away.

A tall blond gentleman, smelling of bay rum and expensive cigars, approached the coat check, his diamond stickpin gleaming in the dim light. "Well, well," he drawled, his eyes lingering a moment too long on Echo's neckline. "Looks like Zhang finally got himself a real looker."

Echo grinned. "Beauty's in the eye, darling. And you seem to have a discerning one."

"He leaned closer, mischief in his eyes. "Care to join me for a cocktail? I'll make it worth your while."

Zhang materialized, smiling, gracious, ushering the man away. "Mr. Harrison, your table awaits."

When Zhang returned, his smile had vanished. "You draw attention, little bird. Good for business. But we sell drinks, not girls."

Echo tilted her chin. "Wouldn't dream of it, boss," she replied with a stunning smile. But defiance simmered. She was done following orders. Echo would play the Peking her way. And Zhang would be none the wiser.

Chapter 23

1919

Silver price $1.12 per ounce

Chicago, Illinois. "Snap out of it, Silver Dollar." My bloodshot eyes stared back from my haggard reflection in the mirror. My fingers trembled as I reached for a brush, a futile attempt to tame the wild mane that mirrored the tornado raging inside me.

Why was I the one left to pay the bill for Echo's late-night escapades? Her crazy antics always left their penalty; the dullness of my skin, dark circles under my eyes, hangover jitters, churning in my gut. Thank you for nothing, Echo. You were supposed to protect me.

I pushed away from the mirror, the room rushing past in a rogue wave of nausea. My head throbbed with a raging ache. It had been two weeks since Carl promised to pick me up for the studio party. Two weeks of silence from him. Why had he abandoned me with Colonel Selig? Why should I care, anyway? But the sting of his rejection lingered.

Heaps of torn stockings, feather boas and garish fringed and sequined shifts lay discarded on the floor, remnants of Echo's fever-dream nights fueled by alcohol ... and whatever else she could find to fly her balloon, drifting in the starry sky. A blurry memory of a mirrored ball, low fedora's shadowing men's lusty leers, a jumbled puzzle I couldn't complete. Did Echo eat anything besides Chinese takeout? Now the smell of Chinese made me want to puke. And the very thought of facing the streets of Chicago gave me the heebie-jeebies. What if I saw one of her boyfriends on the street? My underarms smelled like gin, my tongue tasted like Brillo pads, my insides felt raw as ground beef. I couldn't let Carl see me like this. Couldn't let him know how his absence had shattered my fragile state, and Echo took the reins. With a groan, I sank to my knees, gathering up the empty bottles and grimy takeout boxes. The stench of stale duck and hoisin sauce filled my nostrils, triggering a fresh wave of nausea. "Damn you, Echo," I muttered. "What have you done to me?"

Chapter 24

1919

Silver price $1.12 per ounce

CHICAGO, ILLINOIS. ECHO'S COAT-CHECK TIP JAR overflowed, the audience seated and drinking. But why hadn't the band arrived? She found Zhang outside, in a cloud of reefer smoke.

"Where's the band? It's nine bells already." She took a puff of his cig.

Zhang scanned State Street, sweat beading on his brow. Chan, the lanky usher, scurried down. "Mr. Zhang, the crowd's getting' antsy. Some want their dough back."

"Give 'em hooch on the house." Zhang huffed. "Crank that Victrola. Maybe they'll be too soused to notice."

Chan bolted, his brocade slippers light on the stairs.

"That dame from the Tribune's up there," he muttered, fiddling with his hat. "Florence Lawrence. She'll tear us apart in the newspaper tomorrow."

Opportunity knocked in her ears. "Don't sweat it, Zhang. I'll keep 'em entertained till the band shows."

She darted to the cloakroom, heart pounding like a drum roll. "Coat check girl brings down the house with one daring dance." A sizzle surged through her veins. This was her big break, and she wasn't about to let it slip through her fingers. Shedding her uniform with trembling hands, she reached for the kimono, the silk cool against her feverish skin. A final touch of crimson lipstick, a deep breath to steady her nerves, and she was ready.

The phonograph needle dropped on "Chinatown, My Chinatown." No turning back now. Echo emerged on stage, a vibrant splash against the hazy smoke. Gasps from the tipsy audience. She swayed to the music's pulse, moving with the graceful fluidity of a Chinatown dancer. "Heh, China doll," a man hooted.

Echo soaked in their cheers, her hips swaying with newfound confidence. Step left, sway left. Step right, sway right. Then, a flourish—a twirl, a snap of her wrist, and the blue silk unfurled like a blossoming flower, landing in a puddle of sapphire at her feet. Beneath, a blazing orange robe set her ablaze under the spotlight. The crowd roared, their cheers reverberating in her heart.

Fueled by the audience's energy, Echo danced with abandon. Her fingers grazed the floor as the orange kimono slipped off her shoulders, revealing a vibrant fuchsia layer beneath. She kicked free of the silk, her legs a blur as she whirled and dipped, each movement a tantalizing surprise. The applause intensified, validating every step.

This was more than a dance; it was a metamorphosis, shedding Silver's cocoon and allowing Echo's spirit to soar. She spun, shedding the final kimono to reveal the form-fitting cheongsam. The peony print shimmered as she moved, her bare legs flashing beneath. The audience gasped, their eyes wide with wonder, their cheers a chorus of pure intoxication. Echo basked in their adulation, a potent elixir she could never live without again.

~

FLORENCE LAWRENCE, the entertainment reviewer from the Tribune, bustled backstage, her mink stole quivering with the beady eyes of a sacrificed chinchilla staring at Echo like the rats under Silver's bed.

"Miss ... Echo, was it?" Florence began in a breathless flutter. "My, my! Your performance was something else entirely. Like a magic show and burlesque combined. Those swirls, the shimmies ... they'll be talking about your show all over Chicago! Now, tell me, where did you pick up such skills? Were you with the Columbia or Empire Burlesque Circuit?"

Echo tilted her chin, a sly grin playing on her lips. "Burlesque? Please, darling, those broads couldn't hold a candle to my moves." She paused, searching for a plausible story. "I was the opening act for the Great Houdini at the Hippodrome."

"Houdini? The Hippodrome? My word." Florence dropped her pen and clutched her chest, overcome by the revelation.

Echo pressed her advantage, weaving a fantastical tale. "Before that, I ran away with Buffalo Bill's Wild West, dancing on the backs of galloping horses through Europe. Even met Queen Victoria on her Golden Jubilee."

Florence's pen stabbed the paper with each jaw-dropping revelation. "The Queen! Darling, that is astounding. Tell me, where are you from? Exotic European blood?"

Echo leaned closer, in a conspiratorial whisper. "Actually, I was born to missionaries in China who sold me as a dancer to the emperor, until Buffalo Bill smuggled me out as a cowboy. Yippee ki yay!" She let out a coyote yip that sent a stagehand scurrying for cover.

Florence's eyes sparkled. "A cowboy in China? Extraordinary! You will change the very face of entertainment!" Scribbling in her notebook, her mind raced with this incredible story.

Echo grinned impishly. Each outlandish detail she added painted a more vivid legend where once there was only a blank page. She was no longer just the warm-up act, the chorus girl, the forgotten fan dancer. She was the headliner, the showstopper, the magical burlesque extravaganza wrapped into one mesmerizing package.

When the Tribune printed this fantastical tale, it exploded

across Chicago, each word ringing with an undeniable (if entirely fabricated) truth. After all, in the dazzling world of show business, who was to say it wasn't? This was Echo's life now, and she would not give it up to play nursemaid to Sad Sack Silver for love nor money.

Chapter 25

1919

SILVER PRICE $1.12 PER OUNCE

The morning of the studio party I stood in the Selig wardrobe room, clad only in a lacy brassiere and tap pants, painting my body with tiger stripes. The scar on my belly blended nicely. My front, legs, and arms were easy, but I had to ask Carl to paint my fanny and back.

When he declined, I handed him the paint palette, kneeled over the director's chair, and stuck out my bottom, watching his reaction. He stared as if seeing me for the first time, not just with desire, but with a kind of worship that set my nerves alight. "You sure you want to do this?" he said.

"Scared as a rabbit at a magic show." My voice quaked. "But the bigwigs won't notice me if I play it safe."

Carl dipped the paintbrush in the gold and got busy. The first cold stroke of paint on my spine sent a shiver down my back, a nervous giggle escaping my lips as the earthy scent of pigment filled the air. But as he gained confidence, he painted with such concentration you'd think he was painting the Mona Lisa.

I watched his reflection, how he bit his bottom lip, the furrow of his brow, the flush on his face as he finished the tiger stripes. I closed my eyes, the soft strokes of the brush against my skin sending a warmth through me that had nothing to do with drying paint. Each stroke was a tentative question, a sensual exploration, and I found myself leaning into his touch, craving more.

When Carl finished, his breath hitched, mirroring the unspoken longing in my heart. We looked at the finished result in the mirror together. His eyes were wide, filled with a mixture of awe and something else I didn't quite understand.

"You don't need to go naked to be noticed, Silver," his low rumble that resonated within me. "Look at yourself. Pouty lips, hair like midnight, those eyes of yours ..." His gaze melted on me, making my breath catch in my throat. He reached for a long swath of gold gossamer and draped it around my painted body like a Grecian gown, kneeling at my feet. The delicate caress of the fabric against my skin sent a wave of goosebumps across my flesh.

"You're covering up your work," I teased, breathless.

"You are a gift, Silver." He looked up at me. "And a rare gift is always gift-wrapped. The anticipation makes the unveiling that much sweeter."

His words were a lightning rod. On impulse, I leaned down, the scent of his cologne and licorice mixing with the earthy paint, drawing me closer. I felt the warmth of his breath on my cheek, his eyes searching mine. The urge to close the distance, to taste the kiss that hungered between us, was irresistible.

But a recent memory haunted me: the stolen kiss in the Selig Zoo that overwhelmed me with panic, the shameful flight from the studio, leaving Carl with confusion and pain. That kiss had exposed a darkness within me, a losing battle against Echo's control. Another kiss now, with the same unresolved anxieties clawing at me, would only push us further apart. And Carl deserved so much more than this, more than the broken pieces I was barely holding together.

So I tilted my head away from his mouth, tracing a featherlight path on his cheek. A shiver rippled through me, a tantalizing taste of what could have been. I pulled back slowly, our gazes locked with the ghost of our almost-kiss, regret heavy on my chest.

"Pick you up at seven o'clock then." A pained hurt in his voice before he walked away.

My bravado evaporated, leaving me shivering in the wake of his departure. Had I made a mistake? A tornado of doubt threatened to unravel my ambitious appearance tonight.

But, then I caught sight of my reflection in the mirror, the tiger stripes gleaming under the studio lights. A surge of defiance coursed through my veins. I would not wallow in remorse tonight. This was my night, my chance to seize the spotlight and claim my destiny. I couldn't let anything, not even the longing in Carl's eyes, deter me from my path. Taking a deep breath, I steeled myself against the ache in my heart. Time to face my dream of being a star head-on, to embrace the opportunity that lay ahead. Time to become the Silver Dollar I was destined to be.

∽

Limousines stretched down the block like a gleaming black dragon, its polished scales catching the moonlight as it unloaded passengers at the Selig Studio entrance. Red-uniformed doormen snapped to attention. They opened doors for producers and directors with their dates, all dripping in silk and fur.

I smoothed down the front of my golden gossamer over my tiger stripes, the cool night air raising goosebumps on my bare skin. Beside me, Carl fidgeted with his tie for the eleventh time.

"Quit fussing with that." I brushed his hands away. "You're giving me the willies."

He looked sharp, even in a rented evening suit shiny from overuse. But who'd notice under the evening lights? Besides, it was my outfit, or lack thereof, that would turn heads.

I re-tied his tie with a practiced hand. "What's got you so jittery, anyway?"

"Aren't you?" Carl snorted. "With the Great War looming over our heads, Colonel Selig hasn't announced a new motion picture. I can't afford to wait around. I need a job, Silver. I've sent out resumes and nobody's responded."

I patted his hand. "Something's bound to turn up."

He raked his fingers through his blond curls. "Don't you read anything except *The Standard & Poors?* America can't hide its head in the sand any longer. We have to join the Great War."

"Maybe so, Carl." I pointed to the Selig studio all lit up, the glass ceiling shining. "But tonight's a grand studio party and we're going to celebrate."

Photographers set off their flashes, capturing the tuxedoes and designer gowns in a loud, sharp crackle. Each burst of light froze the glamorous laughter and sparkling sighs, destined for the morning papers.

The driver opened my door, and I stepped out, bracing myself for the onslaught of flashbulbs. But my heart plummeted as the photographers barely glanced my way, their lenses focused on the more illustrious guests.

Carl offered his arm, a reassuring smile on his face. "No worries, the night is young. Plenty of time to make a splash." He led me under the gleaming gold Selig Polyscope sign, a beacon of hope in the deepening twilight.

Inside, he helped me off with my black satin coat with a cool whistle. "Wow, Silver, that tiger motif ... Captivating. Still can't get the image out of my head." He handed my coat to the check girl and pocketed the ticket.

"You were probably right to wrap me in gold gossamer. Adds a touch of mystery." I twirled around, enjoying the stares thrown my way. A sudden stab between my breasts made me wince. "Ouch, that stings." I reached for Mama's silver pick and shovel pin I'd worn to keep her close to my heart when I met Tom Mix, our idol. Now the pin was lodged into my breastbone.

"Stand still." Carl pulled out the pin, eyes still fixed on my body. A small bead of blood welled up. He dabbed it away and licked his finger. "Better?"

"I will be." Snatching two lavender-colored drinks off a waiter's tray, I handed one to Carl.

"The Shooting Star," the waiter announced.

I gulped it down, the gin sparking through me like fireworks.

Carl held up his lavender glass to the chandelier. "You said you quit drinking."

"Tonight's a celebration." I finished the drink, my shoulders relaxing. "One more, please." I took another and knocked it back. A cocktail or two wouldn't hurt to calm my nerves.

The studio buzzed with excitement; bright, shiny people flitted like fireflies. The mezzanine floor offered a bird's-eye view of the sets, perfect for the bigwigs to watch the action. At the far end, a sixteen-piece jazz band played Joplin ragtime. Another Shooting Star slid into my hand from a passing tray. I needed this. Tonight had to be a turning point.

"Slow down, Silver." Carl frowned. "There are a lot of important people here that can make or break your career."

"Then I don't want to be bland, now do I?" I kissed his nose, the alcohol fueling a boldness that eluded me this morning. "Where's Tom Mix?" My eyes searched for his famous face. "If we can meet him, maybe we'll both get hired for his new series."

Carl scoffed. "Mix films shoot in New Mexico. You'd dry up and blow away like the sand."

"Oh, you worrywart," I teased. "New Mexico is a stepping-stone to Hollywood. Aren't you always saying Hollywood's the future of motion pictures?"

A spark of hope ignited in his eyes. "You'd come with me to Hollywood?"

"Of course, I'd go to Hollywood." My arm arched like a theater marquee. "My name up in lights? You said you'd make me a star, remember?" I giggled and took his hand. "Now, look alive,

Carl. We're going to own this room. By the end of this evening, we'll both have new jobs."

Each movie set blazed before us, a dazzling hodgepodge of worlds. Hawaii thrummed with ukulele music and the aroma of roasted pig. The Orient beckoned with rickshaws and the whiff of opium smoke. Rome overflowed with chianti and laughter under the painted Colosseum.

Carl and I flitted between these pockets of make-believe, cocktails our currency, smiles plastered on tight. We found Colonel Selig amidst the guests, but his usual booming laugh was replaced by a distracted tug on his mustache, eyes strangely vacant.

"What'll happen to Selig Polyscope now with the Great War?" Carl asked the Colonel.

"They're drafting single men under thirty. That'll wipe out the motion pictures indefinitely."

The Colonel's gloom was drowning everybody's dreams of silver screen stardust, but I wasn't about to drown with them. I entertained him with stories of the Tabor Grand Opera House, Bernhardt's coffin theatrics, Lily Langtry's glass-breaking voice, Oscar Wilde's drunken revelry down in the Matchless. The crowd around us pressed close, hungry for a taste of that old, glittering magic, instead of the precipice of war.

"I'll be back." Carl squeezed my hand. "There's a chap over at the bar. Might have a lead on a new project." His eyes darted away, hinting of desperation. "I have to try, Silver." He waded into the sea of starched shirts and sequined dresses.

A fire of ambition and liquid courage churned in my gut, fanning out the calling cards I'd painted, each a miniature work of art. I'd drawn myself within a heart of crimson, my tiger stripes the only barrier between me and the world. I offered my calling cards to the bigwigs, their shocked gasps and delighted laughter just what I'd hoped for.

Colonel Selig's eyes lit up when he saw my card. "Let's go find Tom Mix," he said excitedly. "He never stays long at parties."

I waved to Carl across the packed bar. He turned around, holding two fizzy cocktails. His smile dropped when he saw the Colonel leading me towards the grand staircase. But we couldn't get down; people were sprawled all over the steps.

"Oh succotash." Selig snapped his fingers. "Tom Mix is moving toward the door. I told him you were perfect for his next series. A real western girl with a pedigree." His fingers gripped my arm.

Through the shimmer of party lights strung over the ground floor, I spotted Tom Mix, a lone cowboy amidst a swarm of actresses fluttering around like butterflies. Mix was the real McCoy. Tall and handsome, his white duster and chaps set him apart from show-business glitz and glamour. His honest gaze did not flirt or tease, more comfortable on a horse than at this party.

Carl found us, cocktails in hand. "Here you go, Silv—"

"Thanks, son," Colonel Selig interrupted, snatching the second drink with a wink.

I sipped the icy concoction, trying to figure out how to get down to Mix before he left. Party light strings stretched across the room, attached to the mezzanine railing on both sides. The memory of my Slide for Life across Lake Rhoda flashed through my mind. The crowd's gasps, the thrill of the wind ... A shiver of fear ran down my spine, quickly replaced by a rush of adrenaline. Was it time for an encore?

∽

THE PARTY BANTER, the band's jazz music, the clinking of glasses ... it all faded against my racing heart. The room spun before my eyes, a dizzying carousel of lights and laughter. The air grew thick and cloying, each breath a struggle as if the very walls were sweating. Despite all this, I couldn't let this opportunity pass.

Ripping the bright string of lights from the hook, I wound

them around my body like a Christmas tree, under my arms, around my breasts, twisting my waist, coiled around my spine.

A shiver chased by a flush, Echo's voice slithered through my mind. "Oh, sweet pea, I'm sure everyone will be enthralled by your drunken acrobatics. Just picture it: you, tangled in Christmas lights, flashing your painted pelt to the whole studio. A real class act."

A fire ignited inside me, fueled by years of pent-up frustration and ambition. "Shut up, Echo. I'm not letting you win this time." I climbed out on the precipice.

Carl grabbed my arm, his eyes wide with alarm. "Silver, what are you doing?"

"Taking fate into my own hands." Breaking free from his grasp, I launched myself from the mezzanine. Air rushed past my face, my long hair trailed behind me like a comet's tail, lights blurring into a dazzling vortex. A scream ripped from my throat, a wild, unbridled cry for freedom. I was free falling toward my fate, Echo's laughter ringing.

My breath hitched as the gold gossamer snagged on a hook with a sharp rip, unfurling behind me like a shimmering banner, exposing my painted tiger stripes to the sea of upturned faces. Their mouths gaped in gasps and shrieks that filled the vast studio. The air crackled with electricity as the floor rushed up to meet me. I braced for impact.

Then, strong arms enveloped me, smelling of leather and sagebrush. Tom Mix.

"I'm Silver Dollar," I declared, meeting his surprised gaze with a confident smile. "Your next leading lady."

"Well, I've never had a leading lady drop in quite like that!" Mix chuckled, then turned to the press cameras, a dazzling smile already in place. "Smile, Silver Dollar."

Flashes exploded, capturing the image of Tom Mix holding a nearly naked, tiger-striped girl ... a picture destined for every newspaper tomorrow. Mama would be so proud, if she could look past the lack of clothes. Lily would have to eat her judgment and envy. This was it, the moment that would change everything. Searching for Carl, needing to share this moment with him.

Colonel Selig appeared beside Tom Mix. "We'll make film history with you two." With Selig's stamp of approval, the deal was sealed.

Carl shook his head, his eyes searing with betrayal. I'd tossed him aside, like yesterday's newspaper I hadn't read.

Tom Mix held me tight, camping poses for the photographers surrounding us, flashing his brilliant smile.

Carl turned away, his blond curls disappearing into the crowd, leaving a hollow space where my heart used to be.

∽

GOOD RIDDANCE to this fleabag apartment. I was headed to Hollywood. I slammed the lid of my worn leather suitcase, its brass clasps groaning in protest as I forced it shut. Inside, nestled among mismatched stockings and a chipped compact mirror, were a few treasures I couldn't bear to leave behind: Mama's silver pin, cool and smooth against my fingertips, a few faded photographs, and a bundle of letters from Lily, their once-warm words now brittle with silence.

I flung a pile of silk kimonos and embroidered dresses onto the trash bin. Each garment of Echo's a specter haunting the corners of my mind. Let them be buried beneath the avalanche of takeout boxes spilling from the trash.

My fingers danced across the cheap stationery, an irony considering the words I was about to write.

Dearest Mama,

Tom Mix chose ME as his leading lady! The Selig party was a whirlwind of envious eyes and a wailing jazz band that made the champagne glasses tremble. Soon, I'll be a star, Mama. No more cleaning up after mangy tigers and irritable elephants. I'll make the Tabor name shine brighter than any shooting star.

A smile tugged at my lips as I imagined Mama, her weathered hands trembling with pride as she read my letter aloud to the congregation at Annunciation Church. She'd write to our aunts and uncles with triumphant vindication, silencing the whispers of shame that had haunted our family.

Perhaps my success would thaw the frost that had settled around Lily's heart. What poison had Rockwell dripped into her ear, twisting her love into bitter resentment? An arrow of sorrow shot through me, a sharp pain I couldn't shake.

The memory of Carl's disgust twisted my heart. Maybe I could convince him to come with me. A fresh start, a chance to escape the shadows of our past ... who knew what opportunities might blossom for him?

With a deep breath, I sealed the letter, a silent prayer on my lips. It was time to leave the ghosts of this cramped apartment behind and embrace the glittering unknown. Tom Mix awaited, and I was ready for my close-up. The world would soon know my name.

∼

MARCHING INTO SELIG STUDIOS, I expected the usual creative chaos. Instead, an eerie silence hung heavy in the air. The stages were dark, sets torn down like forgotten toys. The smell of stale dust and sawdust clung to my nostrils. I spotted Big Otto, lugging a crate of animal gear.

"What's going on?" I demanded, the knot twisting in my stomach.

Otto just shook his head. "Best you talk to the Colonel," he muttered, patting my shoulder.

That didn't bode well. Nausea washed over me. What was

happening? Selig's office was a disaster zone, the Colonel slumped in his chair like a deflated balloon.

"What's everyone so miserable about? Something happen over the weekend?"

Selig sighed. "Mix is ... gone, kid. Jumped ship to Fox Films. The gall of that bushwhacking whippersnapper." Every word pounded a nail on the coffin of my dreams.

"But he can't do that." I sputtered. "He's your big star. Where's his loyalty? You made him what he is."

The Colonel let out a wheeze like film unreeling from the spools. "Kid, in this business, loyalty's worth about as much as a painted backdrop in a rainstorm. Don't take it personal, unless you want to fade away before you've had your chance."

The silence that fell was thick and icy, the air suddenly heavy. The dismantled studio swam around me, the loose cables like seaweed tangling my feet. Echo hissed in my ears, "You're canned, sardine. Time to *fish* for a new gig!"

Tears pricked my eyes, hot and stinging. I blinked, the studio lights smearing into blurry streaks. "I ... I don't understand," I choked out. "What am I supposed to do now?"

"Fox will use their own actresses." Selig sealed up a box, avoiding my gaze.

"But what about Selig Polyscope?" I must be dumb as a rock.

"Closing the studio and waiting out the war," he said.

"Looks like your closeup got cut, Silver sweetheart," Echo lisped. "What a crying shame."

Selig's words stung. "I'm sorry, kiddo. It's a tough business." He plastered on a showbiz smile. "Plenty of factory jobs these days. Get a job making gun parts. You can be a star helping our boys over there."

"So your leading man rode off in the sunset without you," Echo chided with malicious glee.

My glorious debut, the envy back home, the letters to Mama. All of it shattered.

"Poor Silver," Echo sighed. "Always too trusting. Too ... naive."

Anger flared, a hot coal in my chest. I didn't need Echo's pity. I needed Carl. He'd know how to fix this, how to turn this disaster into a triumph.

∼

THE ONCE-VIBRANT ZOO had become a cacophony of destruction: metal clanged against the concrete, saws squealed through wood, panicked animal cries pierced the air. Carl wielded a hammer, breaking apart crates. His eyes, turbulent as thunderheads, reflected the chaos.

I ran to him, holding back tears. "What are we going to do now?"

He dropped the trunk with a thud, thrusting a paper into my hand. "I ship out to bootcamp in two days." His jaw clenched, his eyes glistening.

The news hit me, unreal and horrific. Carl was leaving for some bloody battlefield half a world away? My throat closed. What if he didn't come back?

"No, Carl, not you. You can't leave me." I grabbed his sleeve and he jerked away. He was the only anchor I had in this crazy town.

"Oh, so now you need me." He scoffed. "Get off it Silver. You made your decision at the studio party, and it didn't include me."

Guilt riddled my gut. "I was going to ask you to come with me."

"Follow you like a puppy dog? No thanks." He opened the truck and threw in harnesses, batons, balls, hoops. "Heck, it's better this way, Silver. You were never going to stick around. You've got your head in the stars. You'll be fine. You always land on your feet somehow."

No good to argue. He was probably right, anyway. I started

helping him pack. We worked in strained silence, the sun beating through the glass studio ceiling. For a few fleeting hours, I pretended nothing had changed, if I only kept going, brushing his hand, forcing a weak joke when I could think of one.

But the war's shadow was inescapable. Images of mud-soaked trenches and barbed-wire snares filled my head, the smell of gunpowder mingling with the odor of horsehair. Each slam of a hammer felt like a bullet aimed at Carl.

Workmen built wooden crates, drilling the tiny air holes, a cruel reminder that the tigers were leaving, too, and my blood boiled.

"That's not enough air for them," I snapped, their carelessness infuriating me. "Those crates will kill the wildcats before they reach California."

A carpenter sneered at me. "Mind your own beeswax."

Carl straightened; his shoulders squared. "You heard the lady. Add more ventilation if you want to keep the tigers alive."

"And the tigers need to see out," I said. "Or they'll be afraid and tear into each other."

The workmen ignored me and hammered on.

Carl's jaw clenched; his hands balled into fists. He kicked the crate, a guttural roar erupting from deep within him. The force of his blows sent splinters flying, but it wasn't enough. He lunged, his body a weapon. The crate groaned and buckled under the force of his blows, sending splinters flying. With a feral growl, he slammed into the wood again and again. The workmen scrambled for the studio guards.

I stood frozen, not believing what I was seeing. My heart hammered against my ribs. Echo's icy-hot breath on my neck. "Are you just going to stand by and let them take everything from you?"

The paralysis broke, replaced by a fierce determination. A war cry escaped my lips. I seized a crowbar, the weight of it felt good in my hands. I unleashed my fury on the crates, each blow a cathartic release of the helplessness that had consumed me. A tornado of splinters and sawdust filled the air as we ravaged the wood together. The once-solid crates crumbled beneath our onslaught, leaving behind only the smell of broken wood and the taste of sawdust. Carl's eyes locked on mine, raw emotion whirling within, his fury combined with the tenderness that always smoldered between us below the surface. The aftermath of our rage left me trembling, a fragile shell amidst the settling sawdust. In the fading light, Carl's face, etched with a profound sorrow, seemed both heartbreakingly familiar and impossibly distant.

A sob tore through me, my body collapsing under the weight of grief. His strong arms encircled me, his ragged breaths mingling with my own. Carl was my anchor, unwavering strength amidst the madness. As the red haze of our anger lifted, a chilling realization dawned upon me. The rage that had overwhelmed me wasn't fueled by a stolen job, or a lost dream, or even the sad fate of the tigers. It was the looming threat of losing Carl that destroyed me.

∞

Hearing people coming, we pulled ourselves together, straightening up, wiping our faces.

"Is this the tiger you were asking about?" Colonel Selig showed off the tiger cub, my sweet Topaz, to a swank businessman.

I'd recognize him anywhere: Dante Rossi, the investor I'd sent to Mama at the Matchless. Slicked-back hair under an ivory fedora, the red carnation, the cleft chin. What the dickens was he doing here? Especially now? His mirror-shined shoes and heavy gold signet ring were badges of the underworld, but it was his eyes, hidden behind wire-framed sunglasses, that truly gave him away.

He flashed me a dazzling smile. "Say, Silver Dollar, quite a stunt you pulled at the party, diving down into Tom Mix's arms. I wanted to congratulate you."

"You were there?" I felt Carl moving away and I grabbed his hand, wanting him close.

"So I imagine you're going with Mix to Fox Films?" Rossi asked. "Dirty deal if you ask me. Selig invented Tom Mix and now he joins another studio?"

Colonel Selig coughed. "Silver Dollar lost the Mix deal when he switched studios." Selig shoved his fists in his pockets. "So, do you want the tiger? Two-hundred cash and she's yours."

"Wait." I stroked Topaz's head between his eyes. "You're not selling the tigers, are you?" Everything I counted on was changing so fast with the studio and war.

"We can't fit all the animals on the train," Selig said.

"But these three tigers can't be separated. They're family." My family. We'd worked together all year. I couldn't lose them along with everything else. It was too much.

Rossi squinted. "Then I'll take them all, if you throw in Silver Dollar as their trainer." He peeled several hundred from a money roll and handed the bills to Selig.

"The Colonel doesn't own Silver." Carl stepped forward. "Let her speak for herself."

I squeezed Carl's hand in silent thanks, but my gaze drifted to the floor, uncertainty churning in my chest. In the blink of an eye I'd let go of my apartment, lost my job, lost Carl.

Rossi turned his money roll on me, the bills crisp and green as if they were hot off the press. "And, I'll double whatever the Colonel was paying you."

I squelched a gasp. Double my salary? Sounded too good to be true. But the money would give me a chance to build a life for myself. Especially with Carl at war and the world on hold until it was over. Could I trust Rossi, though? "Where would we keep the tigers?" I asked.

"Warehouse on the North Side," he smirked. "There's a flat for you there as well."

Carl sucked in his breath and turned away.

"I figure you're worth it, right?" Rossi held out his arms. "How many tiger wranglers can I find in Chicago on short notice?" His chuckle sounded like picking ice.

There had to be a catch. "What would my duties be?"

"Take care of the cats by day and show them off at the Colosimo nightclub at night."

Carl grabbed my shoulder, pleading with urgent eyes. "You don't want to get in bed with guys like this, Silver. Trust me."

The warmth of his hand, the concern in his eyes ... I was torn between Carl's warnings, my loyalty to the tigers, needing money. But he was the one leaving me behind.

"Excuse us, gentlemen." I pulled him into the oversized crate and closed us in, dark and quiet enveloping us in our own netherworld. "What am I supposed to do while you're gone?" I reasoned. "Go home to Leadville and dig dirt? No thank you. This man's offering a big salary to take care of the cats. That's all. When you come back, we'll go to Hollywood and kick open a few doors."

He grasped the nape of my hair, his passion taking me by surprise. My head bowed to meet his lips, tenderly at first, then exploring with a hunger I'd hidden from myself. Now that I tasted it, I wanted more, my mouth moving over his cheeks, his nose, his eyelids.

"Just want to keep you safe." His breath bathed my face with sweet warmth.

"I'm not the one going to war." I tasted his lips, lingering. So lost in the moment, we almost forgot where we were.

Rossi's fist pounded the crate. "Hey in there! What's your answer?"

I entwined my fingers with Carl's, a silent vow passing between us. "I'll be counting the days until you come back to me." My lips brushed his cheek, leaving a trail of warmth. I squared my shoulders "It's a deal, Rossi. I'll care for the tigers like royalty, and they will be the stars of Colosimo's nightclub."

I traced the line of Carl's jaw with my fingertips, a silent reassurance. His arms encircled me, drawing me close, and I melted into his embrace.

~

It was midnight by the time we got the tigers settled into their cages in Rossi's warehouse. My heart felt like a boulder lodged in my chest. Carl would be leaving in the morning, just as I'd realized how deeply I cared for him. I put aside all my excuses. Tonight, I'd make sure he wouldn't forget me.

The oak staircase groaned with our steps up to the hidden loft Rossi kept for ... whom? Clients? I hoped it was warmer than the brick warehouse below. A low growl echoed from the cages beneath us, and I shivered. What had I gotten myself into here? Carl squeezed my hand as we climbed, a fleeting comfort.

I fumbled for the light switch, and light cascaded from ivory tusk chandeliers and silken lampshades, revealing a den of intoxicating luxury. We stood frozen for a moment, drinking it all in. Zebra-skin rugs lay scattered across the polished ebony floor, and cheetah hides adorned plush divans. The walls featured a gallery of taxidermized wildcats: tigers, panthers, lions, their glass eyes gleaming in the soft light. Ceremonial masks and hand-carved tribal sculptures guarded the intricately carved mahogany bureau and cocktail tables. The silence was broken only by the guttural snarls of the real tigers below, unused to their new home.

"Heavens to Mergatroid," Carl whistled. "And here I thought the tigers had it good."

As I walked through the luxurious loft, my fingers brushed against the dark carved wood and plush upholstery. Crystal pendants on delicate chains hung from the ivory chandeliers, catching the light and scattering it in a thousand shimmering reflections across the room. Captivating, yet unsettling, a reminder of the human desire to possess forbidden treasures. A jungle scene was woven into the massive tapestry above the fireplace, the tiger watching us with keen eyes.

Carl gripped my shoulder. "Silver ... you can't stay here. It's too dangerous." His voice was thick with worry.

Clutching the rosary in my pocket, I yanked the rose quartz beads through my agitated fingers so tensely the string might break. "Don't worry about me, Carl. I'll handle Rossi. I'm calling the shots now." A brash statement if I ever heard it; but Carl needed to believe I would be okay. It would take every ounce of grit, glamour, and gumption I had to hold my own with these hoodlums. And that's if I was damn lucky.

Seductive scents of sandalwood, musk, and African violets wafted from gleaming bowls, sensuous and alluring. I sank onto a plush divan, a dozen silk cushions soft as a lover's touch and beckoned Carl to sit by me.

"Please Silver," he pleaded. "Go home to your mother in Colorado. It's safe there."

Safe? My worst moments were in Colorado. Echo's vicious attack ... Rockwell's vacant eyes. "Nowhere is safe anymore. Not with the world at war. I'm better off waiting for you here where I have a good job with the tigers and a roof over my head." The soft click of my rosary beads.

"I wish I didn't have to go." He shook his head, his eyes filled with concern. "Just promise me you'll be careful. I don't trust them."

I laid my head on his shoulder, hiding my distress. Rossi's world was a viper's nest of vice and sin. How could I possibly work for these men without being drawn into their lair?

The ceremonial masks stared with frightening grimaces. Easy to imagine Echo watching us from behind, making me quiver. Would she watch over me? Protect me? Could I trust her?

"Let's not waste this night." I jumped up, smiling and teasing, pulling him toward the ebony canopy bed. Its sheer mosquito netting and intricate beadwork promised a night of sensual dreams. Pushing him onto the down feather mattress, I fell beside him on the billowing cloud. Caressing his face, I tangled my fingers in his soft blonde curls. "I want you to dream of me when you are over in France," I whispered against his lips, my hair spilling over his chest like a waterfall. "And I will dream of you."

His eyes, usually so gentle, burned with a hunger that matched my own. Our kiss ignited a bonfire of desire.

But Echo breathed in my ear, a chilling zephyr against my burning skin.

"You're mine," Echo's voice hissed through the hollow chambers of my mind, the venomous serpent. Her presence wrapped around me, crushing my chest. A strangled sob tore from my throat, raw and guttural. Was she taking over?

Carl pulled back, his eyes wide with alarm. "Silver? What's wrong?"

"Nothing," I lied, my voice shaking. "It's just ... it's all so overwhelming."

Carl gently cupped my face in his hands. "Hey, it's okay. We don't have to rush. We can just hold each other."

Not at all what I wanted. I pulled him closer, shoving the insidious whisper of Echo deep down inside. Would Carl still want me if he knew about her? Of course not. Poison seeped into the sweet moment. I silenced it with a fierce kiss, forcing Echo to leave us alone in this stolen haven.

Our clothes melted away, his strong arms encircling my waist, pulling me down onto the cool silk sheets. Skin met skin, searing through layers of longing. His lips found mine, the fire of our passion reclaiming us. The scent of sandalwood and musk mingled with his warm skin, making me dizzy with desire. We moved as one, our heartbeats drumming in concert with the tiger's roaring below. The sound of passion. The world narrowed to the feeling of his curls caressing my cheek and the heat of his body pressed against mine.

But then Carl perched up on his elbows, his brow furrowed.

"Silver ... where did you go when you weren't at home? Your neighbor mentioned ... she said you had a lot of gentlemen callers."

My heart hammered in my chest. He knows. A wave of nausea washed over me. "I was with you most nights, working on the screenplay," I choked out.

His shoulders hunched, heavy with disappointment. "Why does it feel like you've been keeping secrets from me?"

Echo's laughter taunted me. A knot of desperation tightened in my chest. I needed to drown out his doubts, to reclaim our passion before it slipped away completely. "Don't," I touched my finger to his lips. "Don't let her ruin this night."

His eyes filled with pain and longing. "Her?"

Panic reared up from my core, and I pulled him on top of me, our limbs tangling in a desperate dance against time. His muscles rippled under my fingertips, a map of strength and vulnerability. His thighs gripped mine, the exquisite friction of skin on skin. Our gasps confessions of love. Our thrusts, desire I'd foolishly denied. Why had I wasted precious years, when this was what I yearned for?

"Eat your heart out Echo LaVode, I am not your plaything anymore," I told her. "Carl is mine, and I am his, and you're not invited."

I shoved her grumbling down and sighed, a fragile contentment settling over me as I fell asleep in Carl's arms.

∽

MORNING LIGHT STABBED through my eyelids, revealing the empty bed beside me. The sheets still held his warmth, but he was already up, humming softly as he packed.

Seeing my reflection in the dressing table mirror, I almost screamed. Tumbleweed hair was not the farewell image I wanted to leave him with. I rummaged through my trunk and pulled out my blue silk kimono, slipping it on. I hunted for the tortoise shell hairbrush Carl had given me, a Christmas treasure. Beside the brush, I caught sight of the only photograph I possessed: me, in my sailor dress at Lake Rhoda, a sweet smile on my face, JD Rockwell's arm slung possessively around my waist. A tremor ran through me. That image, a wretched memento of the girl I'd been.

But I needed something to give Carl to remember me by. I tore the photo in half, severing myself from that past. Good riddance. Buried Rockwell's half in my trunk. On the back of my image I scribbled: "You promised we'd go to Hollywood, Carl. I'll keep my bags packed." Drew a heart, a desperate plea, a fragile hope.

I sat at the mirrored mosaic dressing table, my reflection fractured across countless tiny tiles. My hair was a tangled mess, resisting even the gentlest strokes of the brush.

"Need some help with that?" Carl stood behind me, his hands gentle on my shoulders.

I nodded, unable to speak. I watched him in the mirror, working the knots and kinks out of my hair. So methodical, so patient and kind. Soon he was able to stroke through the entire length, the rhythmic feeling on my scalp soothing my frayed nerves.

"Keep this with you." Handing him the torn picture, I watched his reflection.

He smiled, then ran his finger down the tear. "Who was in the other half?"

"No one important," I choked out.

Echo's voice was like ice water in my veins. "Tell him the truth. See if he still wants you." I clenched my jaw, the taste of bile rising in my throat as I pushed her back.

A sob escaped my throat. "Please, Carl, just come back to me." I wrapped my arms around him, a warmth I couldn't bear to let go.

His body tensed beneath my touch, questions in his eyes. But I saw a glimmer of the love that had blossomed so fiercely hours before. He cupped my face in his hands, his thumbs brushing away the tears on my eyelashes. "I will," he rasped.

Our lips met in a last desperate kiss, filled with longing and uncertainty. Our hearts pressed together, the photograph clutched between us, a frail promise in a world on the brink of war. As we pulled apart, the reality of his departure broke my heart into a thousand pieces.

Chapter 26

1932

Silver price $0.28 per ounce

Leadville, Colorado. "You could never write the Tabor motion picture without seeing the silver vein that made the Matchless a legend." Baby Doe helped Carl onto the lift. "And soon the vein will be all mined out. A hollow cavern in the mountain."

Sweat beaded his lip. "You sure we have to go down there? Can't you just tell me about it?"

"Come along now, don't be a scare baby." His fancy suit would be no match for the mine's chill. The tenderfoot had no idea what cold truly meant.

With a lurch and squeal, the hoist plunged them into the inky belly of the earth. Passing inches from their faces, the walls of the shaft displayed ancient seashells and strange shelled worms embedded in the rock whispering of an age only this mountain truly knew.

"Get a whiff of that, Carl?" She inhaled deeply.

He grimaced. "Like rotten eggs."

"That's pure mountain in your nose: copper, lead, iron, silver. My husband always swore this mine wasn't just about what we pulled out; it was what good we could do with it." She pulled her sweater up over her neck. "We meant well. Schools, firehouses, churches ... Fair wages, even when times were tough. Donated Denver's post office and a headquarters for the suffragettes. Folks forget that, try to tarnish our name."

Carl stared up at the disappearing patch of sky. His breath hitched in his throat. "I can't do this, Mrs. Tabor." He clutched his chest, gasping for air. "Take us up. I ... I can't breathe."

"Slow your breathing down, son." Her voice softened with motherly concern. "Short, steady breaths. You'll be alright."

Carl's chest heaved as he tried. But instead of his breaths, they heard a rhythmic tapping from a shadowed tunnel. "What's that?" he cried.

"Tommyknockers." She chuckled, remembering Silver's fascination with mountain lore. "Mind your pockets, city boy. Tommyknockers sticky fingers are quicker than you'd think."

"Pickpockets? Down here?" He whipped his head around, searching the shadows.

"Mine gnomes. Mischievous little critters. A missing tool here, a stolen lunch there."

A gust out of nowhere almost extinguished the lantern, causing Carl to shriek. "What do they look like?"

"Small gnomes with heads as big as melons. Didn't Silver Dollar tell you about them?"

His eyes softened, a flicker of pain passing across his face. A sudden jolt made him stumble. "God Almighty," he gasped, gripping the railing tightly.

"Don't be taking the Lord's name in vain. You may need him later," she said. The lift lurched to a stop, swinging precariously in the shaft, scraping the sides and dislodging a shower of rocks.

"What's happening?" he mumbled, swaying with the lift.

She peered upwards, but they were too deep in the shaft to see anything. "I'm sure the hoistman will get it sorted out and we'll be on our way," she said, trying to sound reassuring. But the silence stretched between them, heavy and ominous in the darkness.

"Never felt so closed in before," Carl's voice trembled as he crossed his arms against the cold. "From what Silver said, I thought this would be more of a lark."

"Silver never did shy away from an adventure, that's for sure." She forced a laugh, but longing pierced her heart, remembering her daughter's daring spirit and contagious laugh. Since they were trapped down here, it was a perfect opportunity to question him. "Carl, what really happened to my girl in the end?"

He swallowed hard. "I've told you what I know." His eyes darted away, like a cornered animal.

Was he protecting Silver? Or himself? "You said Silver was hanging around with the wrong sort of men in Chicago … like that investor she sent me? … Dante Rossi? What was their relationship?"

He scoffed. "You know you're killing me with these questions, don't you? She certainly never consulted me on who to date, and whether her choices were good for her. She was going to do what she was going to do, regardless of my feelings." By the lantern light, his eyes glistened with rejection and bitterness. Baby Doe felt a pang of guilt making him recall the agony Silver caused him.

"She was close to Rossi, is all I can say," Carl said. "But she was close to plenty of other men as well. Let's just say she had a devoted stable of men, and I was stupid enough to believe I was special." He looked up at the patch of sky above and cupped his mouth to yell. "Hey, up there. What's going on?"

Below them she heard the annoying Tommyknocker taps, as if dozens of gnomes were chiseling in the tunnels. Yet Baby Doe knew no one was down there.

Carl yelled, "Hey, get us out!"

"They're several stories up, Carl. They can't hear us. Maybe they think we reached bottom."

"We've reached bottom alright." He wiped his brow with his jacket sleeve, biting his lip.

She leaned over, holding the lantern over the railing but

couldn't see the bottom. A paralyzing fear pooled in her stomach. What if they left them suspended here in the dark? What could she do?

A tense few minutes passed, then a sudden jolt and the agonizing screech of the hoist wheel sent the lift shuddering violently. A fleeting moment of relief washed over her, quickly replaced by sheer terror as the lift plummeted down the shaft in a stomach-churning free fall. "Brace yourself!" she screamed.

They landed hard on the rocky ground, a jarring impact that sent pain shooting through her joints. The lantern in her hand miraculously remained lit, casting shadows that danced across the rough walls.

"Get me off this thing!" Carl groaned, stepping off and clutching his head.

Baby Doe followed cautiously, struggling to keep her balance on the uneven rock floor. "Stand clear of the lift and let me get my bearings," she said, pulling him toward the chiseled wall. "Breathe slow and deep, Carl. The air's even thinner down here."

No sooner had she taken a shaky breath than the lift lurched with a metallic screech and ascended, leaving them stranded in the darkness below.

"It's coming back, isn't it?" Carl asked. "They're not leaving us here."

Truth be known she had no idea what was going on up there, but worrying about it would make things worse. She lifted the lantern and stepped into the even darker tunnel, the lantern shedding light a couple feet ahead. "There's an ore cart down here somewhere that will take us to the vein I want you to see."

Carl chuckled nervously. "Ore cart in the dark? Sounds like a joy ride to me."

Caution prickled under her skin. "What you're about to see, I've only seen a couple of times myself." She lifted the lantern tighter. "You have to promise to keep this secret until it's mined, or I'll have a horde of greedy swindlers snooping around."

He leaned into the light, his expression sincere. "You have my word."

"Then I'll show you the secret that Horace Tabor hid from the world." Guiding Carl through the darkness, cold, damp air clung to her skin, sweat rolling down her temple. No matter how brave she was trying to be, fear clawed at her, a chilling whisper to turn back to safety. But turning back was never the way forward.

Part Three

"Life ... is too hard.
It brings too many pains,
disappointments,
and impossible tasks.

To bear it,
we cannot do without
powerful deflections
which make light of our misery;

substitutive satisfactions
which diminish it;

and intoxicating substances
which make us insensible to it."

~Sigmund Freud, Civilization and Its Discontents

Chapter 27

1932

SILVER PRICE $0.28 PER OUNCE

LEADVILLE, COLORADO. Down in the belly of the Matchless, Baby Doe led Carl into the ore cart. "Watch your noggin. Gets real low in this tunnel, and these wool caps don't protect much."

Carl's face was pale, sweat beading above his lip. His breath caught in tight, shallow gasps. She understood that creeping sense that all this rock above them could come crashing down at any moment. Add to that, the suffocating air, the taste of grit, the groan of shifting earth. Enough to break the toughest mind.

And then, of course, there were the cave's usual occupants: albino crickets, beady-eyed woodrats, their whiskers twitching nervously, and most terrifying of all, the bats. The way they shrieked and swarmed ... and bit.

The ore cart rattled and jittered along the rusty rails into the tunnel's maw. Icy drafts whistled past their ears and raised goosebumps on their necks. An eerie squeaking grew louder from somewhere deeper in the mine's belly.

"You smell like Silver Dollar," Carl said.

A thrill ran through her. "She still wore vanilla?" Baby Doe swallowed hard. "I always dab some on in the morning."

"How much farther is the vein?" Carl gripped the sides of the cart.

"Thirty yards around that curve. Keep your head down."

Suddenly the tunnel shuddered and shook the ore cart. The shifting earth roared like a beast awakening. Rocks rained down, ricocheting against the tracks. Her heart crashed against her ribs.

"Mother of God, save us!" She crossed herself, praying the cave-in was small. She wasn't afraid of dying, but buried under rocks like a prospector's ghost? Not the end she envisioned.

Rocks on the tracks brought the ore cart to an abrupt stop.

"We going to die down here?" The lantern shone on his pale face like a ghoul.

"Not today." She held the lantern high. "Out of the cart and hold me tight." She followed a faint scent of fresh air somewhere ahead.

"Sure we can we get out this way?" he whispered.

"Nothing's sure down in a mine." She pushed on though the dark, the lantern casting eerie shadows against rock walls. Her heart labored with exhaustion, lack of air, and the growing anticipation of that eerie squeal echoing from deeper within the mine.

"What's that?" a strangled whimper from Carl.

A thousand thrumming wings filled the tunnel. Screeching, diving, leathery bodies brushing their faces. The smell of bats thick and choking. Carl flailed uselessly as they clawed at him.

She thrust the lantern out like a sword. "Get back!"

The swarm exploded, vanishing into the blackness with terrifying cries. In their wake, a deafening silence fell, broken only by Carl's ragged breathing.

"Even though I walk in the valley of death, I fear no evil," she prayed. Water covered the ground now, their boots squishing in the sediment. Groundwater seeping through?

"I envy your faith," Carl whispered.

"When you get to my age, you'll see there's not much else to hold onto."

Rounding a corner, a beam of sunlight pierced the darkness. "Glory be! There's our way out!" Her excitement bounced off the rock walls.

They emerged into a majestic chamber of stone, sunlight spilling through a crack in the ceiling like a divine spotlight. A waterfall whispered its secrets to the rocks, its water collecting in shimmering pools on the cavern floor. Baby Doe's breath hitched. It was just as breathtaking as she remembered, yet now, with Carl by his side, it held a different kind of magic. "Look over there, son," she said with reverence. "This is what we came for." The sunbeam illuminated a magnificent vein of silver, a jagged scar across the rock face, gleaming with the promise.

Carl's jaw dropped, his eyes wide with wonder. "Astounding."

Leaning against the craggy rock wall, she remembered the moment Horace had first shown her this breathtaking sight. The sheer wonder of such a natural masterpiece, something God had crafted and hidden deep within the earth for millennia. Took her breath away now, as it had then.

But the monster vein, a gleaming treasure in this subterranean world, had also cast a long, dark shadow over their lives. It had promised riches, power, a life beyond their wildest dreams. But it also brought greed, obsession, envy and a devastating heartbreak she still felt in the depths of her soul.

"This silver vein ruled our lives." Resentment and regret weighed heavy on her. "A beautiful tyrant my husband called it. He gambled everything to chase its promise." And in the end, he'd lost. The vein, a dazzling display of nature's bounty, had been their salvation and their damnation.

Carl waded through the icy pool. He craned his neck, tracing the silver vein's path up the cavern wall, his face alight with child-like wonder. A stark contrast to the hardened greed she'd seen in countless prospectors. But as his fingers brushed the gleaming surface, a shadow eclipsed his joy. Did he see a reflection of her daughter in that shimmering silver? A future they'd both hoped for, now impossible.

This jagged vein cut her to the core. Silver wasn't just a geological wonder. It reflected the hopes, dreams, and shattered illusions they all carried, leaving them grasping at shadows.

Suddenly, a boulder dislodged from the waterfall, crashing into the pool and sending a spray of icy water over them.

Her nerves buzzed in warning. "We have to go. Water makes the rock unstable."

"But how do we get out?" He scanned the cavern walls.

"Good question." The sunlit hole was impossibly high. Her gaze darted across the rock wall, searching for any handhold. A narrow ledge sloped upward, barely visible, offering hope.

"Follow me." Clutching the lantern, she hoisted herself up on the ledge. Testing each foothold before stepping, her fingers dug into the rough groove above.

Carl followed hesitantly. "My foot cramped," he cried. His sudden jerk dislodged a shower of pebbles clattering into the pool below. His leg dangled precariously over the edge.

"God have mercy." Her heart plummeted with the falling rocks. "Put your other foot behind mine." She reached out, her fingers closing around Carl's wrist just as the lantern slipped from her grasp, plunging into the darkness.

"Hold tight, Carl." Panic was a luxury they couldn't afford. Her muscles strained as she sought the next handhold. The rock face was slick, but finally, her fingers scraped against rough stone finding the groove—too smooth to be natural. Pushing against the surface, a thin sheet of rock slid with a groan, revealing a hidden cavity. Recognition shot through her.

"Lord Almighty." Horace's secret vault, a place only she knew existed. She spied something gleaming in the crevasse. What could possibly be in there?

"What's wrong?" Carl asked.

"My husband's secret hiding place," she murmured. "He

showed it to me that night with Oscar Wilde." A memory flashed: Horace's bad jokes, Wilde's mischievous grin, the clink of crystal glasses, the smell of fine whiskey, the magnificent silver vein looming over them.

With trembling fingers, she pried a damp paper loose, an envelope. Had Horace hidden it here, tucked away from prying eyes and greedy hands? What secret had he left behind?

The ledge crumbled beneath their feet, the abyss yawning below. No time to dwell on it. She tucked the envelope into her blouse, a mystery to be unraveled later.

"Almost there." Her voice barely a whisper above the creak of the treacherous ledge. Her heart pounded in her ears against the silence of the mine. Just a few more feet. A few more agonizing inches. Sunlight beckoned, a sliver of hope against the yawning abyss.

Finally ... blessed relief. Sunlight flooded their vision, warm and comforting, chasing away the chill that had clung to them like the specter of death itself. They had made it. They stumbled out onto solid ground, blinking against the sudden brightness, the world tilting and swaying beneath their feet. But they were alive. She had kept Carl safe. That was all that mattered.

Chapter 28

1919

Silver Price $1.12 per ounce

Chicago, Illinois. Echo squinted at the 29th Street Beach as the beating sun made the sand sparkle like a chorus girl's rhinestones. A welcome change from the smoky haze of the Peking Club. But the stark division created by the taut rope, a cruel demarcation between 'White' and 'Colored', was a harsh reminder of the reality she couldn't escape.

Echo trailed behind Daisy and Marlena, her housemates. Daisy, a whirlwind of giggles and ragtime tunes, chirped, "Last one in the lake's a rotten egg!" and took off like a shot.

Marlena, cool as a cucumber under her cloche hat, just chuckled. "Don't get your bloomers in a bunch, Daisy. We're coming!"

Pure happiness bubbled up in Echo's chest. "This dame's about to make some waves!" Two months without Sad Sack Silver, and, finally Echo had her own friends and was living her own life. This was her time to live, and she was grabbing it by the horns and steering the whole damn bull.

Echo's gaze snagged on the new bathing pavilion. A beautiful building, but its doors were closed to folks like Daisy and Marlena.

A cop, puffed up like a peacock, jabbed his club toward Echo.

Silver Echoes

"You with the pale skin. This ain't your side of the beach, see? Keep to your own kind, or there'll be trouble."

Echo's stomach lurched, but she held her ground. "Don't you know it's rude to poke a lady with your stick, copper?"

The cop's face flushed. "Other side, sweetheart."

Daisy waved from the divide, her smile strained. "See ya later back at the boarding house."

Rebellion simmered in Echo's chest. Why can't the world be like the Peking Club? Black, white, they all got along there. When the cop turned away, she slipped under the rope, a thrill buzzing through her. But as the girls spread out their towels near the water's edge, another worry niggled her. Her pale skin stood out against the darker complexions around her. She didn't belong here.

They waded into the cool water, tossing a beach ball between them. The smell of coconut oil and sizzling hot dogs mixed with the joyful sounds of children playing and the rhythmic lapping of the waves against the shore.

Suddenly, a rock whizzed past Echo's ear, raucous jeering from the white side. Young white men, their faces contorted with hate, hurled more stones. A large, jagged rock struck a Black teenager square in the forehead, and he cried out, clutching his head, blood trickling down his face. His flailing arms triggered her protective instincts. She lunged forward, reaching toward him, even as more rocks flew, the mob closing in. Another rock hit the teenagers temple, and his eyes fluttered back in his head before he slipped beneath the waves, leaving a spreading stain of crimson.

Echo recoiled, a scream tearing from her throat. The sound amplified by a chorus of other shouts and cries. The once-joyful laughter turned into a terrifying cacophony of panic. The water around her churned with terrified bodies, a frenzy of thrashing limbs and buldging eyes as she pushed through the crowd.

The shore was no better, a full-out brawl engulfing the beach in a wave of violence. Fists flew, bodies collided, and the air crackled with unleashed rage. The stench of fear, thick and sour, choked out the sweet smell of the lake. Glass bottles shattered, wielded like weapons, shards skittering across the sand.

"Daisy! Marlena!" Echo shouted for her friends, swallowed by the deafening mob. Police swarmed like locusts through the crowd, swinging billy clubs with brutal force.

Echo ran, the taste of bile rising in her throat, sand stinging her bare feet.

∽

BACK IN HER ROOM, Echo collapsed on the bed, sobs wracking her body. Tiger Lily, her stray cat, nuzzled against her chest, the soft purr a silent comfort she desperately needed. Echo's ears strained, listening for the familiar sounds of Daisy and Marlena returning, but the boardinghouse remained eerily quiet.

"I thought I'd finally found my place, Tiger Lily," she choked out, burying her face in the cat's soft fur. "The Peking, the boardinghouse ... I almost felt like I belonged. But today ..." The screaming, the blood, the hate ... "It showed me I don't belong anywhere. Without Silver Dollar."

She smothered her face into the wet pillow. Would she ever find a place where she truly belonged? With friends, a life of her own, a world not sliced apart by invisible lines?

The next morning, the newspaper boy's cries outside the window woke her: "Two killed, Fifty Hurt in South Side Race Riots."

She remembered the sneer of contempt on a policeman's face when he swung his club into a boy's head. The crimson stain spreading across a young woman's sundress. The shrieks of terror. Sickening thud of fists on flesh. The papers called it a race riot, but it was just plain war, fought against the God-given color of our skin. Everyone out for their own. Weren't they all Americans on that beach? Weren't they all God's children? Echo needed to know what Silver would think of what happened. But that was impossible now.

~

A BALL of fire crashed through Echo's window. Gasoline-soaked rags exploded on the wood planked floor. The sizzle of flames ignited her bedspread. Windows were breaking everywhere. People screaming. Panicked faces at the windowpanes.

Smoke choked the room; where could she go? Her heart bolted like it would break out of her chest. Echo scooped up Tiger Lily, the small cat clinging with sharp claws as she bolted for the door. The staircase was crammed with screaming, wailing residents, Daisy and Marlena nowhere to be seen.

A white mob, faces twisted with menace, marched down the street. A lynched scarecrow swung from a lamppost, a grim foreshadowing of their intent. Their chants were a litany of hate: "White supremacy forever! The only good negro is a dead negro! No Jews, no blacks, no Catholics!"

"Catholics?" But, wait, Silver Dollar was Catholic. They hate religion, too? The mob's blind hatred terrified her. But defiance reared up within her. She had to be stronger than fear.

Recoiling behind a garbage can, gasping from smoke, eyes stinging. Had to run. Tiger Lily wriggled free, disappearing into the chaos. "No, come back." She chased her through the alleyway unable to find her.

The mob's chants grew louder, a chorus of hate echoing through the streets. The air crackled with shattering glass and splintering wood, the smell of smoke clinging to her clothes. Echo's lungs ached, her legs heavy, but she forced herself to keep running, dodging rioters smashing doors and torching cars. Their howls bounced off the walls, a pack of rabid dogs, heckling chants.

Disoriented, she realized she'd run in circles back to her own block. A spark of hope, maybe her friends were back. But her apartment building was an inferno now, flames licking the sky. Her lungs burned as she ran toward the blaze, desperate for Daisy and Marlena.

The doorknob seared her hand. Flames devoured the building, a hellish inferno. Tiger Lily, a streak of orange, vanished into the blaze. "No!" Echo sobbed, waves of heat forcing her back.

Then, a blinding flash and roar. The explosion hurled her across the street, the night bursting into fire. A searing pain ripped through her, shards of glass in her hair, a blur of blood and cinders.

Chapter 29

1919

Silver Price $1.12 per ounce

Chicago, Illinois. A diamond ring on every finger glittered under the lights as the king of the Chicago underworld, the owner of this glittering den of iniquity, approached the stage. "Silver Dollar, don't let me down." Diamond Jim's cold, calculating eyes met mine, his lips curling into a smirk. "Rossi tells me you're the best in the business. I'm eager to see if you live up to the hype."

"I'll do my best to entertain, Mr. Colosimo." I pasted a confident smile on my face, though my stomach churned. I'd never performed a tiger act; Rossi had only seen me rehearse.

Diamond Jim turned away, returning to his bride, Miss Dale Winter, the last headliner in his club. Taking him out of circulation, thank God.

A poster caught my eye, lined with lightbulbs: "Silver Dollar Tiger Tamer!" My breath hitched. This was the lion's den, and I'm the fresh meat. Oh Carl, where are you when I need you? Thank goodness the club was only open Friday and Saturday nights, leaving me free for Sunday confession. Mother of God, I was gonna need it.

At least the tigers felt familiar, the scent of animal musk and their husky rumble. But I'd miscalculated their behavior. The film studio sets were contained, predictable. But here in the nightclub, the neon lights, the drunken shouts, the swirling smoke, the reek of booze and sweat made them agitated and erratic. I'd left baby Topaz at home, too volatile to handle this. But Timber and Tamber paced, their nails scraping the floor, their eyes glinting with a restless hunger. As much as they'd grown accustomed to me this past year, their fierceness could turn on me in an instant. One wrong move, one missed cue, and I'm cat food. Can't let them sense my fear. Not now. Not ever. I swallowed hard, fighting back roiling nausea.

Checking for treats in my pocket, I straightened my top hat and grabbed my baton. Fishnet legs flashed beneath a tuxedo jacket as I waited backstage.

"Ladies and gentlemen, hold onto your hats and brace yourselves!" the MC boomed. "For the first time on the Colosimo Café stage, a spectacle that will leave you breathless. Prepare to witness the raw power and untamed beauty of Silver Dollar Tiger Tamer!"

Taking a deep breath, I strutted on stage, heartbeat thrashing against my ribs. I struck a pose, planting one shiny Mary Jane on the gleaming gold pyramid center stage. Anxious applause from the crowd triggered my fear. Would the tigers betray me, their jungle urges overcoming their training?

Cigar smoke curled between Rossi and Diamond Jim, a yellow haze hanging over the front row table. I'd witnessed their brutality during rehearsals: a gut punch here, a bone snapped there. If he hated my act, there'd be no escape. My future would be measured by the length of the coffin.

The stagehand fumbled with the lock, trying to open the cage. Finally, the door swung open, and he jumped back like a startled rabbit. My pulse hammered in my temples, a frantic rhythm matching the click of the tigers' claws on the wooden stage. Timber and Tamber's eyes gleamed like polished amber in the harsh footlights, suspicion radiating from every muscle.

I prayed my strained smile masked my terror. Timber let out a deafening roar, a primal sound that made the chandeliers tremble. The audience shrieked, their faces a mix of fear and exhilaration. Dear God, what have I done? I could almost see it: the tigers, overcome by instinct, leaping into the crowd, tearing into the soft flesh beneath the expensive furs. Screams, blood, chaos.

As fear rippled through me, the familiar chill of Echo tickled my ear: "Don't shrink, Silver girl. Show these tigers who's boss."

New boldness seeped into my bones, and I raised the shiny steel hoops. "Jump," I commanded, and their massive bodies surged forward. I almost felt their claws, so close, yet somehow, they soared through the hoops.

Big Jim clapped, and the crowd joined in.

The tigers circled me, deep rumbles in their throats. A flick of my arm, the hoop in place, and they jumped again. Circled around and jumped through, again. The routine I'd drilled into them at the warehouse. One wrong move, and I'm a tiger's midnight snack.

Finally, it was time for the pyramid. With steady eyes locked on the tigers, the ultimate test of my command, I ordered them up the shiny gold steps. "Stand," I commanded, and they teetered on their massive hind legs. "Dance." Their precarious hops and prancing drew laughter and wild cheers from the crowd. Even Diamond Jim stopped chewing his cigar, mesmerized.

I tapped my baton. "Tamber, down." Then Timber. Both of them obeyed, thank goodness. Now if I could just get these overgrown kittens back in their playpen without losing a limb, I might actually survive this night.

"Play fetch," Diamond Jim yelled and threw a crumpled napkin at my feet like a ball, for heaven's sake.

Is he insane? Does he want a bloodbath?

The tigers lurched toward me, eyes glowing with voracious hunger. No time to think, I fished meaty bones from my pocket, wrapping the napkin around them. "Fetch!" I hurled the napkin and bones into the open cage. The beasts leaped in front of me, grazing my body with stripes and snarls, and I slammed the door shut, the lock clicking into place.

My knees buckled and I leaned back against the bars, my breath heaving, the gnashing and breaking of the bones behind me. Could have been my gams instead of those bones.

"What will you do next time Diamond Jim says jump?" Echo hissed in my ear. "Ask him how high?"

I broke away and took center stage, sweeping off my top hat, and letting my long hair tumble loose. With an exaggerated wink toward Diamond Jim, I bowed my deepest.

A slow grin spread across his face. He leaned forward, slapping the table with his glaring rings. "Well, I'll be damned. That took some moxie, lady. Rossi, get this girl a drink on the house."

The crowd erupted with wilder cheers.

Rossi brought the cocktail; his glinting smile couldn't hide the coldness in his eyes. "Watch yourself, Silver. Mr. Colosimo doesn't like to be shown up by a dame. Remember that."

Rossi's words stung, a reminder of my precarious position. I tilted the glass back and drained it in one swallow, cheap liquor burning a trail down my throat. Now I was part of the gangsters treacherous game. But Papa taught me poker, and I was good at it. Let them think they're winning, then sweep the pot.

∽

MY THIRD NEGRONI burned a fiery trail down my throat, but it did nothing to dull the ache in my heart. Rereading the letter I'd just penned to Carl, a stray tear escaped. I wrote him every week, but his replies were sporadic, like whispers carried on the wind.

I slumped at the gilded dressing table where Carl brushed my hair before he left, his warm reflection in the mirror. He'd practically fainted when he saw me at the Selig Polyscope gate, my hair chopped short like some flapper. Now it was long again, cascading down my back, but tonight's performance had left it a snarled, tangled mess.

I yanked the tortoise shell brush through my hair, wincing as it snagged on knots. Damn those tigers and their playful swats. Frustration bubbled up, hot tears stinging my eyes. What's the point of anything without Carl here? I threw the brush down, strands of hair tangled in the bristles.

The silken sheets felt like ice against my skin as I tossed and turned, haunted by his absence. Maybe he wasn't coming back. Maybe the horrors of war had stolen him from me forever.

Unable to bear the suffocating silence any longer, I went to the window. Chicago sprawled beneath me, a glittering tapestry of lights and shadows. The city throbbed with life, a symphony of laughter and music, while I stood here, clutching the remnants of my dreams.

Back in my lonely bed, sleep remained elusive. Carl's face, his infectious grin, the warmth of his embrace ... danced just beyond my grasp, taunting me. Did he feel this same aching loneliness?

I paced the room like a caged tigress, trying on different hats and scarves, draping a feathered boa around my neck, searching for a reflection that wasn't just ... me. And then, summoned by my own desperation, Echo's sultry presence slithered into my thoughts.

"Feeling caged, Silver girl?" Her laughter was a dark caress against my mind. "Wallowing in self-pity won't get you anywhere, darling. A little danger is all you need to spark that fire within. Or are you too afraid? Because if you won't seize the night, I sure as hell will."

I watched as Echo, a vision in a shimmy of fringe and a cloud of Jardin de Nuit, sashayed out the door, ready to paint the town red.

And honestly? It sounded like just what the doctor ordered.

Chapter 30

1920

Silver price $1.01 per ounce

Chicago, Illinois. Echo's adrenaline charged through her as she swooped up the ribbons, the Peking Club her stage, hers alone. Spotlit, silk organdy ribbons shimmered like emerald fire as she danced center stage. The jazz beat pulsed in her veins—every step, pure energy, every whirl mirroring the joy exploding inside her. Tonight, she was free. Free from Colosimo's, the knife fights, the guns, the violence that radiated from them like heat off asphalt. Free from jealous girlfriends with talons like buzzards. Free from Silver Dollar's whole gangster world, its smoky haze and menace. Here, eyes drank her in, but held no power. Tonight, she was pure spectacle, alive.

Men hooted and threw silver dollars at her feet. She bowed again and the men threw more silver dollars. She scooped them up in her drawstring bag, getting heavy.

Zhang appeared at the back of the theater, the hall light silhouetting him. He tromped down the aisle with two burly policemen behind him, blowing their shrieking whistles, their bulbous caps bobbing, navy frock coats and big brass stars on their chests.

"That's her." Zhang pointed to Echo, then crossed his muscular forearms.

The music screeched to a halt. Her heart thundered, desperation clawing at her throat. She had to escape. But how? Her gaze darted to the back exit, but a sea of gawking faces blocked her way. No. They couldn't take away the Peking Club from her. The one good thing she'd found.

A figure materialized through the parting crowd. Broad-shouldered and imposing, his white Stetson low over his face. A glint of silver flashed from his belt buckle. As he strode closer, the details clicked into place. The unmistakable walrus mustache, the glint of revenge in his eyes. The star of sapphire ring he'd taken from Silver's papa. A jolt shot through Echo. This was the man she'd strangled years ago. The man she'd tried to kill.

"Hello, Silver Dollar," JD Rockwell said.

"Wrong gal, sugar. I'm Echo LaVode." This can't be happening.

"You're wanted back in Colorado for jewel theft," the baby-faced copper said. The handcuffs clicked shut. Cold metal bit into her wrists.

"Don't know what you are talking about," Echo said.

"Tell it to the judge back in Colorado." The red-bearded copper pushed her down the stairs to the restaurant. The smell of greasy eggrolls and fish oil made her gag.

"Zhang, can't you talk sense into them?" She stumbled down the stairs, her sparkly shoes pinching her toes. *He owes me. He can't just let them take me.*

"Have a club to run. Can't be hiding no fugitives." Zhang stared fixedly at the cash register, refusing to meet her eyes. The rat.

∼

THE GEEKY TRAIN PORTER, all smiles and striped trousers, swung open the compartment door. "Golden Coronet, folks! Just like you asked, Mr. Rockwell."

The metal handcuffs bit into Echo's wrists, making her wince.

She shot a glare at Rockwell, who only smirked back, his silver belt buckle gleaming in the low light.

"What's she in for?" the porter ogled her spangled dress and sparkly heels.

"Attempted murder," Rockwell drawled. The train jolted.

The porter's smile faltered. He quickly recovered, tipping his cap. "Enjoy your trip, sir."

Echo sank into the plush seat, her fingers digging into the velvet. The opulence of the cabin a stark contrast to her predicament. She could feel Rockwell's gaze on her, predatory and possessive.

"Veuve Clicquot?" he offered, brandishing a bottle. "To freedom."

Echo scoffed. "How can I drink with these?" She lifted her cuffed wrists.

"No funny business."

Rockwell leaned in, his breath hot against her skin. The click of the lock was deafening. She rubbed her raw skin, an unpleasant memory flooding back. Silver's sixteenth birthday. Rockwell's wandering hands. The shame she'd carried in silence.

"Silver was pregnant," Echo spat with disgust. "Because of you. But don't worry, Uncle Rockwell." A bitter laugh escaped her lips. "She lost the baby."

"I ... I didn't ..." His jaw clenched, and his hand tightened on the champagne bottle. "Silver, stop this nonsense. Why are you talking about yourself in the third person?"

Echo glared at the monster. A tense silence filled the compartment, broken only by the train's rhythmic chugging.

As the train slowed for the Burlington, Iowa station, Echo excused herself for the lavatory, Rockwell guarding the door. She climbed onto the toilet, her heart drumming in her ears. The window was small, but she was desperate. When the train lurched to a stop, she squeezed herself through the window. But as she tumbled onto the ground, she heard a shout behind her.

"Hey! Stop her!"

Gravel scraping her palms, Echo scrambled to her feet. The stench of burning coal burned her nostrils. The tang of blood filled her mouth.

She sprinted into the twilight, the sound of pounding footsteps chasing after her.

∼

Echo needed a hiding place, fast. Thank goodness she knew Burlington like the back of her hand after her time with Takka Chance. She found a barn west of town, reeking of pigs. It would have to do. She climbed the ladder, nose pinched against the stench. She scratched at the itchy welts on her legs, cursing the prickly hay. Hives sprouted across her neck and arms. Damn allergies. She raked the hay away with a pitchfork, unearthing the hard floorboards. It wasn't exactly the Ritz, but it beat being locked up with Rockwell, the bastard.

Night fell, thick and black, and Echo shivered with cold and fear. A rat scurried across her knuckles. She screamed, and the rodent scuttled away. She curled into a ball, listening to the owls hooting.

Echo squeezed her eyes shut, trying to summon Silver Dollar. Felt so empty without her. Usually, it was Echo who soothed Silver's anxieties. Wouldn't she extend the same kindness? Was Silver Dollar too caught up in her own ambitions to offer a shred of warmth? Or had she forgotten about Echo altogether? She closed her eyes, recalling Silver's tales of the Tommy Knockers, their laughter echoing through the mine shafts, their pranks that made the miners scratch their heads.

The wind screamed through the barn's cracks, chilling her to the bone, leaving her yearning for laudanum. But tonight, all she had for comfort was her freedom. Although Rockwell wouldn't give up until he found her. She could almost hear his heavy footsteps echoing in the distance. If he ever got her alone in a train car again, she'd scratch his eyes out.

∼

The next morning, Echo woke to voices. Peering through a crack, she felt a jolt. Rockwell, with the local sheriff and deputy in tow. And there was that damn stench of his cologne.

"Ran away from her husband, Sheriff." Rockwell gestured wildly. "Women get these notions, you know. Always had a touch of wanderlust, just like her poor mother."

The farmer scratched his head. "Ain't seen no runaway wives 'round these parts, Sheriff.

"Mind if we have a look around?" the sheriff asked.

The farmer glanced at his field. "I gotta pick that corn, or it'll be worthless."

"Go ahead," the sheriff said. "We'll take a peek and shut the barn behind us."

Echo heard the door screech open and scrambled under the haybales. Hay prickled her nose, bringing on a sneeze. She pinched her nostrils so hard her eyes watered. Hives swelled in her throat, making it difficult to breathe.

The loft shook. Someone climbing the ladder. Just leave.

"Any sign of her?" Rockwell yelled.

A boot thudded down mere inches from her nose, and her cheek snagged a splinter from the rough loft floor. He grunted, hefting the pitchfork. The prongs pierced the rustling hay near her hand. Rats scurried out, squeaking and skittering through the bales, their beady eyes gleaming in the dim light. The pitchfork stabbed down again, spearing her sparkly heels and wrenching her ankle. She bit her finger, but a strangled cry still escaped as the rats scattered.

The sheriff jumped. "Lordy." He jabbed at the rats with the pitchfork.

Echo curled into a ball, wishing she could dissolve into the floorboards. Soon, the ladder shook as the sheriff climbed down.

"Nothing but a rats' nest," he said.

Echo's breathing struggled against the swelling hives. Her ankle throbbed. She'd rather die than go back to Colorado with that monster. Slipping out of the barn, she limped across the damp grass. Sprained ankle, ripped dress. Doesn't matter. Only one place to go.

Chapter 31

1932

SILVER PRICE $0.28 PER OUNCE

LEADVILLE, COLORADO. BABY DOE AND CARL approached the headframe as a dozen miners were working on the hoist, JD Rockwell barking orders.

She gripped Carl's arm, her voice low and urgent. "Let's keep what we saw down in the mine between us, alright?"

He chuckled nervously. "The secret hiding place or the monstrous vein?"

"I mean it," she swatted him playfully, her tone firm. "Not a word. Especially not to my lawyer, Rockwell."

Carl frowned. "Deal."

Rockwell spotted them, the stump of his arm tucked into his dangling jacket sleeve. "God almighty, woman! Where've you been?"

Her mind flashed back to when she'd first asked about his missing hand. He'd blamed a vague hunting accident, but later she learned he'd spent weeks in a Chicago hospital fighting infection.

He chomped on his unlit cigar, his impatience evident. "The boys were worried sick when you didn't come up from the shaft.'

"Had to climb out on the other side of the mountain," she

explained, wringing out her soaked denim jacket. "One of the East tunnels sprung a leak. River water's seeping in."

Rockwell yelled to Charlie. "Flood below. Shore it up immediately or the excavation's dead in the water."

Charlie and the men stared loading the lift with sledgehammers and timber.

"That's ridiculous." She jutted her chin at Rockwell. "It's too dangerous to send them down now. The tunnel could collapse."

Obeying Rockwell's order, Charlie lowered the lift into the shaft. The squeal of the hoist reverberated through her skull, a blow to her composure. "Blood on your hands," she spat at Rockwell.

"I'm not letting this ship sink now after waiting all these years for a payout." Rockwell's belly strained against the buttons of his suede vest.

"Maybe you should see how serious the leak is before you send men down," Carl said.

Rockwell glared at him. "Who's this guy shooting off his mouth?"

"Carl Erikson." Carl held Rockwell's gaze, defiance in his eyes. "I met you with Silver in Chicago ... Johnny Torrio's birthday party."

Rockwell flinched, his neck reddening.

"When did you go to Chicago?" Baby Doe strained above the din.

"I had business there." He waved dismissively. "So, I thought I'd check on Silver for you."

Carl's eyebrows knitted together, suspicious.

"You know how she was." Rockwell talked fast. "Always drawn to the bright lights. Bootleggers, brothels, the whole sordid scene. And now, we have her friend Rossi breathing down our necks, threatening to take over the Matchless if we don't get a return on his investment soon."

That last bit stuck in her craw. "Now you're blaming Silver for bringing Rossi and his thugs into our lives?" Anger sparked in her chest.

Rockwell shrugged. "Silver vouched for him. How'd I know he was a gangster?"

She crossed her arms. "Isn't that what I've paid you for all these years? To check credentials of potential investors?" Her voice dripped with frustration. "You've been leading me into shady deals for as long as I remember."

Carl stepped closer to her, squaring his shoulders.

"You needed money for the Matchless, and Rossi had it." Rockwell slid his cigar to the side of his mouth. "Silver Dollar was digging her own grave there in Chicago. I protected you from what she got herself into. If I told you the vile details, you'd never scrub it out of your mind."

Carl stepped forward. "Have some respect."

"Rockwell, I don't need your protection from my daughter," she spat. "The good Lord protects me, just like he protects Silver Dollar in the convent."

Rockwell grimaced. "You don't believe that cock-and-bull story. Come on, Baby Doe. I'm your oldest friend."

"I've reconsidered my friends, Rockwell, and you didn't make the cut." She jutted her chin.

Rockwell stomped off, shouting orders to the crew. "Get ready to go down, pronto."

"Gee willikers." Carl's hand patted her shoulder. "Now I know why Silver didn't like him. He's a bully." He sighed, his shoulders relaxing.

She clucked her tongue. "Come inside, Carl. Dry off by the stove." Though she never let anyone inside the cabin, Carl had become family. Still, something bothered her. "Why didn't you tell me you met Rockwell in Chicago?"

A shadow crossed Carl's face. "Actually, I wasn't invited to Torrio's shindig. I just wanted to see how he'd react." His voice turned somber. "Silver told me later about Rockwell insisting she sign an agreement with Lily. She was worried about it and asked my opinion. I told her you probably knew about it. Did you?"

"Never heard a word about it." Baby Doe put the kettle on the woodstove. Something was very wrong about all this. "Doesn't make sense that Lily was at a gangster's birthday? Lily's a homebody."

Carl fed the fire, the crackle of damp pine struggling to catch fire. "Rockwell brought Lily there, trying to get Silver to sign some Matchless papers."

The room spun and she gripped the table for support. "When was this?"

Carl glanced at the ceiling. "I'd come back from the war, and Silver was a big star in Torrio's club. Must have been 1921." His head dropped to his chest. "Oh my God." He gasped. "Just realized. The man in Silver's photo ... it's Rockwell."

Her fingers went numb. "What are you talking about?"

Carl pulled out his wallet and handed her two halves of a picture. "Silver tore this photograph in two so I could take her picture with me to war." His voice wavered. "Isn't that Rockwell on the other half? They found it in her apartment after she died."

She ran her finger along the ripped edges. Her breath caught to see Silver Dollar in her sailor dress from so long ago. "Why would this photograph seem suspicious?"

"Look what she wrote on the back of his half." His hands scrubbed his face.

"In case I'm killed, arrest this man," Baby Doe's voice trembled. "For he will be responsible for my death." The photograph slipped from her fingers, fluttering to the floor. Rockwell? The man who'd been like a father to Silver? Disbelief warred with a sickening sense of dread.

"No ... it can't be ..." she whispered.

Carl shook his head. "The police thought the man in the photo was one of Torrio's men, a bar owner. But he had an alibi."

"Are you suggesting Rockwell was mixed up in Silver's death?

He'd never harm Silver. He loved her like a daughter." Baby Doe choked a sob.

The shrill whistle of the teapot pierced the silence of the cold, mountain cabin, and she moved the kettle off the stove.

"Maybe Silver misunderstood about the Matchless papers."

"She did have a flair for the dramatic," she admitted, her old, veined hands pouring tea into chipped cups. But the image of Lily and Silver entangled with Rockwell refused to fade. It had to be more than coincidence. The weak tea scalded her tongue. "Oooh, watch out," she warned.

She set down her cup with a decisive clink. Carl looked as lost as she felt.

"I can't ask Rockwell about the papers now. He'll just lie." All she could do was watch Rockwell carefully, and when the moment was right ... she would know what to do.

∼

WITH EVERYTHING that had happened that day, it was late before she remembered the envelope she found in the mine, smelling of mildew. She opened it by the light of the candlestick, the damp envelope almost disintegrating in her trembling fingers. Why hadn't Horace told her something was there? If she hadn't taken Carl down there, it would've been lost forever.

Last Will and Testament.

Disappointment lodged in her belly. Horace's will would be worthless after so many years of debt piled on them. This will couldn't be of any use. Yet, curiosity won out. She unfolded the document, her eyes scrutinizing the spindly, old-fashioned penmanship. This wasn't Horace's handwriting. Under the flickering candlelight she made out the signature. Horace's mother?

For my one true son, Horace Austin Warner Tabor ...

She gasped at the amount his mother willed him so long ago. $2,500,000? God Almighty. Her fingers clenched the edges. A question burned in her mind: Why on God's green earth had Horace hidden it? He was estranged from his mother, but still, this money would have saved their empire.

She racked her brain for reasons and finally landed on the only one that made sense. Horace hid it because Rockwell and the bankers would have used it to pay their outstanding debt.

Money hadn't brought them joy, had it? After the terrible year after the silver crash, they'd found happiness for a time. Horace working as a postmaster, the girls safe in Catholic school, Baby Doe cooking and cleaning. Watching the sunset from their Windsor apartment, holding hands.

But then Horace died. She dragged the girls up here to the Matchless. Everything unraveled, Lily moving to relatives and Silver chasing whispers only she could hear. Now, Baby Doe realized, she'd been obsessed with regaining the Tabor wealth and glory and single-handedly destroyed what was left of their family. She slumped against the wall, the weight of the past crushing her. Money had torn her family apart, and this inheritance would be no different.

Still, thoughts of what the money could do ... bring the mine up to working order without Rockwell and Rossi's investors? Too late fore that. She kicked off her decrepit boots, newspaper falling out of the soles.

She found Silver's rosary and went outside to sit on the stoop. A million stars in the inky sky were the only sanctuary she needed. A prayer for guidance filled her heart in the quiet of the night.

It wasn't long before the answer came, clear as the heavens above.

Chapter 32

1920

Silver price $1.01 per ounce

Chicago, Illinois. A streetcar clanged, adding to the roar of engines. "Sorry we're late, Silver," Dante Rossi said, as the setting sun glinted off his sunglasses. "Sammy just got the truck from the paint shop."

A thrill shot through me. "Silver Dollar Tiger Tamer" blazed across the truck, smelling of fresh paint. Me, larger than life, tigers leaping at my command. My pride swelled imagining my fame spreading through the city streets.

I handed off the tigers to Sammy, our driver. "Twenty minutes I stood on the corner with tigers on leashes," I shot Rossi a pointed look. "Traffic, gawkers ... Timber nearly bit an old lady."

My stomach churned. "Don't jinx it, Dante," I retorted, palms sweating. "Colosimo will have our heads."

The city pulsed around us. Honking cars, shouting vendors, the rumble of the L train overhead. Tonight, I'd tame tigers. But first, I had to tame Diamond Jim.

Sammy slid in the front seat, bugging out his big brown eyes at me in the rearview mirror, black pupils shooting warnings like bullets.

Only then, did I notice Rossi was wearing the same white suit as yesterday, now crumpled and filthy, his carnation wilted and smashed, sending off a sickly-sweet smell. A dark, rust-colored stain marred his white tucked shirt.

"I hope you have a fresh suit at the club," I said. "What happened to you?"

Rossi pulled his torn white jacket over his ribs like a shield, wincing as the fabric brushed against his bruised jaw. "Tough job last night, that's all."

Sammy swerved out into the street. Cars, streetcars, buses moved willy-nilly, but he navigated through it all.

"Trouble collecting again?" I hated Thursdays, the roughest of their circuit it seemed, rival gangs competing for territory.

He darted me a dark look as he held his bruised jaw. "Make sure you're dynamite tonight, and all will be forgiven. Colosimo has a short attention span."

Rubbing a sponge in my pancake makeup, I patted his cheekbone. Rossi flinched.

"Hold still." Another bruise formed on his temple, and I smoothed the makeup over like a pencil eraser. If only all wounds could be covered so easily. It felt good to do something for Rossi. Over the past year he'd done so much for me. Covering his bruises was the least I could do.

Sammy slammed on the brakes. An unstoppable force swept down Michigan Street, a legion of women marching in lockstep. "Women's Christian Temperance Union," I read their banner aloud. And then I saw her, Lily, my own flesh and blood, clutching the banner's edge.

My breath hitched. Righteous Lily, marching against alcohol and speakeasies. Marching against me. Wouldn't you know it.

I ducked down, my cheeks burning. "Why are they still marching?" I questioned Rossi. "The Volstead Act passed, didn't it?"

He snorted, his split lip curling. "Women. Can't let a thing go."

I bristled. "I'm a woman."

"Not like these bible-thumpers," he scoffed.

Sammy swerved onto a side street, but the protest snaked on, blocking our path. Their voices rose in a chorus of condemnation: "Prohibition is God's will!" "Alcohol is the devil's work!"

Guilt gnawed at me. Was my quiet faith a betrayal? No. My bond with Mother Mary is my own. It wasn't their righteous anger that drew me to Holy Sepulcher at night. It was the need to wash away the scent of smoke and cheap perfume, to find solace after the adrenaline rush of the show, the ever-present fear of the tigers' claws.

As we finally pulled up behind the Four Deuces, the tigers roared, their impatience like my own. I threw on my black cloak, a shield against the judging eyes of the world, and slipped through the back entrance. The smoky haze of the club enveloped me, sounds of clinking glasses, raucous laughter, and a lone piano playing a melancholic tune. I inhaled the familiar scent of whiskey and perfume, a strange comfort. Tonight was my night. I could feel it in my bones.

Rossi punched my shoulder playfully. "Knock 'em dead, Silver."

"Remember to change your suit." I kissed his cheek and rushed to my dressing room. Rossi had become my shield, my bodyguard in a den of wolves. Of course, he was over the moon about the Matchless investment I'd arranged for him with Mama. Especially since silver prices were up big time since the war started.

The Tabors are back, baby.

∽

IN THE MIRROR BACKSTAGE, I straightened the seams of my fishnet stockings, a shiver of anticipation running down my spine. Buttoning rhinestone buttons on my sequined tuxedo jacket over satin tap pants, I tilted my top hat, a flourish of defiance against the shadows.

Peeking through the curtain, the tiered theater rose above the stage lined with blinding footlights. All I could see of the audience were jack-o-lantern faces lit by table lamps. The clinking of glasses and the low hum of conversation mixed with the discordant notes of the band, creating a chaotic symphony that mirrored the unease in my heart.

Glamorous men and cackling women drank like Prohibition had never started. The head table was closest to the stage. Rossi's fedora hid his expressions. The women wore expensive beaded dresses from Chanel and Lanvin. Diamond Jim brought his new wife, Dale Winter, showing off her five-carat diamond ring to Mayor Thompson, whom I recognized from the newspapers. What was the mayor doing in a speakeasy during Prohibition? Disgust simmered in my belly.

The MC took the microphone. "Welcome Ladies and Gentlemen to the Four Deuces. Tonight, we bring you a very special act." He took a deep breath and bellowed. "Silver Dollar Tiger Tamer!"

The jazz band launched into "Tiger Rag." Clarinet, piano, drums, trombone, and cornet, lighting a fire under the audience, making their toes tap and slapping their thighs. My heart hammered as I strutted out on the stage. I wish Carl was here. A pang of longing pierced through the adrenaline. But I have to do this on my own.

As the curtain rose, I gestured right and left to the tigers' cages that sparkled under the roving spotlights. The tigers paced, agitated at the unfamiliar music and crowd noise, their tiger musk heavy in the air. They roared restlessly, which in turn inflamed the audience. I glanced at my tools: jeweled collars, props, a gold baton. I tucked bags of meat in my pockets and approached Timber, who snarled and snapped his head, his massive body agitated.

"Brought a treat for you, Timber." I fed him a chunk of meat from my palm. He gulped it down, his golden eyes challenging mine. I slipped the jeweled collar around his neck, my hand trembling slightly as I felt the warmth of his fur against my skin.

The mayor jeered through the music. "Look. That tiger is eating out of her hand."

"That's just because the tiger's not hungry enough to eat her hand yet." Dale Winter's sharp wit cut through the laughter. The mayor guffawed, sparks flying from his cigar.

Each chunk of meat, each gentle stroke, forged a silent promise with the tigers. These simple acts were the language of trust that would guide them through the spectacle to come. With a flick of my wrist, I sent balls soaring. The tigers, massive and sinuous, chased them down, returning them with playful swats.

At my signal, they vaulted onto the colossal spheres, their massive bodies teetering precariously. The crowd held their breath, a hush falling over the room. I raised the baton. "Up!" The tigers lifted their torsos, their powerful muscles rippling as they balanced on their hind legs. "Roll." They moved their feet on the spheres, a breathtaking display of strength and grace as they rolled them forward and back across the stage.

Shading my eyes, I leaned over the footlights to a waiter with a caterpillar mustache. "We're mighty thirsty up here," I said. "May I?" I snatched the tray from his startled hands and set it on the pedestal. Downing my glass, I nodded toward the tigers. "Drink up, friends. It's top-shelf bubbly."

The tigers obeyed with gusto. Their long tongues lapped up the champagne, a comical sight that elicited laughter from the audience. Prying another glass loose, I downed it with a wink and a giggle. The audience howled and applauded. Mixing fun with danger. That's how I've lived, wasn't it? That's how I'll perform.

Next came the hoops. Sawdust from the arena floor tickled my nose as I hefted a large wooden hoop in each hand. With a crack of my whip, I ordered Timber to jump first, then Tamber. Like a matador, I struck a pose, hoops held high, challenging the sleek beasts. Their muscles rippled beneath their fur, their powerful leaps a blur of orange and black. Timber cleared the lower hoop, the scent of wet fur mingling with the smoky air.

Again and again, I dared them to fly through the hoops, one high, one low. Far apart, a menacing near-miss. The audience gasped, their eyes glued to the spectacle. The tigers never faltered, their obedience a testament to the bond we'd forged. Yet, beneath my outward calm, my nerves snapped like firecrackers. The crowd's cheers were deafening, but inside my head Echo whispered, "Don't be an idiot, Silver. You'll get yourself killed."

The applause faded, leaving a ringing silence in its wake. A bone-deep chill seeped into my bones, cold sweat beading on my skin. Echo slithered in, cold as ice and sharp as a razor. "That show was nothing." Her venom shot through my veins. "Together, we could ignite a fire that would consume this city, this world."

My jaw clenched, a muscle ticking in my cheek. "I've faced down tigers, Echo," I thundered. "You're nothing but a shadow, a figment of my own fear. I don't need you anymore."

Dante bounded backstage, grabbing my arm. "What are you yelling about? We could hear you out front."

"I ... I was talking to Sammy," I stammered between ragged gasps.

Dante searched the empty stage. "Sammy? You sounded ..."

I pulled away, stepping through the curtains for another bow.

∾

THE CROWD ROARED when I appeared again. But strident chanting from outside silenced them. The audience glanced around anxiously listening.

"Down with the demon drink. Saloons must fall." Their chants reverberated through my brain. Remembering Lily carrying the banner turned my veins to ice. Lily must be right here. Right outside our doors.

Diamond Jim stood and held his whiskey high. "Cheers to the Temperance ladies! And to Prohibition!"

Jeers, applause, chanting … a cacophony of noise. Straining to hold the tiger's leashes, the smell of their musk rising with the tension. I felt their rumbling against my fishnet thighs, my bones trembling with their warning. Any moment, they would break free, their agitation unleashed on the crowd.

With a sharp whistle, I signaled Sammy. Silently, he took them and locked them in the cages, none too soon.

Police and Prohibition agents stormed the front doors, flooding the speakeasy, guns drawn. "Raid! Raid! Freeze right where you are!"

Screaming, panicked, the drunken crowd scrambled like rats. Agents closed in, forcing patrons to their feet, hands held high in surrender.

Curses and cries filled the air. The crack of billy clubs punctuated the chaos. Whistles shrieked. Glass shattered. The tang of fear mingled with the smoke of hastily extinguished cigars. Officers dragged Diamond Jim and Rossi out of the club.

The Temperance Union women stood shoulder-to-shoulder at the top of the theater piercing the chaos with their chants. "Godless sinners! Heathens! Repent! Agents of the Devil!"

Lily stood at the forefront, screaming at the top of her lungs, shaking her fist in righteous fury. But then, her eyes bulged. Her face contorted with disgust.

"It's you!" Lily's finger jabbed accusingly at me. "You flaunt your sin for profit! You'll burn for this, harlot!" Her gaze, once filled with sisterly warmth, now burned with contempt.

My brazen tuxedo, the armor of my success, symbol of dominance, suddenly weighed on me like a shroud of shame. My lungs seized up. Everything turned black and white like a slow-motion film reel of war. My heart flailed like a trapped bird.

Shoving through the Temperance protesters, I bolted for the stage door. Their strident hymns chasing me into the freezing night: "Oh, the saloons are hotbeds of sin. They're the breeding places of crime. They're the homes of the devil's own brood".

Echo murmured in my ear, honeyed and soothing, "Don't worry, Silver sweetheart. You have me. Lily can't see you anymore. You're cursed, broken. But you're mine."

My legs were dragging through thick honey, the crowd blurring into an indistinct swarm. My hands gripped the railing of Holy Sepulcher, but my fingers stuck, unable to move. I tried reciting the Rosary. "Hail Mary ... full of ... no, stop ... please ..."

Despite my prayers, Echo's pricking presence descended on me like a hive of wasps. Stinging my neck, my arms, my eyelids, her poison seeping into my blood. My hands swatted them away, growing weaker with each feeble attempt.

"Hush little baby, don't say a word." Echo sang the old lullaby so sweetly. "Rest, now, Silver. I'll handle things for a while, darling. Just close your eyes and leave it to me."

Chapter 33

1920

SILVER PRICE $1.01 PER OUNCE

CHICAGO, ILLINOIS. Echo's hacking cough echoed through the smoky haze of the White Elephant, a grim counterpoint to the raucous laughter and clinking glasses. The room swam before her eyes, familiar faces blurring into a grotesque carnival. She clutched the bar, her knuckles white, as another coughing fit wracked her body, leaving her gasping for breath.

Eddie, a splash of color in his African shirt behind the bar, juggled bottles and glasses with his usual grin.

"Hey, doll," he called, sliding her a rum and lime. "Thought you'd be celebrating soldier boy's return."

Another cough wracked her body, a deep, rattling sound that she felt inside. "I don't think he made it Eddie," she rasped, swiping away the tears threatening to spill.

Eddie patted her hand, his eyes scanning the room filled with the usual collection of regulars and ne'er-do-wells. "No show at the Peking tonight?"

Echo shook her head, triggering another coughing fit that racked her chest with pain. She couldn't admit that Zhang had turned her over to Rockwell, leaving her without a job and a roof over her head. She tugged self-consciously at her rummage-sale dress, grateful the lights were low. At least they wouldn't see how thin she'd gotten, the bones protruding from her skin.

Eddie fed an orange garnish to the parrot in the bamboo cage on the bar, the bird's squawks momentarily drowning out the sounds of the band tuning up. "They're hiring at The Gaiety."

Echo's heart plummeted. "The strip club?" The thought of baring her body for strangers turned her stomach, but the hunger gnawing at her was a powerful motivator.

"Beggars can't be choosers." Eddie shrugged, a spark of pity in his eyes.

"What makes you think I'd get a job there?" She sounded more curious than she intended.

"Legs up to your neck." Eddie winked. "And a mouth that could charm a snake right outta its skin."

She seemed to bring out the worst in men, their prurient instincts rising to the surface. A fact she'd used to her advantage. Her chest tightened, another cough threatening to erupt.

A man in a minty green jacket, his smile a bit too eager, slid onto the stool next to her. "Buy you another drink?" He pushed his wire-rimmed glasses up his nose, pointing at her empty glass with a hand that still bore traces of ink from his fountain pen.

She nodded. What did she have to lose?

"Name's Hubert Buck," he said, extending a hand with a surprisingly firm grip. "District Supervisor for Fuller Brush. Best damn brushes in the business." He beamed, proudly adjusting his Fuller Brush lapel pin.

"Broom or mop, Hubert Buck?" Echo teased, amusement bubbling up through her exhaustion.

"Linoleum or hardwood floor?" Hubert grinned over his glass. "A mop is much better for hardwood floors. It gets into all the nooks and crannies."

Echo played along. "But a broom is so much easier." She took a sip of her drink, savoring the warmth spreading through her body.

"Easier, but not as effective," Hubert countered. "A mop will leave your floors cleaner and shinier." He popped a handful of nuts into his mouth, wiping his hands on a napkin. "I can arrange a no-cost demonstration at your home."

Echo stirred her swizzle stick, popping bubbles like her fading hopes. "That would be swell if I had a home. My apartment burned down in the race riots."

Hubert's nose wrinkled. "That's terrible. What are you going to do?"

Dizziness overcame her, the room swaying, the clinking of glasses sounding distant and muffled. She clutched the bar for support, her cough erupting in a violent fit.

Hubert reached out, his hand steady on her arm. "You can stay at my place tonight," he offered.

A niggle of doubt. A man's apartment? Men were wolves in sheep's clothing. But his touch, warm and gentle, offered a fleeting comfort, and the thought of another night shivering on a park bench sent chills down her spine. Each breath felt like inhaling fire, a painful reminder of her weakened state. "Can I trust you?" She searched his salesman smile, not bad, even if he did have horsey teeth.

Hubert shrugged. "Would a dishonest man offer you a free mop demonstration?"

Could have been the craziest thing anyone ever said to her, but what other choice did she have? She couldn't take over Silver's gig, tigers scare the heebie-jeebies out of her.

She offered her arm. "Alright, Hubert. Lead the way. But just so we're clear, I prefer feather dusters. They're much more ... ticklish."

At least the scent of pine cleaner in Hubert's apartment was a welcome change from the stale beer and smoke in other joints. She sank onto his plush sofa, her cough grumbling like a the grim reaper. Maybe Hubert, with his earnest smile and clean habits promised a brighter future, a lifeline she desperately needed. A warm meal, a soft bed, a respite from the relentless cough that rattled her bones. Perhaps this Fuller Brush man was her ticket to survival.

~

ECHO'S COLD clawed its way deeper into her lungs, each breath a burning rasp. Days turned into a feverish blur of Hubert's endless fretting over dust bunnies and fingerprints. The view outside his window offered no escape: a bleak canvas of gray-on-gray, where towering buildings cast long shadows, smoke choked the air, and the relentless rumble of trains echoed through the streets.

Dr. Lawton, looking more like a ghoul than a physician, diagnosed Echo with pneumonia. His treatment? Bloodletting? This quack is a century behind the times! She winced as the needle pierced her skin, a spark of defiance in her chest. Hubert, however, fainted dead away. Figures. The big strong man can't stomach a little needle. A bitter laugh played on her lips. If she could survive this circus, she could survive anything.

Hubert, once hovering with chicken broth and blankets, now grumbled about her 'unladylike' coughing fits and the dust motes dancing in the sunlight. When he was away on his next business trip, an eviction notice arrived, a crisp, white rectangle, its words a death sentence. Three days to vacate. Apparently, Hubert had found a cleaner apartment, leaving Echo with nothing but her cough and mounting despair. Feverish and desperate, she scrawled a plea on a scrap of paper:

"*Mama,*

The Fuller Brush man was a bust. Men are all the same, Mama. They promise the world, then vanish like smoke. I'm trapped in Chicago, coughing up blood, each breath a battle. The doctor says my lungs are failing. If you don't hear from me again, know that I loved you always. Please, Mama, send what you can to Echo LaVode, General delivery, Chicago. It's my only hope.

Your loving daughter, Silver Echo"

She sought out Dr. Lawton, her last resort. With nothing left to offer but a few trinkets and scraps of finery, she bartered for his dubious care. His solution, a nightly swig of gin, burned like fire down her throat, yet offered a fleeting respite from the relentless pain. Salvation woven from desperation and burning juniper berries. But it wasn't enough. She needed Silver Dollar.

Chapter 34

1920

Silver Price $1.01 per Ounce

Chicago, Illinois. When Diamond Jim finally reopened the Four Deuces after the raid, folks couldn't get enough of my Silver Dollar Tiger Tamer show. Hottest ticket in town.

After the show, Dante Rossi appeared with an Art Deco vase of tiger lilies. "Compliments from Diamond Jim." He set them on my large vanity, the spicy scent overpowering the dressing room. "Killer show tonight, Silver Dollar. Good to have you back." He lowered his gold-rimmed glasses, revealing murky eyes. "Looks like you finally kicked that cough of yours."

I swigged gin from my flask and smiled. "Just what the doc ordered."

Leaning down to smell the tiger lilies, Rossi's leathery cologne mixed with fiery fragrance of the flowers. "How would you like to entertain a very special guest?"

A slow smile spread across my face, as I applied lipstick in the vanity mirror encircled by lightbulbs. "Important client with a taste for brunettes and tigers, perhaps?"

He spoke in a conspiratorial tone. "Dale Winter. Mrs. Diamond Jim Colosimo herself. Jim's got some business to attend to tomorrow night, and he wants to make sure she's ... occupied."

Understanding dawned. Dale Winter, the trophy wife with the smart mouth and fiery temper, was to be my captive audience while her husband conducted his illicit affairs.

"Should be a real hoot," I said, forcing a smile.

Rossi slipped me a wad of cash thick enough to choke a horse. "Have it catered, something real nice. Chinese, she loves it."

"I told you, I hate Chinese."

He wagged a finger, his smile vanishing. "Keep her company until after nine, at least."

I raised an eyebrow. "You mean keep her busy while her husband plays cops and robbers."

◈

THE FOLLOWING EVENING, I slipped into a crimson silk cheongsam, its high collar and elegant slits a nod to the Chinese feast I picked up from the Peking. I watched from behind my filmy curtains as Dale Winter's black and gold Pierce Arrow pulled up to the curb. She emerged, draped in an ermine coat. The chauffeur escorted her to the door, a reminder of the servants I'd grown up with.

I descended the narrow staircase, the silk of my cheongsam brushing against my legs with each careful step, and opened the door. Dale was checking her compact, our eyes meeting. Tall, too thin, with those piercing eyes and a pouty mouth painted a dangerous shade of red.

"Welcome, Mrs. Colosimo," I greeted her. "We're just upstairs."

"Isn't there an elevator?" she asked, eyeing the stairs with disdain.

"It's a walkup," I replied, trying to hide my amusement.

She grumbled something under her breath and followed me up, her fur brushing the walls with every step.

Inside, silk lanterns flickered, casting shadows on the tapestry hangings adorned with fierce tiger eyes. A black panther, mounted above the fireplace, seemed to watch our every move with its unnerving gaze. Bronze tiger statues stood guard on the mantel; their snarling expressions mirrored in the polished silver tray laden with delicacies from the Peking Club. The air was thick with the scent of sandalwood incense.

Dale slung her fur over the back of a cheetah chaise lounge, revealing a slinky, figure-hugging bias-cut satin gown in a champagne hue, exuding elegance and sophistication. Her eyes scanned the room, lingering on the ceremonial masks and statues. "Who's paying for all this?"

"I earn enough at the Four Deuces," I retorted, my pride stung.

"I don't think so," she sneered. "I did that gig, and I know what they pay."

"Perhaps things have changed." Cracking ice with a silver pick, I shook the lychee martinis.

We settled onto the plush velvet sofas, the tension between us as thick as the smoke curling from the incense. Over the next hour, Dale peppered me with questions, her words laced with suspicion and jealousy.

"So." Dale swirled her second martini. "Tell me, Miss Silver, what's your angle? Replacing the big boss's wife? Or perhaps you're simply trying to climb the social ladder by befriending her?"

A playful smirk tugged at my lips. "You flatter me. But I assure you, my talents lie in taming tigers, not climbing ladders."

"Clever girl." Dale's eyes glittered like splintered glass. "I used to say something like that. Keep your intentions hidden. But I see the way you shine when he's around."

I chuckled, a low, throaty sound. "Perhaps your husband's the one with wandering eyes, Mrs. Colosimo," I said, meeting her gaze. "Or maybe it's you? Freud says it's not uncommon for those who feel guilt to project it onto others."

Dale slammed her glass down, a sharp crack through the room.

"Listen up, Silver Dollar. I won't tolerate competition, especially not from some circus floozy."

My cheeks flushed, my jaw tightened. "My dear Mrs. Colosimo, such accusations are unbecoming of a lady of your stature. Besides, I'm sure a woman of your ... experience ... knows how to keep her man satisfied."

Dale fingered her five-carat diamond ring. "Oh, I do. You can bet on that."

But a defiant streak made me challenge her. "A little competition can be good for the soul, don't you think?"

The ticking Chinoiserie clock the only sound as our gazes locked in a battle of wills.

"Rest assured," I said. "If I was going to choose a lover, it wouldn't be Diamond Jim."

Dale glared at her. "I'll be leaving now."

"What about dinner?" I asked. "Peking duck."

"I never eat dinner." Dale found her handbag and stood. "If all I am is arm candy, then I'm going to be the most irresistible arm candy I can be, for as long as I can."

"Suit yourself, honey," I retorted, a sly grin tugging at my lips.

She snatched her coat, pausing to stab a finger at my chest. "Don't even think about going after Jim." She flashed her giant diamond ring in my face. "Or the police just may find my stolen ring among your things."

Her accusation hit like a gunshot as I clutched my chest.

"You'll be in city jail faster than you can say Pikes Peak." Dale swept down the stairs and slammed the door, the lingering scent of Chanel No. 5.

Only Rockwell could have told her. Panic clawed at my throat.

Echo's voice a cruel taunt in my mind. "She knows what you did. She knows everything ..."

But how does Dale know Rockwell? I squeezed my eyes shut, fighting back tears. What did he want from me?

"You know what he wants." Echo's laughter was bitter wind. "Rockwell wants his revenge."

I downed the rest of my martini, burning down my throat and leaving a bitter taste in my mouth.

∼

Diamond Jim Colosimo's black and gold casket was draped in black velvet trimmed in gold cord and topped with an ostentatious floral arrangement in the shape of a cross. A symbol of Colosimo's wealth and power, but look where it got him. The air in St. Philomena's hung heavy with the mingled scents of frankincense, gardenias, and Tabac Blond perfume. The sweetness cloaked the underlying stench of death, a morbid reminder of the man lying in the gilded casket.

What would his death mean for the Colosimo Cafe and the Four Deuces? Would I have a job after this?

I leaned over to Rossi, pale and haggard, curiously wearing a white suit for his friend's funeral. "No open casket?" No sunglasses for once. I took it for respect.

He tapped his cheek. "Couldn't make his face decent." He pressed his watering eyes.

Was it sorrow or remorse? "Where are your sunglasses?" I whispered.

"Broken," Rossi said, wiping his eyes with a handkerchief. Diamond Jim's horrific shooting affected him more than he admitted. Then again, Rossi never admitted anything.

Dale Winter sat in the front row surrounded by men who'd sat with Diamond Jim at the front table at my last show. She checked her watch, distracted.

Who's that woman and girl across from Dale?"

Rossi's breath tickled her ear. "Diamond Jim's daughter and ex-wife. Victoria Colosimo runs brothels on the South Side."

The Madam sat with studied composure. Only the faint tremor of her bejeweled hand betrayed her. Perhaps not all of Jim's secrets had died with him.

The service began and Father Dominick praised Colosimo as a 'pillar of the community' and a 'good man'. He urged the congregation to 'turn away from a life of crime' and 'live honest lives'.

"Save your breath, Father," Rossi whispered beside me.

The sanctuary crackled with an unspoken promise of revenge. Blood would be shed for this. Between whispered Hail Marys and the low drone of the rosary, the capos and their lieutenants weren't focused on salvation, but retribution. Capos, their jaws clenched tight, exchanged curt nods with their lieutenants. Fingers traced the outlines of concealed weapons beneath expensive suits.

Rumors snaked through the congregation, punctuated by the rustle of new pinstripe suits against polished pews and the nervous shifting of feet. Was it the Genna brothers? Or had Torrio finally made his move? A woman's voice, sharp and insistent, cut through the murmurs: "My money's on Victoria herself who made the hit, to get back at Colosimo for dumping her."

Finally, the service concluded. Victoria and her daughter approached the closed coffin to pay their last respects, bowing and crossing themselves before sweeping up the aisle. Beneath a mask of heavy makeup and thick false eyelashes, Victoria's full lips curled into a triumphant smirk that belied her mourning attire. She fluttered her lace handkerchief at acquaintances in the congregation like a queen surveying her subjects.

Dale Winter bent down and kissed the coffin, then wrapped her arms over it and sobbed. A large man came to walk her down the aisle. Who was that? Her new protector?

Colosimo's widows stood like sentries at the church doors, buxom Victoria on one side, young Dale Winter on the other. A silent battle for loyalty played out as mourners were forced to choose. Dark gloomy clouds gathered outside the door.

"These people are sucking up my air." Rossi's grip was tight on my hand as he pushed through the crowd. The Outfit, the bosses, the widows.

He kissed Victoria's hand and waxed eloquent condolences. But I chose Dale, shoulders slumped under the fur, her purple lidded eyes cast down. What should I say? We weren't friends. But Dale's pathetic expression touched me. I grasped my rosary in my pocket and said a quick prayer to Mother Mary.

"You!" The grief in Dale's eyes changed to cold fury. She lunged forward, her red pointed fingernails raking down my cheek. "You were in on it." Spittle flew from her mouth as she jabbed a red-tipped finger at my chest. "You and your tigers, your fancy drinks ... a smokescreen while those animals murdered my Jim."

"Dale, I had no idea!" I wiped away the warm, sticky blood that welled up.

Across the aisle, mourners surged towards Victoria Colosimo, avoiding our brewing confrontation.

"You conniving witch!" Dale lunged at me, her nails digging into my arms as she shoved me to the cold, unforgiving marble floor. My shoulder felt jammed into the socket. Stunned, I felt the icy chill of Echo to my rescues.

"Scratch her eyes out, Silver!" Echo roared in my ear. "Let her know that messing with you comes with a price."

Fueled by rage, I kicked and bucked, digging my nails into Dale's expensive fur coat. We rolled across the cathedral floor, a tangle of flailing limbs and curses. The world dissolved into a chaotic blur of red. Her lipstick smeared across her cheeks, my blood staining the marble.

Dale straddled me like a pony, her eyes blazing with fury. "You couldn't stand that I had what you wanted." Her hands clamped around my throat, her thumbs digging into my windpipe.

A strangled gasp spewed from my lips. The room swam, the faces of the onlookers blurring into grotesque masks. A chilling realization dawned on me. This is how it ends. Just like Rockwell.

The irony was as bitter as the bile rising in my throat. You reap what you sow. I'd tried to take a life, and this was my just reward.

But, suddenly, Echo's cold fury surged through my limbs and I bucked my hips, throwing Dale off balance, and scrambled to my feet.

"Mrs. Colosimo, let me help you." Rossi lifted Dale up. He made a big fuss of putting her fur around her shoulders.

I gasped for breath, sucking air into my lungs.

Dale straightened her black cloche, its netting torn and dangling. Her mouth was a macabre smear of red lipstick. Her eyes glowed hot as a blacksmith's iron as she pointed a broken fingernail. "Watch your back, Miss Silver Dollar Bitch. I'm coming for you."

I straightened my back, wincing at the pain but refusing to let it show. Dale Winter had underestimated me, but she wouldn't make that mistake again. Silver Dollar Bitch. Despite my aching throat, I smiled at my new nickname.

∾

The rain, cold and relentless, seeped through my thin coat, mirroring the chill that had settled in my heart.

"Right cheek." Rossi handed me his handkerchief, while he opened his umbrella, the black canopy a shield from the world.

I daubed at my face, streaks of crimson across the linen. "If she wasn't inheriting millions, I'd feel sorry for her."

We descended the church staircase, rain now slicking the worn marble.

"She won't touch a red cent, if she knows what's good for her."

"Then who'll inherit Diamond Jim's millions?" The air between us, wet and heavy.

He scoffed. "You can't still be this naïve, after all you've seen of his operation."

So, the Outfit would take everything, and Dale Winter would be left with her engagement ring for her trouble. I wasn't so different from Dale Winter. Tomorrow, it could be my life that was dispensable.

"So, I'm working for Johnny Torrio, now," Dante said.

So the rumors were true. Torrio knocked off Diamond Jim. Vicious as a fox, Torrio. Cunning, too. I vowed to avoid him at all costs.

"Big Jim never approved of bootlegging. Made enemies of certain people. Dale Winter's lucky to be alive."

"Something tells me she'll survive." Lightning flashed, painting the wet street silver. I shivered, remembering the feral glint in Dale's eyes. Could I be that fierce if I needed to be? A requirement in the underworld. "What about my job now?"

Rossi shrugged. "Johnny Torrio's the new boss. He's a leg man, so you should be fine." He punched my arm playfully.

Truth was that Torrio's new attention made my skin crawl. His girlfriend's jealous glare was even worse. I had no desire to become the target of Josie's wrath.

Rossi pulled me aside to avoid a jagged crack in the sidewalk, water gushing through it to the gutter. "Just keep your act fresh and pack the speakeasy, and you have a golden ticket."

There was the rub; the golden ticket felt tarnished. We'd been performing the same old razzle-dazzle for a year, and while the joint was jumping, the show was losing its bite. The roar of the crowd was starting to drown out the growl of the tigers. The tigers themselves were getting increasingly agitated, cooped up all day in the warehouse and performing at night under the harsh gaslights, surrounded by raucous people and smoky air. It was nothing like the open spaces they had at Selig, or the tropical rainforests they'd been captured from. I often wondered if they dreamed of it. Time to up my game, but I was so tired.

The rain pounded the umbrella as we maneuvered through

slick streets. "How'd your mother like the pomegranates you sent?" Rossi said.

I grimaced. "Mama said the seeds stuck in her teeth."

He laughed as we crossed the street. The Peking Club's neon sign ahead glowed in the rain, its red and gold characters shimmering like a siren's song. The scent of grease and roasted duck wafted out, clinging to me like a ghostly embrace. Had Echo walked these streets before? A chill made me shiver, desperate to escape the unsettling familiarity of somewhere I'd never been.

"How about some lunch?" Rossi said.

"You go ahead." I pointed to my awning down Washington Street. "I need to check on Topaz. She didn't look herself when I left." The tiger cub was fine, but I needed time to think.

He narrowed his eyes. "You okay?"

"Right as rain." I stepped into the street just as a tan Buick swerved into me, tires squealing on the wet pavement. My hands slammed on the hood, fingers spread wide. The car stopped; windshield wipers blurred the windshield. The engine revved and the car surged forward. I jumped back up on the curb.

The Buick screeched away, leaving me shaking. A hair's breadth from oblivion. Someone out to get me? I closed my eyes, trying to erase the glare of the car's headlights. Was this my future? A life lived in constant fear, always looking over my shoulder? Ice flooded my veins. "They'll use you up and discard you," Echo whispered. "Just another pretty bauble in their game."

Rossi bolted toward me, but I held him back. "Who was that, Dante?"

"Hell, if I know." Tension pulsed in his jaw. Didn't believe him for a second.

Thunder crashed above us, followed by a lightning bolt splitting the sky. "Let me buy you lunch at least. Their Peking Duck is out of this world." Rossi waved me under his umbrella that had felt like a safe haven before, now a trap.

"Chinese makes me sick." I waved him off, splashing in the flooded sidewalks, feeling his eyes on my back.

"That car was meant for you," Echo hissed.

"Shut up," I spat at her. How had I become part of this shadow world where I needed to watch my back, threats were a promise, and murder was an everyday occurrence? The rain soaked my hair, dripped into my eyes, and down my neck, making me shiver miserably. Was a life on stage worth the lies and lust? At least Echo was on my side. Wasn't she? I didn't know who to trust anymore, or which version of myself was real.

∾

THE RAIN-SLICKED ALLEY STRETCHED ENDLESSLY, reflecting the streetlights in a distorted shimmer. My muffled sobs were lost in the deluge as I trudged toward Holy Sepulcher church, two blocks away. Prayer always helped when I felt so lost and alone.

"Hello Silver." His voice husky with emotion, years of unspoken feelings. "I didn't know what to do when you didn't answer the door."

The rain blurred my vision, distorting the figure before me. "Impossible." My heart quickened, hope flaring against the odds. Could it really be him? The war had etched new lines on his face, a beard now covered his jaw. His uniform, once crisp, hung loose on his thin frame. But it was still him. "Carl!" A relieved laugh burbled up from my throat. "I thought I lost you."

His eyes filled with tears as he caught me in his arms, and for a moment, we held each other close, the rain beating down around us. His familiar scents of licorice and Brylcreem, now mingled with gunpowder and mildew. Memories of our nights spent huddled over his typewriter, his fingers flying across the keys as we whispered ideas about the Tabor script, flooded my mind. Those simple joys seemed a lifetime ago.

I wrapped my arms around his neck, burying my face in the

rough stubble of his beard, smothering him with kisses. "You came back," I whispered against his wet skin. "You came back."

His arms tightened around me, a haven against the storm. His warmth chased away the chill, his chuckle a melody of hope. Held so close against his heart, I felt the sinister darkness lift from my shoulders. I could face any threat, any storm, as long as I had Carl by my side.

Chapter 35

1932

SILVER PRICE $0.28 PER OUNCE

LEADVILLE, COLORADO. BABY DOE SMILED AS A PLUME of exhaust announced Carl's arrival. It had been a few weeks, and she'd missed their conversations, their shared connection to a past that felt both distant and achingly close. She included him in her prayers like family since he had courted Silver. If things turned out differently, he would have been her son-in-law. Wouldn't that have been grand?

The Tin Lizzie rattled to a stop in the rutted driveway, its engine sputtering into silence. He took off his driving cap, his gaze sweeping across the bustling scene, miners hammering and sawing, the air thick with the scent of fresh-cut pine.

"All this work for that little leak?" he shouted over the noise.

She shook her head. "Not just the leak, they're shoring up the mine so we're ready for Silver Purchase Act."

"What a boon for silver." Carl handed her the greasy brown bag. "I have good news too."

"Stopped at Hatties?" She clucked her tongue playfully and peered into the bag inhaling the sugary aroma. "That's always good news."

Carl flashed white teeth that gleamed like the movie stars'. "A little birdie told me you liked milk chocolate because it reminds you of the chocolates your husband used to buy you."

She clucked her tongue. "Hattie's clairvoyant, reading people by the donuts they choose." She pointed at him. "You like caramel coconut."

His jaw dropped. "How'd you guess?"

She reached over and swiped the coconut stuck to his lips.

"That wasn't my news, thrilling as it was." His eyes sparkled. "Warner Bros. bought the Tabor movie script."

Complex emotions washed over her, a pang of loss that their shared moments were over, a flash of pride for Carl's success, and a touch of apprehension about how the film would portray her beloved Horace. "That's fantastic, Carl. Truly. What did your family think?"

His ears reddened, a trace of hurt crossing his face. "My parents ... they don't approve of the movie industry. Devil's work, they say."

She felt a pang of regret. He'd brought her his shining success, and she had carelessly dimmed its luster. "Well then." She clapped her hands together. "We'll just have to celebrate ourselves!" Enthusiasm bubbled up in her. "How does fresh Rainbow Trout sound? There's a little creek not too far where you can catch them and cook 'em right there."

Carl's eyes lit up. "Like Huck Finn? I've never done that."

Grabbing fishing gear and the bag of donuts, they climbed the path further up the mountain. A warm breeze blew through the canyon, blue spruce shaded them from the summer sun. They set up in a sandy spot among the rocks. A raven cawed, its shadow flitting across the sunlit rocks.

"Silver Dollar caught our dinner up here plenty of times," she told him.

Carl shook his head. "I have a hard time imagining her here. She was always so glamourous, meant for the big silver screen."

"We all have different sides to us, don't we?" she said. "I lived among stage stars and presidents, but all I need now is what the good Lord provides." She dug her fingers into the silt, pulling up a wriggling worm, and threaded it on the hook. The smell of the ore-rich soil hinted at the promise of wealth, always tantalizingly close, yet just out of reach.

Carl waded barefoot into the creek. She watched him cast the line, a smile tugging at her lips. How Silver Dollar had loved to fish. Sun dappled on her shoulders. Their worries floating away with the tumbling creek. The chipmunks chittered nearby. The bees buzzing around the hive above. The mountain stream jumping and splashing. The air crisp and sweet.

Wasn't too long before Carl hooked a silvery trout. "Not going to starve today, Mrs. Tabor."

They built a small fire near the water's edge. She boned the trout, stuffing it with a sprig of wild chives and speared it with a multi-forked branch. Carl held the glistening fish over the crackling flames, the scent of woodsmoke mingling with the crisp mountain air. A wistful smile played on his lips, but a shadow flickered in his eyes. Was he thinking of Silver, of the dreams they'd once shared? Or perhaps the bittersweet taste of his success, achieved without her by his side.

They slid the grilled fish onto plates, smelling savory and making her stomach growl. They ate with their fingers. "Sweet and tender," he said, "Delicious."

When they finished, she settled back on a boulder, brushing the velvety moss with her fingers. "Tell me more about the filming. Who'll they cast as Horace?" Sticking her nose in the donut bag, she inhaled the sugary dough, choosing the chocolate one and handing him the bag.

He peered in and took one. "Maybe Tom Mix?"

She savored the chocolate. "Really? That would be swell. Mix is tall and commanding like my husband."

Carl sat up tall, shoulders back, chin lifted, mischievous grin.

Twirling the donut on his forefinger. "The Old West is not a certain place, it's in the heart."

She laughed breathlessly. "I remember that quote!"

"Did Silver tell you how she met Tom Mix?" Carl giggled.

"She told me she was starring in his movies." She huffed and rubbed a mound of kinnikinnick, smelling like sage. Another of Silver's fantastical stories.

His eyes danced. "You know Silver, always looking to make a splash. It was a big Selig studio party. We were up on the mezzanine, and she wanted to meet Tom Mix down on the floor below. Mix was surrounded by celebrities and directors, cameramen trying to take his photograph."

Baby Doe tried to picture the glamourous scene.

Carl kneeled beside her, his hands drawing the scene. "So, Silver wrapped a string of party lights around herself." He giggled. "Then, in front of God and everyone ..." Tears streamed from his eyes. "She climbed over the railing and jumped."

Baby Doe gasped, pride surging in her chest. "That's my Silver, going for broke."

"Tom Mix pushed people aside to catch Silver in his arms." Carl shook his head.

She marveled at the story. "So that's how Silver landed a part in a Tom Mix film? I thought she made it up because I never heard another thing about it."

"Naw, Mix went to another studio. Tough break for Silver. She was devastated."

"Why didn't she tell me that?" her voice cracked, her fingers tracing the worn fabric of her overalls. "She rarely wrote of her own struggles, her own dreams. It was always about the Tabor name, about making us proud." A heavy sigh fled her lips.

A cool breeze whispered through the trees as Carl set down his half-eaten donut, staring at the grease stain on the paper bag. "Silver always talked about the Tabor legacy. Bringing back the glory days. Restoring your rightful place. It became this ...

consuming idea for her. Maybe that's why she latched onto show business so fiercely. Her opportunity to shine so bright, everyone would remember the Tabors again."

Gazing up at the mountain peaks, he heaved a deep breath sounding suspiciously like a sob, all the brightness and joy drained from his face. "I should get going, Mrs. Tabor." He seemed eager to leave, have some time alone.

"I think I'll stay until the fire burns out," she said. "Can you find your way back?"

"I'm not that much of a tenderfoot." He walked away, shoulders slumped. The sound of his footsteps faded, swallowed by wind rustling through the aspen.

A twig snapped. A deer bolted through the trees, its white tail a flag of alarm. Following its path, Baby Doe's gaze snagged on a glint of metal half-hidden in the undergrowth on the opposite bank. A tangle of branches and rusted wire barely concealed the skeletal remains of one of their sprawling mine tunnels, gaping like a wound in the earth.

This could have been where the leak had started. The rushing water dug away the soil, water trickling through the rusted joints. Vulnerable and fragile, ready to collapse at the next earthquake or avalanche. Just like humans, she reckoned.

The mountain air whipped at her cheeks as she gazed at the eroding tunnel, a question mark in the burbling water. What would become of the Matchless when this excavation was over? A hollowed-out scar, the earth's treasure plundered? Then what was left of the Tabor legacy? A glimmer of doubt crossed her mind, quickly extinguished by a steely resolve. She couldn't trust it to Rockwell's hands, that was for damn sure.

Chapter 36

1921

Silver price $0.63 per ounce

Chicago, Illinois. The jazz band, their faces slick with sweat, slid into a frenzied rendition of my signature song, "Tiger Rag." Flappers in shimmering dresses and men in sharp suits swayed to the rhythm.

Carl Erikson was missing from the audience. Thank God. He'd been distant and edgy since his return, lost somewhere on the front lines. I wasn't ready for him to see my new act.

Gone were the sequins and lace; shiny leather hugged my curves, sheer black stockings gleamed, and my kohl-lined eyes held a dangerous allure.

From the cage, I heard Tamber's restless pacing, her roars amplified through the club, mingling with the screams and giggles. Timber snarled at the bars, his frustration seething. The speakeasy's chaos fueled their primal instincts. A cold knot formed in my stomach. Would they be able to focus on their new, treacherous tricks?

"Ladies and Gentlemen," the MC crooned; a snare drum grumbled through the smoky haze. "Get ready for the show of your life: Silver Dollar, the Tiger Tamer!"

I emerged in my leather tuxedo, a thin veneer of control over my trembling beneath. The bass drum pounded a jungle rhythm as the spotlight hit me, searing white. I lifted my top hat, letting my midnight black mane cascade down. Thunder from the crowd fueled my hunger for the spotlight. The tigers roared, eager for their cue. "Showtime," I said, opening the cage.

With surly glances at the sea of faces, the tigers followed. The audience gasped, their eyes wide with fear and fascination.

Two oversized balls gleamed under the spotlights, their polished surfaces reflecting the nervous excitement in the room. I gestured to Tamber. "Hop up, honey! Show 'em your fancy footwork!"

She gingerly placed a paw on the wobbling ball, then hesitated.

"Allez-Oop!" I cracked the baton against the cage.

With a defiant snarl, Tamber leapt. Four paws gripped the ball, precarious and unstable beneath her, claws digging into the surface. The ball wobbled dramatically, drawing gasps from the crowd, but Tamber regained her balance, a reluctant queen atop her perilous perch.

I pointed my baton towards Timber. "Your turn, big boy! Show 'em what you're made of!" Another crack of the baton, and Timber launched himself onto his sphere with a powerful leap. His claws dug into the rubber, a display of raw strength. The joint went wild, clapping in a frenzy of appreciation.

"Now, dance!" My voice a velvet whip cracking through the noise. The jazz band transitioned into an ominous calliope tune, its circus-like melody heightening the suspense.

The tigers waltzed, a mesmerizing dance of power and grace. The calliope melody soared, every eye in the hushed speakeasy glued to the stage. Tomorrow, the city would buzz with the memory of this night.

At the upswing of my baton, both tigers paused for a heart-stopping moment, their muscles coiled, their breaths misting the air. The calliope reached a crescendo, its notes hanging in the pregnant silence. With a commanding nod, I arced the baton over my head, commanding: "Over the rainbow!"

The tigers coiled on their haunches and sprang from the spheres, their bodies blotting out the stage lights, a terrifying eclipse of muscle and claw. Time stretched, every detail agonizing: the flash of fangs, the ripple of muscle, the sheer immensity of them hurtling over my head ... on a collision course. The crowd gasped in horror.

Miraculously, the tigers brushed past each other, landing with a synchronized thud that shook the stage, the audience leaping to their feet, their applause a thunderous roar.

I stumbled, catching myself on the edge of the stage, forcing a smile. I turned to my tigers. "Good cats," I rewarded them with chunks of raw meat, their powerful jaws snapping them up. The familiar ritual grounding me.

But an icy-hot chill crept down my spine. "Death wish, I tell you," Echo hissed. "You barely escaped disaster. Quit while you're ahead."

Echo wasn't wrong. I was about to attempt a finale more dangerous than any I'd ever tried. The knot in my stomach hardened. Would this be the peak of my success, or the beginning of my downfall? The line between courage and recklessness blurred, leaving me teetering on a knife's edge.

The lights fell, the snare drum pulsing in time with my heartbeat. Carrying two enormous, fuel-soaked hoops, I stepped onto the stage, the kerosene stinging my nose. Leather gloves on, I gripped the handles. Struck a match. A whoosh of flames, nervous chirrups from the crowd. Holding the flaming hoops out by my sides, they radiated an intense heat, my leather tuxedo offering only minimal protection.

"Alley-oop!" I shouted, my voice a whip crack. Tamber charged forward, a blur of orange and black, sailing high through the fiery ring with a triumphant roar.

The second hoop awaited. "Your turn, big boy!" But as

Timber charged, the flames flared, shooting a searing blaze towards me. I couldn't move the hoop or I'd burn Timber. The heat deepened, the leather of my tuxedo shrinking and curling, burning my arms. Gritting my teeth against the pain, I held my ground, my gaze fixed on Timber as he cleared the hoop. The crowd roared, oblivious to the near-disaster. Despite my pain, I couldn't stop now, not when I held the audience in the palm of my hand.

I circled the flaming hoops, whirling them like fiery windmills, my heart racing. The tigers' eyes locked on the moving targets. "Alley-oop!" I cried, and they leapt in unison, their massive bodies impossibly graceful as they bounded through the moving flames. Again, I spun the hoops, and again they jumped, the heat licking my skin.

My turn to tempt fate. I hopped through the twirling flaming hoops like a jump rope, their heat an almost unbearable caress. Tamber and Timber followed me, their powerful bodies leaping with an ease that belied the danger. The crowd held its breath, their gasps swallowed by the crackling fire. My lungs burned, my skin prickled, but exhilaration surged through me, a defiance of death itself.

I led the tigers to their cage, rewarding them and turning back to the crowd with a triumphant smile. Stepping into a hidden tray of water, I raised the flaming hoops above my head and let them fall over me into the water. A hiss of steam rose, baptizing me in a mystical veil.

The speakeasy exploded with deafening cheers, the stomping of feet shaking the very foundation of the building. Tiger lilies rained down on the stage like confetti, vibrant orange petals.

Then, I saw him. Carl. Leaning against the bar, his eyes, once warm and full of laughter, now held a chilling distance. It hit me like a slap: I wasn't the girl he'd left behind. I'd become a creature of fire and shadow, someone he no longer recognized, someone he no longer approved of.

While he was haunted by war, I'd embraced the rush of adrenaline that came with dancing on the edge of danger. A storm of grief washed away my joy, the cheers of the crowd fading into meaningless noise. We were two different people now, separated by disillusionment. Tears stung my eyes, hot and bitter. We'd both made choices, me chasing the spotlight, him clinging to ghosts of war. Maybe our love was just another casualty, lost in the flames.

∽

Admirers clamored for autographs, their voices a meaningless buzz. My gaze was locked on Carl. The infectious spark that once lit his eyes was replaced by a haunting emptiness. Gin and war's lingering injury had taken their toll.

The Tabor screenplay, our shared Hollywood dream, lay untouched. Now, he spoke only of moving away, settling down, dragging me into a life I never wanted. The pressure to conform, to surrender my dreams ... it suffocated me.

Reaching him, I kissed his cheek, the scent of licorice and gin heavy on his breath. "You were supposed to be home, resting," I scolded gently, ordering a Kismet for myself, the sweet fizz a fleeting distraction.

Dante Rossi materialized at my side. "The tiger truck's waiting," he announced, barely acknowledging Carl.

"Dante, you remember Carl ... my ... friend." The hurt in Carl's eyes was palpable.

"Yeah, sure. You made it back alive," Rossi said with a dismissive wave. "Outside in two minutes, Silver."

Carl's frown deepened. "I made us reservations for dinner."

"I'm booked for Mr. Torrio's birthday bash tonight." I tweaked his nose, a desperate attempt to rekindle a spark. I pulled him into a hasty kiss, a bittersweet nod of our past passion.

When I pulled back, he touched his lips, hope flickering in his eyes. "So, I'll see you later tonight?"

Time to rip off the bandage. "Raincheck for tomorrow?"

His expression crumbled, and guilt twisted my heart. A final, fleeting touch to his cheek, then I fled to the waiting truck, the cold night air a harsh reminder of my betrayal.

As the truck pulled away, I caught a final glimpse of Carl's silhouette at the door. A cold lump formed in my throat. When he'd come home, I'd hoped for a new beginning. Now, it felt like an ending, instead.

I needed Torrio's party, the roaring crowd, the thrill of the performance to numb the ache in my chest. As I slid into the truck, Rossi sneered. "You don't need losers dragging you down." He offered me his flask.

"He won't be a problem," I lied, the whiskey burning a trail down my throat. I loved Carl. Or at least, the memory of who he'd been. But was that love enough to sacrifice my dreams, the spotlight, everything I'd come to Chicago for?

∼

MY TIGER TRUCK pulled up to a house pulsating with life. Red lanterns cast a seductive glow on the ornate facade, while lace curtains veiled the windows, hinting at the pleasures within. The air hummed with a sultry energy, laughter, and the whine of a jazz band.

"What is this place? Have we been here?" I turned to Rossi.

"Not unless you're moonlighting," he chuckled, reclaiming his flask.

"Feels like déjà vu." That same creepy sensation I'd felt before. I shivered with a sudden icy chill, pressing my fingers to my temples, trying to rub away the electric buzz. Echo must have been here. I never knew where she went or what she did when she took over, but when I sensed déjà vu, I knew she'd been there before me.

"This is Victoria Colosimo's Brothel. Johnny Torrio's her nephew." Rossi took a swig.

Torrio. Hazy memories flashed warning signals in my mind.

His smooth-shaven cheeks, polished manicure. Vicious grin. Dead eyes. "Strange place for a birthday party," I muttered, heart racing. Echo had been with Torrio. Now I understood why he looked at me with those bedroom eyes. He wasn't flirting. He was remembering. Mother Mary, save me.

Sammy opened my door. I slipped him a silver dollar, a habit from my father.

"Drive Topaz around back, Sammy," Rossi instructed. "The boys will help you unload." He took my arm, leading me up the stairs.

"What if baby Topaz isn't ready for a crowd like this? No stage, no boundaries with the audience. No telling what she'll do."

"Improvise." He snickered. "By the way, an old friend of yours is in the audience tonight."

"I don't have any friends," I quipped, gulping from the flask. "Just me, myself, and I."

He wiped a drop from my lips. "JD Rockwell is here. Your lawyer friend from Denver? He's brokering business with Torrio now. Guns. Seems your Rockwell is a man of many talents."

Nausea twisted my gut. "I forgot you knew each other." Rossi had invested in the Matchless with my approval. But Mama had introduced Rockwell, and I couldn't stop her. "He's no friend of mine," I spat. "I only play nice because he holds a lien on the Matchless Mine."

Rossi's sunglasses glared from the lights. "He brought papers for you to sign. Says you owe him. What dirt's he got on you?"

My heart sank. "I haven't a clue what that weasel's up to. But you can bet it involves blackmail, misery, and nothing good for me."

"Let me know if you need help," his tone edged with danger.

My spine straightened. "I can handle Rockwell." This was between me and that snake.

The brothel interior was a decadent fever dream of red velvet, black leather, and crystal chandeliers. Victoria, the madam, greeted us, a long cigarette holder dangling from crimson lips like a smoldering exclamation point. "Welcome, Mr. Rossi." Her eyes, sharp and knowing, flicked to me. "And the multi-faceted Silver Dollar ... or are we calling you Echo this evening?" A slow smile curved her lips, and she held my gaze a beat too long. "I haven't forgotten your ... performance at my ex-husband's funeral."

My smile felt brittle. "Always happy to provide a spectacle, Madam."

"Torrio wants to see you," Victoria purred to Rossi.

I crossed the room to the grand piano, its gleaming black surface reflecting my agitation. Echo in a brothel? Don't even want to know.

Scanning the audience, my eyes locked onto Rockwell in his ivory leather hide cowboy hat and walrus mustache, seated at a corner table with a woman. May as well get the party started. I marched over, my voice clipped, "Five minutes. Then you need to vamoose."

"Silver Dollar! My, my, you've certainly made a name for yourself." Rockwell chuckled, mocking me. "Always said you were destined for greatness, didn't I?"

My blood ran cold in my veins. His companion was none other than my sister. "Lily? What are you doing here?" I grabbed her forearm. "Is it Mama? Is something wrong?"

She jerked away. "Papa would roll in his grave knowing his daughter has become a cathouse floozy."

Fury shot through me. "I'm an entertainer, Lily. The Tabors were always in show business."

"Not this kind," she said, as Rockwell slid a document across the table. "Just sign these papers, Silver, and we'll be on our way."

Rossi found me. "Showtime, Silver Dollar."

"What is all this?" I snatched the papers and started to read.

"Standard agreement." Rockwell stroked his mustache. "Ensuring all profits from the Matchless Mine are reinvested back into the company for new equipment and operations."

My stomach lurched. "All profits reinvested? What about Mama? What will she live on?"

"She'll be fine," Rockwell scoffed. "As long as silver stays strong."

"Just sign it," Lily urged. "You should be ashamed of yourself. Mr. Rockwell told me how you beg Mother for money. You don't deserve rights to the mine at all."

Her words stung. "I never ..." but I had to face the fact I had no idea what Echo did. I peered at the legalese, the words fuzzy. Why would I trust Rockwell?

"I read it Silver. It's no big deal." Rossi's sunglasses reflected the contract as he handed me his fine ink pen. "We can't keep Johnny Torrio waiting."

I'd come to rely on Rossi, and he'd never steered me wrong. With trembling hands, I scrawled my signature, the pen scratching like a raven's claw.

"Atta girl, Silver." Rossi steered me away. "Wait until they see you perform. You'll bowl them over."

"But what did I sign, Dante? What consequences does the contract have?"

A shadow crossed his face. "Now that the price of silver is so high, Rockwell needs better equipment to keep up the work. The silver market's exploding, and we don't want to miss the opportunity, now do we?" His smile felt more like a threat than reassurance.

∼

VICTORIA'S CLANGING bell cut through the brothel, silencing the rumble of laughter and clinking glasses. "Tonight, we celebrate the birthday of the new Boss. My nephew, Mr. Johnny Torrio."

Torrio emerged at the top of the stairs, a figure as dark and imposing as midnight. His black sharkskin suit and blood-red cravat exuded an air of menace. A lusty grin spread across his face as he raised his fists, basking in the adulation of the crowd.

Torrio's captains, the men who ran his gambling dens, bars, bootlegging operations, brothels ... they were all here, hailing their new king, kissing his ring. The same men who'd arranged Diamond Jim's demise. Even Rossi. The tightness in my chest coiled, ready to strike. Lily and Rockwell's disapproving glances were the least of my worries in this den of vipers.

Victoria sliced through the tension once more. "And tonight, Johnny brings us his star from the Four Deuces." The spotlight swung to me. "Silver Dollar, Tiger Tamer!"

A white-hot beam pinned me in its embrace. Tommy's bluesy tune snaked through the smoky room, a sultry invitation. My hips answered, swaying in a tantalizing shimmy that drew every eye. Topaz watched from her cage, her golden gaze burning with anticipation. My heels clicked on the polished floor as I circled the piano. A silent pact passed between us as I unlocked Topaz's cage.

A flick of my wrist, a playful bow, and Topaz rose, mirroring my dance moves with unexpected grace. We waltzed, a synchronized dance of woman and beast. The audience's gasps replaced their raucous laughter. Topaz, all 165 pounds of adolescent energy, moved with delicate precision. The crowd leaned forward, captivated, conversations paused as they watched the touching spectacle.

I caught Lily's eye; her jaw hung open watching my dance, and pride swelled in my chest. I was thrilled to have her see my talent, my command of the stage. No frightened child begging for her attention.

Holding Topaz's paws, a joyful tremor in my arms, we danced. She twirled, tail swishing, a playful swat sending me into a graceful dip.

But just as the applause thundered, a horsefly caught the light, buzzing an insistent, angry drone. Topaz reacted, her paw lashed out, becoming entangled in my hair. Pain seared my scalp as her claws dug in, her panic twisting the movement into something frantic and desperate. The graceful dance devolved into a chaotic struggle, Topaz's high-pitched snarls and growls piercing the music. I felt the warmth of blood trickling down my neck as the audience gasped. Faces, once filled with admiration, contorted in horror. Some started to rise from their seats, their cries of alarm mixing with the panicked screech of my trapped cat.

My heart pounded against my ribs, a frantic drumbeat against the chaos. Get her off! Get her off! Fear clawing its way up my throat. But how? Topaz was a fury of fur and claws, her usually graceful movements now wild and unpredictable.

The music faltered, the pianist unsure what to do. The thick aroma of Topaz's musk mingled with the fear of the audience, creating a sickeningly sweet odor. I felt the strands of my hair ripping from my scalp, each tug a jolt of agony.

"Topaz, let go!" I choked out, my voice barely audible above the chaos. "Please, let go!" But we'd never rehearsed for this, never imagined such a terrifying turn of events.

Torrio descended the stairs, each slow, deliberate step echoing ominously in the silent room. The dim, flickering lights cast dancing shadows on his face, accentuating his menacing expression. His hand, a pale inched closer to the gleaming pearl handle of his revolver. A cold, calculating glint flashed in his eyes. Torrio was a man of volatile whims, but my trapped tiger was a force of nature, poised to strike.

"Sit tight, everyone. I'll handle this." He drew his gun and aimed for Topaz.

Had to do something to stop him. "Wouldn't want to spoil that gorgeous suit with tiger blood, now, would we?" I purred, straining to control my voice. "Don't worry, Mr. Torrio. This is what you hired me for, isn't it? A little excitement for your birthday dinner?"

Gently, I pried Topaz's claws loose. "It's okay, girl." I snapped on her leash, locked her in her cage, and turned my sunshine on

Torrio. "That was the bravest thing I ever saw. Risking your life to protect your guests!" I whipped the crowd into applause, Torrio basking in their praise.

A disaster averted, but the terror lingered. My scalp throbbed, blood matting my hair.

Torrio's kiss seared my lips, his breath reeking of tobacco and power. "Come sit at my table, sweetheart." He pinched my derriere.

"Nothing would make me happier," I told him. "Give me a minute to freshen up." I needed to talk to Lily, find out what the contract really meant.

Torrio cuffed my chin. "Don't keep me waiting, gorgeous."

But Rockwell and Lily had vanished from their booth. Panic clawed at my throat. I bolted out of that smoke-filled cathouse, lungs burning for clean air. Pounding the pavement, the city lights swirled into a dizzy mess, mirroring my chaotic thoughts. Rockwell, that slimy weasel! What the hell did I just sign? And Lily ... siding with him? The nerve!

I walked the twenty blocks to the flat, pounding the pavement, the city lights swirled into a dizzy mess, mirroring my chaotic thoughts. I slipped into Holy Sepulcher. No one around. The smell of incense and absolution. I lit a candle ... for my soul, and watched it burn into a pool of molten wax.

Chapter 37

1921

Silver price $0.63 per ounce

Chicago, Illinois. Since Torrio's party, Silver had spiraled into a comatose slump, not going to the club, not answering the door, no food in the joint, leaving Echo to fend for herself.

The Peking Club looked worse for the wear, sticky carpet and stench of stale frying grease. Zhang fingered his Fu Manchu mustache. "Wish I could help you, Echo, but things ain't what they used to be. New clubs poppin' up everywhere, stealin' my customers. Hired a new dame to bring in some fresh talent. You know, the shimmy-shake kind."

Echo swallowed her pride, along with a desperate craving for the Peking duck. "Let me audition at least, Zhang. Maybe a splash of old Shanghai with some fresh ideas can spice up the act." She shimmied and shook, but her hands quaked with hunger that hollowed her out.

He puffed on his clay pipe, his sphinxlike eyes narrowing. "Frankly, Echo, you look famished."

"A bit of rouge, a few egg rolls, and I'll be a fresh peach. Please, Zhang? I won't let you down." She forced a spark in her eyes.

He jerked his thumb upstairs. "Ask for Tiny Kline. She's the boss."

Surprise jolted Echo. "Tiny's here? We danced together years ago." She climbed the narrow, dark staircase, the walls closing in like a tomb, the distant clatter of dishes from the kitchen below.

In the theater, familiar smells of hot metal, gaslight, and musty velvet curtains thrilled her. The spotlight illuminated Tiny Kline, a four-foot-ten dynamo, twirling in her iridescent costume. Bending over backward, she walked her legs over, several times in a row. Leaping across the stage like a baby deer, she turned and stopped in the spotlight, her large eyes flaring. "Hey, hey, hey! No peekers in the theater during rehearsal!"

"I'm here for an audition." Echo walked down to the stage.

Tiny shielded her eyes from the footlights. "We're already chock-a-block with dancing dames this week, sister. Ain't no room for another."

Echo bent over the footlights. "It's me, Echo LaVode."

Tiny slapped her face, a sharp crack through the empty theater. "You stiffed me on the hotel bill, you little grifter!"

Echo slapped her back. "You left me at the hospital. How'd I know where to find you?"

"I joined the Ringling Bros." Tiny's face flushed. "Didn't know where to write you."

Holding her smarting cheek, Echo stepped forward, instinctively reaching out to embrace Tiny. Five years and a slap and a hug later, they were back where they started.

Echo pulled back, lowering her eyes. "Please, Tiny. Just let me dance. Old time's sake?"

Tiny sat cross-legged on the wood planked stage. "I dunno, doll face." She examined her sparkly talons. "This ain't some two-bit hoochie-koochie show like Takka Chance."

"You know I'm a quick study."

Tiny arched her painted-on eyebrows. "I'll give you a shot, on one condition, see?"

"Name it."

"You gotta teach me that Slide for Life razzle-dazzle you were always yappin' about. I need a showstopper for Ringling's next summer, see?" She spread into the Russian splits and started stretching.

"When can I start?" Echo hacked a dry cough, vestiges of pneumonia.

Tiny planted her elbows on the floor between her splayed legs. "Go get some shut-eye, doll. Be back here at nine bells sharp tomorrow, and we'll see if you still got the chops."

Echo grabbed her small muscular hand. "Thank you, Tiny. You're a real gem."

Only problem was, Echo had nowhere to sleep. Going back to Silver's pad wasn't an option. What if Torrio showed up? She walked up to the coat check. The wooden rod creaked ominously under the weight of the forgotten coats. Dark, warm, private. She shut the door behind her and made a mattress and covers from the coats.

"Tomorrow's a new day," she told herself. But who was she fooling? The rough wool of a coat scratched against her cheek. The memory of Silver's Slide for Life disaster surfaced, the terror, the near drowning, the screaming crowds, the abject disappointment. A heavy sigh escaped her lips. If Silver Dollar failed at The Slide for Life, what chance did Echo have?

∼

By morning, Echo had transformed two coat hangers into sturdy triangles, paper menus covering their sharp edges. She stood precariously on a chair, attaching the makeshift mouthpieces to a creaking pulley. With a grimace, she clamped her jaw over the cold metal mouthpiece, the metallic taste of blood filling her mouth as she bit down. Then, with a defiant kick, she sent the chair sprawling and hung there swaying, her neck muscles pulled taut.

She counted to ten, the burning in her jaw growing unbearable. But she kept going.

A scream from above. Tiny, a blur hurtling down the aisle. "No, no, no, no. Don't do it!"

Echo let go of the mouthpiece and landed in a heap.

Tiny climbed the stage stairs and hugged Echo with her strong arms. "Echo, darling, I didn't realize it was that bad. We're going to fix that face up and make you a star. Don't you worry about a thing. I was thinking about it all night. We're going to do our sister act and be all the rage."

Echo doubled over, shoulders shaking with laughter and tears welling up in her eyes. "You're hysterical." Tiny pulled back her hand to slap her.

But Echo jumped up, grabbing the wire triangle. "I wasn't killing myself, silly. I was testing the mouthpiece for the Slide for Life."

Tiny reached up to touch the gruesome-looking triangle. "Show me how. I can use it tonight in my act."

Echo scoffed. "It's not that easy. It takes weeks to build up your neck and jaw muscles to hold your body." The pain in her jaw flared. "Ready to give this a shot?"

Tiny raised her arms, and Echo lifted her sturdy, compact body. "Grab the mouthpiece with your teeth and hang. I'll time you." Echo counted under her breath; the tendons in Tiny's neck strained taut as banjo strings. Her moans and wriggles started at ten seconds.

"Keep going," Echo said. "You're doing great."

Tiny let out a high-pitched squeal, then mewed like a kitten, a tear tracing a path through her pancake makeup.

"Twenty seconds." Echo grabbed the other mouthpiece.

Tiny let go with a defeated groan, collapsing onto the stage in a heap of feathers and sequins.

"That was torture." She snorted and rubbed her neck.

Echo bit into the mouthpiece and hoisted herself off the chair, dangling. She focused on the electric sensations starting at her jaw and teeth and radiating outward to her fingertips and her toes. Redemption pulsed with the throbbing in her jaw.

"Okay, smarty pants show me what you've got." Tiny took a pocket watch from her bag, counting the seconds which seemed like hours.

Echo posed in an arabesque; the graceful ballet moves from Silver's childhood flowing through her with newfound strength. Every muscle thrummed as if it was being played like a violin.

"Thirty seconds," Tiny chimed.

Echo undulated, her torso swaying like a swirling leaf. Her muscles prickled with new intensity, sharp and electrifying, unlike anything she'd felt before.

"One minute," Tiny chirped. "What else can you do while you hang up there?"

Echo lifted her legs to a right angle, then whipped them around creating a whirlpool effect, spinning and twirling. The lights blurred as she spun faster and faster until the theater and lights and Tiny disappeared. Her jaw ached, but she kept going, swinging her arms in counterpoint to her legs. She opened them to the splits and spun around.

"Two minutes." Tiny's mouth dropped open in awe.

Echo whirled her legs and swung across the stage, transported back to when Silver had danced for her Papa and his friends, pirouetting and leaping across the floor. The smell of cherry pipe tobacco and scotch. The pride on his face as he bragged about his daughter.

Echo jackknifed her hips and flipped over, releasing her teeth from the iron. She landed on stage in a dramatic lunge, the taste of blood in her mouth, her jaw throbbing. It was worth it.

Zhang's applause cracked like a whip in the empty theater. "Echo, doll face, where've you been hidin'? We'll change the show to 'Echo's Slide for Life!' That'll bring 'em in by the dozens!"

Felt so good to be back in Zhang's graces, back in the spotlight, not to mention back in the money she desperately needed.

Tiny whirled on Echo, fury twisting her features. "Should've known you'd pull this. Should've never given you the chance to steal my spotlight. Backstabber, that's what you are. Always biting the hand that feeds you."

Zhang clapped Tiny on the back, a patronizing gesture. "Now, Tiny, let's not get dramatic. Show business is a fickle mistress."

"Them's the breaks, kid." A brittle smile stretched across Echo's face.

"I thought we were friends. I guess not." Tiny's footsteps pattered up the aisle.

Echo had betrayed Tiny, no denying it. But what choice did she have? She had to survive, to make her own way.

"Don't worry about it, Echo. Your act'll have 'em clamorin' for more!" Zhang waved his jazz hands and left.

But victory tasted sour. Could applause substitute for the warmth of Tiny's friendship? Unlikely. And with Silver missing in action? Echo was better off alone anyway. "I'll show them all." A bitter laugh burst from her lips. "I don't need anyone." The vast emptiness of the theater swallowed her words.

Part Four

"No tree,
it is said,
can grow to heaven

unless its roots
reach down to hell."

~Carl Jung, *Aion: Researches into the Phenomenology of the Self*

Chapter 38

1932

SILVER PRICE $0.28 PER OUNCE

LEADVILLE, COLORADO. The first breath of autumn painted the aspens with gold, amidst swaths of blue-green pines. The September sun held a waning warmth, but the freezing nights warned of snow that could bury their mining operation overnight. Baby Doe shivered, not just from the mountain chill seeping into her old bones, but from a deeper worry. The task of shoring up the mine's crumbling tunnels had become a huge ordeal, draining their resources and fraying everyone's nerves. The incessant clanging, buzzing, and suffocating dust was enough to drive anyone to the brink.

Carl's arrival was a welcome distraction, with that mischievous glint in his eye and something hidden behind his back. "Going for broke, are we?" He gestured toward the activity.

"Rockwell insists," she replied. "He's convinced we must prepare for Silver Purchase Act immediately." She coughed. "He claims all the contracts will be snatched if we dilly-dally."

Carl's smile broadened. "Roosevelt buying silver again? Just in time for the Tabor movie premiere! Couldn't have scripted it better myself." With a flourish, he presented a flat blue box from behind his back. "Bauer Chocolates. For my dearest Mrs. Tabor."

They made a game of guessing the flavors, their laughter a respite from the harsh realities of the mine. The taste was so creamy and delicious that for a while the weight of the world lifted from her shoulders. This year had brought unexpected joys: her friendship with Carl, the resurgence of the Matchless. If only her daughters could share in it.

"Another chocolate?" Carl offered, his eyes twinkling.

Placing a hand on her stomach, she feigned a groan. "I'm utterly spoiled. You've outdone yourself."

Carl's gaze drifted to the miners loading building materials onto the shaft lift, their faces creased with exhaustion, their clothes caked in grime. The mules musky scent mingled with the acrid smell of blasting powder, a reminder of the dangers lurking beneath the surface. His brow wrinkled and eyes narrowed.

Was he emembering their narrow escape from the mine's depths? This Hollywood man clearly wasn't cut out for the gritty reality of mining life.

"They finally cast for the Tabor movie." He sounded strained.

She grasped his wrist. "Tom Mix? He'd be perfect for Horace! Tall, handsome, a natural leader. Who is playing me?"

"Bebe Daniels. Glamorous, blonde, with a personality as big as yours."

"But can she ride a horse? Swing a pickaxe?" Her words crackled. "I want them to know I wasn't just a delicate flower clinging to Horace. I lived with the rigors of the mountains, the mines, the hardships."

Carl nodded. "I've made sure the script reflects that." He watched the braying mules descending on the lift, the hoist groaning and creaking under the weight. "When do those poor animals get a break? It seems cruel to keep them down in the mine."

"No breaks until the excavation is finished. If the mules came up every day, they'd be scared to go back. A necessary evil, I'm afraid." One of the cruelties of mining she'd learned to live with.

"Scared of the dark, or scared of the harsh light of day?" Carl gripped the split railing. "Just like most of us, I suppose. Too scared to face the truth staring us in the face."

An enormous crack and rumble shook the earth, and she jumped up, knowing that sound was no good. Dust billowed from the mine like a monstrous exhalation. The miners scattered, panicked as the warning bell clanged, piercing through the din. A miner, his face streaked with grime, stumbled toward them. "Cave-in!" he gasped. "Charlie and a bunch more are trapped."

Her heart jumped to her throat. She jumped off the stoop, striding toward the shaft, calling out orders. "Clear the tunnel! Bring picks, shovels, anything we can get our hands on!"

Carl followed her. "What can I do? I want to help."

"Get to the Tabor fire station," she commanded. "Tell them there's been a cave-in. Bring their firetruck and the longest ladder they have."

As they rallied around the billowing shaft, fear and determination on their faces, Baby Doe tasted the ore dust of the mine. The hopeful morning had turned into a fight for survival. One thing for certain: the longer the men were trapped, the fewer of them would see the light of day.

Chapter 39

1922

Silver price $0.72 per ounce

Chicago, Illinois. Peeking out from the velvet stage curtains, I spied Carl under the juddering neon sign, drumming his fingers on the bar. The memory of his proposal still haunted me: him kneeling before me, the Burdeen's box open, the small diamond winking up.

"Marry me, Silver Dollar," he'd said with such sincerity I wanted to cry. But things had gotten even more complicated since Echo took up with Torrio, and of course, he thought she was me. I had no choice but to go along.

I'd laughed off Carl's proposal. "Torrio would kill us both," the excuse burning like cheap gin. Still, the dream of grasping Carl's ring, the promise of normalcy, appealed to me. But no way I'd survive it. Better to break it off now, while I still held sway with Torrio.

After all, I was Silver Dollar, the name on everyone's lips, reigning supreme in his hottest speakeasy. But exhaustion burrowed into my bones. Echo, my volatile alter ego, devoured the weeknights, leaving me drained, fighting for control. The roar of the crowd, the spotlight, the money ... all I ever dreamed about. Even if it meant living dangerously, dancing on the razor's edge. As

Torrio's secret paramour, he kept a watchful eye on me. Josie, his mistress for years, would undoubtedly be by his side tonight.

Carl's wave from the audience was a knife to the gut. The last time he'd be in the audience, off to his Hollywood dreamland soon, a brand new scriptwriter at Warner Bros. A hot tear traced a burning path down my cheek, smudging my thick liner. Damn Echo for putting me in this mess, forcing me to turn down his sweet proposal. No going back now. Tonight, I would shine so bright Carl would never forget me. Never forget what we had.

I inhaled the scent of smoke and perfume. The stage waited. The Echo that haunted me, the ambition that drove me—it was all I had left.

The drumroll rumbled. I opened the cage, stroked the tigers' velvety ears and snapped on jeweled leashes. The MC grabbed his microphone. "And now the woman you've all been waiting for: Silver Dollar, Tiger Tamer!"

I kicked through the curtain, leading Timber and Tamber. Gangsters whistled, pockets bulging with Torrio's cash. Rossi, in cream suit and a red carnation, kept Josie occupied while Torrio's eyes devoured me. The tigers strutted beside me, orange and black against my shimmering magenta costume ablaze with rhinestones. My black hair unfurled like a temptress's veil.

I'd amped up my act considerably for Torrio, and he rewarded me for it with a wad of bills thick enough to choke on. His brothels thrived when the crowd got riled up, and my bonuses, well, a girl could get used to them. Even if it meant the poor tigers had become nothing but props.

With a captivating smile, I sent the tigers to their pedestals and swirled off my cape. The drunken men gasped. When I ripped away one jacket sleeve, baring my glistening shoulder, a man climbed the stage and was hauled away. The audience went berserk. I had them.

Ripping off the other sleeve, I winked at Torrio in the front row. Next to him, green daggers shot from Josie's eyes. I stared back challenging her. Her five-karat ring flashed as she flipped me the bird. I turned to Torrio, a slow smile creeping across my face. He gaped, his eyes devouring every curve of my body. This was my show. Josie wasn't going to diminish my performance.

Moving with the sinuous grace of a wild animal, my body in perfect sync with the tigers, I growled and hissed, my eyes blazed, the crowd roared in response. I twirled around the tigers in a flash of fire and smoke. I leaped over them, slid beneath, a seduction of their rippling power. I crawled under their bellies, fur brushing my skin, their musky scent filling my lungs. Then, a daring caress of their faces, feeling the rumble of a purr vibrate through me.

The men's nostrils flared, their breaths panting rapidly. Playing with fire, I tempted fate. The tigers brushed their claws through my waist-length hair, the audience gasped. I felt my scalp burning, a shudder of pain down my spine. But the crowd ate it up. A ecstatic grin spread across my face.

My gaze locked with Torrio's as I prowled across the stage, every step a silent invitation. The springboard propelled me into a graceful arc, landing me atop the tigers with a triumphant flourish. The crowd erupted, their cheers fueling my every move. The music throbbed, a sensual pulse echoing the wild beat of my heart. I became one with the beasts, my body a sinuous extension of their own. An arabesque melted into a handstand, my legs parting slowly, seductively, until I straddled their backs. The air hung heavy with the scent of danger, a wild, triumphant drumbeat in my chest. Torrio's dark gaze locked onto mine, burning with desire.

My stomach fluttered, a mix of guilt and a dangerous thrill I couldn't suppress.

At the next table, Carl cheered louder than the rest, his eyes bright with pride, intense longing shadowing his smile. I bit my lip, a pang of guilt stabbing my heart, but I pushed it down.

My sharp whistle sliced through the tense air. On cue, the tigers sprang up, joining front paws, forming a magnificent archway. They roared in unison, the sound vibrating through me as I launched into a back walkover. With another roar, my tuxedo jacket ripped free, raining sequins like scattered diamonds.

Next, a front flip, sailing through the tigers' living arch, and the second layer snapped off, magenta silk swirling in the air. The tigers swayed with me, their eyes burning with a shared passion, roaring with each dramatic reveal. It was a dangerous dance of daring and rebellion.

With a final, gravity-defying flip that sent a gasp through the crowd, the last layer of fabric tore away, revealing a scandalous black G-string and cascading silver tassels. This wasn't vulnerability; it was a defiant roar against expectations. The spotlights narrowed, a blinding halo erasing everything but me. The frantic music, the tigers' receding forms, even the intoxicated cheers of the crowd, all vanished as I became the spectacle. My spinning tassels pulsed with the power to fill that aching void inside, my purpose ignited in the spotlight's blaze. This was where I belonged. The eruption of applause surged through my veins. I soaked in the swell, savoring every whistle and cheer. Torrio, a dark specter amidst the faceless blur, blew a torrid kiss. I returned it, the motion automatic. Only the spotlight mattered.

Finally, the lights blinked out, darkness falling. Sammy's touch startled me as he placed the fur coat around my shivering shoulders. The roaring adulation left behind a silence so profound I felt it in my empty soul. Why did the high of the performance always fade so quickly, leaving behind a craving even fiercer than before?

In the cabaret's dim haze, Josie stood, silhouetted by the lights, her red sequined headband a devil's crown. Her face, contorted with rage, twisted toward the stage. With a snarl, she yanked a Little Humdinger from her garter, aiming it squarely at my heart. "The show's over, Silver."

In an explosion of light and sound, the gun blasted, spitting fire and lead. The jazz band screeched to a halt. My heart pounded in my throat as the bullet traveled through the haze, aimed directly at me. Josie's eyes glittered with hate and triumph.

A man raced with impossible speed, the surrounding scene in slow motion. As Carl shoved me aside, a gasp tore from my throat. The bullet ripped into his upper chest at full force ... spurting blood through his shirt. He fell in a crumpled heap at my feet with a sickening thud that shook the stage. The reverberation rang in silent waves as the audience watched, mouths open. Carl writhing. Silence. My ears ringing without sound.

Then suddenly the percussion set toppled, cymbals, drums, maracas clamoring on the floor, the band running with their bass and saxophone and brass. Women screamed and tore at their hair, running out. Men drew their Colt 1911s and .38 Specials, the glint of steel catching the light, aiming at the stage. Yelling. Cursing.

I knelt beside Carl, my hands trembling on his cheeks. Blood blooming on his chest. "He's shot! We need help!" I yelled, pressing Carl's pocket square against the wound. The coppery scent of his blood filled my nostrils and throat as it soaked through the fabric in seconds. Frantically, I grabbed his jacket, pressing it against the growing stain.

"Everyone out!" Rossi barked. "Take the boss and his girl!" His thugs hustled Josie and Torrio away.

"Hold on, Carl," I begged, the stench of blood and gunpowder overwhelming.

Sirens wailed. "We gotta go!" Rossi grabbed my arm.

"No!" I pulled away. "I'm not leaving him!"

Police flooded in. Rossi cursed and fled. Blood pooled around Carl, vivid evidence of the violence I'd invited into his life.

"Help him!" I screamed, the world screeching to a halt. Carl, my sweet Carl.

Police restrained me as they carried Carl away, leaving a trail of blood on the wood floor. My vision swam with tears. "Carl ..." A sob escaped my lips, a raw, guttural sound. He didn't deserve this. I brought him this pain. If he dies, it's on me. And with that realization came a surge of determination. I won't let him die. And if he lives, I will let him live the life he deserves to live, without all this darkness. Without me.

∽

The scissors felt cold against my skin, their sharp points a tempting invitation. In the dressing table mirror, a stranger stared back. Hair a tangled mess, eyes hollow with despair. The tigers roars below, once my pride, were now a reminder of the blood I'd spilled for fleeting fame.

Echo's voice slithered through my thoughts. "You deserve peace." A lie coated in honey, tempting me towards oblivion. But what awaited me on the other side? Would it be the sweet release of heaven, or the eternal torment of a soul lost in the abyss?

A sharp knock at the door made me jump. Torrio, ready to claim his revenge? The police? Another knock. I was trapped. By Torrio, by my choices, by this mess of a life.

The lock clicked. Heavy footsteps on the stairs. No place to hide from my fate. I dug the scissors into my flesh, the sharp points biting deep. At least I'd be the one to end it.

I was shocked to see Carl in the doorway, his arm in a sling, head bandaged. He shouldn't see me like this. His gaze snapped to the scissors, his face draining of color. He stumbled toward me, his hand reaching out to ward off the unthinkable.

I forced a laugh, hoping he bought it. "Just cutting my hair. It's such a mess from the tigers."

Relief flooded his face, quickly replaced by a flash of hurt. "Why didn't you say goodbye at the hospital?" His breath was ragged. "Taking a bullet for you doesn't count for much now?"

My cheeks heated, ashamed of what happened. Ashamed of leaving him. Ashamed of my life. "The nurse told me you were sleeping after they extracted the bullet from your shoulder. Told me to come back tomorrow. They released you?"

"Walked out." He shook his head. "I figured I needed to get out of here, before Torrio comes after me." He winced, shifting slightly. "I can recover on the train."

"You're still going after all this?"

"It's Hollywood, Silver." He stood behind me, his reflection in the dressing table mirror a mix of hope and regret. "Warner Bros.? Doesn't get much better than that." He took the scissors from me, setting them on the dressing table. "Don't even think about cutting your hair. Everyone knows your act by that ebony mane." His tone was wistful.

"There won't be an act after tonight." I scoffed, bitterness rising. "Torrio will shut it down."

A frown creased his brow. "No need to pretend with me, Silver. Everyone knows you're Torrio's now. Next, you'll tell me I was foolish to think we had something special." His voice shook with anger and pain.

I flinched. The air crackled with words I wasn't ready to say. Carl saving me from the bullet was a selfless act wasted on someone like me. I had to face it. I was a liar, a cheat. To Carl, to Josie, to myself. Was Carl here for an apology? Or was he trying save what we had? Regardless, Torrio would never let me go. Not now.

"Here, let me brush your hair out." Carl picked up the tortoise brush, a Christmas gift last year. "Heat up some hot oil later, it'll loosen the tangles. Think how much better it'll look on stage." His touch, once comforting, now a poignant memory of a happier time. "My train leaves soon."

I touched his hand. "Don't go." The words stuck; it wasn't fair to hold him back.

"Even if I stayed, would it change things between us?"

I glanced away, unable to meet his honesty. He brushed through the snarls, his touch gentle as he worked through the tangled mess. Our silence stretched, fragile. Finally, our eyes met in the mirror, and I saw the miserable truth in his gaze. He knew the darkness in me now, the choices I'd made. A sob tore from my throat, raw with shame, with a sudden, painful understanding.

He finished brushing, my mane bright and shining. A miracle despite my betrayal.

"Please stay," I choked out, my hand reaching for his. "Get another job."

"Who pays your bills, Silver?" he scoffed. "Torrio wouldn't appreciate his girlfriend having a roommate, especially not me." Sorrow shadowed his face. "Silver, even if ... I don't know how anything could be the same between us." He checked his watch, grimacing. "I'll miss the train."

"Then write to me," I pleaded. "Send your address."

He leaned in, his kiss featherlight on my cheek. Before he could pull away, I clung to him, my lips crashing against his. My pulse raced, a frantic drumbeat of love and despair. I might have broken us forever, but a desperate hope flamed within me.

He pulled away, his gaze lingering, a storm of longing and resignation swirling within its depths. With a sad shake of his head, he tossed me the apartment key. The brass clamored on the vanity like a death knell. My fingers traced the cold metal, once a symbol of shared dreams, now a mockery of the love I'd traded for fool's gold. Shiny, but worthless.

Chapter 40

1923

SILVER PRICE $0.67 PER OUNCE

CHICAGO, ILLINOIS. THE FOUR DEUCES WAS SHUTtered, Torrio and Josie fugitives on a luxury liner to Italy. Silver, shattered, retreated into the labyrinth of her mind, leaving Echo to seize the opportunity to shine at the Peking Club.

Tiny's brilliant red curls bobbed as she descended the aisle, her eyes fixed on Echo's rehearsal as if engraving each move on her brain.

"So are you stalking me or trying to steal my act?" Echo asked. The question, sharp with longing for their lost friendship, hung in the vast theater.

"You backstabbed me and snatched my spotlight, you two-faced floozy!" Tiny said.

A twinge of something like guilt, but Echo would not admit it. "What if we worked up an act together?"

"Oh sure, and we can call it 'Beauty and the Fairy'." She poked Echo's chest. "I'm tired of being the brunt of jokes. I wasn't born with your looks. I have to work twice as hard and kiss a few toads to get anywhere."

Echo's giggle reverberated through the theater. "I've missed you, Tiny girl." Warmth spread through her as her lips lifted in smile. "The audience won't be laughing at you Tiny, I promise."

∼

Echo and Tiny had trained for months, hanging by their jaws on the cables, building up their neck muscles to hold their bodies up on the pulley. When Tiny wanted to quit, Echo wouldn't let her. They were going to succeed and succeed together.

When they were strong enough, Echo taught Tiny the routine. Using fans from Chinatown, they synchronized the movements of their arms and legs, practicing over and over until everything ached. They worked on their costumes, cutting out cardboard wings, and gluing on bags and bags of white feathers. Every night, Echo iced her jaw to ease the throbbing.

Finally, they were ready to perform.

Dressed in feathered wings and sequined white leotards, Echo and Tiny perched on opposite ceiling ledges of the Peking Club. Echo could see the audience shuffling in for the sold-out show.

Echo's heart skipped a beat as she recognized Silver Dollar's cousin Andrew guiding Aunt Tilly into the third row. Silver's mama, Baby Doe, had written about their fondness for vaudeville shows and Andrew's search for a wife in a recent letter with a faded photograph. Perhaps her performance tonight could make a good impression on Silver's relatives. Maybe then, she could win back Silver's heart.

According to Baby Doe's letter, Andrew and Silver had been betrothed, but Aunt Tilly reneged when the Tabors lost their money. But now with the price of silver soaring, Aunt Tilly deemed Silver a worthwhile candidate for marriage.

A sudden ache twisted in Echo's gut. She thought back to her own lost soldier, Jeffrey. She'd come so close to having someone who cared for her, loved her for herself. The prospect of marriage was something she'd never have.

Echo moved her jaw side to side to ease the pain. She heard the audience twittering with excitement, their anticipation palpable. This was it. The moment she and Tiny had worked so hard for. She glanced over at Tiny perched in the other corner of the ceiling, her smile hard, a glint of ambition in her eyes Echo hadn't noticed before.

When Echo heard the opening notes of "Angels Watching Over Me", she signaled Tiny. Together, they bit down on the mouthpieces and leapt off their ledges. They fluttered their expansive wings and glided over the audience on cables. The wind whooshed through her hair, adrenaline coursing through her veins. Flying like this was the freest she'd ever felt. As close to real angels as she may ever get. If her jaw just held out.

Tiny and Echo danced and twirled through the celestial choreography Echo had created; their legs poised in beautiful arabesques. The audience oohed and ahhed at their stunning acrobatics. It made her pain endurable.

But then, a sickening crack echoed through the theater. Echo's molar shattered against the mouthpiece, a jolt of agony radiating through her jaw. Her joint buckled, and with a strangled cry, she plummeted towards the unforgiving stage.

Her foot caught on the wood floor, and her ankle twisted with a pop, not the sharp crack of bone breaking, but a sickening, twisting sensation. No, no, this can't be happening!

Her dance career flashed before her eyes, the countless hours of practice, the triumphs and setbacks, all ending here in a pathetic heap. The audience groaned, their faces contorted in horror.

Tiny landed on the stage and ran over. "Let me help you up."

Echo shook her head, tasting blood and feeling her loose tooth. "Keep going, Tiny."

"I can't do it without you. The dance is two angels, not one." Tears dropped on Tiny's cheeks.

"Then dance for both of us." Echo spit out a piece of her broken tooth.

Tiny returned to the pulley, bit down on the mouthpiece, and the cable rose. As the spotlight found her, Tiny transformed into a dazzling angel. Dancing above the fallen Echo, her angel wings glowed, her tears fell like diamonds to the stage. Tiny's eyes sparkled as the audience gazed up awestruck, applauding.

Cousin Andrew knelt beside her, concern wrinkling his handsome brow. He helped her up with strong arms, and she hobbled on her sprained ankle.

"Mother and I insist on taking you home with us, Silver Dollar." Andrew was gentle, but firm. "We're family after all." His strong arm lifted her and carried her to their carriage.

Warmth spread through her, a flicker of hope ignited in her belly. Echo, nestled in the carriage's plush seat, felt a glimmer of something unfamiliar. Hope. She'd always been the bad girl, a thrill for men, but perhaps this was a chance to be something more.

∼

ECHO'S ANKLE pulsed with a dull ache from the fall. Yet, the crutches Andrew offered became an unexpected key, unlocking a world previously unknown. Each Wednesday and Sunday, they'd make their way to Our Lady of Sorrows. The heady incense and mournful hymns were foreign to Echo, but for Silver, they were a lifeline. Echo played along, mouthing unfamiliar prayers, her mind a whirlwind of plans.

The charade went beyond church. She was now Silver, the doted-on niece, swept up in Aunt Tilly's extravagant shopping trips. Each new purchase—dresses, gloves, scarves, stockings—was another layer of disguise, another step away from the girl who'd danced for her supper. "In for a penny, in for a pound!" Tilly's motto mirrored Echo's survival instincts.

Evenings were spent sipping mint tea on the porch, the fragrant steam a poor substitute for whiskey. Gin rummy with

Tilly replaced the smoky haze of the club, but Echo found a new thrill in outsmarting her aunt and Andrew.

Dinner, served by silent staff, was a vast improvement from the take-away food she'd known in Chicago. The clinking of silverware, the hushed conversations, the warmth of belonging—it was intoxicating. Could this be her life? A life of ease, far removed from her precarious past?

Andrew's thick spectacles magnified the earnestness in his eyes, while the subtle scent of bay rum from his hair pomade wafted toward her. Could she truly make this work? Could she bury the truth of her past deep enough to forge a life with this man?

She confessed to the priest about her desire to marry her cousin. A heavy silence lingered in the confessional and then he strictly forbid it. Why couldn't she? Lily had done it! Echo rose from the confessional, her jaw set. She would find a way.

⁓

AFTER AUNT TILLY retired for the night, Andrew led Echo into their grand library, his sanctuary for after-dinner reading. Towering shelves held countless leather-bound volumes with gold-leaf titles. Echo could imagine spending hours nestled in the wing-back chair by the leaded-glass window, lost in worlds of words and imagination.

Her fingers trailed along the book spines. "Do you have a favorite Jack London?"

"*The Call of the Wild*, of course."

"Too brutal. Too sad." Echo shivered. "I prefer *The Valley of the Moon*. A couple finds paradise in California. It made me dream of such happiness."

Andrew slid open a hidden panel, revealing a well-stocked bar. "Choose your poison. Canadian whisky, rye, or brandy."

"Andrew, you're full of surprises," Echo said, impressed. "I'll take the rye." These weren't the usual bootleg brands, but the genuine article, smuggled from Canada—likely by Silver's connection, Torrio.

He poured generous portions into crystal tumblers, slipping something into hers before handing it over. "To surprises." Their glasses clinked, his owl eyes steady on her through his thick lenses.

Something glimmered at the bottom. "What's this?" Echo fished out a diamond solitaire, its sparkle unmistakable compared to the paste jewels she was accustomed to. Heat rose in her cheeks as she met Andrew's eyes.

"It was my grandmother's," he said softly. "But it's yours now."

Echo examined the small, flawless gem. "Is this a proposal?" She took a gulp of rye.

"I asked Mr. Rockwell for your hand," Andrew confessed, his cheeks flushing. "He gave me his blessing."

Echo choked on her drink. "Why would you ask him?"

"Mother insisted. He's your father's power of attorney, after all."

"I'm a grown woman," Echo retorted. "I can make my own decisions."

Andrew finished his rye. "It wasn't so much about marriage as it was about the dowry."

"Dowry? I have nothing to offer."

"Mother thought it prudent to inquire about the Matchless Mine. It's doing quite well, you know. Of course, Baby Doe could stay on, but she's getting on in years. Mother thought we all could move to Leadville and oversee the operation."

Her smile faded, her grip on her glass tightening. "So that's why your mother wants this marriage?" Her throat constricted, the dream of her new life shattered.

Andrew's Adam's apple bobbed. "To be blunt, this house is facing foreclosure. A loan, with the Matchless as collateral, could save it."

The words pierced Echo's heart like shards of ice. She was no woman with dreams, but a commodity, a key to unlock the Matchless Mine. Her life—laughter, love, freedom—shattered, leaving a familiar hollow void. Echo was a pawn, her value measured not in warmth or wit, but in cold, calculating silver.

She refilled her glass, her hand trembling. The rye whiskey burned a fiery trail down her throat, its spicy warmth a stark contrast to the icy realization settling in her stomach. "You and Aunt Tilly are the only family Silver Dollar has in Chicago." The words rang hollow.

He winced. "Must you refer to yourself in the third person?"

"My goodness," Echo struggled to maintain her composure. "This rye packs a punch."

"I like you dizzy." He poured her another. "Mother is quite fond of you, as am I." He raised his glass. "To keeping it all in the family."

"All in the family." Echo's anger burned her throat as she drained her glass. She excused herself, her mind racing as she packed her new wardrobe into her trunk.

Later, in the quiet of the night, she found Aunt Tilly's Chinoiserie jar of petty cash. She slipped a few bills out, then hesitated. "In for a penny, in for a pound," she murmured Tilly's words. She took the entire roll, then called for a taxi on the house phone.

As the cab sped away, Echo pressed her cheek against the cold window. Her fingers tightened around the money. She wasn't innocent, not by a long shot. But she felt no shame. Instead, a bitter amusement rose within her. Echo was swindling them even as they tried to swindle her.

Chapter 41

1932

SILVER PRICE $0.28 PER OUNCE

LEADVILLE, COLORADO. THE WIND CARRIED THE ACRID scent of ore as Baby Doe gazed into the collapsed mine, a jagged tomb that had swallowed the lives of five good men. Beside her, Rockwell, his empty sleeve flapping around the end of his arm, chattered on about the disaster. Meaningless noise.

Five lives lost. The weight of the mountain pressed down on her chest, suffocating her. Charlie, her rock, lay gasping for air in St. Vincent's Hospital. All for the insatiable greed of tearing silver from the earth.

Fifty years she'd chased this dream, witnessed countless miners die for meager wages, all to line the pockets of mine owners. How many lives had been ground into the dust that had paid for her elegant dinners, her mink slippers, her gilded carriages? She'd mourned them, but now her grief felt hollow compared to this crushing guilt. She had to make amends before it was too late.

Rockwell, oblivious to the blood on his hands, droned on about the Silver Purchase Act, contracts, windows of opportunity, eager to send men back down into the unstable mine.

"No." The word ripped from her throat. "I won't risk more

lives. The earth needs time to settle before we even consider shoring it up again."

"Other mines are snapping up those contracts as we speak." Rockwell scoffed. "Come on, Baby Doe. This is what Horace wanted. We've been waiting for this moment since the silver crash."

The silver that once glittered in her dreams now felt like lead in her gut. Tears blurred her vision. "Horace would never have traded lives for profit," she rasped, thick with sorrow.

"Horace isn't here, Baby Doe," Rockwell snapped. "But I am. And I won't let you squander this opportunity."

She steeled her nerves. "You pompous, one-armed fool! Do you think I'll stand by while you turn my mine into a graveyard?"

"I'm afraid you have no say in the matter." He jabbed his polished boot toe into the ground, kicking dirt into the mine shaft. "You gave me power of attorney. Your daughters signed the same documents. Rossi's group now controls the mining company. I'm managing partner."

Her knees buckled and she grasped the wooden rail for support. "My daughters would never join you against me." Well, maybe Lily would. She never returned her letters. But not Silver Dollar. Never. Her gaze drifted toward Turquoise Lake, but its serenity couldn't soothe the ache of betrayal.

"Let me spell it out for you." Rockwell dripped with condescension. "You gave your daughters twenty shares each. I've accumulated eighteen over the years for my services. And you traded Rossi another twenty for his investment. We all pooled our shares with Rossi." He wiped his dusty glasses on his sleeve with his one good hand.

"You poisoned them against me?" she spat. "Manipulated them, twisted their love into greed." A sob caught in her throat, but she refused to crumble before this vile man.

Rockwell's smirk broadened. "You should be grateful to me, Baby Doe. The Tabor legacy is being resurrected."

Her laugh was brittle. "This is no legacy, you vulture. It's a travesty." Fury colder than the mountain blizzard surged in her. She couldn't let this man destroy everything she'd lived for.

Rockwell shoved past her, nearly knocking her into the gaping shaft.

Baby Doe steadied herself, her grip tightening on the weathered railing. Now was the time to catch him off guard if she ever was going to. "Rockwell," her voice sharp as a pickaxe, "where were you when Silver Dollar was killed?"

His fancy cowboy boots skidded to a halt. He flinched, his one good hand clenching the brim of his hat. The wind howled through the headframe, a mournful echo of her unspoken accusation. Slowly, he turned to face her, his face a carefully constructed mask of composure.

"I could never forget the moment I heard about the tragedy," he said, his voice hoarse. He removed his hat, staring into its depths as if searching for the right words. "I was in the hospital, recovering from the hunting accident that took my hand. I was devastated. You know how much I loved Silver Dollar."

But his performance didn't fool Baby Doe. "You loved her enough to turn her against me?" she challenged.

Rockwell sighed heavily. "You don't understand, Baby Doe. I'm looking out for you as I always have. You'll thank me for this when you get your payout from the excavation." He plunked his hat back on, a final flourish. "Now let me get on with it."

An odd pang of disappointment flared in her chest. So, maybe he didn't kill Silver ... But her anger remained, a white-hot flame. He stole control of the mine. Manipulated her daughters. Sacrificed the lives of innocent miners. This was a betrayal of her trust, a desecration of everything the Tabor family stood for. The Matchless Mine would not become a monument to Rockwell's greed. Not on her watch. "I will not go down without a fight," she vowed, her heart pounding. "Not while I still draw breath."

Chapter 42

1924

Silver price $0.69 per ounce

Chicago, Illinois. "Hey, Silver Dollar! You look like you could use a shine." Josie filed her nails, dripping sarcasm as I rehearsed the tigers.

Torrio had returned with her from Italy and reopened the Four Deuces, installing a gilded cage on stage to separate me and the tigers from the audience. Three years his prisoner, choking on the stale air thick with the stench of desperation. Each thud of the bass drum hammered spikes of fear through my chest. I longed for the fresh air, the trees, and the flowers of the nun's garden at Holy Sepulcher—my only refuge.

And the tigers. Those poor, magnificent creatures with their haunted eyes and mangy fur. They used to roam free in the fields behind Selig Polyscope. Now they were nothing but props, their spirits broken. My heart ached for them.

I'd begged Torrio to return them to the Selig Zoo near Hollywood, where Carl lived. Torrio just laughed, his teeth sharp and eyes cold. The tigers were his property now, he said, and when they got too old or crazy, he'd simply replace them. Just like he did with women. Besides, Carl rarely answered my letters anymore.

Josie, finished with her nails, slithered over to Torrio, draping herself on his arm like a prized possession, a smug reminder that she was Torrio's favorite. They exited, her laughter drifting behind them. Now he kept three of us on leashes: his dutiful wife in Oak Park, Josie the mistress, and me, locked away like a jewel in his crown. I seethed with indignation at my plight. Josie loved to flaunt her status, her painted face a sneer of triumph. I craved something more than this sordid, gilded life, where I was merely a trophy. I never knew when Torrio would show up, lustful and demanding, though his visits had become less frequent, which bothered me also.

I retreated to my cramped dressing room, the scent of tiger musk and sweat hung in the air. My muscles ached and my eyelids heavy. Two shows a night on weekends, and whatever Echo was up to during the week drained me empty.

"Face it, honey, those wrinkles are canyons now," Echo hissed. "Your hands are like claws. Look at those showgirls, half your age, twice as pretty. Torrio's going to trade you in for fresh meat soon enough."

I squeezed my eyes shut, trying to block out her poisonous words and the images they conjured.

But Echo wouldn't be silenced. "Think he'd marry you after all this time? You're damaged goods."

A sob welled in my throat. As much as I hated to admit it, Echo was right. I'd be thirty-five in December, and the new girls had creamy skin and figures that stopped men in their tracks. I had to starve myself to keep up, and the wrinkles were starting to show.

My rosary beads, once a source of comfort, now brought only discordant arguments in my head. I needed Madam Theodesia. It'd been too long. Could she see a future for me beyond Torrio's clutches?

The scent of cinnamon and incense mingled in the dimly lit room. My eyes gradually adjusted to the vibrant tapestries and towering plants. We sat in wicker peacock chairs, a carved elephant table between us, its polished surface reflecting the swirling depths of the crystal ball.

Madam Theodesia, swathed in purple and gold, had aged since our last encounter. Her once-vibrant eyes were clouded, a milky veil obscuring their depths. Her wrinkled fingers, adorned with heavy rings, traced the crystal ball. After several minutes, a deep frown creased her brow, her fingers pausing as if snagged on an unseen obstacle.

"Is everything alright?" I whispered, anxiety tightening in my chest.

"Ah, child, your spirit is heavy with the weight of jealousy and longing." Madam Theodesia's prediction, honeyed and soothing, was never-the-less disturbing. "But do not despair, for even the darkest night holds a hidden moon."

A cold fist squeezed my heart. "That's why I'm here, Madam. My rosary beads used to bring me peace, but now they feel like empty stones, my prayers drowned out by doubt and confusion." Echo's mocking laughter rang in my ears, the cruel sound of her hold on me.

"I see the man in your thoughts, a flame that still burns within you. But the path you chose led you away from him, into the arms of another. And now, your heart yearns for escape, for a life lived in truth and not in shadows."

"Escape." A sigh of longing. "To be free of this deceitful life, to build something meaningful, something I can be proud of. But honestly, I don't even know what that looks like anymore." An anvil weighed down my chest. "And the tigers ... What will happen to them if I leave."

Madam Theodesia sighed, her milky gaze reflecting a lifetime of sorrows. "The path ahead is murky, child. It takes time to find your way back after straying so far. There is something else, a force within you, resisting the change you seek."

A chill prickled my spine, goosebumps rising on my arms. "It's Echo. Can you make her shut up?"

"Hush, child. She's part of you. You can't ignore her, only learn to live with her. Embrace her fire, her passion." Her milky eyes seemed to pierce through me. "She was your protector, but you pushed her away. Now she's hurt, lashing out. You gotta make peace with that part of yourself you're hiding from."

My stomach knotted, a familiar ache of guilt and shame. "How?" I choked out.

"Find a quiet place, somewhere pretty. Sit with your Echo, listen to what she's trying to tell you. Learn to love her, even the parts that scare you. That's the only way you'll find peace, and the will to build the life you want."

A sliver of hope pierced the gloom. "Thank you, Madam Theodesia. For everything."

Her smile faded, replaced by a worried frown. "Be careful, child. This ain't gonna be easy. There's trouble ahead you don't even know about."

Outside, the city was a cacophony of noise and lights. I tried to picture Echo next to me, not as a monster, but as a wounded part of myself who wanted to be seen and loved. Maybe the old lady was right. Maybe running away wasn't the answer. Maybe I needed to face my demons head-on.

But can I really do it? The taste of doubt bitter on my tongue. Can I forgive Echo for all the damage she's done? And even if I could, would it be enough to silence the storm raging within?

∿

GLASS SHATTERED IN THE NIGHT, yanking me from a fitful sleep. I lunged for the window, the frigid air biting at my exposed skin like a swarm of angry bees. The street below was a sea of white, the pointed hoods bobbing like grotesque buoys on a tide of hate. My stomach clenched, a wave of nausea rising in my throat as the chant of "White supremacy forever!" reached my ears. A noose swaying from the makeshift gallows sent a jolt of terror through me, cold sweat beading on my skin.

A chilling sense of déjà vu washed over me. I'd lived this before. The shouting, the anger, the sickening dread. But it wasn't *me* who'd experienced this firsthand. It was Echo. Her terror, a specter from the past, melded with my own, amplifying the fear until it pulsed through my veins.

The realization that they were marching toward Holy Sepulcher hit me like a punch to the stomach. Had to warn the nuns.

Fear turned my legs to lead, but adrenaline surged, propelling me forward in a desperate flight. Barefoot on the icy floorboards, I snatched my coat and rosary, fumbling down the creaking back stairs. The alleyway was a nightmare of shifting shadows. Splintered wood shards crunched underfoot. The guttural roar of hate ricocheted off brick walls. A broken bottle glinted in the moonlight, reflecting the flames of a burning cross. The perfume of moon flowers couldn't mask the stench of smoke. They were everywhere, a chaotic wave of hatred spreading through the streets.

∼

WHEN I REACHED HOLY SEPULCHER, the heavy doors were barred. I pounded on them, my heart a frantic bird in my chest. The footsteps and hateful shouts grew closer. With shallow breaths, I ran to the side gate, ringing the bell wildly. But inside, the sisters sang hymns, oblivious to the approaching storm.

Panic flooded my veins. I yanked at the iron gate, its unyielding bars a cruel reflection of my own trapped life. What would they do to the nuns? I wriggled between the cypress trees, their sharp needles tearing at my skin, a penance for my sins. The mob pressed against the church doors, their collective breath a hot wind carrying their venomous words. Squeezing deeper into the prickly refuge, I prayed the trees would shield me. But surprisingly, there was no fence. I slipped into the convent's embrace.

"Miss Tabor, what are you doing here?" Startled, I looked up to see Sister Paulette. Her crisp coif and shadowy gray habit made her seem an heavenly figure in the sinister night.

"Sister, there's an angry mob outside. I was worried they'd break in."

"No one may enter except nuns who've taken vows. We're a cloistered convent."

"But you don't understand. It's the Klan. They hate Catholics." I cleared my throat, the words catching like thorns.

"Go home, Silver Dollar. You'll be safe there."

"But I'm Catholic. Let me stay. I want to stay. Please let me." I fell to my knees, desperation clawing at me.

Sister Paulette's eyes softened. "You must take vows to stay here. Commit to poverty, chastity, and obedience. I don't think you're ready for that, dear girl."

"Sounds impossible." I winced as shouts and pounding erupted nearby, closer now.

A touch of sadness graced her smile. "For some, shedding the world's sins is pure bliss."

Sister Paulette led me into the cloister, the convent's private heart. The scent of roses and honeysuckle offered a welcome respite from the burning hatred beyond the walls. Was there no escape from this darkness?

"You'll find sanctuary here, child, amidst the garden. May their beauty remind you that even in the darkest of times, hope can bloom." Sister Paulette's eyes lingered on the vibrant flowers before she turned and left.

A riot of blossoms spilled over the ancient stone archways.

Crimson roses, defiant and bold; yellow lilies, whispering of hope; velvety purple pansies, a quiet strength. Their vibrant beauty soothed me in a way I didn't quite understand. Gravel crunched softly under my feet as I ventured deeper into this haven.

Sinking onto a stone bench, my fingers traced the cool marble. I prayed my rosary for understanding. Weren't we all just people struggling with our lives? Where was the compassion for each other? I prayed for a way to reconcile the warring factions within me, to find harmony between my despair, and Echo's smothering protection that had become a prison which I could not escape.

∽

In the morning, sunlight dappled my eyelids, coaxing me awake, where every blossom seemed to exhale peace. Dewdrops clung to petals, shimmering against the vibrant green. Birdsong filled the air, drowning out the terrors of the night. But the moment was fleeting.

Echo's persistent whine shattered my tranquility. "Are we done with this peace and quiet crap yet?" She sneered. "I'm bored. Let's get back to the real world. I want to rumble."

I longed to remain in this tranquil oasis, to bask in the warmth of the sun and the sweet scent of roses, to let Echo fade away into the gentle rustling of leaves. Maybe if I came here every day, bathed in the serenity of this garden, I could find the strength to silence her. Maybe I could pray her away, banish her to the shadows from whence she came.

"Not likely," Echo spewed bitterly. "I deserve to live. And you have nothing to say about it."

My shoulders slumped, a heavy weight settling on my chest. Was I doomed to forever battle this demon? Was there no escape from her relentless whispers, her insatiable thirst for chaos? *No.* I clenched my fists, a flicker of defiance sparking in my eyes. I won't let her win. I'll find a way to silence her, even if it's the last thing I do. I'd seek solace in prayer, in the rituals that once brought me peace. I'll search for the strength to banish Echo's darkness. One way or another, I will be free.

Chapter 43

1924

Silver price $0.69 per ounce

Chicago, Illinois. Echo sashayed into Murphy's Bar, a smoky Irish joint where dreams drowned in bootleg gin. The air hung heavy with the scent of stale whiskey and sawdust, but it did nothing to dampen her spirit. Not tonight. Not when there were pockets ripe for the picking.

"Kismet, please," she declared, taking a drag on her cigarette holder.

Murphy, a bear of a man with a walrus mustache, eyed her with amusement. "Feeling fancy, eh?" He winked, a glint of lust in his hazel eyes. "You know better than to order that fancy stuff here, sweetheart." His shaker rattled with practiced ease, gin, honey, lemon. "But a Bees Knees for the Queen Bee? Closest thing to kismet you'll find in this den." He slid the glass toward her, the liquid catching the flickering gaslight.

The first sip was a glorious blaze that chased away the Chicago chill. Just the fuel she needed for the night ahead.

"Where you been? Your regulars are getting restless, Echo. Had to palm them off on the other girls."

A shadow caught her eye. Mrs. Murphy, a gaunt woman with a widow's peak of iron-gray hair, stood sentinel at the far end of the bar. Her eyes, sharp as broken glass, pierced the smoky haze, fixing on Echo with a chilling intensity. The gin's warmth evaporated, replaced by a prickling unease under Mrs. Murphy's stare.

"A lady's gotta spread her wings, Murph." Echo tilted her chin in defiance.

"Don't forget you owe me a date," Murphy whispered, thick with a threat that made her skin crawl. Rossi's deal still hung over her head, the price of Murphy's cooperation.

Echo traced the jagged scar on his cheek. "How about you take me to White City, and we'll go from there?" she purred. Anything to postpone the inevitable.

"Your apartment would be a little more private." His gaze lingered on her decollete.

"Sure, Murph. Whatever you say." She winked, relishing the idea of getting under Mrs. Murphy's skin. It was a dangerous game, but Echo thrived on the thrill.

The marks flocked to Echo, desperate to fill their voids with lust and liquor. She looked the part but the emptiness inside her was a bottomless pit. Emptiness, it turned out, was her greatest asset, keeping her pockets lined. A bluesy lament from the corner piano set her toes tapping.

"So, what's got you so tense tonight, Echo?" Murphy asked, glancing toward his wife.

"Can't a girl have a life outside your glorious establishment?" The truth was, Echo's life had become a jumble of smoky rooms and forgotten faces. Tonight, she'd lose herself in another honey-sweet gin. "Extra honey this time, Murph," she said.

Murphy gestured toward the poker table. "See that mark? Beaver fedora? Billy Ryan, Cleveland money. Pockets over-flowing."

Echo's gaze snapped toward the newcomer. His expensive suit and flashy rings screamed easy target. Another night, another way to chip away at the hollowness inside. In a single glance, she saw their entire encounter: the flirtation, Billy boy too eager to notice the hungry gleam in her eyes, and finally, the taxi ride back to his hotel room, where she'd relieve him of his excess cash.

"What's his game?" she asked, out of habit than genuine interest.

Murphy snorted. "What's it matter? Planning to settle down?" A sharp intake of breath from the doorway—Mrs. Murphy hadn't moved an inch.

"Is that a proposal?" Echo retorted with a wink. Sliding off the stool, she shimmied toward her prey. "Mr. Ryan, I presume?"

He tipped his hat, eyes glittering with anticipation. "And you would be?"

"Echo." The name danced on her lips. "I believe you and I have some business to discuss."

The Charleston pulsed through her veins as she moved with him, their feet kicking up dust on the linoleum. Mr. Ryan might have been clumsy, but he was eager, and for tonight, that was all that mattered. She caught sight of her reflection in the mirrored ball above. Still fierce, but fractured and fading around the edges. So what? she thought defiantly.

Echo was made for this life. The bootlegger gin, the smoke, the fleeting thrill of laughter with men she'd forget by morning. Tonight, she'd dance beneath the shattered light of that mirrored ball, her laughter ringing out above the din, a defiant challenge to the creeping shadows of tomorrow. Tomorrow? Tomorrow can kiss her satin fanny.

Chapter 44

1932

Silver price $0.28 per ounce

Leadville, Colorado. The moon, a sliver of bone in the obsidian sky, cast long shadows as Baby Doe Tabor trudged up the mountain. The rusted ore cart squealed, its burden heavy, but not as heavy as the fury that seized her. Rockwell had stolen everything. Revenge would be hers. She tightened her blue bandana against the biting wind, her breath misting in the frigid air. If Charlie were here, he'd try to stop her. But he still lay in St. Vincent's Hospital, his life hanging by a thread, a victim of the Matchless Mine's insatiable hunger.

The hill was steep, the path treacherous, but she pushed on, fueled by a silent prayer to Horace and a burning resolve. An owl hooted mournfully from the pines, a lonely lament that mirrored her own sorrow.

"Look what Rockwell's become, Horace," she rasped, ragged with grief and anger. "Greedy as a coyote, turning our own daughters against us. But not for long."

Inside the cart, nestled amongst sacks of ore, were crates of dynamite. Their weight was a ominous reminder of her mission. "Horace, I promised you to bring back the Matchless. And I tried, I truly did. You wanted that silver for your family, to make us happy again, to restore our fortunes and leave a legacy for our daughters. But Rockwell's twisted your dream into a nightmare." A tear froze on her cheek. "Has to end, Horace. Even if I end with it."

With a final grunt, she pushed the cart over the crest of the hill, the swollen river below roaring like a hungry beast. Reaching the spot where she and Carl had once fished, she saw the exposed timbers, the rusted steel joints, the festering wound where the river gnawed at the mountain.

She hesitated, Horace's last words engraved on her mind: "Hang onto the Matchless." He believed it would make millions again. But at what cost? Her hands shook as she set the dynamite, but her eyes remained focused and determined.

Working quickly, she burrowed into the silt and rocks, her fingers raw and bleeding as she placed the dynamite. She set the timer for dawn way before the miners would be arriving. By then, it would be too late.

The river, swollen with winter runoff, would rip through the weakened supports like matchsticks. The ore cars would be swept away, the tunnels flooded, the monstrous vein buried forever. A watery grave for Rockwell's avarice, a fitting end to his twisted scheme.

Her riches, her fame, her family—gone. All gone. Swept away like so much river silt. But as she turned her back on that roaring water, the moon shining down like a silver dollar in the sky, a deep peace settled over her.

She'd saved the Matchless, sure as shooting. Not for the silver, but for something far more precious. It would become a whisper on the wind, a tale told around campfires, a legend of the love she and Horace shared, and the heartache that came with it. The Matchless Mine wasn't just a greedy hole in the ground no more. It would live on as a testament to the love and loss that had shaped its destiny.

THE FRIENDLY CHATTER of the Saddle Rock Cafe couldn't drown out the ticking in Baby Doe's ears. Not the clock on the wall, but the one she'd set earlier that morning, nestled among the timbers of the Matchless Mine. Her heart hammered like a woodpecker against a hollow tree, a mix of fear and exhilaration. Seven minutes to seven. Right on schedule. A nervous smile tugged at her lips as she sipped her coffee, the taste of chicory doing little to calm her nerves.

The jangle of the cafe door made her jump. Carl hurried toward her, a silk scarf around his neck, a cap perched over one eye.

"Mrs. Tabor!" A worried frown creased his brow. "Got your message. Are you alright? Why the change of plans? Weren't we supposed to meet at the mine in a couple of hours?"

She forced a chuckle. "Nothing wrong at all, Carl. Just a change of scenery. Thought we'd celebrate the film with a proper breakfast." She patted his hand as he slid into the booth, hoping he wouldn't notice the slight tremor in hers.

"Nothing happened?" he pressed, worry furrowing his brow.

"Not yet." Her gaze darted toward the clock. Six minutes. "But Rockwell's got a surprise comin' his way this morning, so I thought we'd enjoy a little pre-celebration."

Breakfast arrived with a clatter. The waiter, with a flourish, popped the cork on a bottle of Veuve Clicquot, filling two coupes.

Carl blanched, staring at his plate. "What exactly is this ... creation?"

"A Hangtown Fry!" she said. "Back in the gold rush, when a fella struck it rich, he'd head to the nearest fancy restaurant and order up the most expensive thing on the menu. A mess of eggs, oysters and bacon, all scrambled together."

Carl grimaced. "But oysters make my throat swell up like a prizefighter's hand after a brawl."

She felt a pang of disappointment but quickly recovered. "Well, what would you like then?"

A sheepish grin spread across his face. "I'm a sucker for pancakes with real maple syrup."

She waved down the waiter. "Tall stack of pancakes, and don't be stingy with the syrup." She popped an oyster into her mouth, savoring the briny flavor, her eyes never straying from the clock. "Horace would've been tickled pink to see his life on the big screen." Her tension barely concealed.

"So would Silver Dollar," Carl's eyes glistened. "She wanted to show the world the real story of the Tabors. Your tenacity, pluck, and hard work—those years of struggle, not just the Hollywood version. That's the American dream."

Pride swelled in her chest, momentarily eclipsing her anxiety. "And the picture show is still premiering at the Tabor Grand in Denver?"

"Indeed." His eyes danced. "Grand affair. Warner Bros. is pulling out all the stops."

"Here's to you, Carl." She held her glass to his, her hand trembling. "For not letting anyone twist your dream into something unrecognizable."

He took a long sip, a shadow of sadness passing over his face as he thought of Silver. Baby Doe reached across the table, her hand finding his.

"We keep her in our hearts, Carl. That's where Silver Dollar lives on." The ceramic clock chimed seven. Her heart leaped into her throat.

Suddenly, a thunderous boom shook the cafe, rattling plates and glasses. Someone in the kitchen screamed. Diners rushed onto the porch, their faces pale. A series of smaller explosions followed, rumbling from the direction of the Matchless.

She gripped Carl's hand, her knuckles white. A wave of nausea washed over her, but beneath it, a cold satisfaction pulsed. She'd done what she had to do.

He lurched to his feet, a gasp of horror from his lips. "The Matchless! I'll get the car!"

"Let things settle," she said. "No one was hurt. The miners don't arrive for another hour."

A plume of smoke rose from the mountain, a dark smudge against the morning sky. It was the signal she'd been waiting for. She closed her eyes, a silent prayer of thanks escaping her lips. A sense of peace settled over her born of resolve and sacrifice. Her plan had worked.

"Why are we still sitting here?" Carl's eyes narrowed with a dawning realization.

She held his gaze. "Rockwell and his investors took over the mine yesterday. Let him deal with it. Seems the Lord decided the Matchless had given all it could."

Sirens wailed in the distance, rising above the rumble of the explosions. She raised her glass with a smile. "Now, where were we? Ah, yes, celebrating." She clinked Carl's glass, the sound ringing through the chaos. "Perhaps I will come to the movie premiere, after all."

Chapter 45

1925

Silver price $0.69 per ounce

Chicago, Illinois. Two in the morning, a thunder of fists against the door downstairs. Rossi's wolfish grin filled the door, reeking of expensive cigars and whiskey. "Silver, get dressed. Command performance," he rasped. "Torrio's Denver gun dealers are on their way."

My fingers dug into my braid, panic twisting my stomach. "Not a good idea at night, Dante. The tigers are nocturnal. Restless, dangerous. And they haven't been good lately, anyway."

He scanned the approaching headlights. "Showtime!" A convoy of Torrio's cars rolled to a stop, the Rolls, the Duesenberg, the Bentley. Men in fancy suits spilled out, laughing too loud.

"Tell them I'm out," I closed the door, but Rossi's hand shot out, fingers bruising my arm. "Want a one-way ticket to the graveyard? Torrio's made you a star, and this is payback time."

"It's not like that," I seethed. "Torrio and I, we're tight."

"Then you know to play by his rules." He sneered. "I'll bring them into the tiger cages."

Upstairs, I splashed cold water on my face, trying to ignore Echo's taunts. "You really think you can escape this, Silver girl? You're fooling yourself. You're nothing but a has-been now, a faded flower. How long until Torrio finds another doll to dress up and parade around?"

Frustrated with Echo's relentless taunts, I slammed down my brush, my nails digging into my palms. I had to silence this she-devil once and for all, not with words, but action.

A swipe of lipstick, a twist of hair. This was the price of fame: Four Deuces weekend shows a grotesque circus, my body a spectacle. The crowd's jeers filled Torrio's pockets, carving out a void in me that Echo filled with gin and laudanum. I was a puppet, strings jerked by Torrio and Echo, my body their battleground. I longed for Carl's laughter instead of the lude and sneering smiles I endured. And now, Torrio shows up in the middle of the night expecting me to perform for his cronies?

Even my beloved tigers had become sad shadows of their former selves. Their restless pacing had worn paths in the sawdust, their once-glossy fur now matted and dull, their eyes clouded with despair against the cruelty of their captivity.

I paused at the top of the stairs, the air thick with tension. Squaring my shoulders, I descended into the smoke-filled holding cages, the stench of stale whiskey burning my nostrils.

Torrio, eyes glassy with icy amusement, slammed a fist on the table. "Gentlemen, behold!" he roared. "My Silver Dollar Tiger Tamer!" A cruel smirk twisted his mouth. "Give these Denver boys a show they won't forget." His cigar breath filled my nostrils as he gripped my jaw. Before I could react, his lips were on mine, a rough, wet assault tasting of Seagram's and the chalky Milk of Magnesia he favored. Could use a shot of that about now.

Whistles and catcalls erupted; sloppy jackets revealed holstered weapons. The stench of lust was suffocating. I could make a run for the door, but I'd felt Torrio's brutality enough to know I wouldn't make it far.

Timber's roar rattled the bars, pacing restlessly. The other tigers slept in separate cages in the back; no need to rile them.

Rossi herded the men toward plush chairs, their drunken slurs polluting the air. Torrio's fingers dug into my waist, pulling me close. "Pipe down, boys," he barked. "Or Silver Dollar here will make you the main course."

Then, like a gut punch, I saw that damned cowboy hat, the silver bolo, my papa's gold watch, the graying walrus mustache. The man who'd violated me. The man who held my mother's fate in the palm of his hand.

"Rockwell?" His name tasted like poison. He glanced away. What was he doing with Torrio? That's right. Rossi mentioned Rockwell was dealing guns. Rockwell must be the dealer's lawyer. Was he afraid I'd expose him, somehow? I scoffed, considering a plan. Blowing his deal would be perfect revenge on the bastard. But the atmosphere already teemed with danger: Timber's growls, drunken gangsters with guns. Not smart to go off half-cocked and get more people killed. Not even for sweet revenge.

Timber rose up on hind legs roaring with full fury, his fangs bared. The drunken men exchanged wary glances.

Torrio's order was a whipcrack. "Get this show on the road, Silver."

"Yes, sir," I saluted him glibly and sashayed over to Timber's cage. The only way to keep these bastards safe was to perform inside the bars. I grabbed my baton and entered. The men's laughter died in their throats, their eyes darting nervously.

I gripped Timber's mane, his muscles taut beneath my touch. A low hum escaped my lips, a futile attempt to soothe the wildness in his eyes. With a shaky breath, I swung my leg over his broad back. He tensed; every muscle coiled. My heart hammered as he lurched forward, his powerful stride a reminder of his strength and speed.

"I won't bite unless you do," I murmured, stroking his ruff. He stretched, a magnificent beast showcasing his power. My feet found his haunches, his low chuff vibrating against my thighs. A warning tremor, but I had to continue.

I arched backward, legs kicking high, then twisted, straddling him in reverse. His golden eyes, burning with a restless fire, held the gangsters captive as we paced. The men fidgeted, their gazes hungry, silenced by the intense tension.

Torrio leaned toward Rockwell, a glint in his eye. "Mesmerizing, wouldn't you say?"

Rockwell's mouth opened and closed, a soundless gasp before he finally managed to croak out, "Intoxicating."

I used Timber's movement to swing my legs sideways, a flash of turquoise silk against his fur. My movements became bolder, provocative. The men hooted and cheered. I laid back against Timber, hoisting my legs in the air, then jackknifed, flipping my feet to land against his powerful back. With each move, Timber picked up the pace, his agitation growing from the noisy crowd.

The men's stench mingling with the tiger's musk, a nauseating cocktail. I needed to finish this show and get them out of here. Crouching on Timber's back, I tapped his skull. He ignored me, his ears flattening against his head, his tail twitching with barely contained fury. I tapped again, harder. With a vicious snarl, he turned his head, his dilated pupils fixing on me, a low growl rumbling in his chest and chomped down on my baton, snapping it in half in my hand.

Fear gripped me, cold and numbing. He was not playing anymore.

I raised the splintered baton, my voice trembling. "Timber, down."

He didn't move, his growl deepening. I murmured the familiar lullaby I used to soothe Topaz. But Timber's eyes were wild, restless. "Easy, Timber. Easy, boy."

The men leaned back in their chairs, gripping their drinks tighter, knuckles white.

Oblivious to the danger, Torrio clapped with great gusto. "Told yous fellas she was something else." He beamed at me like I was a prized possession.

Rockwell's smile didn't reach his eyes. "Perhaps a homecoming performance is in order, Silver Dollar." He offered a handshake through the bars, knowing I couldn't refuse in front of Torrio. "Wouldn't your family in Denver just love to see what their little girl has become?"

Torrio's grin turned predatory. "Actually, her show's run its course here." He met Rockwell's gaze with a challenge. "Maybe you'd like to buy her from me. For the right price, of course."

They were playing me like a wild card, and I had no say in the game. "Buy me? Or buy the show? What are you saying?" I yanked my hand away from Rockwell's grasp.

In a flash of orange and black, Timber lunged toward Rockwell's hand. There was a sickening crunch, as he bit into his wrist. Rockwell screamed as he stumbled back and fell into the chair, scraping against the floor. A raw stump where his hand had been. Blood spurted in a crimson arc, splattering Torrio's immaculate suit, splashing on the wood-planked floor. Rockwell's severed hand lay in the cage, fingers still twitching. Timber, blood dripping from his jaws, snatched the prize and disappeared into the corner.

A moment of stunned silence hung in the air, broken only by Rockwell's ragged gasps. Then, chaos erupted. Men scrambled for their weapons, the sinister clicks of safeties disengaging. Torrio roared in fury, his face contorted in rage. Several guns were trained on me and Timber, the glint of steel reflecting in their cold eyes.

Rockwell lay in a growing pool of blood, his face crumpled in agony. The tang of blood hung thick in the air. I held up my palms to the gang, extracting myself from the cage, locking it behind me.

"Party's over fellas." Rossi snapped his fingers at the men, ushering them out.

"Rockwell needs a doctor, fast," I held my voice steady.

Torrio turned his gun on Rockwell. "Too much heat. He sleeps with the fishes tonight."

"No, Johnny. I can't have his blood on my hands," I said. "He's my family's lawyer." To kill Rockwell once was a nightmare;

to see him die again, unthinkable. I went to him and bound his wrist with my kimono tie.

Torrio glared at me like I was crazy. "So, you're giving orders now?" He swung his gun on me.

Rossi returned, his eyes riveted to Torrio's gun. Sweat traced his jawline. "Let me take care of this, boss. No need to dirty your hands."

Torrio stared at me, the gun unwavering. Seconds stretched into an eternity, the silence a taut wire threatening to snap. A bead of sweat trickled down my temple. I held my breath, my muscles frozen. Finally, with a guttural grunt, he lowered the weapon. "Clean this mess up, Rossi," He jerked his thumb toward me. "Including the girl."

Just like that, Torrio discarded me. Relieved and giddy, a strange irony surged in me. "What? No goodbye kiss?" I blew him an exaggerated kiss like a heroine from one of my dramas.

From his hateful glare, I knew the final curtain had fallen.

Chapter 46

1932

Silver price $0.28 per ounce

Leadville, Colorado. Baby Doe and Carl watched the sheriff climb the hill toward the cabin. His scarecrow shadow stretched like accusing fingers across the wreckage of the explosion.

Apprehension coiled around her like a rattler. From the nervous twitch in his cheek, she knew he'd found evidence. One thing would lead to another, and she'd be locked away for the rest of her days. She brushed off crumbs from the snickerdoodles Carl brought from Hattie's. Probably the last she'd taste on God's green earth.

The sheriff took off his dingy hat and wiped his forehead, grimacing. "Not the news you want to hear. But we've combed the rubble the best we could for evidence of foul play and turned up nary a clue."

Pressing her trembling hand to her chest, she hoped he took it for grief and not relief.

"Wish I could tell you we found out more," the sheriff said, harboring doubt in his eyes. "But an accident like this, with no one around … it's hard to swallow. Unless you can think of anyone who would do this."

She shook her head. "Who in their right mind would sabotage

the mine before it got going again? Least of all, the investors. You gave it your best, Sheriff." She'd endured them poking around the boulders and timber for clues for near a week now. Time they cleared out.

"But how could the mine explode if no one blew it up?" Carl asked. For once she wished he'd keep his questions to himself.

The sheriff wiped his brow. "Maybe someone left old dynamite down in the tunnel that corroded over the years and exploded by itself."

She clenched her jaw, her fingers tightening around the pickaxe handle. "Good thinking, Sheriff. Nitroglycerin sweatin' outta those sticks, turns 'em brittle and treacherous. One good freeze, like that night, and the crystals explode." She slapped her hands together. "Kaboom. Destroyed everythin'. The river wreaked the rest. Thank the Lord my cabin is on the west side, or I'd be pushin' up daisies."

"Maybe the Tommyknockers set it off." Carl grinned, chomping on a cookie.

She forced a chuckle.

The sheriff squinted at Carl, rubbing his stubbly beard. "Can't help thinking what a blessing it was that you two were at breakfast the morning it happened."

"Praise the Lord." She lifted a busted pickaxe beside the porch and propped it beside her.

"She ordered Hangtown Fry," Carl grinned.

"Oh? What were you celebrating?" the sheriff asked, wiping his sunglasses on his shirt.

Carl licked his fingers. "The Tabor movie's coming out soon. Very big deal."

"Saw the poster in town." The sheriff studied him. "That'd be cause for celebrating, I s'pose. Good thing the explosion happened before the miners showed up for work."

"A blessing." She squelched the satisfied smile of a gambler with an ace up his sleeve.

"Okay then." The Sheriff tipped his hat. "I'll let Mr. Rockwell know we're leaving."

"Rockwell's long gone. Heard Rossi was on his tail after the blast, so he skedaddled." Baby Doe couldn't help but enjoy the sight of the predator becoming the prey. She knew it was wrong to take pleasure in another's misfortune, but Rockwell had it coming.

The sheriff scuffed the dirt. "Sorry about the Matchless. You'll manage, though?"

"I'll manage," she insisted.

He studied the dark gray rubble left by the explosion, not a hint of bright shiny silver. "A shame." A frown creased his brow. "Well, we'll be off then." He touched the brim of his hat.

"About time." Charlie brushed past him, heading for the porch.

"Just doing his job, Charlie," she told him, her voice catching in her throat.

Charlie cast a sidelong glance at Carl, resentment glinting in his eyes. "They found this down by the river." He held out her blue bandana, the corner ripped, the once-bright fabric smudged with ash and dirt.

Her breath hitched, and she snatched it from him. That darn thorny Hawthorn branch must have snagged her bandana when she climbed up the riverbank.

"Shouldn't we give that to the sheriff?" Carl said. "The scarf might be evidence of who blew up the mine."

"Belongs to me." She tucked in her overalls. "Charlie was protecting me." She couldn't meet Charlie's eyes.

"Told them I must have lost the bandana," he said, pride ringing in his voice. He watched the trucks haul away equipment, their headlights cutting through the deepening dusk. "See you, Monday."

She felt a pang of guilt. "I can't pay you anymore, Charlie, now that our investors have pulled out. But with the Silver Purchase coming, you can find a good job anywhere."

"I'll be here, Monday, just the same." He stooped to pick up a gray rock. Definitely not silver by the dull surface. He stuffed it in his pocket and headed out with a wave.

The wind whistled through the mine's shattered timbers as Baby Doe watched Charlie disappear down the hill. The setting sun cast long shadows across the wreckage, mirroring the emptiness that had settled in her heart. The Matchless had always been the bond between her and Charlie, the rhythm of their days. Now, with the mine in ruins, a chasm opened between them wider than any collapsed shaft. Too late to change that, dust settled and done. She'd been so consumed by the Matchless, by her movie schemes and memories of Silver Dollar, that she'd never truly seen Charlie. The thought lingered with her, like the tune he whistled constantly.

∽

Dusk settled over the mountains, a chill creeping into the air. Baby Doe brought out Ute blankets for Carl and herself.

"We're wrapping up the edit this week for the movie," he said. "You're going to love it. Bebe Daniels was gorgeous and played you so well. Have you decided about coming to the premiere? It would mean so—"

Carl may never come back, and she was no closer to answers about Silver. "The first time you came to visit, you claimed Silver was dead. But you never fully explained why you thought that."

Scrubbed his hands over his face. "I heard the testimony at the coroner's inquest." He gazed at the sunset as if it would help him. "No question she was dead."

"Go on Carl. What'd they say?"

He stared into the gray rubble the explosion had unearthed around them. "I can't ... can't go through that again."

Her veined hand covered his. "Please, Carl. I need to know."

Swallowing hard, his breath caught in his chest. "Well, the

coroner suspected foul play, so they pulled in everyone who knew her to an inquisition." He shook his head. "Some blamed the bootleggers, others said it was a jealous wife. Or one of Silver's boyfriends. But they couldn't pin it on anyone. The whole investigation was a mess."

"But how'd they find her?"

"Dr. Lawton testified someone called him to her apartment late at night. I ... I was there earlier." He wiped a hand across his eyes. "We'd made a date meet for lunch the next day. She stood me up ..." His voice cracked, and he turned away. "I had no idea ..."

She grabbed his hand. "What else did the doctor say?"

A heavy sigh. "Lawton testified she was going by Echo LaVode." His jaw tightened. "Claimed she changed names like she changed underwear."

"Heavens sake ... her underwear?" She clutched her blanket under her chin but could not stop shivering. Silver's letters flashed through her mind, proof her daughter's restless spirit. "I could've sent her more money if she'd just settled down."

Carl scoffed. "Silver was a headliner, Mrs. Tabor. Top billing at the biggest club in Chicago. She wasn't hurting for money."

What was going on? "What else did this Dr. Lawton say?"

"Lawton swore her death was an accident, but he worked for the Chicago Outfit, so I didn't trust him."

A sob tore from her throat. "But Silver was scalded to death. What kind of accident is that?" She wanted to believe her daughter's letters describing the peaceful convent garden. Was her hope crumbling?

"Silver always used heated hot oil to condition her hair." Carl looked down at his trembling hands. "Lawton said the pot burst into flames. And she spilled it on herself."

The image seared into Baby Doe's mind. Silver, screaming, enveloped in flames. A hot wave of nausea gutted her. Boiling oil, burning flesh. The image was unbearable, Silver's agony beyond comprehension.

Carl's breath shuddered, sweat beading his forehead. "Dr. Lawton said by the time he got there ... burns so bad ... she was unconscious ..." He covered his face.

Baby Doe's heart fluttered against her ribs like a bird flying against a window. "Who else did the coroner question?"

"The coroner put the screws to me, of course, the jilted boyfriend." Carl huffed. "And they questioned Rossi since he was Silver's booking agent."

"Dante Rossi?" Her hand flew to her chest "My investor? He just poured a fortune down this mining hole. This explosion ruined him."

"I doubt he's ruined," Carl said. "Rossi has his claws in too many pies to count." He leaned against the cabin watching the North Star piercing through the clouds. "There was another suspect they grilled for a while. Murphy, a bar owner tied to the Outfit. They thought he was the man in the picture with Silver."

"But, that was Rockwell in the picture."

"Strange what Silver wrote about him, isn't it?" Carl raised an eyebrow.

"She must have resented him acting as her father." A lump lodged itself in her throat.

"Anyway, Murphy got off with his wife's alibi. She testified that Silver was really Echo LaVode, a working girl who picked up tricks at the bar."

"They called her a prostitute?" She felt for Silver's rosary in her pocket. "Mother Mary full of grace ..." She mumbled, oblivious to Carl. She'd prayed for the truth so many nights, but never imagined how painful it would be. Silver and Echo ... Echo and Silver ... she thought she had stopped it when she was little. When she finished praying, Carl's eyes and nose were rimmed in red, shaking his head, staring into the sunset.

"I figure the doctor and the coroner were in the Outfit's pocket," Carl spat the words, his voice thick with disgust. "Swept the whole damn thing under the rug. Accidental death my eye." He slammed his fist on the bench.

On the mountain above, the train's whistle startled her, like a wake-up call to her heart. As the train rumbled past, she finally understood she'd deceived herself. One letter from Silver about seeking refuge at Holy Sepulcher, had become the foundation of a lie that took on a life of its own. Each time Baby Doe reread those faded lines, she'd painted a picture of peace that didn't exist.

The pieces fell into place. Silver's tear-stained letters, the desperate pleas for money that Baby Doe so readily believed. They were Silver's pleas for attention, cries for help Baby Doe had not answered. Had she failed to keep her motherly love burning just when Silver needed it most?

As the last rays of the sunset faded, and the stars began to twinkle in the night sky, Carl's shoulders slumped, his grief pulling him down. He stared vacantly at the blackened ruins of the mine, his eyes reflecting the shattered hopes and dreams that lay buried beneath the rubble.

It was clear he'd loved her daughter, truly loved her. His pain was raw and real. Baby Doe hesitated, then gently placed her hand on his arm. He turned to her, his eyes glistening. Without a word, he sank into her embrace, his body wracked with sobs. She held him close, her own tears flowing freely, their shared grief witnessed by the vast night sky.

Chapter 47

1925

Silver price $0.69 per ounce

CHICAGO, ILLINOIS. ROSSI'S SILVER-TONGUED CHARM evaporated like morning mist. "Forget about leaving, Silver Dollar. You're staying put until Torrio gives the word. Help Sammy keep those tigers docile until I figure out what to do with them."

Despair mingled with a bitter relief. I'd been spared immediate execution, yet Torrio's motives for keeping me alive remained murky.

The days blurred into a monotonous routine of feeding, grooming, and whispering hopeful lies to the tigers about the freedom they'd never know. Rossi, meanwhile, booked a new act for the Four Deuces. Chinese contortionists dubbed "The Limber Lizards of Lijiang." He described their suggestive poses and daring escapes with a sadistic smirk, reminding me that I was just a spectacle, now forgotten.

My once-cherished warehouse flat had transformed into a prison of my own making. The vibrant colors of the room had muted into the grays of my despair. Dust specks danced in the stale air, undisturbed by any breeze. I felt my sanity fraying like the carpet beneath my feet.

Echo, a venomous parasite, had infested my sanctuary, filling every waking moment with foul propositions and cruel taunts. Even sleep offered no respite, as her whistling whispers invaded my nightmares.

The success I'd clawed my way to, now lay shattered around me. My splintered baton, once a magic wand summoning applause, now tinder for the fire. Torn fishnet stockings, once a symbol of my allure, lay in a fraying pile, a testament to my unraveling sanity. My once-proud mane, now a tangled mess thanks to Echo's drunken escapades and the tigers' playful mauling, mirrored the feral chaos raging within my mind.

Forbidden by Torrio to attend church, I clung to my rosary, repeating Hail Mary as shields against Echo's whispers. Against the madness threatening to consume me.

The apartment reeked of Jardin de Nuit perfume and bootleg gin, a sickening reminder of Echo's presence. Discarded clothing and broken promises littered the floor like the aftermath of a tornado. Scrawled on a Murphy's Pub napkin, a stranger's phone number ... one of dozens Echo had collected.

The unmade bed, a silent witness to sweat-soaked betrayal. Her overflowing ashtray filled the air with the acrid stench of failure, a fitting epitaph for our bond. Everywhere I turned, reminders of Echo's disdain assaulted me.

Propped on the mantle was the torn half picture of Rockwell. Every time I tried to discard it, Echo would retrieve it, a trophy of the night she nearly killed him. Beside it, a sunburst of colorful swizzle sticks mocked me, a shrine to her power. In a fit of rage, I swept them across the room. The glass shattered against the brick fireplace, a cacophony of defiance. Glittering shards danced in the firelight, a declaration of war.

The gauntlet I'd thrown down filled me with grim determination. But what would this war against Echo demand of me? Was I willing to sacrifice my sanity, my soul, even my life, to silence her venomous whispers once and for all? The path ahead was shrouded in uncertainty, but I would see this through to the bitter end, no matter the cost.

∼

FINALLY, a glimmer of hope pierced the oppressive darkness. Rossi had sold the tigers back to Colonel Selig, and Carl was coming to take them to Hollywood. This could be my chance to escape. But first, I had to prepare.

My heart skipped with a tumultuous mix of anticipation and dread, love and resentment. Carl was coming. Part of me still yearned for him. Had he only come back for the tigers, or did an ember of love still flicker beneath the ashes of our past?

Focusing on the task at hand, I gathered the torn fishnet stockings and broken baton, remnants of a life I desperately wanted to forget. I swept up the shattered swizzle sticks, erasing the evidence of Echo's chaos.

The dressing table mirror startled me. My reflection was a feral creature, caged and snarling. I plunged my fingers into my tangled mane, desperate to regain control, but they snagged and twisted, trapped like a fly in a spider's web. Each tug only tightened the strands, a twisted grip mirroring the hold Echo had on my mind.

Echo's laughter, a relentless drumbeat of madness, pounded against the walls of my sanity. "You can't escape me, Silver Dollar," she hissed. "We're intertwined forever, you and I."

My lungs seized, and my hands shook uncontrollably. Was I truly trapped, a prisoner of my own tangled mind? No. I wouldn't let Echo win. With a fierce growl, I ripped my fingers free, tearing through knots and snarls. Pain seared my scalp, but it was a small price to pay for freedom. I would reclaim my dignity, my beauty.

"First," I muttered at the mirror, "I have to fix this damn hair."

∼

CARL CAME SOONER than I expected, my hair still tumbleweeds, while he breezed in like a leading man. For a second, I barely recognized him. A sharply tailored, midnight blue suit, peak lapels gleaming. A rakishly tilted fedora. Hollywood. That confidence he'd always struggled with, he'd found in spades. While he entertained me with stories about his new life, I pinned up my hair in glittering hair combs at my dressing table. His eyes lit up with each Hollywood tale, and I hung on his every word. The lovestruck boy I'd known had bloomed into a charismatic ladies man. Maybe it wasn't too late for us after all.

Swept up in his excitement, the hopelessness of the past few months faded some. Sammy helped us load the tigers into the truck, and, afterwards, Carl asked about my act. Part of me couldn't resist bragging. I painted a picture of daring feats and roaring crowds, the exhilaration of the spotlight. Yet, the truth lurked beneath the surface. The bone-deep exhaustion. The Torrio affair that ended abruptly. Echo's relentless heckling fueled by bathtub hooch and enough opiates to bring down a horse. Nights that left bruises I couldn't explain. Fistfuls of cash hurled on my bed. My world had grown warped and dark, so far from the starry-eyed girl he'd met in Colorado. I didn't want Carl to know any of it, especially not about Echo.

"What are you going to do now?" He sounded genuinely interested, but the question twisted a knife in my heart.

"Oh, I'm working up an exciting new nightclub act. Something exotic and beautiful. Something French." A story to hide how low I'd sunken. "Do they like French acts in California?" I grimaced. What was I thinking? Echo LaVode is French and she's definitely not invited to come along. I couldn't bear another morning waking up with strangers. My sobbing confessions and hours of repentance at Holy Sepulcher, the soothing scents of lilies and frankincense. Praying to find a way to exorcise Echo from my being, so I could survive.

Carl offered me a licorice, the familiar smell grounding me. He chattered on about glamourous premieres, bustling backlots, the thrill of working alongside rising stars. Douglas Fairbanks swashbuckling through *The Thief of Bagdad*, Lillian Gish in *The White Sister*.

His enthusiasm was contagious, his words sparking the old creative fire we'd shared crafting the Tabor film. "The Warner Bros. backlot is bathed in golden California sunlight, humming with energy. They build fantastic sets and everyone's buzzing about talking pictures. It's all so ... alive."

As he spoke, I sensed that vitality I'd always felt working with him, humming through my veins like life itself. How had I ever let him go? My fingers brushed his sleeve. My laughter joined his. Somewhere between his larger-than-life dreams spun into celluloid and my desperate lies, our eyes caught each other's, our hands found reasons to touch, the very threads of our connection started to weave together again, even stronger this time.

"Tonight, Sammy and I will have to get the tigers settled into the train cars," he said. "How about tomorrow we grab a bite? Somewhere special." A charming smile played on his lips. "The Palmer House?"

My heart did a little tap dance. "Rainbow Sundae?" I flirted, recalling our first date. "I'd love that." Tomorrow, I'd tell Carl I've decided to go with him. His dazzling world would become ours.

Some hopeful part of me craved his arms around me. That day in Lake Rhoda so long ago, he'd hauled me out, kept me alive. Held Echo's taunting at bay. Could he do it again? Maybe a kiss, being close to him, could drag me out of the darkness, keep Echo at a distance.

I lunged forward, my lips finding his. Carl kissed me back, his loving hands like I remembered, on my cheeks, on my back, on my waist. His smell, clean soap and licorice cut through the tigers' odor. But when Carl reached out to stroke my hair, his hand snagged in the tangles.

He pulled away. Confusion clouded his eyes, guilt replacing

the warmth. "Annette would love to hear your stories. She's fascinated by animal acts."

"Annette?" Heart plummeting, my arms fell to my sides.

His gaze fell away. "I didn't mention her? My fiancée."

Reality crashed through my fantasy of us together again. My cheeks burned, a hot flush of embarrassment spreading across my face.

Why'd I ever think Carl would wait for me? I'd let my ambition blind me, and let Echo take me down. Chasing delusions instead of what was important.

"I'm sorry I didn't tell you sooner," he whispered.

The sting of his unanswered letters should have warned me. On instinct, I sought the rosary in my pocket. Beads slid beneath my fingers, a familiar rhythm against the rising tide of panic. Each bead clicked, a whispered Hail Mary against the pain, but not loud enough to drown out Echo's insistent counsel. But, this time, I wouldn't let her. She would not come between Carl and me despite the agony I felt.

I tried to ignore the pity in Carl's eyes as he retreated. I clutched the rosary, chanting fervent prayers, each Hail Mary a desperate plea for strength. I couldn't stop, not with Echo's furious chatter in my ears demanding attention.

In a fit of rage, Echo ripped the rosary from my grasp. The old string snapped with a crack. Delicate Murano glass beads scattered across the floor like tears. The crucifix, a symbol of my faith, lay twisted and upside-down. I was too stunned to speak.

To my surprise, Carl bent down and gathered the beads, carefully wrapping them in his handkerchief. "There's a jeweler in the Palmer House," he said softly. "I'll have it fixed for you by tomorrow, good as new."

"Thank you." I wiped my eyes, forcing a smile. "I'll meet you at noon."

He kissed my cheek. I covered my eyes, couldn't bear to watch him leave. A cold, empty ache spread through my limbs like poison. The sound of Carl's hesitant steps down the staircase were a death knell to my foolish heart. I'd pushed away the one person who truly cared about me.

My hands pulled at my hair. Hideous. Rage flared within me, hot and bitter, a wildfire consuming the last vestiges of hope. "Damn you, Echo. You did this to me. You stole everything from me." I clamped my hands over my ears against Echo's venomous whispers hissing and rattling, coiling for her next attack.

The silence that followed was deafening, flooded with longing for Carl and the love I lost.

∼

I STARED AT MY REFLECTION, the sharp points of the scissors shaking against my throat. My hair spiraled with tangled snakes of my hair, a grotesque likeness of Medusa herself. No wonder Carl left me. He'd seen too much of my darkness, even before the haunting presence of Echo took its toll.

"What are you waiting for, coward?" Echo slithered into my thoughts, her icy chill infiltrating my nerves like a disease. "Become Echo LaVode, and escape. Chop away the past like you did after Rockwell's attack." She wheedled herself inside my brain like a parasite.

But I fought her off. "Not this time." I put the scissors down, a jolt of defiance coursing through me. The oil I was heating to condition my hair sizzled on the stove, smelling acrid and bitter. A way to tame the snakes in the mirror.

A fleeting image of Carl's face flashed in my mind, a bittersweet reminder of what I'd lost. Tonight, I'd detangle my hair into something beautiful, something Carl might recognize. A fresh start, a chance to reclaim myself.

Tiger musk like glue, burrs, and dried blood matted to my tangled mane. It stretched down past my waist, a frightful mess. Carefully, I dipped a paint brush into the bubbling oil and dragged it slowly across my scalp. I planned to leave it wrapped in a towel overnight and wash it out in the morning. Why was I even bothering to salvage my appearance for Carl? Maybe I could remind him of all we shared and change his mind somehow? Maybe he still cared?

As I applied the hot oil to my head, Echo's icy hot needles prickled my arms, her calling card. "You don't have a snowball's chance in hell with Carl," she hissed. "He's found a normal girl. Not like us, Silver, sweetheart. The best you can hope for is a farewell romp to keep him dreaming of you."

I scoffed at the idea. "My consolation prize?"

Downstairs, the front door banged open. Too early for Rossi's evening check in.

"You with anyone, Echo?" An Irish brogue, slurred and demanding, called out. Footsteps, heavy and uneven, thudded up the wooden stairs. "It's Murphy. Came to collect my payment." He blurted a drunken laugh and slipped off a step. Cursing, and recovering slowly.

Fear rippled through me. Murphy. Murphy's Pub from the Echo's napkin. One of Echo's clients? I pulled up my silk kimono and tightened the tie.

Echo's presence enveloped me like a warm blanket. "Don't worry Silver, sweetheart. Murphy's quick on the draw as they say. I'll protect you like always."

"Echo isn't here." I yelled back, quivering. "She's at the pub." I slathered more oil on my hair, hoping the sight would frighten him. "Said she'd meet you there."

He reached the landing, floorboards groaning with each step.

"Please, God, let me escape this," I prayed, my mind racing for a way out.

Echo laughed hysterically in my ears. "Nowhere to go. Nowhere to hide."

The man burst through the doorway, a hulking figure in the dim lamplight. "There you are, Echo, baby," he slurred, the stench of stale alcohol wafting off him. "Torrio said you were the best, and he never lies."

"What does Torrio have to do with this?" I backed against the dressing table.

"Torrio said you were free game now that he dumped you. Remember the deal he made for you? Free dates for bringing in the marks at Murphy's. You admitted it yourself." He lurched toward me, his meaty hand reaching out.

I tried to dodge him, but he was too fast. His greasy fingers closed around my arm, pulling me close. "Stay away from me." He wouldn't get what he wanted. I'd die first.

He slammed me against the dressing table. Heaving his bulk on me, he crushed my lungs so I couldn't breathe. My body went cold and still. Déjà vu moved over me like a glacier. Rockwell, his crushing weight, the memory forever frozen in my bones.

My fingers clutched the sides of the table, my nails brushing against the pot of oil. The burning smell hung acrid and thick in the air.

Echo emerged, shielding me from his brutal attack. "Step back, Silver. This is my job. You're just in the way."

"Don't play games, Echo," Murphy grunted. "You owe me bigtime." He forced a bruising, slobbering kiss.

I tasted the rot of his teeth, felt the slimy trail of his tongue.

Echo bit hard on his tongue, and he howled like a coyote.

"You hellcat." Murphy slapped me. "You deserve this." He unleashed his belt, tearing at his pants. His weight crushed me, his breath hot and fetid against my face.

Echo wrestled her hand free and grabbed his neck, forcefully squeezing until he gagged and coughed.

Murphy lifted his head, eyes popping like Rockwell's had. He yowled like a trapped animal, screaming in my ear.

Adrenaline flooded me. My hands spasmed, each finger tightening, crushing. His red bulging face blurred, his eyes rolling back in his head.

"No, Echo. We can't. You can't. I won't live through this again."

Echo's long nails scratching at his eyes. "Let me protect you!" Her shriek blended with mine.

Murphy growled and grasped between my legs.

Had to stop her. Cannot live with that guilt. Grabbing the handle on the boiling oil, I lifted it over our heads. I hesitated. But if I didn't do it, I'd never be rid of her. A pain worse than death. An epiphany struck me like lightning. I would never be free of Echo. Not unless I killed her. And to kill her, I had to kill myself.

Tipping the pot, I unleashed a torrent of boiling oil, a searing cascade that engulfed us. The agonizing heat ripped through my skin, sounds of sizzling flesh and stifled screams.

I kept pouring the golden liquid, honey dripping straight off the comb, the buzzing of bees around my head. My oiled hair, now a glorious autumn bonfire, crackled and hissed as it burned.

Murphy punched the pot out of my hand with a shattering clang. He jumped off me. "What the hell?" He clutched his sizzling arm, black hairs burning like a prairie fire.

Echo screeched a raw, primal screech that tore through the room, a sound no human throat could make.

Molten oil cascaded down my face and body, a baptism of fire that blistered my skin and filled my nostrils with the stench of seared flesh.

Blinded by the burning oil, I could only make out the vague shapes of Echo's oil-slick hands flailing in agony. She was screaming, crying for mercy. But she was losing the battle, the flames eating the skin on her face, her chest, her arms. Echo was dying, my fierce companion and enemy, protector and tormentor. The agony seemed to slow down, each of Echo's gasps for air stretching into an eternity. I watched, detached, as if it were all happening to someone else. Was this grief? Or relief?

Murphy watched, his face a death mask. He reached out, then jerked his hand back, fear and anguish warring in his eyes. "Oh

God, oh God," he choked out, the words barely audible over the roar of the flames. Murphy yowled and grunted, his pounding footsteps retreating down the stairs. In the brutal silence, only the burning oil pool around me crackled and hissed.

I surrendered to the engulfing flames, a final offering for my sins. The flames licked at my skin, a searing caress like the pain Echo had inflicted on my soul. My burning hair smelled of sacred sacrifice. My vision wavered, sparks scattering against the comforting darkness that beckoned. In that inferno, I saw a reflection of my own tormented spirit, finally finding release.

Mama ... I'm sorry. I only wanted to make you proud.

Molten oil and flames, a heavy blanket pulling me under. Echo was truly gone ... only silence ... A single tear of pain and regret traced a scorching path down my cheek. Was this peace? Or surrender?

"Blessed Mother." A hoarse whisper. "Forgive me."

The screams of the past echoed in my ears, growing fainter as the flames consumed me. The tigers... free now, at least. And Carl ... wish I could have loved you the way you deserved.

A final, wheezing gasp escaped my lips as the flames devoured me. Then ... only the sound of crackling flames. The world dissolved into a rainbow of light and shadow, a final dance before darkness claimed me.

Chapter 48

1932

Silver price $.28 per ounce

Denver, Colorado. The Tabor Grand Opera House shimmered against the velvet night, a beacon in the swirling snow. Baby Doe's heart pounded like a sledgehammer against rock. Her daughter's name, emblazoned on the giant marquee, shone brighter than any silver strike.

SILVER DOLLAR!

If only her Silver could see this. Pride swelled in Baby Doe's chest, then twisted into a bittersweet ache. Below, a sea of faces churned, their anticipation a palpable hum in the air. Newsboys darted through the crowd; their cries swallowed by the eager murmur.

The crowd around the entrance was suffocating. Denver society had swelled beyond recognition. Had the audiences always been this large? Or had she simply become invisible, like a faded sepia photograph of the past?

"Look at this, Horace darling," she whispered, wiping her cheek. "Our theater in all its glory, up and running again." A whisper of his Creed cologne teased her senses. And for a fleeting moment, she felt his warm embrace.

Carl led her to the VIP door, a whirlwind of energy in his

tailored tails and top hat. Gone was the young man who'd interviewed her; this was a rising Hollywood star. She'd miss their quiet meetings, their shared love for the Tabor story. Tonight would change everything. Why would Carl visit an old eccentric woman when he belonged to this glamourous scene? She'd once belonged too.

A flashbulb exploded in her face, momentarily blinding her. A man in a houndstooth jacket thrust his card at her. "*Variety Magazine*, Mrs. Tabor. Can I schedule an interview for tomorrow?"

Carl held up his hand. "Save your questions for the press conference."

A thrill pulsed through her at the mention of an interview. It'd been so long. But she tamped down her pride. "Smart, Carl. Let them devour Bebe Daniels and Edward G. Robinson."

"Trust me." He smiled at her. "It's you they'll want to talk to. Hear the whole story from Baby Doe herself."

"I'm not that woman anymore. Let them see the Tabors young, bold, and reckless in your movie. Not this old, worn-out prospector. I don't want to dredge up the past and all their gossip about us. Especially not about Silver Dollar. Let her rest in peace."

Carl nodded glumly at the mention of Silver, forever a bruised spot on his heart.

Suddenly they were in the lobby she'd designed. The theater was more magnificent than she remembered. The thick Brussels carpet, the moire taffeta wallcoverings, the gilded moldings—all her choices, a testimony to a different lifetime. Memories flooded her: the gleam of mahogany, rich brocade, opulent marble, and wood paneling set off by gold. She hadn't seen the Tabor Grand since they lost it.

The chandeliers dimmed three times, signaling the guests to enter the theater.

"I need to get you settled in our seats, Mrs. Tabor. They want me on stage with the director and producer."

He led her to the front box seats, the same seats she used to sit in when the Tabors entertained dignitaries, senators, governors, and her friends like the Vanderbilts, Marshall Fields, opera stars, actors, writers and artists.

"I'll be back after the introduction." He stepped up to the stage, leaving her alone.

She tightened the lace mantilla over her face. Why expose herself to their scrutiny? This wasn't her life anymore. She'd come here to represent the Tabor family, but without her husband and daughters, she felt like an imposter. She couldn't claim the glory of their lives without them.

When the theater lights dimmed, she slipped up the side aisle to the back of the theater where she could watch the movie in anonymity.

She reached the back row, a nun in a white habit and veil sat alone. Seeing empty seats around her, Baby Doe felt the sense of peace she'd been craving. It seemed like a sign. "Mind if I sit with you?"

The nun shook her head, her face mostly hidden behind a pristine white coif and a stiffly starched wimple. Her hands, clasped in her lap, were rough and calloused, a mirror to her own. Yet the nun's upright shoulders spoke of a much younger woman. As she settled into the seat, a whiff of frankincense mingled with the elusive scent of lilies, hovering just beyond the reach of memory like a half-forgotten dream. Her heart skipped a beat.

Applause drew her eyes up front where Carl walked across the stage, bathed in a warm spotlight. His tuxedo shimmered like that monster silver vein in the Matchless mine, now buried forever from the explosion. Carl adjusted the microphone, his gaze sweeping the audience. A wave of warmth washed over her. He cleared his throat, and she noticed a slight tremor in his hands. A bittersweet ache settled in her heart.

"Good evening, everyone. Tonight, we share a story that has haunted me for years. The rise and fall of the Tabor dynasty. Baby

Doe and Horace Tabor." He raised his arm out to her empty box seat. His brow furrowed. "Ah, Mrs. Tabor seems to have stepped away for a moment."

Baby Doe winced. Guilt pricked at her for abandoning her seat, but this was Carl's night to shine. His chance to share the Tabor story, a story he'd woven from memories, love, and a few facts, and a broad brush of Hollywood sparkle. She wasn't about to steal his thunder.

"The Tabors weren't just chasing a fortune; they built an empire," Carl continued. "Mines, theaters, railroads, firehouses—their investments touched every facet of society. They lived a life fueled by a burning passion, a fire that forged their dreams into reality. And maybe, that's the true treasure we can find in their story. Even when the world crumbles around you, don't abandon the dream. Cling to love, live with reckless abandon, and leave your own indelible mark on the world, just like the Tabors." He huffed and looked at the floor, then recovered. "That's the legacy the Tabors leave behind, a legacy that resonates, even today."

The nun beside her sniffled, a soft, mournful sound, as she watched Carl speak with rapt attention. A tear escaped, tracing a glistening path down the weathered lines of her cheek. "Why such sorrow?" Baby Doe wondered, a wave of empathy washing over her. Was it Carl's words that stirred such deep emotion within the sister? She gently touched the nun's arm and offered her a crisp, lavender-scented linen handkerchief.

The nun took the hankie, her face remained glued to the stage. "Thank you."

The slight lisp, the melodic tone ... Baby Doe's breath caught. From the plush velvet seat, her gaze was drawn to the nun's ravaged features: a long nose, enormous dark eyes starkly devoid of lashes and brows, a stark contrast to the serenity of her habit. In the warm glow of the crystal chandelier, the network of red, ropy scars stood out in stark relief against her pale skin—a chilling reminder of the headlines that had once screamed across the nation: "Death by Scalding."

"Silver Dollar?" The name escaped Baby Doe's lips in a breathless whisper. A moment stretched. "Is that you?"

The nun's warm, strong hand enveloped hers. Scarred fingers intertwined. A sob tore from Baby Doe's throat, a raw, guttural sound of years of suppressed grief. Silver. Her Silver Dollar had returned to her, but so different.

"Yes, Mama." The nun's voice was thick with emotion. "I'm Sister Rose Mary, now."

Baby Doe gasped, squeezing her daughter's arm. "The nun I've been writing to at Holy Sepulcher about the women's shelter?" Laughter and tears mingled, a torrent of relief and disbelief. She crossed herself, tears streaming down her cheeks.

"You didn't know?" Sister Rose Mary asked, a gentle smile gracing her lips.

"I did feel something," Baby Doe's voice was thick with emotion. Of course she must have known. A mother always knows. "Rose Mary ..." A sudden memory sparked: Silver Dollar as a young girl, twirling in her tutu across this very stage. "Rose Mary Echo Silver Dollar ... You kept your name?"

"Yes, Mama." A soft glow seemed to emanate from her face in the dim theater. "Rose Mary was the part of me that felt untarnished."

"Thank God, my child. My prayers are answered." She squeezed Silver's hand, fresh tears welling up. "I knew you were alive in my heart." She clutched Silver's sleeve. All those years hoping and praying her daughter was alive.

"Mama, I was sure you knew it was me when you sent Holy Sepulcher that donation for the women's shelter." Silver's fngers traced the lines on Baby Doe's palm. "Your donation touched so many lives. I'm a cloistered nun, Mama, but Mother Superior granted me a visit here to thank you in person."

Baby Doe beamed. "It was my pleasure, dear."

Silver's brow furrowed. "Did that donation really come from the Matchless? I knew silver went up in the twenties, but I never imagined the Matchless would produce like that again. That was amazing."

"Consider it a last gift from your papa." A bittersweet smile touched Baby Doe's lips as she thought of Horace. "Your father hid his inheritance away in a Matchless tunnel. That's what he was trying to tell us when he died."

"You always believed in him, Mama, even when no one else did." Silver glanced down at her. "And you always believed in me."

Baby Doe squeezed her hand, feeling Horace's presence with them, a comforting warmth. In the dim light of the theater, surrounded by the ghosts of the past, she finally felt the love she'd craved, the circle complete. Her Silver Dollar, reborn as Sister Rose Mary, was safe.

"I want you to know I learned my lesson, Mama," Silver said. "I wanted stardom. I wanted fame. I wanted applause. And when I got it all, I turned my back on love." Silver's head riveted to the stage, finding Carl with deep longing in her eyes.

"He still loves you, you know," Baby Doe whispered.

Silver shook her head, a curl escaping her coif. "No, Mama. Carl loved the woman I was when we first met," she said wistfully, her voice catching. "My heart belongs to God now."

"I understand your soul belongs to the Lord, sweet girl." Her hand found Silver's and gave it a reassuring squeeze. "But the heart has a memory all its own."

Silver's grip tightened. "Tell Carl it wasn't his fault, Mama. He's carried a guilt that was all mine. Tell him I'm happier now. Finally at peace."

Deep sadness clouded her eyes, a shadow passing over her features. Her daughter looked so sad, but Baby Doe knew she was right. True happiness resided in faith, not the fleeting joys of the world. Yet, regret pooled in her heart. Regret for the life they all could have shared together, a life filled with laughter, love, and the joyful chaos of family.

"And now," Carl boomed, his arms outstretched, "the stars of our movie, Bebe Daniels and Edward G. Robinson!" Bebe Daniels, a whirlwind of glittering sequins, captivated the audience with her dazzling smile. Trailing slightly behind, Edward G. Robinson, a man who seemed to carry the weight of the world on his shoulders, surveyed the crowd with a keen, knowing gaze.

"Your papa would roll in his grave to be portrayed by Robinson," Baby Doe said.

"Wouldn't he though?" Silver laugh sounded like sleigh bells.

Baby Doe intertwined her fingers with Silver's. The scars and scrapes from working with their hands. They were kindred spirits, dreamers who'd learned the value of a humble life.

She watched the movie through her daughter's eyes. Now she recognized what Silver and Carl meant to each other. And why Carl was obsessed with the Tabor story. It was their story ... blind ambition leading to a life lived on their own terms.

It was an extraordinary sensation, watching her own life flashing on the silver screen like a divine review. Every scene was more beautiful, nostalgic, and heart-wrenching than the last. Horace, once a hopeful prospector, materialized on-screen. She blinked back hot tears. Memory pierced the darkness. The earthy smell of the mine shaft. Horace's exultant cry as he swung the pickaxe, revealing the first gleam of silver ore. His strong back gleamed with sweat, a grin splitting his dirty face. Harrowing wagon rides over narrow ledges of mountain stagecoach trails, the wheels creaking precariously close to the edge, the wind whipping through her hair. Backbreaking thrills of chipping away at a gleam of silver in dark tunnels. Exhilarating, exhausting years of the political fight between silver and the gold standard.

And success was fickle. Horace, fueled by wealth and power, became a stranger working dozens of mines, crooked bedfellows, and the next big strike. Their daughters' faces, a source of such happiness, appeared on screen. A pang of guilt pierced her. Had she, too, been blinded by ambition? The silver crash came in a terrifying freefall, stripping them bare of the trappings of wealth. The mansions, carriages, horses, servants ... every possession auctioned to cover the debt. Horace, a broken shell of the man she loved. Such loss.

And yet, she realized that even amidst the pain and the regrets, there was a beauty, a simplicity, a love that burned brighter than any silver. On the screen, the image shifted from the opulence of the Tabor mansion to a quiet scene of domesticity. From the ashes, something precious had emerged. She saw them gathered around a worn wooden table, sharing a meager meal, laughter filling the small space. In their eyes, she saw a quiet strength, a faith that had weathered the storm. Like a wildflower pushing through the cracks in mountain rock, a new life had blossomed from the ruins of the old, bringing a different kind of beauty, a resilient richness.

∽

AT THE END of the movie, the audience jumped to their feet. The ovation, a thunderclap of applause, seemed to shake the very foundations of the theater.

Silver's hands twisted in her lap, her knuckles bone white. "After Papa died, how'd you ever have the courage to move us to Leadville?"

"Leadville was our sanctuary," Baby Doe said softly. "The fresh mountain air, the view of Turquoise Lake ... I thought it would heal us."

"But why'd you move us into the mine cabin?" she pleaded. "Lily hated it and left us."

"You must have been lonely when Lily left, I know. But Lily wanted a different life than I could provide. I couldn't blame her for leaving." Though it killed her when Lily denied she was a Tabor to the Chicago newspapers.

Silver's shoulders caved in with a heavy sigh.

Baby Doe cringed, guilt twisting in her gut. Losing her father, then her sister ... it was too much for a young girl to bear. Sadness overwhelmed her as she caressed her daughter's scarred cheek, guilt for not recognizing the depth of Silver's pain all those years ago. "When you were sad," she said softly, "I tried to encourage your creativity, writing, dancing, acting, singing." You were talented from the time you were little. My shooting star, Silver. A light so bright no one could ever dim it. You had your own dreams to follow."

Silver sighed. "I made such a mess of it, Mama. You have no idea."

A thousand mangled dreams hung between them. "Looks like you found your way." She patted her hand. "You were destined for great things, my darling. And you found them." Even though a part of her ached with the knowledge that their paths, once intertwined, now diverged like the branches of a tree reaching for the sun.

As the house lights came up, Silver's hand darted to her wimple, smoothing it nervously as she watched Carl walking toward them. Baby Doe watched her daughter, a knot tightening in her throat. Silver's shoulders were tense, her gaze darting between Carl and the exit.

"I have to go." Silver's coif revealed a red and blotchy complexion. She pulled the wimple forward, as if to hide her turmoil. "Peace be with you, Mama."

Silver glided past, her habit brushing Baby Doe's knees, igniting a panic within her. Goodbye forever? Would she ever again hold her daughter, feel her embrace, hear her laughter?

But before walking away, Silver locked eyes with Carl, hers filled with unshed tears, his with disbelief and longing. The air thrummed with unspoken emotions, years of yearning and regret. Carl's hesitant wave broke the spell. Silver Dollar's answering smile was faint, her hand trembling as she squeezed Baby Doe's shoulder.

"Tell him, he did it, Mama. Tell Carl the film was all that I ever dreamed of and more." Her hand flew to her mouth, stifling a sob. Then, she was gone. The rustle of programs and the murmur of voices muffled the sound of Silver's retreating footsteps. A dark figure swallowed by the sea of faces, disappearing into the anonymity of the crowd.

Baby Doe's throat swelled. Silver's touch lingered on her shoulder, a phantom warmth in the cool theater air. Carl threaded through the crowd towards her, his eyes searching frantically.

"That was Silver, wasn't it?" He clenched his jaw, running a shaky hand through his hair. "Is she coming back? What did she say?"

He deserved the truth, but what was the truth? Was it the lingering embers of love in Silver's eyes, or the resolute acceptance of her chosen path? Each truth held its own kind of pain, its own potential for heartbreak. Baby Doe swallowed the lump in her throat, the weight of her decision heavy in her heart.

"She wanted me to tell you that nothing that happened was your fault," she said, gently. "And you're not to bear the weight of the past. She wants you to be happy."

Carl collapsed onto a plush seat, his hands behind his neck, his voice hollow. "She's gone? I don't even get to talk to her?"

"She's a cloistered nun, Carl. She chose her life."

He expelled a great huff. His gaze, lost and searching, soared across the ornate ceiling, searching for solace amidst the painted cherubs and billowing clouds. "Did she like the movie, at least? God, I did it for her ... because of her." His breath was ragged. "All these years, I thought I could have saved her ..." He pounded a trembling fist against his chest. "Silver loved her family so much. I just wanted her to know ... somehow, that she was right to be proud."

Baby Doe choked back the sob rising in her throat. "Silver

thought the movie was perfect, Carl. Exactly how she would have wanted it." She squeezed his arm.

He looked up, his eyes glistening.

"You poured your heart into this film," she said. "Tonight, we celebrate your triumph." But as she guided Carl into the lobby, the flash of cameras capturing their every move, she knew none of them would ever forget this moment ... a moment teetering between what was and what might have been.

∼

The opulent Tabor Grand buzzed with excitement as Carl escorted Baby Doe through the grand archway, a radiant smile illuminating his face as he offered her a glass of champagne. All eyes were on them; him, the rising star, and her, the enduring legend. The crowd erupted in applause, warmth breezing over her like a zephyr.

Baby Doe lifted her chin, a smile curving her lips as she watched Carl receive the recognition he so deserved for the film. And, it was more than just a film, wasn't it? It was a testament to perseverance, and a reminder that even the deepest wounds could heal and lead to unexpected triumphs.

Carl's smile lit up like a Christmas tree, his glass raised in a private toast, "To Silver Dollar, the woman who inspired me to make this film, and to the remarkable Baby Doe who had the courage to live it."

They drank their champagne, their eyes meeting over the brims, a secret passing between them that no one else in the room would ever know. The unspoken truth that lay beneath the surface of this celebration ... the truth about Silver Dollar, the woman who'd been lost to them until a few minutes ago. They'd witnessed Silver's return at the premiere, radiant and serene, a world away from the troubled young woman who'd vanished years ago in scandal and shame.

As Carl was pulled away by the film's producer and director, the orchestra struck up "The Band Played On". A song that had always held a special place in her heart, a reminder of the resilience and joy that could be found even in the darkest of times.

Subtle scents of lilies and frankincense wafted through the soft murmur of the crowd, drawing her gaze toward their source. Her eyes landed on the nun by the front doors. A serene grin turned into a beaming smile on her daughter's lips. Silver raised her scarred hand in more of a blessing than a goodbye, before she turned and slipped into the night.

Baby Doe's eyes danced over the crowd, a sea of shimmering gowns and smiling faces. It was a night of celebration, a culmination of a lifetime of dreams. She thought of Horace, her rock, and Lily, who had chosen a different path. But it was Silver Dollar ... She had wrestled with her own demons, her ambition and restless spirit. Faced the fire and come out stronger, braver.

And it was her love for Silver, unwavering, that gave her strength to go on. A love that had endured. A love that now held the promise of peace. Baby Doe stood tall, her heart filled with gratitude and a quiet determination to embrace the future, whatever it might hold.

THE END

There are hardly any exceptions to the rule
that a person must pay dearly
for the divine gift
of the creative fire.

~Carl Jung, *Modern Man in Search of a Soul*

Epilogue

Leadville, Colorado. As Baby Doe peeled potatoes for a humble Colcannon on her porch, an uneasy acceptance settled over her. She'd weathered the storm of the past month the best she could, memories flickering like the movie in her brain. The Matchless Mine explosion had sent the miners and investors scurrying for a new mine, leaving her alone in the cabin. The whirlwind of the movie premiere was behind her, now left her with the monotonous rhythm of her lonely life. A stubborn ache of longing dragged heavy on her heart, knowing she might never see her daughter's face again. But the memory of their tender reunion and shared purpose at the women's shelter brought a measure of solace.

Old Charlie, bowlegged as ever, ambled up the lane from town. He presented her with a muslin bag filled with rocks, a gap-toothed grin on his face.

"The queen's jewels?" She peered inside, plucked out a dull gray rock, and gave him a skeptical look. "Surely not silver. More fool's gold to mock me, Charlie?"

He swept his arm across the vast expanse of rubble around

them, all the same dull stuff stretching as far as the eye could see. "Same rocks as all these," he said, his grin widening.

She scratched her head, a spark of curiosity igniting in her chest. "Well, there must be a point to this. Out with it, Charlie."

"Just got back from the assay office down in Denver." Charlie puffed out his chest. "These here rocks are Molybdenite."

"Molyb-what-now?"

"Molybdenite. They use it in steel to make it stronger, harder, less likely to rust through."

She turned the rock over in her hands, unimpressed. "Never heard of it."

Charlie chuckled. "That's why your investors paid no mind to this ore when the Matchless exploded and laid these beauties right in front of their eyes like an Easter egg hunt. They were too damn busy chasing that shiny silver to see they'd exploded a fortune from the mine."

A sweet, familiar thrill coursed through Baby Doe's veins. "So, we've got work to do?" She extended her hand for a shake. "Partners? Fifty-fifty?"

He countered with a mischievous glint in his eyes. "Hold on now, I discovered it. Should be more like sixty-forty in my favor!"

She tilted her chin, a spark of the old fire burning. "But I own the Matchless, Charlie. And the land it sits on."

He stroked his beard thoughtfully. "True enough. But what about all your investors? Won't they be wanting a cut?"

Holding a finger to her lips, a sly smile spread across her face. "Who's talking to 'em?" She tossed the rock in the air and caught it with a wild giggle. "You sure you want to start all this again, Charlie?"

But in her heart, she knew the answer. It was what they were born for. The thrill of the chase, the taste of possibility, the chance to turn the ordinary into something extraordinary. As the sun dipped below the horizon, casting long shadows across the scarred landscape, Baby Doe felt a spark of hope ignite within her. The spirit of adventure was alive and kickin'.

Author's Notes

The life of Silver Dollar Tabor is shrouded in contradictions, a tale whispered in hushed tones and riddled with conflicting accounts. Few historical figures have been as misrepresented and misunderstood as this enigmatic daughter of the legendary Silver Queen, Baby Doe Tabor. A woman of immense talent, young Silver Dollar captivated audiences as a writer, actress, and singer, even performing for President Theodore Roosevelt. Yet, her brilliance was overshadowed by a life marked by instability and tragedy.

The tale most often told about Silver Dollar is one of a promising show business career tragically derailed by addiction and a cruel death in Chicago. But her mother, Baby Doe Tabor, clung to a different story, claiming Silver Dollar had joined a convent.

It was in the letters Silver Dollar penned to her mother, spanning her ten years in Chicago, that I finally glimpsed a different version of "the truth." Each letter was signed "Your loving child, Silver," but they were written from a different name and address, with shifting details about her life: her work, her relationships, her friends. She was a chameleon, constantly changing, with no stable identity or sense of belonging.

This discovery led me to re-examine the known events of Silver

Dollar's life, searching for the roots of her instability. The family's financial ruin and the public shame of losing everything, followed by her father's death and the isolation of the Matchless mine, created a deep sense of loss for Silver Dollar. This was further compounded by Lily's abandonment and the traumatic abuse she suffered at the hands of their family lawyer.

While a definitive diagnosis is impossible, Silver Dollar's shifting identities and fragmented sense of self resonate with modern understandings of Dissociative Identity Disorder (DID). Though DID was little understood in her time, her struggles with identity speak to the intense human struggle to define ourselves, especially in the face of adversity.

In *Silver Echoes*, I explore this fragmented self, not just as a medical condition but as a reflection of her human experience. After all, don't we all have different parts to our personalities? And when the going gets tough, don't different parts emerge? Silver Dollar's story, though rooted in history, speaks to the enduring question of who we are when life forces us to reinvent ourselves.

About Dissociative Identity Disorder

In dissociative identity disorder, the awareness that different personalities, or "alters," have of each other can vary significantly. Here's what is generally understood:

- **Amnesia is common:** Often, alters have amnesia for periods when other alters are in control. This means one personality might not remember what happened when another was "out."
- **Awareness can vary:** Some alters may be completely unaware of others. Some might be aware of another alter and even observe their actions as if watching

someone else. Others might have a more interactive relationship, even communicating internally.
- **Complex inner worlds:** In some cases, alters exist within a complex inner world where they have relationships and roles. The level of awareness and interaction within this inner world can be quite intricate.
- **"Host" personality:** Often, a primary or "host" personality exists that identifies with the person's given name. This host may be unaware of the other alters.

It's not quite accurate to say that the "bad" behavior of an alter in DID is simply the result of trauma in the host personality. Here's a more nuanced explanation:

- **Trauma's role:** DID itself is strongly linked to severe and often repeated trauma, particularly in childhood. This trauma can be physical, sexual, or emotional abuse or other forms of significant adversity.
- **Alters as coping mechanisms:** Alters are thought to develop as ways to cope with overwhelming trauma. Different alters may embody different aspects of the trauma or serve different protective functions.
- **"Bad" alter's function:** An alter that exhibits "bad" behavior may be carrying the anger, aggression, or self-destructive impulses that resulted from the trauma. They might act out in ways the host personality cannot or will not.
- **Not just the host's trauma:** It's important to remember that each alter, in a sense, has their own experiences and responses to the trauma. The "bad" alter's behavior might be a direct reaction to their own perceived role or experiences, not just a reflection of the host's trauma.

Think of it this way: Imagine a group of people who survived a terrible disaster together. Each person might cope with the trauma in different ways. Some might become withdrawn, others might become caregivers, and others might become angry and lash out. In DID, these different coping mechanisms can become embodied in separate alters.

It's crucial to avoid stigmatizing any alter, even those with challenging behaviors. They are all parts of a person trying to cope with overwhelming experiences. Therapy for DID often focuses on

understanding the roles of different alters, processing the underlying trauma, and working toward integration and healing.

Sources:

For a general understanding of DID:

- *The Dissociative Identity Disorder Sourcebook by Deborah Bray Haddock:* A comprehensive overview of DID for both individuals with the disorder and their loved ones.
- *Understanding and Treating Dissociative Identity Disorder by Elizabeth* **F. Howell:** A more academic approach, exploring the theory and treatment of DID from a relational perspective.

For trauma and its impact on DID:

- *The Body Keeps the Score* by Bessel van der Kolk MD: While not solely focused on DID, this book explores the profound impact of trauma on the mind and body, offering insights relevant to understanding how trauma contributes to DID.
- *Trauma and Recovery* by Judith Herman MD: A

classic text on trauma, including discussion of complex trauma and its relationship to dissociation.

For the perspective of individuals with DID:

- *When Rabbit Howls* by The Troops for Truddi Chase: A powerful first-person account of living with DID, written by a collective of alters.
- *The Sum of My Parts: A Survivor's Story of Dissociative Identity Disorder* by Olga Trujillo JD: A memoir offering insights into the internal world and experiences of someone with DID.

Learn More About Silver Echoes

Want to delve deeper in the world of Silver Echoes? Follow me on Facebook @Rebecca Rosenberg Novels, and Instagram @Rebecca Rosenberg Novelist.

Visit the blog on my website, for fascinating back stories:

- **Silver Dollar's escapades:** Discover the truth behind her scandalous burlesque shows and her movie career in the silent film era. Discover the wild Motion Picture Zoo of Selig Polyscope in Chicago.
- **The dark side of Chicago:** Explore the hidden lives of 1920s gangsters Diamond Jim, infamous Madame Victoria Colosimo, and Johnny Torrio. Learn the fate of the dazzling performer, Dale Winter. Learn of the chilling reality of the Ku Klux Klan's presence in the city.
- **Relive the prohibition wars** between the gangsters and the Women's Temperance Movement.
- **Uncover the real-life characters in** *Silver Echoes*: the delightful Tiny Kline, a famous circus performer,

who slid across Time Square by her teeth! And the real tiger tamer who inspired me, Mabel Stark.
- **The untold stories:** Uncover the secrets of Carl Erikson, the screenwriter behind the controversial film *Silver Dollar*.
- **The legacy of Baby Doe:** Journey into the famous Matchless Mine and experience the heartbreaking story of Baby Doe's final years.

Join the conversation and uncover the hidden history behind *Silver Echoes*!

Acknowledgments

With gratitude from the bottom of my heart:

To Rae Blair, author, and my Sydney writing buddy. Rae, your insights on character development were invaluable, and your unwavering belief in this story kept me going through countless rewrites.

To Cindy Conger, my publicist, the magician, editor, writer, and hand-holder. I couldn't have done any of this without you in my corner.

To Stephanie Rabell of Books and Wine Marketing, your infectious enthusiasm and uncanny ability to promote and find readers made the publishing journey a joy. I was eternally grateful for your guidance and support.

To my editor, Tiffany Yates Martin of FoxPrint Editorial, your sharp eye and insightful suggestions helped me polish this story to a shine.

To The Book Designers, thank you for capturing the essence of *Silver Echoes* in such a stunning cover.

To my husband, Gary, who read *Silver Echoes* and assured me it was riveting (and who hardly ever complained when I disappeared into my writing cave for days on end). Your love and support meant the world to me.

To my friends, Lori Fantozzi and Pam Schlossberg, your early feedback helped me shape the emotional core of this story.

To my beta readers, Matthew Lawrence, Barb Bryzgalski, Susan Peterson, Deborah Harpham, Courtney Salmon, Irene Tan, Nicky Lees, Jennifer Van Hook, Vivian Gerber, Janet Wright, and Dave Kanzig. Your insights were invaluable.

To my many author friends who offered to read, blurb, and spread the word on about *Silver Echoes*, your time, generosity and support were truly appreciated. Thank you so much.

To my blogging, social media, and street team friends who welcomed *Silver Echoes*, thank you for spreading the word.

This novel would not exist without the incredible reading and writing community that surrounded me. I am deeply grateful for your friendship and support.

~Rebecca

About the Author

Rebecca Rosenberg is a champagne geek, lavender farmer, and multi-award-winning and bestselling author of several historical novels about extraordinary women. Her novels, including the Gold Digger series and the Champagne Widows series, celebrate the strength and spirit of women who dared to defy convention. Growing up in Denver, Colorado, she was captivated by the story of Baby Doe Tabor, a woman whose life mirrored the boom and bust of the Wild West, and her daughter. Silver Dollar, the subject of her latest novel, *Silver Echoes*. When not writing, Rebecca can be found sipping champagne, stomping grapes, or exploring ghost towns!

Read the First Chapter of Gold Digger

One look at Baby Doe Tabor and you know she was meant to be a legend of the Wild West and Gilded Age! She was just twenty years old when she came west to work a gold mine with her new husband. Little did she expect that she'd be abandoned and pregnant and left to manage the gold mine alone. But that didn't stop her! She fell in love with an old married prospector, twice her age. Horace Tabor struck the biggest silver vein in history, scandalously divorced his wife, became a US Senator, and married Baby Doe at the US capitol with President Arthur in attendance. Though Baby Doe Tabor was renowned for her beauty, her fashion, and even her philanthropy, she was never welcomed in polite society. Her friends were stars they hired to perform at their Tabor Grand Opera House: Sarah Bernhardt, Oscar Wilde, Lily Langtry, opera star Emma Abbott. Discover how the Tabors navigated the worlds of scandal, greed, wealth, power, and politics in the wild days of western mining.

Enjoy this sample of *Gold Digger, the Remarkable Baby Doe Tabor.*

Chapter 1
Trans-Continental Railroad
1878

Tumbleweeds scraped across the Colorado prairie as Lizzie looked out the window of the Pullman railcar, rushing along the rickety tracks, too fast, too far, ever farther away from her family.

The ache under her breastbone deepened as she remembered Da back at the train platform, dour as a pallbearer. Ever since the Oshkosh fires ripped through their haberdashery, their theater, and even their home, the light went out of his Irish eyes. He should have hugged her and wished her Godspeed, but he just pressed a cameo locket into her palm.

On the train, Lizzie opened the locket hanging over her heart, staring at her parents' faces.

"You are such a tease." Harvey Doe, her husband of two weeks, reached across and caressed her décolletage like it belonged to him, which maybe it did."

A bead of irritation trickled down her neck, the July morning already stifling. "My stars, are you as ravenous as I am?" Lifting a profusion of red-gold locks, Lizzie fluttered a peacock feather fan. "I'll go find out when breakfast is served." Maybe fresh air would clear away her homesickness.

"Elizabeth McCourt Doe, just sit there and look beautiful." Harvey's bowler hat topped dark blond curls framing a face so thin-skinned his blue veins showed through. Lizzie's father had tailored his natty three-piece suit to perfection. His starched shirt still held its press for the third day on the Union Pacific, headed west to Central City, Colorado. "No wife of mine will be wandering around the train looking the way you do."

"What's wrong with how I look?" She leaned over to the wall mirror and pinched her cheeks for color. Her beauty was a gift from God, Mam said, a gold-plated guarantee she'd marry a gentleman of means and wouldn't have to take in mending. She tied her hat ribbon under her chin, her bosom inches from Harvey's eyes, wielding her power over the boy.

He pinned her to the seat, sweet-clover breath close to her own. His trembling fingers traveled down her face, pulling back her curls until it hurt and kissing her breathless.

"Lizzie, I'll make you the richest woman in Colorado. I swear I will. The Fourth of July gold mine will strike it big. Just wait and see."

Richest woman in Colorado. He said it again. She didn't need to be the richest, just enough to pull her family back from the precipice.

"But, we'll be back for Christmas?" She spread her fingers through his hair.

"Sooner, if I can help it."

The train porter strutted down the aisle ringing his brass bell, wearing the same blue uniform with frayed cuffs he'd worn the whole trip. "Breakfast is served...in a quarter hour," he said, his Southern cadence melodic to her ears.

Harvey traced the crocheted trim on her plunging neckline with a bitten fingernail.

"Enjoying the scenery?" the porter asked.

Harvey retrieved his hand and studied it for a hangnail.

Lizzie laughed. "Why, yes, we are, Mister George."

"Just plain George." He pointed to the nametag on his lapel.

"Seems like all the porters are named George," she said.

"They calls us that after George Pullman, inventor of this here sleeper car." He smiled.

"George it is, then." She gazed outside the window, bothered he wasn't allowed to use his real name.

Two bare-chested men rode horseback on a barren hill. "Land 'O Goshen." She pressed her palms on the window. "Are those real Indians?"

"Pawnee, I reckon." George plucked whiskers on his chin, eyes fixed on the horsemen. "Pawnees looking for a Morning Star sacrifice. Not a subject fit for ladies."

"You have to tell me now," she said, irked when he looked to Harvey for permission.

"She won't leave you alone until you do," Harvey said. "She questions everything."

"Don't say I didn't warn you." George's voice dropped an eerie octave. "When the morning star rises, a Pawnee brave shoots an arrow through the heart of a young woman."

She felt the soft spot between her ribs where the arrow could penetrate.

"Then, the Pawnee carves a star around her heart and lays her in the field to drain her blood out to nourish the prairie."

"You're trying to spook me." Lizzie hiccuped and grabbed the Dr. Mackenzie's Smelling Salts from her handbag.

"Indians aren't the only varmints in the West," George nudged Harvey. "Keep her away from bandits like Jesse James. They'll steal a girl out from under your nose." Lizzie swallowed a hiccup and changed the subject. "What's the next stop, George?"

"The Mile High City."

"He means Denver," Harvey said, puffing out his chest.

"Why do they call it that?" she asked.

"Denver's a mile higher than sea level," George said. "Don't you feel it? Hard to catch your breath." He continued down the aisle, ringing his bell.

Ready for breakfast, Lizzie and Harvey jostled through the narrow passageway of the train. Her shoulders bumped one side, then the other, until the end. Harvey insisted she jump first between the railcars, so he could help if she had trouble. It scared her, all right, the whirring of wheels on tracks, the link-and-pin coupler holding the cars together, the ground rushing below.

She jumped before she dared think of the consequences. The impact of the metal floor on the balls of her feet sent a whoosh of exhilaration through her. Harvey stood on the opposite platform, watching the flickering tracks below.

"Just jump," she shouted above the roaring train.

He squeezed his eyes closed and leapt, one boot landing on the platform, the other skidding off the edge. Panicked, she pulled him to her, his heart flailing against her own.

The sweat on his lip belied his smile. "See? You did just fine," he said, opening the door.

His bluster annoyed her, but a fight wouldn't help her find out more about the mine. Why did his eyes glaze over whenever she brought up the subject?

As they passed through the dining car, folks turned to stare. She'd grown used to people's reactions to her over the years, and now her boyish husband seemed to amplify the effect. All eyes devoured the fetching damask gown Mam had sewn for her trousseau.

Mam. Lizzie swallowed hard as her fingers grazed the real silverware, crystal, china, smoothing the white linen, while, back home, her mother struggled to put food on the table.

They'd left behind the abundant Oshkosh trees that cradled the sky with lush foliage. Trees were scarce here on the western plains; the bleak horizon stretched a hundred miles in every direction. Even the sky's color had changed from eggshell blue to a vibrant turquoise that hurt to look at it.

A sizzling platter of pan-fried steak and eggs arrived at the table. "Ohhhh. That smells divine." She took a bite, mulling over what she wanted to ask him. "You never told me how your father found the mine."

"Always the questions." He tweaked her chin.

"Maybe if you answered I wouldn't have to pester you."

"Okay, okay." He held his palms up. "Father met this prospector, Jenkins, who needed money to build a mine, so he backed him."

"But why is he sending you to the mine?" She bit into the steak, too tough to chew.

He pushed eggs around his plate. "Some things are better left unsaid."

"Tell me," she pushed.

"My father wanted us out of Oshkosh, okay?" His face reddened.

"What do you mean?"

"Father never even mentioned the mine until I told my parents I was marrying you, and mother left the room in a conniption. Then he poured me a Glenlivet and said, 'Time to cut the apron strings, son. Take your beautiful bride out west for a honeymoon and work the gold mine until your mother simmers down.'"

"She nodded slowly. "Your father is a smart man." What a relief to get away from Mrs. Doe who never looked Lizzie in the eyes. Her backbone stiffened. She'd make a good wife and strike it rich at the same time. "What makes your father so sure we'll strike gold?"

"Father says Central City is the richest square mile on earth." Harvey leaned back, elbows splayed, hands behind his head. "He'll meet us there after he finishes up some business in Denver."

"What will he want me to do?" Lizzie said, anxious to get started."

"Stay home and sit pretty, most likely," he said.

"Come on, Harvey." She laced her fingers with his. "I'll do anything to help." Anything to help her family.

He kissed her knuckles. "You can count the gold."

"I'll be good at that." She smiled; the bookkeeping she'd done for Da would come in handy.

As the train pulled into Denver's outskirts, the double-time pace of the city thrilled her. Hundreds of carriages, supply wagons, horses and buggies traversed the brick street. A milk wagon dodged the streetcar running down a wide boulevard flanked with stores."

"George was right about the altitude." Harvey jerked his collar, sucking in dry, sparse air.

His mother had warned about his asthma, instructing Lizzie to distract him from his tight chest. So, she read the signs on the storefronts. "Robertson Art Gallery. Larimer Butter & Cigars, Walker Whiskies & Wines. Whoa. Look at that one, House of Mirrors."

A revolving red light glared off a million mirrored tiles behind a woman in a lacey bustier gyrating up and down a brass pole.

Lizzie had read about tainted women in the Bible, but never imagined them so…striking.

"House of Mirrors." Harvey's eyes bulged. "We don't have places like that at home."

"Because we don't need them, do we?" She turned his head and kissed him with all the fervor she could muster. The best kiss they'd had, ardent and satisfying.

Afterward, Harvey's eyes still followed the red light.

∼

AT THE FOOTHILLS, they transferred to the General Sherman, a narrow-gauge train just three feet wide to squeeze through the steep and winding mountain tracks. American and Colorado flags fluttered from the locomotive, black smoke billowed from the smokestack, the bell clanged.

Harvey heaved trunks to the porter, then doubled over, wheezing. "I can't go on."

"The train is leaving, we have to go." Lizzie helped him up the steps, determined not to turn back. She settled him on the front-row bench, and the train lurched forward. Rubbing Harvey's back soothed him.

After a few miles, his breath resumed a halting rhythm and he patted her hand. "You're a good wife, Lizzie."

She smiled, things would be fine. Never mind the altitude zinging her eardrums with pain.

They passed a waterfall cascading down jagged rocks and plunging to the river. "Ever see anything so glorious?" She turned to Harvey, but he slept, bowler tipped over his forehead, sweet mouth pursed for a kiss.

Mam was right; she could learn to love this boy. Harvey Doe, son of the mayor of Oshkosh, had walked into Da's haberdashery, proud and flirtatious, bragging about his father's gold mine in Colorado. Mam had set her cap for him right then. Not-for-nothing had she coddled Lizzie, excusing her from chores, and dressing her like a porcelain doll. Harvey Doe was the gentleman of means she'd been groomed for.

Lizzie figured they'd return to their families after a few months at the gold mine, and with the money she brought back, she'd help Da open a new haberdashery.

As the train threaded Clear Creek Canyon, sheer rock walls rose like a formidable fortress, grand and terrifying, nothing like the gentle hills of Wisconsin. Layers of rock ranged in color from blood red to charcoal to gold. One enormous peak overlapped the next, obscuring the distant view. The majesty of it all cracked her heart open as surely as if the Pawnee had, pouring her hopes onto the magnificent mountains.

When the conductor called the next stop was Central City, Harvey stretched and smiled, apparently feeling better.

The train pulled around the last bend, whistle shrieking

through the canyon. They chugged to a halt, billowing clouds of steam.

Breathless and light-headed, Lizzie rushed to see the legendary Central City. Her new home. Her gold mine. Raising her petticoats to step down, she imprinted the red soil with buttoned boots.

The sulfuric breeze seeped into her lungs. Ramshackle buildings had been thrown up haphazardly over the rising slopes. Piles and piles of discarded ore littered the barren hillsides. Pine trunks had been hacked at their base, clear-cut for lumber. The stench of burning garbage and burping fumes gagged her. She pulled out her rosary beads and prayed for strength.

If this was the richest square mile on earth, it certainly didn't look like it.